The Wasp Trap

Also by Mark Edwards

The Magpies Series

The Magpies
A Murder of Magpies
Last of the Magpies
The Psychopath Next Door

Other Novels

What You Wish For
Because She Loves Me
Follow You Home
The Devil's Work
The Lucky Ones
The Retreat
In Her Shadow
Here To Stay
The House Guest
The Hollows
No Place To Run
Keep Her Secret
The Darkest Water

With Louise Voss

Killing Cupid
Catch Your Death
All Fall Down
Forward Slash
From the Cradle
The Blissfully Dead

The Wasp Trap

MARK EDWARDS

MICHAEL JOSEPH

PENGUIN MICHAEL JOSEPH

UK | USA | Canada | Ireland | Australia
India | New Zealand | South Africa

Penguin Michael Joseph is part of the Penguin Random House group of companies
whose addresses can be found at global.penguinrandomhouse.com

Penguin Random House UK,
One Embassy Gardens, 8 Viaduct Gardens, London SW11 7BW

penguin.co.uk

Penguin
Random House
UK

First published 2025
001

Set in 13.4/16pt Garamond MT
Typeset by Falcon Oast Graphic Art Ltd
Printed and bound in Great Britain by Clays Ltd, Elcograf S.p.A.

The authorized representative in the EEA is Penguin Random House Ireland,
Morrison Chambers, 32 Nassau Street, Dublin D02 YH68

A CIP catalogue record for this book is available from the British Library

HARDBACK ISBN: 978-0-241-72102-5
TRADE PAPERBACK ISBN: 978-0-241-72103-2

Penguin Random House is committed to a sustainable future
for our business, our readers and our planet. This book is made from
Forest Stewardship Council® certified paper

For Sara

Prologue

July 1999

It was the last Friday in July and I was trying hard not to panic about the deadline when Lily made the suggestion that would change everything.

'I've had an idea,' she said, in that measured tone of hers. 'I want to devise a test that will tell us if someone is a psychopath.'

There were only three of us left in the library: Lily, Sophie and me. The others had gone outside to smoke or get some air while we carried on working, though at least we were cool in that dark-panelled room that the sun barely touched. The library was now a makeshift office. Antique tables and chairs with wobbly legs had been dragged in from other rooms, and cables snaked across the floorboards to connect the fruit-coloured iMacs that we'd been sitting in front of since first light.

We were spurred on by the date that was written on a whiteboard and propped on a shelf in the fiction section. The launch date, just four weeks away. The fiction section was apt because there was no way the site would be ready by then. But we kept hearing rumours that our rivals were going to beat us to the punch, that *they* would revolutionize online dating, not us. 'No prize for second,' Sebastian kept saying, and we could always tell when he'd been on the phone to his chief investor. He would march into the office, sweat gleaming on his creased brow, and demand to know exactly what we had achieved that day.

'This is our revolution,' he said to us many times. 'We can't let them take it from us.'

I could hear the professor upstairs in his study now, pacing from one end of the room to the other. I looked up. One of the dogs, sitting by my feet, lifted his head too.

'I want to help him,' Lily said, following my gaze towards the ceiling. And that was when she came up with her suggestion. A test to identify psychopaths, a subject I had been obsessed with over the past couple of weeks, since we'd been up there, in Sebastian's study, searching through his papers and scouring the psychology periodicals that he still subscribed to. 'We could ensure it was reliable, trustworthy, something he could use in his other work. What do you think? Will? Sophie?'

A test. Hadn't we done enough of those this summer? I'd been tested before I even met the professor and since coming here, to his house, I'd spent hours in front of the computer, completing questionnaires, trying to figure out how much I agreed or disagreed with statements like *I feel comfortable around strangers*.

'How would you go about it, Lily?'

That was Sophie. She was seated across from me, leaning forward with her elbows on her desk, her wavy black hair tumbling around her face; a face I found it hard not to stare at.

Lily smiled. 'I haven't quite figured that out yet. I'll have to make sure it's not easy to fool.' I could almost hear the crackle of that remarkable brain, the firing of synapses, as she grabbed a pad and pen and began making notes. Sophie and I got up from our desks and peered over Lily's shoulder. She scribbled fast: a flow chart, arrows and question marks. Beyond the library I could hear chatter and laughter.

My colleagues. After a month at the professor's, I was still unsure how many of them I could call friends.

'What do you think?' Lily asked, when she'd finished making notes.

I picked up her notepad and tried to make sense of it. I quickly put it down again. It was like being a work-experience kid on the Manhattan Project.

'Will?'

I chose my words carefully. 'It sounds . . . interesting. And I want to help the professor too. But aren't we busy enough? Everything we're here to do. Our stock options. All of it. We're already running out of time.'

She had the smile of a benevolent dictator. 'It will be fine. I have the capacity, Will. I'll base it on the same algorithm we're using for the site. It's just another form of psychometric testing, really. And if I can't pull it off, we won't have lost anything.' A pause. 'So? Shall we do it?'

I caught Sophie's eye, thinking about another test we'd taken and the results it had spat out, and I wondered if that would ever lead to anything or if work and pressure would get in our way. We still had so many problems that needed fixing. Words that had to be written and polished. Bugs squashed.

I was about to tell Lily we were too busy, that it would be too difficult. A test to catch a psychopath? I had faith in her genius, but did she really have time? And could she really create a test that a psychopath wouldn't be able to fool?

But as I opened my mouth to put forward my argument, Sophie said, 'I'm in. I think it's a brilliant idea. Surely you do too, Will?'

They both turned to me and I swallowed my words.

I simply couldn't say no to them.

'Let's do it,' I said, and both Sophie and Lily clapped their hands.

'What's all the excitement about?'

Georgina came into the room, followed by the others, smelling of cigarettes and sunshine, the spaniel rousing himself and running over to greet them, tail a happy blur. Once everyone was inside, Lily began to tell them about her idea, explaining that we would all need to take part, volunteer to be tested, just as we'd acted as guinea pigs for the dating site.

As they listened to her, the ceiling creaked again. Sebastian, still up there, pacing.

I looked over at my colleagues. Sebastian's six hires and the other two, spending all our time together, sunrise to sunset and sunset to dawn.

No one had protested, not then anyway, although there were one or two frowns of doubt, signs of disquiet that would come out later. At that point, though, there were no arguments, and I knew that, at some point in the coming weeks, we would all risk exposing a darkness in ourselves. A difference.

I looked around again, as the conversation turned towards the evening, to plans, to beer and wine and a dip in the lake. The genius. The lothario. The salesman. The affluent couple, the joker and the local girl. Finally, me, the wordsmith, whose role was to write it all down.

If any of us were a psychopath, I already had a good idea who it would be.

Part One

Chapter 1

February 2024

Of course Georgina and Theo lived in an enormous house. Out of all of us, they were the ones who had always been the most likely to achieve success. As individuals, each would have made something of themself, I had no doubt of that. But as a couple? They were unstoppable.

Still, even after the invitation had landed on my doormat and I'd checked the address on Google Maps, I hadn't expected the Howard residence to be quite so impressive. It was a Georgian townhouse, four storeys plus a basement, the last one on a row of imposing terraces in Notting Hill. The house to its left was covered with scaffolding that appeared to have been there some time, green netting flapping in the wind. Next door to the right, set just a little way apart from the row of terraces, was a grand detached house that seemed empty too, its windows dark, the wrought-iron gate secured with a chain and padlock. Between these two unwelcoming buildings the Howards' home stood even prouder and taller, its front windows illuminated, the white paintwork immaculate, a family home that happened to belong to two people I had once known but hadn't seen for over twenty years.

It had taken a death to bring us back together.

You are cordially invited to a dinner party to celebrate the life of
Sebastian Marlowe
Hosted by Theo and Georgina Howard
RSVP

The invitation was printed on thick ivory card, a little grubby at its edges now where I had examined it so many times. Beneath the RSVP was an email address and, on the back, in looping cursive handwriting, a personal message written in blue ink:

Dearest Will. Please come! All the old gang will be there and it will be lovely to remember the professor. Can't wait to catch up. G xx

Catch up. Tell us what you've been up to for the past twenty-five years.

It would take twenty-five seconds.

And it was that thought, picturing Georgina's attempts to suppress the pity she felt for me, that almost sent me back to the tube station, back to my little flat south of the river, where I would spend another evening in front of the TV, waiting for the Deliveroo driver, sharing my dinner with Bernard, my cat – my sole companion since Danielle had left. Bottle of supermarket wine and the optimistic opening of my laptop, the blinking cursor on the blank page.

Waiting for me to tell my story.

That blinking cursor was one of the main reasons I'd accepted the invitation.

'Will?'

The voice, male, came out of the darkness. It was a voice I hadn't heard in a long time but was instantly familiar.

Rohan stepped into the sodium light, brandishing a piece of card that matched mine.

'Mate,' he said. 'I'm so happy to see you. I thought I might be the only one stupid enough to come.'

He grinned as I put out my hand.

'A handshake? Come on, man. Bring it in.' He pulled me into an embrace, patting my back before releasing me and saying, 'You're still as skinny as ever.'

'You're looking good,' I said, though I wasn't sure I meant it. It's always a little depressing to meet up with people you haven't seen in over twenty years; a reminder that youth is a speck in the rear-view mirror. There were dark smudges beneath his eyes, like he'd suffered through a few sleepless nights, and he'd filled out since I'd last seen him. But in other ways, Rohan looked distinguished: his black hair was streaked with silver and he was dressed well. I told him so: 'Looking *sharp*, I should say.'

He held his overcoat open. 'The suit? You like it?' Beneath the streetlight I could see it was midnight blue, well made. 'My brother-in-law's a tailor.'

So he was married. I was going to ask the customary question about whether he had kids — a little later in the evening I would find out that he had two boys, aged nine and eleven, and that he'd been married to Anika for thirteen years — but before I could say anything he let out a whistle as he swivelled on his heels and took in the house.

'Look at this place.' He leaned forward conspiratorially. 'Know how much it's worth?'

He told me. It was the kind of figure that's hard to comprehend, mind-boggling even for London.

'What do they do?' I asked, somehow knowing he would have looked it up. 'For a living, I mean?'

'Theo is in investment banking. Do you remember James? Sebastian's angel investor? Apparently, he gave Theo his first break.' I did remember him. A flash bloke who drove a Porsche and couldn't keep his eyes off Sophie. 'I'm not sure about Georgina, but her family were loaded, weren't they?

9

Probably inherited a fortune. Whatever – can you imagine? Being able to afford a place like this?'

'How do you know *I'm* not loaded? I might have flown here in a gold helicopter.'

He laughed. 'I've been keeping an eye on the bestseller lists, mate. Waiting to see your name. Hasn't happened.'

'Not yet.'

'But when it does you'll be able to afford a gaff like this, right? Maybe a decent suit.'

I tried not to look offended. I was wearing my nicest clothes: a shirt that Danielle had bought me the Christmas-before-last and a smart pair of Levi's. My coat, which had seen me through several wet English winters, was a little thin though, especially in this biting wind.

'Do you know who else is coming?' Rohan asked.

'All the old gang, apparently.' These words, quoted from the back of the invitation, sent a little shiver through my veins.

'Nice. I saw Lily a few years ago at a conference. She's married with kids too. I think she told me her wife is a lawyer.'

'You sound surprised.'

A shrug. 'I never pictured Lily getting married.'

I hadn't either. For someone who had worked for a dating site, Lily had been remarkably uninterested in romance.

'What about Sophie?' I asked, trying to sound casual. 'Do you know what she's up to?'

'Yeah, married to a firefighter. Eight kids.'

'Oh. I never—'

He erupted with laughter. 'Mate, your face. I haven't got a clue what happened to her. She's not on Facebook or anything.'

I already knew she wasn't on social media, not in a way that was easy to trace, anyway. I'd looked for her several times, late at night when I'd had a couple of drinks and started thinking about the past.

'Have you stalked all of us?' I asked.

'Of course. Actually, I sent you a friend request about ten years ago. Guess you never saw it. Or maybe you didn't want to be friends with your old colleague.' He thumped me playfully on the shoulder. 'It's all right, I don't hold grudges.' A wink. 'Much.'

We went up the front steps, Rohan ahead of me. I tried to remember if I'd seen and ignored his friend request. I had no memory of—

A noise stopped me dead.

'Did you hear that?' I asked.

He had reached the top step. 'Hear what?'

I held up a hand. 'Wait.'

We both paused, listening. It had been faint. Muffled. But I was sure I hadn't imagined it. It had sounded like someone crying out. Distressed. Possibly in pain.

'What exactly did you hear?' Rohan asked.

But I didn't get a chance to answer, because the front door opened and there, before me, stood two more people I hadn't seen since the summer of 1999. Theo stepped forward first, pumping Rohan's hand, and then Georgina was there with air kisses, the scent of expensive perfume, her cheek warm against my cold face.

'Just you two?' she said.

'So far.'

'Come in, it's freezing.' Theo gestured for us to go inside.

The three of them went in – Rohan telling Georgina she hadn't aged at all; her half-hearted protests – but I held back, waiting to see if the noise came again.

Cars rushing by on neighbouring streets. The metronome thump of music and a dog barking in the distance. The background hum of London. No cries. No shouts.

I let it go and followed them in.

Chapter 2

Georgina took our coats while Theo closed the door behind us and pressed some buttons on a keypad to its right. The door, which was impressively solid, emitted several clunking sounds, locks sliding into place.

'We have this ridiculous high-tech security system,' Georgina said as she hung our coats on the rack. 'Honestly, sometimes when the postman calls it takes me five minutes to remember how to open the bloody thing.'

'She's exaggerating,' said Theo. 'It's not that complicated. It uses Swiss technology. Controls the doors and windows too. This place is impenetrable.'

'Very cool. Is it biometric?' Rohan asked, and Georgina rolled her eyes as Theo began to explain it to him.

Rohan had always been into gadgets – on his dating profile he'd listed his main interests as Manchester United and 'bleeding-edge tech' – and Theo seemed to be equally enthusiastic. Our host was still in good shape too. Theo had the physique of someone who spent a lot of time working out. I had thought – hoped? – the good life might have caught up with him. It was sickening, really. Rich, handsome and fit. He hadn't even lost any of his hair.

'It's madness,' Georgina said, leading me a few steps along the hallway. It had a gleaming parquet floor and the walls were painted a shade of blue which probably had a name like

'existential light'. 'It's all controlled with an app. I don't understand any of it. But Theo insisted.'

'There have been a lot of burglaries around here,' he said
in response to his name. 'The place next door is empty and
we're worried it might attract squatters.'

'Which one?' I asked, and Georgina gestured in the direction of the house on the right. The detached one.

'Some Russian oligarch owns it but hasn't been here for
over a year.' There was distaste in her tone.

Theo smiled at his wife. 'Your favourite person, isn't he,
darling?'

A shudder. 'Awful man. He told us he was going to extend
downwards, build an enormous basement.'

'It would have taken a year. Constant noise and disruption.
It's been bad enough having the builders on the other side,
but he was planning major work. He and Georgina had some
full-on rows about it.'

'I think that's a bit of an exaggeration. I stayed civil.'

He laughed. 'Anyway, it all came to nothing. He buggered
off back to Russia and we haven't seen him since. Mixed bless-
ing, really, because now we have to worry about squatters.'

I wondered if that was the cry I'd heard on the doorstep.
Perhaps squatters were already in there.

'So yes, the house on the other side is empty too,' Georgina
said before I could mention the noise. 'The family have moved
out while it's being refurbished, but it's only going to be a
month, thankfully, so . . . Oh dear. Listen to me. It's *so lovely*
to see you.'

Georgina had always been posh, with an accent that firmly
placed her in a certain strata of British society: the country
set. Big, crumbling houses. Boarding schools. Shooting
pheasants during the season. Theo, on the other hand, was a
grammar-school boy from a modest background, the son of

two teachers. A couple of years older than the rest of us, he had been our manager, the guy with the unfortunate task of making sure the rest of us didn't slack off.

Some London had crept into Georgina's accent now. The odd dropped H, a couple of faint glottal stops. Street posh.

That was not the only change. Back then, Georgina had been the kind of young woman who was comfortable in a Barbour jacket and wellies; the sort of thing you might see a young royal wearing. Now, she had a more urban sheen. Her honey-blonde hair made me think she'd just come from a salon where someone had spent hours straightening it. She was wearing a black cashmere polo neck and bootcut trousers, sleek and immaculate. There were very few lines on her face and I immediately thought *Botox*. But there was no denying it, she looked good.

'Something smells appetizing,' Rohan said. 'Which one of you is the chef?'

He looked from Georgina to Theo, who said, 'His name's Callum.'

There was a pause before Rohan laughed and said, 'Oh, you've hired a caterer. Or do you have a live-in chef?'

'Oh no,' said Theo. 'We *do* cook. Well, Georgina does, don't you, darling? I can just about bake a potato. But there's an agency we use for special occasions.'

'Shall we wait for the others upstairs?' Georgina said. 'They shouldn't be long.'

'Let me fetch some vino for while we wait.'

Theo went through a door into what was clearly the kitchen. I could hear clattering from within, a male voice, and the smell of the food was wafting into the hallway.

'This will do nicely,' Theo said, re-emerging with a bottle. 'Château Lafite Rothschild. You both okay with red?'

Georgina raised her eyebrows. *Do you really want to waste that on these philistines?*

'Red's great,' I said.

'Just water for me,' Rohan told him. Of course he didn't drink. He was the only one who'd stayed sober that whole summer, when we'd gone through so much booze the professor had been forced to arrange an extra recycling collection.

I wasn't a big drinker these days, but tonight my nerves needed soothing. It was so strange, being here with people I hadn't seen, except in dreams, for twenty-five years. Unsettling. And the most important person, the one I'd dreamed about the most, hadn't even arrived yet.

'Follow me,' Theo said.

We went up the stairs, the carpet plush underfoot, the walls lined with family photos. There was one of Theo at what must have been the London Marathon, holding up a medal like it was an Olympic Gold. Next along was a wedding photo, Theo and Georgina standing on the steps of a stately home, exactly as I remembered them: fresh-faced, happy. Halfway up the stairs, we passed a window that gave a view of the garden, a large, neatly mown lawn surrounded by trees that were still bare, and a quaint little summerhouse at the far end. The closest houses were a hundred metres to the rear, beyond their own substantial gardens.

I passed a family portrait: Georgina, Theo and two girls, aged about ten and six. They were at what looked like some kind of garden party. The younger girl and Georgina both wore serious expressions while Theo and the older daughter were grinning.

'She's the absolute spit of you,' I said to Georgina, who was ahead of me on the stairs, pointing at the younger girl.

She turned back. 'Hmm? Oh, Mia, yes. Everyone says that.' She touched the frame of the picture. 'She's sixteen now, but don't worry, she's at a friend's house tonight. A sleepover.'

'I wasn't worried at all. I'd like to meet your kids. Is your other daughter here?'

To my great surprise, Georgina turned away without answering. I was certain she'd heard me.

Strange.

We reached the top of the steps and found ourselves in another hallway, a landing, with more polished wood, partially covered with heavy rugs. The sitting room we went into was pristine. It had two high-backed sofas which looked like no one had ever sat on them. There was an ornate fireplace in which, I guessed, no wood had burned for a long time. Standing there, I had the strangest feeling of déjà vu.

'We don't use this room often,' Theo said, pouring me a glass of wine. I took a sip. It was delicious. Rich and oaky, without being too heavy. 'We save it for special occasions.'

'It looks like Sebastian's sitting room,' I said, suddenly realizing why it was so familiar. 'That is, if all the old, tatty furniture he used to have had been restored. Minus that TV you were always watching football on, Rohan.'

Theo grinned. 'Well spotted. We gave the designer a photo. We wanted a souvenir of the place where we fell in love.'

Georgina rolled her eyes as he put his arm around her shoulders. He was twice as broad as her, but he was beaming like a little boy. Standing this close to him, in better light, I noticed the broken veins on his face, the slight ruddiness. Perhaps he wasn't so well preserved, after all.

'Theo is such a romantic,' she said.

I was hardly listening. I had spotted something else. A painting that hung over the fireplace. I went over for a closer look.

'It's Thornwood,' I said.

Sebastian's house. There, hugging the frame, were the woods where we would seek shelter from the heat. Close to the centre of the painting was the little lake with its rowing boat which we would take out in pairs. I had a flash of myself with oars in my hands, Sophie sitting opposite, half drunk on a bottle of cherry wine we'd found in a cupboard, lips stained red, sick from the sweetness but laughing at some joke I'd cracked.

'Sebastian gave us that as a wedding gift,' Theo said.

I turned. 'Did he still live there? When he died, I mean?'

'He did. Just him and a nurse.'

'I wish I'd known about it. I would have liked to have gone to the funeral.'

'Me too.' Rohan frowned. 'We all have a habit of missing funerals, don't we?'

The doorbell rang, saving us from having to pursue that painful line of conversation, although I had no doubt it would come up at some point tonight.

From her place at the front window, Georgina said, 'It's Sophie. Theo, go and let her in.'

Sophie. There was a mirror on the wall, no doubt created by some renowned designer and sourced by one of Georgina's people. As soon as Theo left the room I went over to it.

'You look gorgeous,' Rohan said with a smirk.

'Just checking I don't have anything on my face.'

He laughed, and I saw that Georgina was smiling too. 'Will, you look like a teenage boy waiting for his prom date to turn up.'

That made Rohan properly guffaw, and there were footsteps on the stairs. I took a deep breath and a last look at myself, turning away from the mirror as Theo reappeared.

Beside him was a woman. A fully grown forty-something woman, and she was smiling, her gaze going from Georgina, who approached her with air kisses, to Rohan, who gave her a big hug, and then they both stepped aside and it was my turn.

'Sophie,' I said.

'Hi, Will.'

But before I could step forward to embrace her, something behind her caught my eye. There was someone else, lingering in the doorway. A man.

Sophie hadn't arrived alone.

Chapter 3

Why did I feel so nervous about seeing Sophie? The answer was simple. It was because of how it had ended: messily. I had been upset, confused. Angry, with her and myself.

It had all come back to me recently, following the break-up with Danielle, when I was going through a load of old boxes that had lived for years inside our divan bed. In one Kickers box, I found relics from 1999. Floppy disks. A pamphlet from my graduation ceremony. Then the real treasure: a packet of photographs from the summer of that year. I sorted through them, one by one. Sebastian's spaniels. The office with its colourful iMacs. Sebastian himself, shirtsleeves rolled up. Finally, us. His team, sitting together at one of the tables on the edge of the lawn, raising our glasses to the camera. There on the floor of my bedroom I had a revelation. Wasn't it startlingly obvious that if I was ever going to write something worthwhile, I should do what I always advised my students to do and draw on my own life? Here, in this packet of Kodak moments, was the experience that shone brighter than everything else I'd ever done. And shining brightest at the centre of it all?

Sophie.

First, the revelation, then something like fate. Almost as soon as I'd made my mind up to pursue this idea, the invitation had arrived. I wasn't in the habit of reading obituaries and hadn't even known Sebastian had died.

This dinner party was exactly what I needed. A chance to reminisce. To see how everyone had turned out. My own memories would only get me so far. But almost as soon as I RSVP'd, I started to worry. After all these years, would Sophie be happy to see me?

Or would the shadow of that final night still hang over us?

'Everyone,' Theo said, beckoning the stranger into the sitting room, 'I want you to meet Finn.'

My first thought was *husband*. Of course, she had to be married. I was a little dazed as he shook my hand. He was about ten years younger than the rest of us and very tall. Six foot two, and wearing a black off-the-peg suit. He had a boyish mop of scruffy hair with a ginger tinge and was wearing old-fashioned horn-rimmed glasses. Square jaw. Handsome. He was exactly the kind of person I could see Sophie ending up with. But then, just as I had convinced myself they were a couple, Sophie said, 'We met. On the doorstep.'

'Finn was Sebastian's assistant for the last few years,' Theo told us.

It's ridiculous how relieved I was.

'Georgina and Theo were kind enough to invite me,' Finn said. 'I hope you don't mind. It's just, I never really met anyone who knew Professor Marlowe when he was younger. I was saying that to Georgina at the funeral, and she very kindly asked me along.'

Even though I was relieved Finn wasn't with Sophie, I was a little surprised to find it wasn't only going to be the old gang here tonight. But I didn't dwell on it, or on Finn himself. Because he was standing next to Sophie.

Unlike Georgina, Sophie had laughter lines and creases around her eyes, a natural face for a forty-seven-year-old. But it was her eyes that made her look young. They still had that sparkle. Amused, intelligent, playful. The way she dressed made her seem youthful too. She was wearing black Converse and, above those, black tights, a navy-blue dress that was patterned with daisies, and a leather biker's jacket. Her black hair had been cut short and she wore earrings that were shaped like daggers. She dressed almost exactly as she had when she was twenty-two.

Finn was looking from me to Sophie and back, clearly trying to figure out the dynamic between us. Then Theo appeared with a drink for Finn, and the two of them drifted away with Rohan. Finn towered over Rohan, who was almost a whole foot shorter. Temporarily, I had Sophie to myself, and I couldn't think of a thing to say. It was as if the last twenty-five years hadn't happened and she had just said her last words to me from that summer, spoken through the window of my taxi: 'You need to get yourself a phone.' I wanted to get my iPhone out of my pocket now, show her: *Look. I've got one.*

'Lily not here?' she said, putting me out of my tongue-tied misery.

'Not yet.'

She took a sip of wine. 'This is so weird.'

'The wine? It cost about a million pounds.'

'Oh, that explains it. I only drink cheap shit.' A smile. 'I meant, being here. Seeing you. All of you.' She turned her head, taking in the room. 'I have to admit half the reason I came was because I wanted to see inside this house. Did you see when they were featured in the *Sunday Times* magazine? What did Georgina say? "It's a family home. It just happens to be a family with exquisite taste."'

'Sebastian's taste, in this room at least.'

'Oh yes. They talked about that in the piece. They didn't mention what he did to—' She caught herself. 'Sorry. It's sweet, and I'm just jealous.'

'Why are you jealous?'

There was a whole story in the look she gave me in response. A story of disappointment. Of life not taking the path she'd plotted. But she wasn't going to admit that, not right now, not to me.

'Um . . . have you seen this place, Will? Don't tell me – you live somewhere equally fabulous.'

As I racked my brain for a witty response she went on: 'It's so *clean* too. You should see my house. Mess everywhere. Piles of old books and records. If I ever appear in a newspaper it will be in an article about a woman who was killed when her collection of American *Vogue* fell and crushed her.'

'Where is this hoarder's paradise?' I asked.

'Oh, out in the sticks in Bedfordshire. A little cottage that used to belong to my gran. Tons of her old crap is still there too.'

'All her stuffed animals?'

'You remember!'

Sophie had told us that her gran, her mother's mum, lived in a cottage that was stuffed full of taxidermized corvids and 'witchy paraphernalia', whatever that meant. Sophie had shown us photos of her, along with the rest of her family. Her mum, a white woman from deep in the Bedfordshire woods, had met her dad, a handsome Black man, in Trinidad and married him after a whirlwind romance. Sophie had spent the first few years of her life over there before moving to the British countryside. Her dad, whose photo she carried in her wallet, had already passed away when we met.

'Of course I remember.'

'I banged on about myself a lot, didn't I?'

I laughed. 'We all did.'

This was her cue to say something about how I'd boasted that I was going to be a famous author, but instead she said,

'I'm probably doing the same now. I don't see people very often so when I do it all comes bursting out in a terrible splurge.'

'Do you work from home then?' I asked.

'Yes. I make jewellery and sell it on Etsy.'

'Oh, that's cool.' So she *was* online.

'I don't make any money from it though. This is embarrassing, but my gran left me some money along with the cottage and I've been living off that, getting through it very, very slowly. You'd be amazed how little I spend. I have chickens and – Oh my God, I told you: let me loose among people and I just vomit words.'

To say I was relieved was an understatement. Firstly, her nervous energy was making me feel relaxed in comparison. Secondly, she didn't appear to be harbouring any bad feelings towards me. Perhaps she had forgotten the angry exchange we'd had the last time I'd seen her. It had been a long time, after all.

'So what about you?' she said. 'Can you summarize the last twenty-five years of your life in as many words?'

'Twenty-five words? Let me see.' I counted them on my fingers as I went. 'Moved to London, bought a flat when they were cheap, became a lecturer and moved in with my girl-friend, but we broke up last year. Blimey, twenty-five words doesn't get you very far, does it? Can I try again?'

'Of course.'

'Bought cheap flat, south London. Became a creative-writing lecturer. Co-habited. That's one word, not two. Wrote novels no one wanted. Lost most of hair and all of girlfriend.'

'I think you still have a word left.'

'Okay. Wrote *crap* novels no one wanted.'

'Ouch. Harsh on yourself, I'm sure. But you teach creative writing? That's cool.'

Was it? I worried people would think I was a fraud, even

though I'd been doing it for twenty years now. I taught at a college of further education in south London, and they were always threatening to close the course, especially in recent years, when all the focus was on STEM subjects. It was hard work, with occasional moments that made it worthwhile. One of my students had gone on to publish a string of bestsellers, winning a prize for her comic novel *Cassandra Gets the Ick*. She had thanked me fulsomely in the acknowledgements.

'It must be rewarding,' Sophie said.

'It can be. Especially the work I do in prisons.'

'Oh?'

I explained that I ran writing workshops in several men's prisons across London and Kent.

'Some of the talent I've come across is staggering,' I said. 'They have so much to say and, for a lot of these blokes, nobody has ever encouraged them to share their stories and their opinions before.'

'That's amazing, Will.' She paused. 'Sorry, but I have to ask. Have you taught anyone who's done anything really terrible?' She leaned closer. 'Any psychopaths?'

'Not diagnosed, or they wouldn't be in these prisons. They'd be in psychiatric units.'

'A very earnest answer.'

'Sorry. I realize I sounded just like Lily right then.'

Sophie smiled. 'Did you read Sebastian's book?'

'*They Live Among Us*? I bought it but didn't get around to it.'

It had been published in the early 2010s and marketed as the latest in a wave of 'popular psychology' books about psychopaths and sociopaths. The *Guardian* review, however, said it was too densely academic to appeal to the casual reader. When I had come across the review as I ate breakfast in the college refectory it had given me a shock of nostalgia that had left me feeling out of sorts all day. That was the first time I'd searched for Sophie on Facebook. It had almost made me reach out to the others, but I had decided against it. I had, however, bought the book, flicking through it before deciding the *Guardian* was right. Much of the book was based on Sebastian's studies of psychopaths in Boston, along with theories he had developed later. There was a painful account of what had happened to his wife, Barbara, and how that had influenced him. But much of what followed was too dry to maintain my interest – and, to be frank, I still hadn't quite forgiven Sebastian for what he'd done to us all.

I looked across the room at the others. Georgina had returned with more wine and they were all standing by the bookcase, chatting. Finn had the air of a man who was trying hard to pay attention to whatever Rohan was saying to him, wanting to make a good impression. Perhaps he didn't realize we hadn't seen each other for a long time, that we hardly knew each other. He ought to relax. He was a stranger among strangers.

'Did you talk to Finn outside?' I asked, turning back to Sophie.

'Hmm. A little. He seems pleasant enough. I was taking my headphones off when he arrived and we had a chat about music. He likes jazz, apparently.'

'How . . . groovy.'

I wondered if he'd heard us, because he suddenly looked over and, in that instant, his smile disappeared, just for a second, before our eyes met. He raised his glass, but I didn't return the gesture. Something about that smile, the way it had vanished, made the hairs on my arms stand on end.

Sebastian had written about how the psychopaths he studied were good at social camouflage. A quote, half remembered, came back to me. Something about masks. What had he said? *It's in those moments when the subject believes himself to be unobserved that the mask slips and the true self can be glimpsed.*

'Are you still with us?' Sophie asked. 'You zoned out for a second.'

'Huh? Oh. I was just thinking about psychopaths.'

'A normal thing to do at a dinner party.'

'It was because of Sebastian's book and what you asked me about the prisoners.'

'Of course.'

There was an awkward moment. I longed to talk to her about what had happened on that last night. Maybe, after dinner, I'd gather the courage to bring it up. I also wanted to tell her about the strange moment I'd just had observing Finn, but she might think I was mad.

I had to stop thinking about the past. I glanced over at Finn again. He was chatting happily to Rohan. Completely normal. I put my moment of unease behind me, telling myself he probably felt awkward, that was all. As did I.

There was nothing wrong here. Old friends. A dinner party. Okay, there was a stranger among us, but so what?

I needed to chill out.

Chapter 4

I went over to Theo, who refilled my glass, then found myself standing alone for a moment. Spotting Georgina at the front window, I joined her.

'I'm wondering if Lily is going to turn up,' she said, peering down at the street. 'I texted her, but it hasn't been read.'

'She's probably on the tube. Although—'

'What?'

I found myself voicing a concern I'd had since receiving the invitation. 'I wouldn't blame her if she didn't show. The way everything ended must have been hardest on her.'

She fixed me with a look that took me right back to that final night, the twenty-five years in which I thought I'd grown and matured vanishing instantly. 'It wasn't easy for any of us.'

'You and Theo landed on your feet though.'

She folded her arms. 'We were devastated by what happened, Will. Theo took it as badly as Lily. But you know what? It made him – made both of us – work harder than ever to get the life we deserved.'

She was about to say something else when Theo came over. 'Rohan is asking for a tour of the house.'

'I'd like one too,' Sophie called over.

Georgina demurred until Theo said, 'Come on, darling, I know you're dying to show the place off. We don't have to wait for Lily.'

'Oh – twist my arm.' Georgina stepped away from the

window, leaving me looking down at the street, hoping to see a diminutive figure hurrying along beneath the streetlights.

Sophie fell into step beside me as we left the room and went back into the hallway in pairs. Georgina and Theo, followed by Rohan and Finn, then Sophie and me.

Sophie winked at me, then reached up to tap Finn on the shoulder.

'Do you live near here?' she asked him.

'Quite close. I mean, I was living down in East Sussex until quite recently, but now I'm back in London.'

'Did you live at Thornwood?'

A pause. 'I commuted there from Tunbridge Wells.'

I tried to catch Sophie's eye, but she had already asked a follow-up question. 'You were his research assistant?'

'More of a general dogsbody. Doing admin. Looking after things.'

'I guess he wasn't well enough to work towards the end,' I said. He was being frustratingly vague.

'No. That's right.' Sophie and I waited. Eventually, he said, 'He had a live-in nurse who saw him more than I did.'

We reached the landing and Georgina led us towards a door at the far end of the hallway. 'This is where we'll be eating.'

We took turns to poke our heads inside. The room was so large that even with the long oak table at its centre there was still plenty of floor space, and there were two huge windows, with long curtains, that gave a view of the empty house next door, the one that belonged to the oligarch. The table had been set for seven people, three chairs on one side, two on the other, and one at each end. It struck me that, with Finn as an addition, there should have been nine chairs, but one was gone, one was . . . well, I wasn't sure what had happened to her. Perhaps someone here would know.

'It won't be long before appetizers are served,' Georgina said.

Finn spoke. 'Do you think Lily's going to turn up in time? Have you heard from her?'

Why was this guy so concerned about Lily? I guessed Sebastian must have talked about her a lot so it was natural that Finn would be curious. Along with Theo, Lily had been the professor's favourite.

As Georgina repeated to Finn what she'd said to me, something shot towards us from under the table. A blur of silver-and-black fur that vanished from the room before I got a good look. All I could see was that it had been a large cat.

'Claude! I wondered where he'd got to,' Theo said. 'He usually stays in Mia's room when she's here but he's roaming around looking for somewhere else to sleep.'

Next, Georgina showed us the study, which was beside the dining room, and the first of their three bathrooms, then we all went up a flight.

'The master bedroom and Georgina's dressing room are up there,' Theo said, pointing to the fourth floor.

'The best bathroom too,' Georgina said. 'We just got a new bath. Brushed copper. I could live in it.'

Sophie shook her head in wonder. 'A dressing room too?'

'It's more of a walk-in wardrobe, really.'

'She's got more clothes than Selfridges,' Theo said. 'And how many pairs of shoes? And bags?'

'You're the one who keeps buying them for me.'

'Things rich people bicker about,' Sophie whispered to me.

It was carpeted up here, and more homely. Colourful striped wallpaper and some framed artwork that looked like it must have been by one of their daughters. The cat, Claude, was sitting outside one of the bedroom doors. A silver tabby with enormous ears, it was one of the biggest and cutest cats I'd ever seen. A cuddly monster.

'That's Mia's room,' said Theo, pushing the door open.

Claude, who I was sure was a Maine Coon, slunk through the gap, chirruping as he went, tail as thick as a fox's. There was an iMac, the current model, on the desk on the far wall, its screen black. Theo closed the door behind the cat. 'He'll let us know when he wants to come back out.'

Georgina showed us the spare room, which had apparently been the nanny's room when the children were little, and we all poked our heads into another bathroom, which was beautiful, with a sunken bathtub and a walk-in rainfall shower.

'You'll be interested in this, Will,' Theo said. 'This house used to belong to some famous crime novelist. A contemporary of Agatha Christie's. Rupert Chadwick?'

'Really?' Golden-age crime wasn't my thing, but I'd heard of Chadwick.

'Apparently,' Georgina said, 'he had a secret passage built into the house, but we think that's a load of rubbish, don't we, Theo? We've never been able to find it.'

'That's so exciting though,' Sophie said.

Theo scoffed. 'I reckon it's something old Rupert told people to make himself sound more interesting. Although he did marry five times, so he can't have been that boring.'

'Ooh.' Sophie's eyebrows went up. 'Five wives. Did he murder any of them?'

'Let's go and take a look at the kitchen,' Georgina said, making it clear she found this conversation distasteful.

'What's in this room?' Rohan asked, nodding at the door he was closest to.

Neither Georgina nor Theo replied. Instead, Georgina said, 'I'll introduce you to the chef.'

Finn went with the Howards while Rohan, Sophie and I loitered on the landing.

'Do you think she heard me?' Rohan asked.

'Definitely.' I moved a little closer to the mysterious door.

'I assume it belongs to the other daughter. The one they don't mention.'

'What do you mean?'

They were both looking at me, intrigued.

'There's a family photo downstairs. Theo, Georgina, Mia – whose room the cat just went into – and an older girl. I asked about her and they both ignored me.'

'Oh God,' Sophie said, checking to make sure Theo and Georgina were out of earshot. 'Do you think she died or something and they can't bring themselves to talk about her?'

Georgina's voice came from below us. 'Have you three got lost up there?'

'Coming!' Sophie called. She whispered, 'Don't say anything. If they want to tell us, they will. Okay?'

We went down the stairs, the mood darker than it had been coming up. As we reached the ground-floor hallway, Georgina furrowed her brow. 'What were you whispering about?'

'Just wondering what time we're going to eat.' Rohan patted his belly. 'I'm starving.'

A tight smile. 'We can ask the chef.'

We went into a kitchen which was bigger than my entire flat. There was a small dining area to the left – *the breakfast nook* – with a window that looked out on to the street, though tall hedgerows prevented passers-by from being able to see in. To the right, there was another small area with a retro American fridge and a wine rack that took up a whole section of wall. But I barely took in any of that. I was transfixed by something else. Some*one* else.

A woman stood by the marble-topped island with her back to us, chopping onions. She was wearing a white protective hat, but I could see red hair poking out at the nape of her neck, and the sight of her threw me back in time and space to the kitchen at Thornwood, where another red-haired woman had laboured to prepare food for the rest of us.

Eve?

I almost – *almost* – said it, believing in that moment that Georgina and Theo had tracked her down too, hired her as a reunion surprise. But then the woman looked around at us and even though she was the right age and had the same colouring, it clearly wasn't her, and I was relieved I hadn't spoken, hadn't made a fool of myself.

Behind the redhead, a man in chef's whites was standing by the hob, also with his back to us, stirring something in a pan over a gas flame.

'Callum?' Georgina ventured. 'I'd like you to meet our guests. Will, Rohan, Sophie, Finn. Lily is still on her way.'

He had a craggy face, sandy hair, a man in his mid-fifties with a broad smile. He had forearms that bulged like a cartoon sailor's, and huge hands, which he wiped on a cloth before shaking each of ours in turn, his grip just this side of painful.

'No one has any allergies?' he asked in an Estuary accent.

'Only to bad food,' said Rohan.

Callum clapped a massive paw on Rohan's shoulder. 'A man after my own heart.'

'Sophie and I are veggies,' I said. 'I mean, she used to be . . .'

'I'm a carnivore now,' she said. 'Actually, I only eat raw meat. Oh my God, Will, your face. I'm joking.'

Callum roared with laughter. 'She got you there.' He looked from one of us to the other. 'You two old flames?'

'Just old friends,' said Sophie, and I was sure she deliberately avoided my eye.

'Hmm,' said Callum. 'I sense a story there.'

'A very short one.' She didn't look at me.

'What time are we eating?' Rohan asked.

'Whenever you guys are ready.'

Theo came over. 'Let's give Lily fifteen more minutes.'

'You're the boss,' said Callum, turning away. 'Amber, can you pass the paprika?'

He hadn't introduced us to Amber, who I assumed was his sous chef. Was that the right term? I wasn't sure. But she acted like we weren't there, concentrating on her job, and then we all trooped out of the kitchen.

We passed another door, which Georgina said was 'the cupboard', and were then shown into the 'family room', which had comfortable sofas, a big TV, bookcases that contained paperbacks with cracked spines – a whole collection of Rupert Chadwick's mysteries, I noticed – and a shelf of literary novels that, I realized, contained all the recent Booker Prize winners, lined up in chronological order and all in pristine condition.

'Why don't you all go back up to the sitting room?' Theo suggested. 'I'm going to try to call Lily. See where she's got to.'

He left the room, followed by Georgina, and the rest of us went back up the first flight of stairs, with me taking the rear. As we reached the landing, I heard a harsh whisper from below me. Georgina, saying something to Theo. She sounded annoyed. Sophie, who was ahead of me, turned her head and peered down before raising her eyebrows in my direction. Theo and Georgina had gone into one of the downstairs rooms and were clearly arguing.

Rohan came back to join us. 'What's going on?' he whispered. 'Are they having a domestic? She's probably telling him not to drink so much.'

Sophie and I both looked at him.

'Haven't you noticed? He's already downed two huge glasses of red since we got here. Wouldn't be surprised if he started before that. Not that I want to be judgemental.'

Had Theo been a big drinker back in 1999? We all had been,

apart from Rohan, but I didn't recall him being any worse than the rest of us.

Sophie said, 'If they start fighting, I'm going.'

'I don't want him to get too drunk,' said Rohan.

'Why not?' I asked.

Rohan clammed up and, all of a sudden, I wondered if I'd made the right decision coming here. The hosts were fighting, there was a guy here we didn't know, Rohan was being shifty, and Lily hadn't even turned up yet. As for Sophie – did I really want all those long-dormant feelings from 1999 stirred up again? I wondered if I could bail without seeming unspeakably rude. Did it even matter? Sebastian was dead. He wouldn't care if I left.

I looked along the hall towards Finn. He was standing just inside the doorway of the sitting room, hunched over. What was he doing? Craning my neck, I saw that he was writing in a little notebook.

He caught me looking and quickly put the notebook into his inside jacket pocket.

The doorbell rang.

'Lily!' Sophie exclaimed. She hurried towards the stairs, Rohan following her. I hung back a moment, casting an eye towards Finn, who looked relieved.

What had he been writing?

I let it go and followed the others downstairs to greet Lily, relieved she had turned up but also wondering: now the six of us were here, did that mean we would finally talk about how terribly that summer had ended?

Chapter 5

June 1999

Recent graduates sought for internet start-up that is going to change the world. Intelligence and curiosity more important than experience. Send 500 words about yourself to sebastianmarlowe@yahoo.com

'Curiosity, eh? You know what you'll be doing,' said my friend Philip when I showed him the ad in the local paper. 'Scanning porn in a dingy back room somewhere.'

I had already typed 'Sebastian Marlowe' into the Yahoo search engine. Assuming it was the same person, he had until recently been a professor of psychology at the University of Kent. An unlikely pornographer. Besides, I was intrigued. This was 1999, and every day the papers were full of stories about IPOs and dotcom millionaires, websites coded in bedrooms making their creators rich. There were a lot of people making a lot of money – and right now, a month after sitting my finals, money was the number-one thing I needed.

That night, when I got home from the pub, I sent a long email telling all about my literary ambitions and my longing to get the hell out of my home town of Rye, a tiny place with lots of history but no jobs. I even attached a short story written in the minimalist style I was trying to perfect.

To my amazement, when I awoke the next day I found a

reply inviting me to an interview. It was to take place in a country hotel near Ashdown Forest, not too far from Rye.

I borrowed my dad's car and drove to the hotel, where the receptionist told me to wait upstairs in one of the conference rooms. I was the only person there and I sat, fiddling with my tie, until a guy a little older than me came into the room. He had floppy sandy-blond hair and a big smile. Ruddy cheeks, a rugby player's build.

'Will?' he asked. 'Theo Howard. Project manager. Before you meet the professor, I'll need you to complete these.'

He handed me a sheaf of papers.

'What are they?' I asked.

'Just some exercises. This one is the Belbin. It helps tell us how you would fit into a team. The other is a more straightforward personality test. Nothing to worry about.'

I leafed through them.

'Please answer both sets of questions honestly. Don't overthink it. Don't worry about what you think we're looking for.' He checked his watch. 'I'll be back in twenty minutes.'

I tackled the Belbin first. It consisted of a number of statements, collected into groups. The instructions told me to divide ten points between the statements. For example, one group of statements focused on idea generation. A note told me not to spread the points too evenly.

It was almost enjoyable. I was not one for self-reflection, but I had a clear image of myself as a creative, imaginative person. I had a rich fantasy life and spent much of my time having made-up conversations in my head. I was shy but liked being with groups of people I knew well. I got bored easily and was a voracious consumer of culture. I preferred to have one or two close friends than lots who didn't know me so well. I was romantic rather than rational.

I applied all this to the Belbin and then to the personality test, which was also comprised of statements, though this time all I had to do was agree or disagree with them, on a scale from strongly to slightly.

I enjoy meeting new people. Disagree slightly.

I make decisions based on my feelings. Agree strongly.

I prefer casual encounters to a steady relationship. Disagree strongly.

Theo returned as I was putting my pen down, which made me wonder if he'd been watching me. He scooped up the papers, glanced at them and said, 'Wait here.'

He returned ten minutes later, then led me into another room where two people sat behind a table: a middle-aged man and a young woman. I could see my test spread out before the man, with red pen marks added to it.

Theo joined them behind the table, and the middle-aged man spoke.

'Will. Thank you so much for coming along to meet us. I'm Sebastian Marlowe.'

He had dark hair speckled with grey and eyes that twinkled with mirth, which made me like him immediately. He was dressed as if he was about to board a yacht: polo shirt, unbuttoned to reveal a hairy chest, and shorts. I wasn't surprised by this lack of formality. This was the dotcom world, after all.

'This wonderful person is Lily,' he said, gesturing to the woman to his right. 'She just happens to be a genius.'

With a smile that told me she was secretly pleased by this praise, she said, 'You need to stop hyping me up.' She was also dressed casually, in an olive-green vest top and cargo pants, and wore an open, intelligent expression. Later, I would learn that she had been born in Hong Kong and that her parents had moved to England after the UK agreed to the handover with China, so she had grown up here.

'Lily is our chief coder,' Sebastian said.

'By "chief" he means "only",' Lily said.

Sebastian clapped his hands together. 'Theo, do you want to tell Will here what we're all about?'

I don't recall exactly what Theo said. He introduced the professor, telling me that he had recently decided to swap academia for entrepreneurship, then launched into a spiel about the opportunities that had opened up thanks to new technology. Halfway through, Sebastian interrupted.

'Tell me, Will. Do you have a girlfriend?'

Uh oh. Maybe this *was* something to do with porn.

'Not at the moment,' I answered hesitantly.

'Boyfriend? No? Well, your sexuality doesn't matter. I could tell from the short story you sent us that you have an interest in love. A longing for it, I would say.'

I am sure I turned pink. Theo was concentrating on the table in front of him, making notes in a pad, but Lily was staring straight at me, expressionless. Had they all read my story? It was about a man who was obsessed with a young woman he had seen at the launderette, which was where I'd written half of it, waiting for my underwear to dry.

'I'm sure you want to know how we're going to change the world, yes?' Sebastian said. 'Let me tell you a little story. I know you youngsters think you invented both sex and computers, but I did my postgraduate studies at Harvard in the sixties, where computer dating was created. Operation Match.' His voice was wistful, tinged with the rosy mist of nostalgia. Later, I discovered that after completing his studies at Harvard he accepted a position at another esteemed Boston institution, Fredericks University. 'We had to fill out a questionnaire, seventy-five questions about oneself and another seventy-five about one's ideal partner. Then they fed it all through an IBM that was bigger than this table. It's how I met my wife, Barbara. She lived in the suburbs of Boston and, if it hadn't been for Operation Match, I simply wouldn't have met her.'

Halfway through this anecdote, I saw where he was heading. 'You're setting up an internet dating site.'

'Bravo,' said the professor. He nudged Theo. 'I told you he was bright. Tell me, Will. What do you think of internet dating? Ever tried it?'

'I haven't.' I was hoping my face didn't betray my feelings. Wasn't internet dating something desperate people did? None of my friends had tried it, as far as I was aware.

'He thinks it's sad,' Lily said.

I chose not to lie. 'I suppose I think it's for people who can't find a partner by the, um, normal method.'

'Like going to *nightclubs*?' Sebastian leaned forward. He had very hairy, muscular forearms. 'Not everyone likes clubs, or bars. There are millions of lonely people out there, Will. People of every type. Extroverts and introverts, thinkers and feelers, the quirky and the deeply conformist. Those who love books, like your good self, and those who would prefer to poke at their . . .' He turned to Lily and waggled his thumbs. 'What's that thing called?'

Somehow, she knew what he meant. 'Game Boy.'

'That's the one. The problem is that internet dating in its current form is about as sophisticated as your average Game Boy-poking teen. Have you looked at any of these sites? They're barely better than classified ads in the newspaper. It's as if we've taken a step backwards from the original computer dating that helped me meet my wife.'

Beside him, Lily had opened a laptop and turned the screen towards me. I found myself looking at a dating site I'd heard of but never visited, with a profile of a woman on the page. A photo plus a screed of information about her. A personal statement. *I have a great sense of humour and love picnics in the countryside.* Lily clicked and, slowly, the page changed to another profile.

'You do this,' Sebastian said with a sad shake of the head. 'Click, click, click until you spot someone who takes your fancy. Like internet shopping. And everyone writes the same thing, because they think they know what potential partners want to hear. *Walking on the beach. Fond of puppies and snuggling in front of the telly.* We are going to change all that.'

Lily closed the laptop and leaned back. On the other side of the professor, Theo was still making notes. Appraising me.

'Your job,' Sebastian said, 'will be to create all the words for this site. The user guides, the FAQs, the sizzle we'll need to hook people in. We need a name too. A great one. We're going to start tomorrow.'

'Tomorrow?'

'Timing is everything, Will. You can bet there will be people in Silicon Valley having the same idea right now – we're going to require absolute dedication. That means you'll be living on site for the summer. Living *here*.'

He handed me a printed photograph. A picture of a huge house nestled in the countryside. Living on site? I hadn't expected that.

'That's my home, Will. Thornwood. You'll have your own room, three square meals a day, access to the grounds, the company of five or six like-minded souls, generous compensation and, of course, stock options.' He handed me another sheet of paper, with a number on it. It was considerably higher than I'd expected and I immediately started to think about what I could do with the money. I could find my own place. Get away from my parents.

It was exciting. I found myself being propelled along by the energy in the room, the sense of almost manic purpose coming off Sebastian. Tomorrow? Hell, yeah. I had nothing better to do.

There was still something I didn't understand though.

'How will this be different to the dating site you just showed me?' I asked. 'How are you planning to change the world?'

Sebastian leaned back and put his hands behind his head. 'We are going to harness the power of psychometric and behavioural testing, similar to the tests you sat before you came in here – the results of which we'll discuss with you when you start, by the way. Call me an old hippy, if you like, but I'm a strong believer in love.'

I blinked at him, taken aback by this declaration, which seemed to contrast with the statement he'd just made about taking a scientific approach.

'We're going to use what's here' – he tapped his head – 'to make people happy *here*.'

He thumped his chest, above his heart, and held his fist there.

'And when people are satisfied here and, without wishing to be crude, here . . .' He pointed at his groin. 'I believe they're also satisfied up here.'

He pointed at his skull again.

'So, Will,' he said. 'What do you say? Ready to join our revolution?'

Chapter 6

Lily slipped off her overcoat and handed it to Theo. Her hair was cut short and she was clad in a riot of patterns and colours: a tweed jacket over a leopard-print shirt with blue jeans and mustard Doctor Martens. No wedding ring, despite what Rohan had said.

We greeted her, one by one: Theo, Georgina, Rohan, me, and finally Sophie. 'Still not a hugger?' Sophie said with a laugh at the end of their embrace.

'She's definitely improved,' said Rohan.

'Hardly like cuddling an ironing board at all,' added Georgina.

'Bloody cheek.' Lily was mock outraged. 'My children tell me I'm a brilliant hugger.'

'Look,' I said. 'We're all here. Sebastian's six recruits.'

'The revolutionaries,' said Rohan.

Sophie put her hand to her mouth. 'I'd forgotten he used to call us that.'

Every morning, he would come into the library, which had been converted into an office, and say, 'Good morning, my revolutionaries!'

'I'm so sorry I'm late,' Lily said to Theo and Georgina. 'It's my ex. I arranged for her to have the kids tonight as soon as I got your invitation, but she claimed to have no knowledge of this request.' She let out a sigh that said a thousand words. 'But it's sorted. She's got them for the night, and I can relax. I'm going to have a drink. Maybe two!'

We all trooped back up the stairs and into the sitting room, where Theo handed Lily a glass of red and we stood facing each other in a messy circle.

'Why have we never got together before?' Rohan asked.

'Let's raise a toast.' That was Lily. 'To old friends?'

'To Sebastian,' Theo said, and we all murmured, *Yes, of course.* That was why we were here, after all. Back then, when we met him, he had been ten years older than most of us were now. Strong and quick and in the prime of life. What had he been doing in his old age? The obituary I'd eventually read had been vague. Finn should know more though.

We held our glasses aloft, all of us with wine, blood red and shiny beneath the chandelier, all except Rohan with his sparkling water. 'To Sebastian.'

We sipped our drinks and none of us moved, just looked at each other. The old gang. Co-workers. Hardly revolution-aries, despite Sebastian's best efforts, although we *had* been ahead of our time. The six of us were still here, alive and – on the surface, at least – well. It crossed my mind to mention the other two absent parties. Dominic and Eve had both been there that summer too. But I didn't want to risk puncturing our little bubble of togetherness.

We chatted for a minute, filling each other in on what we did for a living. Theo and Georgina drifted away and Sophie explained the layout of the house to Lily: 'The kitchen is on the ground floor, but the dining room is on this floor – I know, I'd be annoyed if I was the caterer, having to carry plates up the stairs – and the kids' bedrooms are up one more flight, with Georgina and Theo's bedroom right up at the top in the converted attic. Got that?'

During this, Rohan went into the corner and got his phone out. He seemed agitated about something and shot frustrated glances at Theo as our hosts left the room.

'Have you really not seen each other since 1999?' Finn asked. He had remained quiet during Lily's arrival but now came over to join me, her and Sophie. 'What happened? Did you fall out or something?'

'Nothing like that,' Sophie replied, but the way she avoided looking at me as she said this felt very deliberate.

Lily had not yet been introduced to Finn, so I did the honours.

'What was Sebastian working on during those last years?' I asked him.

'Oh . . . not much really. We were mostly putting his affairs in order. Archiving. That sort of thing.'

It seemed like a non-answer to me. A sidestep. But before I could ask a follow-up he said, 'I am genuinely surprised that none of you have seen each other for twenty-five years.'

He said it like he didn't believe us. Had Sebastian said something that made him think we had all kept in touch? Because I hadn't seen or spoken to the professor or any of the others since that summer.

'Did *you* stay in contact with Sebastian?' I asked Lily.

'No, I didn't.' She sounded terse. 'Not after the way things ended.'

I cleared my throat. 'Rohan told me you bumped into each other at a conference.'

'Did we? I don't remember that. What about you two?' She meant me and Sophie. 'Did you stay in contact?'

'No.'

I saw myself on that final night, stumbling along the hallway, praying no one would see me. I snapped out of it to see Finn scrutinizing me.

'What happened?' he asked.

'Didn't Sebastian tell you?'

'No. I mean, I know the website launch didn't go to plan—'

47

'That's one way of putting it.'

'—but I'd like to hear it from you guys.'

'I don't want to talk about it.' Lily was gripping her glass so tightly I feared it might shatter and slice her fingers open. 'I want to remember the professor fondly tonight. The good stuff, you know. Before . . .' Her voice became very quiet and I was only able to make out her final words because of the context. 'Before the bad.'

'Right,' said Finn, obviously disappointed.

'What are you up to these days?' Sophie asked Lily in a bright voice designed to break the tension. 'I imagine you in a massive corner office, minions running around, industry leaders begging your assistant to put them through to you.'

'Ha. Replace that image with one of me on my laptop in Starbucks, trying to get my ex to answer my texts.' She explained that she and her wife, Carrie, had separated a year ago, and that they shared custody of their two children, who were nine and seven. Carrie lived in what had been the family home while Lily was in a one-bedroom flat in Walthamstow.

'It's so unfair and so typical,' said Sophie. 'You're the cleverest person I've ever met. You should be living in a house like this one.'

'I'm really not that brilliant, Sophie. Remember what happened?'

'That wasn't your fault though. If you'd had more time.'

'Yeah, maybe.'

I cringed, wishing we could change the subject because it clearly still made Lily deeply unhappy.

'Anyway, the Belbin said I was an implementer. It's the plants who get rich.'

'Plants?' Finn said.

'Ideas people,' Lily explained. 'Innovators. Free thinkers.'

'Oh. Yes.' But it was clear this was the first time he'd heard

48

this, which was very odd for someone who'd worked for Sebastian.

'We all could have been rich,' Rohan said, fixing Lily with a glare.

'Leave her alone,' Sophie said. 'It was the professor who made the decision, not Lily.'

'We were only ever going to get rich if the company went public,' I pointed out. This was something I'd had to tell myself several times over the years, whenever I'd been tempted to mourn the riches that never came my way. 'And we were a long way from that.'

'Yeah, I know that,' he retorted in a tone that said, *I'm the businessman, you're just a lecturer.*

Finn was observing all this with great interest, and opened his mouth like he was about to ask something else.

Rohan cut him off. 'Do any of you still smoke?'

'I gave up years ago,' I said.

'Same,' said Sophie. 'Don't tell me you're still a smoker, Rohan?'

'Nah, of course not. I vape though. It's practically harmless.'

We all raised our eyebrows at the same time.

'I don't need a lecture, I need nicotine, and I was wondering if anyone wanted to join me.' Ah, that explained his tetchiness. 'I'm guessing they won't want me vaping in the house and I'm frightened to go and ask. They're having a proper domestic now. Listen.'

As a group, we edged closer to the door. It sounded like Georgina and Theo were in the dining room and, though it wasn't possible to hear the words, the tone of their voices made it clear they were arguing again.

'Maybe she *is* telling him off for drinking too much,' I said.

'Who knows,' said Lily. 'I'm a veteran when it comes to marital battles. It could be anything. Rohan, go and ask them if you can go into the garden. They'll probably be glad of the interruption.'

'I'll come with you, mate,' said Finn.

'Do you vape too?' I asked.

'No, but I could use some air.'

'Come on, let's all go,' said Sophie.

The five of us left the sitting room and went down the hallway towards the dining room. I was annoyed with Rohan for the way he'd spoken to Lily, showing that he still bore a grudge. To use a metaphor from Rohan's favourite sport, it was like a lesser squad member feeling aggrieved about missing out on the dream of winning the World Cup because the star player had missed a penalty.

As we got closer to the dining room, Georgina and Theo must have heard us because they fell silent, though not before I heard a snatch of conversation:

—*going to tell them.* That was Georgina.

And Theo, in response, said, *Are you sure we can trust*—

He stopped before he said the final word. *Them*, I thought. He was going to say *trust them.*

Sophie reached the dining-room doorway first. 'Hiya. We were just going to pop into the garden so Rohan can vape. That okay?'

'Actually,' Theo said, frowning at Georgina, 'we were hoping to have a word with all of you. Do you mind waiting five minutes, Rohan? Shall we all go back to the sitting room?'

'Everything okay?'

'Not really,' Georgina said quietly.

We returned to the sitting room. I took one end of a sofa, with Sophie beside me. It felt good having her that close to me. Since she'd arrived I was having to force myself not to keep looking at her.

Georgina sat in one of the armchairs, with Theo perched

on the arm beside her. Was he drunk? His nose was a little pink, but he seemed steady enough on his feet. 'Some of you have been asking, wondering about our eldest daughter, Olivia.'

He turned his face towards his wife, who said, 'So we thought we should fill you in.'

Everyone was staring at them, enrapt.

Theo cleared his throat. 'The thing is . . .'

His voice cracked and Georgina took over.

'The thing is, we have no idea where she is.'

Chapter 7

Olivia Howard was nineteen when her parents last saw her. During the eleven months she'd been missing she had turned twenty. Georgina brought up a picture on her phone and we passed it around the room. She was a striking girl, willowy with light-brown hair, a gap between her teeth that she'd inherited from her dad, a little mole above her lip like Georgina's. In fact, she was a perfect blend of both her parents, as if a piece of software had merged their faces.

'She was taking a gap year,' Georgina explained. 'She had a place at Durham. To read English, much to her father's horror.'

'I wasn't horrified. I wanted her to study a subject that leads somewhere, that's all. No offence, Will.' Theo shrugged an apology in my direction. 'We thought she was going to do the whole backpacking thing. We have friends with properties all over the world, so she could have done it without having to stay anywhere grotty, but she insisted she wanted to do it properly.'

'Hostels,' Georgina said with a shudder.

'She's a free spirit, our Livvy. She has a huge chip on her shoulder about being privileged. You know what this generation is like. Obsessed with social justice. She can't walk past a homeless person without giving them whatever cash she has on her.'

'She has a kind heart, that's all. She was always pestering us to take in stray cats when she was little.'

'She sounds like my type of person,' Sophie said. 'I like this generation. The fact that they care so much.'

Theo took a big swig of wine. 'Yes, well, *obviously*, I support a lot of these causes. My company hosts a charity auction every year, raising money for all sorts. And we always buy Fair Trade, don't we, darling?'

'Do we?'

'Well, we try. The problem with Livvy is that she gets so *emotional* about everything. That was one of the reasons I wanted her to go travelling, so she could see that life here in London isn't that bad. But then she met Felix.'

He spat the name out like it was poisonous.

'Her boyfriend,' Georgina explained, a wrinkle of distaste on her face. 'Actually, she denied that. Said they were just friends who hooked up sometimes.'

Theo grimaced and downed another mouthful from his glass.

'Bad news?' Rohan said. He was seated on the opposite sofa, with Lily next to him. Finn was in the other armchair, leaning towards the Howards but glancing every few seconds at the rest of us.

'Very. For a start, he dissuaded her from going travelling.' Theo had clenched his fists. 'Said it was poverty tourism or some such nonsense. Spending thousands to go and look at poor people.'

'So she cancelled her trip,' Georgina said. 'And I expected her to spend her time out of the house, campaigning or hanging out with Felix. But she actually spent more and more time slobbing around here. Reading. Moping. She kept baking cupcakes that she never ate.'

'Vegan cupcakes,' Theo said. 'Like eating cardboard.'

'Mia and I enjoyed them,' Georgina said, and Theo muttered a half-hearted apology and rubbed her shoulder. This was the first time during the conversation that Mia, the younger sister, had been mentioned.

'It transpired that Olivia and Felix had fallen out. She discovered he was also seeing several other girls and she couldn't handle it. Turns out she thought they were boyfriend and girlfriend, after all.'

'When was this?' Lily asked. She looked distressed, perhaps imagining something similar happening to her own children.

'The Christmas before last. She spent most of Christmas Day locked away in her room with Claude, writing in her journal, while the rest of us sat down here playing board games. We sent Mia up a couple of times to try to persuade her to come down, but she refused.'

'I suspect she was up there obsessing over that little twat,' Theo said.

'We've all done it.' Sophie took a sip of her wine. 'All had our hearts broken, I mean.'

'I haven't,' said Theo.

'That's because you're still with your first love. You two are rare and lucky.' Hurriedly, because of the current topic of conversation, she added, 'In that respect, I mean.'

Rohan piped up. 'Sorry, you're losing me. What happened?'

Georgina squeezed her husband's hand. 'We thought everything was picking up. January, February, she seemed happier. Started eating cheese again. Told us she was thinking of going to stay with a couple of friends from school whose parents have a place in Tuscany.'

'Lovely place,' said Theo. He was starting to slur his words now, just a little.

'Then one day we came home from work and she wasn't here. The messages we tried to send to her phone went undelivered. None of her friends knew where she was. She was gone.'

These words, and the way she said them, sent a chill through the room. Lily turned even paler. Rohan stopped acting like he was waiting for them to get to the point and whispered, 'Shit.'

'She was here when you left for work?' I asked.

'Yes. I spoke to her through her bedroom door before heading in.'

'Where do you work, Georgina?' Sophie asked.

'I run a little yoga studio in Hampstead. I don't go in every day, but I was teaching a class that morning, then I had lunch with some friends.' She shook her head, apparently full of regret. 'When I got home, I went upstairs to talk to Olivia and she wasn't there. To be honest, I didn't think anything of it.'

'What about Mia?' I asked. 'Was she here?'

'She boards during the week. Comes home on Fridays and spends the weekend here.'

Theo took over the story. 'I came home around eight and Livvy still wasn't here, but neither of us was worried. It was only when Georgina texted her around ten to see if she was coming home – we needed to know whether to lock up – and got no response that we had the first stirrings of concern.'

'I tried to call her,' Georgina said. 'It went straight to voicemail. And our texts weren't being read.'

'I have to admit, I still wasn't that worried.' Theo sighed. 'She was nineteen. She often stayed out. I assumed she'd probably gone to a club and there was no signal or had met a boy and turned her phone off.'

Georgina pushed a stray lock of hair out of her face. 'I thought she might have gone to see Felix. That perhaps that was why she'd been in a better mood recently. I'd see her tapping away at her phone. Or writing in her journal.'

'Which is missing too, by the way. We've searched her room, but she must have taken it with her. To cut a long story short, Livvy didn't come home that night or the next morning, and when we tried to call or text her it seemed her phone was still off or out of signal.'

'It was a nightmare,' Georgina said. 'I called the police that morning and they tried to fob me off until I reminded them who we are. A lot of those auctions Theo mentioned are for police charities, and the commissioner's wife has attended my yoga classes. *Then* they started to take it seriously. We contacted all her friends – no one had seen her – while the police went and found Felix. He claimed he hadn't spoken to her since Christmas.'

'Her phone records seemed to back that up,' Theo said. 'It also transpired that the last time her phone sent out a signal, she was here, or in the immediate vicinity. The police think she must have turned her phone off before she went out.'

I was listening to Theo but watching Georgina. There were tears rolling down her cheeks. Sophie got up and went over to crouch in front of her, whispering consoling words.

Then I noticed someone hovering in the door. It was the red-headed woman who had been in the kitchen with Callum. His sous chef or assistant, or whatever she was. Amber.

'Are you and your guests almost ready for appetizers?' she asked, entering the room. 'And would you like me to light the candles at the table now?'

She moved further into the room, glancing at Georgina and obviously wondering what was going on.

'Yes, please do that,' Theo said.

Amber nodded and backed out. Sophie was still crouching before Georgina, who said, 'I'm so sorry. I'm fine. Really. The police believe nothing awful has happened to her. They think she has taken herself off somewhere, that it's probably related to her heartbreak over Felix, though they don't suspect him of anything.'

'Quite a lot of money was withdrawn from her account the

day she vanished,' Theo said. 'Plus, she had a very expensive watch that she got for her eighteenth birthday and some jewellery she inherited when Georgina's mother died. She could have raised thousands by selling it.'

'They think a friend, someone unknown to us, could be harbouring her. All we know is that she must still be in the UK, because her passport hasn't been used.'

'We are certain she's out there,' Theo said. His glass was empty again. 'A runaway.'

'We just have to wait for her to come home.'

A silence hung over the room until Theo stood up and said, 'And that's it. We thought you should all know so you don't waste your time speculating and so it doesn't spoil the evening. But she's out there, we know it, and we also know she's going to come home. When she's ready.'

I studied Georgina's face. She looked very clearly, to me, like someone who was trying very hard to hold it together. Trying to look brave and confident.

'Georgina?' I said.

She stood. 'Theo's right. She's fine, I can feel it. I just . . . I miss her. I think, if I was a better mother . . .'

The tears came fully now. Theo, who seemed shocked, took a step towards her, but Sophie and Lily got in his way, surrounding Georgina and putting their arms around her. Theo hovered on the outside of this group, unsure what to do. He saw me looking at him and came over. We were all on our feet now.

'Are you all right?' I asked.

'Yes. Georgina worries, of course she does.' He held up his empty glass. 'I need another drink.'

'Another? Are you sure?'

'I'm certain of it.'

Rohan followed him over to the cabinet, where he had put

the wine bottles. 'Mate, I'm sorry, it's totally shit about your daughter, but I *really* need some nicotine. Can you let me out the back door?'

'Huh? Oh. Yes, of course.'

He led Rohan out of the room. I thought about talking to Sophie again, but the three women were huddled together. Finn had excused himself a moment. Feeling like a spare part, I drifted out into the hallway, still carrying my drink, and stood outside the small bathroom that was diagonally opposite the dining room. A moment of much-needed peace.

Poor Theo and Georgina. I often wondered what it would have been like to have children, but any regrets I might have vanished when I heard stories like theirs. How could anyone take that amount of worry and heartache. How—

The floorboards above my head creaked.

It was a loud creak too, and I was almost certain it was the sound of someone walking across the floor above. Rohan and Theo were downstairs, and the women were all in the sitting room. The only person unaccounted for was Finn. But why would he go upstairs?

At that moment, the toilet flushed inside the bathroom and, a moment later, the door opened. It was Theo.

'Oh,' I said. 'I thought you'd gone downstairs.'

'On my way now.' He didn't wait. He headed straight down the staircase, and I hurried to keep up. I assumed what had happened was that Finn had come out of the sitting room looking for a loo, found the one on the first floor occupied and gone up to the second to use the one up there. A simple explanation.

We found Rohan waiting by the back door, which opened on to the garden, fidgeting with his vape in his hand.

'I have to disconnect this door from the security system until we go to bed,' Theo said, 'because otherwise it becomes massively inconvenient going into the garden. Letting the cat in and out too.'

He looked up at the key rack on the wall beside the door and made a noise.

'What is it?' Rohan asked.

'It's not bloody there.' He walked back to the foot of the stairs and yelled, 'Georgina.' When she didn't immediately respond, he called her again.

I heard her voice from above. Annoyed. I couldn't blame her. She had been crying, upset about her daughter. Theo was hardly being sensitive. 'What is it?' she called.

'Have you seen the back-door key?'

'No.' A pause. 'I bet Mia accidentally took it to her room and left it there. I'll go and check.'

We waited for Georgina, Rohan growing increasingly fidgety. He had the air of someone who was trying to gather the courage to ask someone on a date. Finally, he said, 'Theo, mate, have I told you about this idea—'

Theo cut him off. 'Maybe it's in the kitchen.'

He walked away, and Rohan tried to rearrange his face, to bring the devil-may-care smile back, but it wouldn't hold.

'Were you about to pitch an investment to him?' I said, my irritation with him lingering. 'Isn't that a bit inappropriate? It's a dinner party. He's literally just told us about his daughter going missing.'

'What do you know?' he said, his aggression taking me aback. 'You've got no family. No responsibilities.'

'Rohan, what's going on?' I asked. I was used to dealing with overwhelmed students melting down before exams or bringing their problems from home into the classroom and I switched into professional mode. 'Do you want to talk about it?'

'It's not fair,' he said, after a pause. 'All I've ever needed is a bit of luck.'

'Are you talking about the dating site?'

'I'm talking about everything. But yeah, it started there. I got screwed over, while some people . . .'

He stared over my shoulder, and I turned to see that Callum had come out of the kitchen, wiping his hands on a cloth and nodding at us.

'Thought I'd better get out the way while Mr Howard searches the kitchen.'

Theo appeared a moment later. He held out his empty palms.

'No sign of it,' he said, glancing at Callum, who went back into the kitchen. 'But don't worry. Georgina will find it.'

I hoped she would. Because right now, I was starting to feel claustrophobic, even in this big house. Rohan kept rattling the door handle, the muscles in his jaw clenching. It was fraying my nerves. Making me feel trapped.

I reached past Rohan and rattled the door too.

Chapter 8

July 1999

It was seven thirty and the morning sun had yet to burn off the mist that blanketed the East Sussex countryside. I rubbed at my eyes. I'd been too worried about missing my alarm to sleep much and the instant coffee in the Thermos my mum had handed to me as I left was weak and ineffective. But now, as my train slowed then pulled into a tiny station, the adrenaline kicked in. I was here.

Moments later, I stood on the platform, surprised by the chill in the air. The mist hung around the edges of the station, turning the trees into grey silhouettes and giving the little ticket office a ghostly glow. Only one other passenger had disembarked: a young woman with an enormous suitcase by her feet. She stood there, looking a little unsure, a mobile phone in her hand, and that made me wonder if she was here for the same reason as me.

A man's voice boomed from behind me.

'Are you Will? Sophie?'

I turned to see a dark-haired guy striding through the station's side gate, car keys in hand. He was about my age, tall, Ray-Bans pushed up to reveal a pair of startlingly blue eyes.

'Uncle Sebastian asked me to pick you up,' he said, watching impassively as I hoisted my holdall on to my shoulder and the woman, Sophie, struggled to drag her suitcase across the platform. One wheel was broken so a corner scraped against the concrete as she pulled it.

'You should have seen me trying to get it through Charing Cross station,' she said with a self-deprecating smile. 'There was a gang of pigeons pointing and laughing.'

'Do you want a hand?' I asked, though I was already weighed down with my own luggage and the driver – Sebastian's nephew, apparently – was unencumbered.

'Yes, please. If you don't mind.'

The nephew made no offer to help. Instead, he regarded us with amusement.

'You sure you want to do this?' he asked.

'What?' Both Sophie and I said this at the same time.

'Just saying – this is your last chance to back out.'

I frowned. 'Why would we want to do that?' I remembered my friend's warning. 'This is real, isn't it?'

'Oh, it's real, all right. Uncle Seb is taking it all very seriously. I just wondered . . .' He trailed off.

'Wondered what?'

'Oh, nothing.' He turned and walked through the gate into the car park, leaving Sophie and me looking at each other.

'Well, I'm not dragging this thing all the way back to London now,' she said. 'Come on.'

I helped Sophie wrestle her suitcase off the platform. Our driver had stopped beside a vintage Jag, a bottle-green convertible with four seats, the top down despite the temperature. With a loud *tut* he grabbed the suitcase and wrestled it on to the back seat. 'Bloody hell. Have you got a body in here?'

'Two, actually. I already had one with me, but then this guy on the train was being really annoying.'

'You're Sebastian's nephew?' I asked, after Sophie had squeezed on to the back seat beside her case.

'That's me.' He didn't offer his name.

'I'm Will.'

'Yeah, got that.'

He climbed into the driver's seat and I went around and got in beside him. 'This is beautiful,' I said.

'Used to be my dad's.'

We had all been instructed to come by public transport and leave our own cars at home, with no explanation why, though my friend Philip – the one who had warned me about the porn-scanning – said it was probably because they wanted to make it harder for us to escape if we got fed up. I thought about what Sebastian's nephew had just said. *Was* I sure I wanted to do this?

Yes. Yes, I was.

We drove out of the car park and I turned around to talk to Sophie, exchanging small talk about where we came from – she was from Bedfordshire – and our journeys. She was wearing a necklace in the shape of a star with a circle at its centre. I'd seen this before: it was an evil eye, designed to protect its wearer from harm. I decided not to remark on it.

Soon, we passed through a little village, with a pub and a post office and an express supermarket. A black cat watched us from its place on the stone wall surrounding a pretty church.

'What are you going to be doing on the website?' I asked.

'As little as possible.' She had large brown eyes. A tiny scar above one eyebrow. 'Oops, probably shouldn't say that in front of the boss's nephew.'

'It doesn't bother me.' He had lit a cigarette and the wind blew the smoke into my face.

'The boring answer is that I'm in charge of user experience,' Sophie said. 'What did the professor call it? UX. Making sure the site is easy and logical to use. You?'

'Copywriter.'

65

'We'll be working closely together then.' She addressed our driver: 'Hey, can I grab one of those cigarettes? Mine are at the bottom of my case.' She must have misread my reaction because she said, 'I know, vile habit. Don't judge me.'

'I'm not,' I said as our driver passed one back. 'I occasionally have one, at a party or something.'

'Ooh, a proper Hunter S. Thompson.' I must have looked stung because she immediately apologized. She lit the cigarette. 'Are you going to be working with us too, Sebastian's mysterious nephew?'

He finally cracked a smile. 'Work? I'll just be hanging out. Uncle Seb gets me to do the odd favour in return for letting me live with him. Like picking you two up.'

I wondered why he lived with his uncle. He'd mentioned this car had belonged to his dad. Had he inherited it? Did that mean his parents were dead?

There was a silence. We had left the village now and were driving along an A-road, hedgerows on either side. The sun was finally coming out and the mist clearing.

'I'm Dominic.' We both looked at him.

'Nice to meet you, Dominic,' said Sophie. As she leaned forward to stub her cigarette out in the ashtray, the wind fanned her hair so it tickled my face. I touched my cheek as if she'd kissed me.

'So what's Professor Marlowe like?' She asked Dominic. 'To work for, I mean?'

'I wouldn't know.' There was a long pause. 'All I can say is he takes all this shit very seriously, so I'd advise you not to fuck around.'

She pretended to take a note. 'Do not fuck around.'

'Did they send you the results of your tests?' I asked her as she sat back.

'Oh, yeah.' We talked about our results for a minute. On

the Belbin behavioural test we were both 'plants', and I also had a strong 'implementer' score – I was good at making sure stuff got done, apparently – while she was a 'teamworker'. After talking about that for a little while we moved on to the psychometric test we'd taken, the Big Five personality test. Sophie closed her eyes as she attempted to remember what hers had said. 'I'm highly inventive, introverted but friendly, completely disorganized, and resilient. What about you, Will?'

'High on inventiveness. Sensitive . . .'

I saw Dominic roll his eyes.

'Half introvert, half extrovert. Half organized, half careless.'

'A halfwit,' said Dominic.

'Very funny.'

Sophie said, 'Did you spend ages agonizing over each statement before choosing "I don't know"?'

I laughed. 'My main personality trait is indecisiveness.'

'Ha. Do you actually agree with that? Let me guess: you can't decide.'

We turned off the main road and found ourselves driving down narrow lanes with room for only one vehicle. Despite this, Dominic drove fast, leaning back, one hand on the wheel. I gripped the edges of my seat and watched the trees blur past. Dominic put the radio on. 'You Get What You Give' by New Radicals was playing, and Sophie said, 'I love this song,' so Dominic turned it up. She sang along softly. She had a good voice, sweet and tuneful.

The song ended and we turned on to an even narrower lane, and then, as we crested a small hill, the landscape opened up ahead of us.

'Oh. Oh, wow!' Sophie said from the back seat.

That first glimpse of Thornwood will be embedded in my memory for ever. The gardens that rolled out into meadows, alive with wildflowers. The woods that circled the estate. The lake, with some mist still hanging over its surface like a cloud fallen to earth. The long gravel drive that led to the house. And, of course, the house itself. It was even bigger and grander than I'd imagined, H-shaped and built from limestone, glowing pale yellow in the sun that had broken through as we'd driven down the lane. On one side of the building there was a tower from which a Union flag flew, and ivy crept up its facade, almost covering a couple of the tall, narrow windows, and to the far right, red roses clung to the masonry. There was a smaller outbuilding across a courtyard and a mix of neatly trimmed topiary and wild shrubs, nature both tamed and untamed.

'You're all going to be sleeping and working in the main house,' Dominic said. 'Uncle Sebastian is in the cottage, which you can't see from here because it's behind the house.'

'Are any of the others here yet?' I asked.

'Theo is. That geeky girl too.'

'Lily?'

'Yeah. I've got two more to pick up later.'

Sophie was leaning forward between the front seats again, eyes wide with wonder.

'This is it,' she said in an awestruck tone. 'This is where the movie of my life finally begins.'

Dominic pulled up at the end of the driveway, wheels crunching on gravel. As we got out of the car, the front door of the house opened and two spaniels came running across to us, barking. Sophie immediately bent to befriend them and then the professor was there, greeting us and asking how our journey had been.

'Let me show you to your rooms,' he said. 'And you must see the office. Lily's done a marvellous job setting it up.' He tried to lift Sophie's suitcase, which made his smile vanish, and his tone changed when he addressed his nephew. 'Dominic, you take this. Do something for your keep.'

Then he was all charm again. 'My dear, let me give you the tour. Oh, what a beautiful morning for you to join us. Perfect. *Perfect.*'

He set off towards his house, Sophie almost having to run to keep up. She glanced back over her shoulder and smiled at me as I stood by the car with Dominic, who glared at the suitcase like it was his mortal enemy, muttering under his breath.

He looked up and caught me watching Sophie as she went up the front steps of the house, the professor animatedly pointing out something inside

'Out of your league, mate,' Dominic said.

Chapter 9

Georgina came down the stairs. 'Sorry. I can't find the key anywhere.'

Rohan swore.

Georgina put her hands on her hips. 'Look, just go and vape in the family room. As long as you're not smoking real cigarettes, I don't care. Then everyone needs to come up to the dining room for appetizers.'

Rohan made grateful noises then went to get his nicotine fix, which would hopefully make him chill out. If he was going to pitch Theo a business idea, couldn't he wait till after we'd eaten? Perhaps he was worried Theo would be passed out drunk.

I went upstairs to the dining room with Georgina and Theo, and found Sophie and Lily chatting with Finn. Seeing me, Sophie peeled away from that conversation. As Georgina made sure everything on the table was exactly how she wanted it, Sophie and I moved into the corner and I told her about Rohan and the locked back door. Then Lily joined us, frowning at her phone.

'I've been trying to text Carrie to check the kids are okay, but there's no signal here. At all.'

She held up her phone and I saw there were zero bars.

Sophie and I got our phones out.

'I haven't got any either,' Sophie said, and mine was the same. 'Weird. It was working earlier.'

'Maybe the network's gone down,' I suggested. 'Which one are you on?'

We compared notes. We were all with different providers.

I noticed that Sophie was looking at me with a little smile on her lips. 'You did get a phone in the end then?'

So she *did* remember her final words to me. That meant she must remember how angry I'd been.

Finn appeared at my shoulder. 'Hey, guys, are you— What's wrong?'

We explained about the lack of reception and he checked his phone.

'Nope, nothing. A dead spot?' Holding his phone up, he walked out of the room and into the hallway, then came straight back. 'Same out there.'

Georgina, who had been attempting to remove a speck of dirt from a glass with a napkin, overheard us talking. 'What's going on?' When I told her, she said, 'Oh, it's this house. Thick walls. Reception comes and goes all the time. The kids are always moaning about it.'

She flinched at her own words. Kids, plural. I think we all realized simultaneously that the lack of mobile signal was trivial compared to what Georgina and Theo were going through, and we put our phones away. Then Rohan came into the dining room.

'Are you feeling better now?' I asked.

'Yeah. I'm sorry, man, I just . . . I've been under a lot of strain recently.'

'Financial strain? It's okay – you don't need to tell me. But do you want to describe the idea you want to pitch to Theo? I might be able to help you. Bring up the subject so it comes naturally into the conversation.'

'I'd appreciate that.'

He began to tell me about his idea. Something to do with a

members' club for small businessmen which also doubled as a shared workspace during the day. I wasn't sure how original it was or how easy it would be to bring it up in conversation, but I promised to try.

As he went off, seeming slightly happier, Amber came in bearing a huge silver platter. I was able to get a proper look at her for the first time. She was wearing a white chef's jacket, short-sleeved, with two columns of buttons, and black trousers. She had removed her head covering and her auburn hair was tied back in a ponytail. About forty, I estimated. Her most distinctive feature by far was the tattoo that covered most of what I could see of her left arm. Just below her sleeve, the face of a woman, eyes closed in apparent ecstasy, tears falling from her eyes towards Amber's elbow, where the teardrops expanded and changed shape to become wolves.

She saw me looking.

'That's really cool,' I said.

She gave me the tiniest smile in history, the kind of look that told me she heard this inane comment several times a day.

'Everyone,' Georgina said loudly, saving me from having to come up with something more interesting to say to Amber, 'we have a charcuterie board for the meat eaters, crudités with dips for the veggies and, as a special treat, a tribute to the professor: miniature lobster rolls.'

There were several exclamations of delight as everyone came closer. Sebastian had been obsessed with lobster rolls, telling anyone who would listen how he had become addicted to them when he and his wife lived in Boston. One night, he had brought in caterers and thrown a 'Boston dinner party': clam chowder, cannoli, lobster mac and cheese; for dessert, Boston cream pie, which was about the only thing Sophie and I had been able to eat that evening.

The mini lobster rolls were snatched up while Amber went

around refilling wine and water glasses. I stood by the crudités and accompanying dips and crunched baby carrots and asparagus. I hadn't realized how hungry I was.

I looked at my old friends: Georgina and Lily, Sophie and Rohan. Theo stood on his own in the corner, munching on a lobster roll and staring into space. I went over to him.

'I just want to say thank you for this,' I said. 'I realize everything must be hard for you and Georgina at the moment, what with your daughter being . . .' I trailed off, deterred from saying more by his expression.

'She's out there. She's going to come home.'

'Do you think this Felix guy might be hiding her?'

He leaned closer. 'Can you keep a secret? I actually spent a couple of weekends trailing him. I'd park outside his flat and watch him, thinking he might lead me to her. But he hardly goes out, and he had several other young women visit him. Can you imagine how it feels to see that? Olivia was in love with him. He broke her heart. And he doesn't give a fuck.' His voice was thick and, although he hadn't slurred his words during this conversation, he was clearly well on the way to getting properly drunk. 'I saw him come out of his flat a couple of times, and the temptation to march over there and throttle the little shit . . .'

He was getting aggressive and I wanted to pull him back. There was also something else I wanted to talk to him about. 'I think it's great that you kept in touch with Sebastian over the years.'

'Hmm? Oh, it was just Christmas cards, that kind of thing. We often talked about getting together, but you know what it's like . . . Years drift by. One minute we're talking about meeting up for lunch, next thing we're getting an invitation to his funeral. Apparently, he'd given his solicitor a list before he got really sick.'

'That's where you met Finn?'

'Yes. Poor chap seemed a bit lost, like he didn't know what he was going to do next. Georgina had already come up with the idea of throwing this dinner, and she suggested that we invite Finn too. Give him a chance to meet some more people who'd known the prof.'

There was a fleck of pink meat clinging to his lower lip. It wobbled as he spoke.

'Do you know how long he worked for Sebastian?'

'A few years, I think. Why are you asking all these questions about him?'

'I don't know. It's just that he doesn't seem to know very much about Sebastian or his work. Like, he didn't know about the Belbin. Seems odd.'

'Oh, I think it's just that talking about the professor upsets him.'

'Really?' My impression was that Finn had spoken about Sebastian as if he were someone he'd heard stories about, a famous acquaintance of a friend. He hadn't seemed emotionally affected by his death at all.

Theo, on the other hand, was growing maudlin. 'I wish I'd made more of an effort to keep in touch with the prof. He was the father I never had, you know. My own dad was always cold and distant. Sebastian was so *interested*.'

I recalled that both Theo and Lily had got to know Sebastian when they were students at Kent. Although they had been studying business and computer science respectively, they had both taken part in a psychology trial overseen by Sebastian and his department, something to do with how people act when their circadian rhythms are disrupted. He had identified something in both of them that had led to him offering them jobs, which ultimately progressed to him asking them to join him when he came up with the idea for the dating site.

75

Theo's eyes were damp. I tried not to look at the meat that refused to leave his lip as he relayed an anecdote about Sebastian, something about the professor taking him aside and giving him advice about how to keep Georgina happy, sharing a story about how marriage had changed his life, made him a new man.

'You didn't bear a grudge then?'

'Hmm?'

'For the way he suddenly shut it all down. Scrapped the website and sent us away.'

It was the first time any of us had mentioned how it had ended. The crushing disappointment that had come at the close of that summer, the morning after the party that had ended up being the last time we all saw each other. I immediately felt a little lighter for getting it out there.

Theo shook his head. 'Of course I was gutted. I couldn't believe it when he told me. But businesses fail all the time. It was nothing personal.'

'It was hard to see that at the time though.'

He finally wiped his mouth with the back of his hand. 'For you, perhaps. But that day, when we left, Georgina and I went straight to a pub and talked.'

'Really?'

'Yes. About the future. About how strong we could be together. And I'd made contacts at Thornwood . . . certain opportunities I could leverage.'

I didn't understand what that meant, but before I could ask he said, 'Excuse me for a moment,' and made his way over to Georgina.

In his absence, I focused on Finn. He moved slowly around the room, stopping to hover close to Sophie and Rohan, apparently eavesdropping. Then he surveyed the room and I followed his gaze to Amber, who had remained in the dining room, refilling drinks and replenishing the platter.

She must have felt his eyes on her because she looked up from the glass she was pouring wine into. Their eyes locked for a moment, and he furrowed his brow, apparently confused.

They know each other, I thought, startled. Or . . . maybe it's just that she knows him?

I glanced at Finn – and he caught me. His expression was troubled, his brow creased, but as our eyes met he rearranged his face into a smile.

It was the fakest thing I'd ever seen.

Chapter 10

'Will, have you— Oh my God.' It was Sophie. She had appeared behind me, making me jump. 'Anyone would think I'd popped a balloon in your ear.'

I took hold of her arm. 'I need to talk to you.'

I led her out of the room, and it wasn't until we were on the landing that I realized I was still holding her arm. Her skin was warm beneath my palm.

She looked at me and raised her eyebrows and I clicked what I was doing.

'I'm so sorry,' I said, snatching my hand away.

She laughed. 'It's fine. I thought you were going to drag me into a cupboard and I was trying to figure out how I felt about it.'

Now I was even more flustered. 'I . . .'

She leaned closer. 'What did you want to talk to me about?'

I looked around. There was a closed door just along from the dining room: the study. I opened it and peered inside, then gestured for Sophie to join me.

The study was so neat and orderly it was hard to believe anyone ever worked in here. The desk bore no clutter and the pens were kept neatly in a mug that bore the legend 'World's Best Mum'. So this was Georgina's office.

'This is very cloak and dagger,' Sophie said. 'I wasn't expecting so much excitement. Not sure if my heart can— Wait, are you all right?'

'It's Finn.' I kept my voice low. 'I think there's something . . . off about him.'

There were two chairs in the room, an office chair and a beaten-up armchair that was the oldest-looking thing I'd seen so far in this house. Sophie sat in it while I took the office chair.

I explained what I'd witnessed, how Finn had gone around the room apparently listening to everyone else's conversations, and also mentioned the way his expression had shifted so suddenly when he'd caught me looking.

I waited for her to respond and, when she didn't, said, 'So? What do you think?'

'I don't know. I mean, he must be nervous, being here with us lot. He's the odd one out. He asked me lots of questions.'

'Like what?'

'Oh, about my life, my work, how often I come to London, how well I know this area in particular.' She stroked her chin. 'Hmm, the more I think about it, the more it feels like I was being chatted up – but by someone who actually knows how to do it. I wonder if he'd told Georgina he was single and she invited him here as some kind of matchmaking exercise.'

Matchmaking? Could Georgina really be trying to set Sophie up with Finn?

'Your face is doing peculiar things,' Sophie said.

'That's what I look like when I'm thinking.'

It made me happy that I was still able to make her laugh. And I wondered: had Finn seen something in the way Sophie talked to me that made him think she was interested in me? Was this about jealousy?

'I still don't get why you think there's something "off" about him. His smile slipped for a moment and he listened in to some conversations. Is that it?'

'No, there are other things. I saw him writing in a little notebook.'

'Don't you do that? Like, when you have ideas for your books?'

'I tap them into my phone.' But that could be an explanation, couldn't it? Maybe he was writing something too. A book about Sebastian? A memoir or a biography?

'What else?' Sophie asked.

'I'm wondering if he's lying about being Sebastian's assistant,' I said.

That made her lean even further forward in her seat. 'What makes you think that?'

'Firstly,' I said, 'he had never heard of the Belbin. How could you work for the professor and not know about that test?'

'Maybe he didn't use it any more. It's not like he was still employing people.'

'Apart from, apparently, Finn. Don't you think he would have made him sit the Belbin?'

'Not if he wasn't going to be part of a team.'

I wasn't convinced. 'What about this? He said Tunbridge Wells is in East Sussex when it's actually in Kent. Surely if he lived there and commuted to Thornwood, as he claims, he would know that.'

'That hardly seems like a smoking gun, Will. It could have been a simple mistake. It's right on the border, isn't it?'

'I think he and Amber know each other too. Or she knows him, at least.'

'Really? Maybe she catered another event he was at.'

I sighed. 'I know. There's a simple explanation for all of it. But when you put everything together, including how evasive and vague he is about anything to do with working for Sebastian, I'm certain he's up to something.'

'Like what?'

'That's what I don't know. Maybe he's casing the joint. Theo and Georgina are loaded. He might be planning a burglary or a con. Some clever way of extracting money from them.'

'Hold on. If that's the case, what was he doing at Sebastian's funeral? You think he's some kind of weird criminal who goes to random services hoping to meet rich people?'

I ran my hands through my hair. 'I realize it sounds far-fetched. But—'

'Oh my God.' She had clearly remembered our conversation earlier. 'You think he might be a psychopath?'

'Don't look so shocked. He could be. What was that stat Lily told us? One in a hundred people. That isn't that rare.'

Sophie stood up. 'I don't know about any of this, Will. Yes, he's a bit weird, a little vague. But you know what, I'm not here for drama. I'm here to see my old friends, including you, and to have dinner. Speaking of which, we'd better get back.'

She moved towards the door. Again, I reached out and touched her forearm. 'I thought you'd be more interested. What happened to the old Sophie? The one who loved nothing more than solving a mystery?'

'That wasn't the old Sophie. That was the young Sophie. I'm tired. I just want to have a nice dinner, without any drama.'

'Okay. I get it. But please, be wary.'

'I promise to be completely paranoid.'

I must have reacted like she'd struck me because she sighed and said, 'Will, let's face it, you were always a bit up and down.'

I stared at her.

'Maybe hot and cold is a better way of putting it. Like the last time I saw you. That morning. What was all that about? Why were you so angry with me?'

Finally. This was the perfect opportunity to talk about it. But the words were still hard for me to say. I hesitated, and then it was too late.

'Let's just enjoy dinner, shall we?' she said.

She slipped out through the door, leaving it ajar behind her.

Chapter 11

I left the study and immediately bumped into Lily, who was coming out of the dining room with her phone in her hand.

'Are you still struggling to get reception?' I asked, pleased to have something else to focus on after the disappointing conversation with Sophie.

Lily held her phone above her head and scowled up at it. 'It's driving me crazy. I promised I'd call the kids around bedtime, and Carrie will be making passive-aggressive remarks to them about how Mummy is too busy with all her friends.'

'I'm sorry it's like that.'

'The cream turned sour.' A sigh. 'Do you think Theo and Georgina will mind if I go upstairs to see if I can get a signal up there?'

She went up without waiting for an answer. I needed the loo. I went in, and when I came out she was back, still frowning. 'It's hopeless. There's nothing at all.'

'Surely the phone networks wouldn't all go down at the same time. Not unless it's the end of the world.'

She grimaced. 'It might be if I can't call my kids. I'm going to go outside.'

'The back door's locked.'

'I'll go out the front then.'

We went down the stairs. As we walked past the kitchen, the chef, Callum, appeared, wiping those huge hands of his on a tea towel.

'How were the lobster rolls?' he asked with a grin that showed his teeth.

'Amazing,' Lily replied. 'The professor would have loved them.'

'They were his favourite, right?'

As they spoke, I was distracted by the sight of movement at the other end of the hallway. It was Finn, going into the family room. I craned my neck. He appeared to be alone.

'Looking for the loo,' he said, coming towards us. Again, I was sure his smile was fake, though I also had Sophie's words about paranoia echoing in my ears.

'Opposite the dining room,' I said, after a beat. If he didn't know where the bathroom was, my theory about him being upstairs a little while ago couldn't be correct. Or rather, the reason for him going up to the floor where the girls' rooms were couldn't be right. Unless he was lying now about trying to find the loo.

'I'm about to serve starters,' Callum said, drawing my attention back to him. 'I was on my way up to talk to everyone, tell you about the menu.'

Lily looked at the front door, then back up towards the stairs.

'It will take five minutes,' Callum said. 'Less. I promise you'll have time to sneak out and have a ciggie or whatever it is you're planning before the starters are served.'

'I just want to call my children,' Lily said. I explained about the lack of reception.

'Oh yeah, Theo told me the walls are so thick they have issues here.'

'The internet doesn't appear to be working either,' said Lily. 'Theo gave me the wi-fi password, but the connection has dropped out.'

Callum tossed the tea towel into the kitchen. 'Coming? Five minutes, that's all.'

As we reached the top of the stairs, Lily said, 'I knew I shouldn't have come here.'

'Don't say that. It's so lovely to see you.'

'It's good seeing you too, Will. But, well, I don't want to sound like Sophie with all her spiritual stuff, but I thought it was a bad omen when I got here and heard that weird cry.'

I had been about to follow Callum into the dining room. Now I froze. 'What?'

'When I was waiting on the doorstep I heard this awful noise.'

'What kind of noise?'

'It's hard to say. I assumed it was a baby in one of the neighbouring houses. Or a fox, maybe? They make horrible sounds when they're mating, don't they?'

'I heard something too,' I said. 'When I first got here. I'm sure it was a person. Was there anyone else around? Anyone else who heard it?'

'No. Will, you're making me even more freaked out. It was horrible. Like someone was in real pain.'

'Are you two coming in?' It was Georgina, leaning out of the dining room. 'And where's Finn?'

'I think he's in the toilet,' I said, but the bathroom door was open. I heard footsteps. Finn was coming down the stairs from the floor where the girls' bedrooms were.

'Did you get lost?' I asked when he reached us.

'Huh? Oh, yes.' He didn't elaborate, and I didn't get time to say more because Georgina ushered us into the dining room.

I sat at the table next to Sophie and mouthed an apology to Georgina. Finn was opposite me. Had he really got lost? Right now, I was more concerned about what Lily had said. Was it a crying baby we'd heard? As the table settled down and the chatter subsided, I forced myself to stop thinking about it and to listen to Callum.

'Everyone hungry?' he said, waiting for our response like an MC at a gig. When we all said quietly that we were, I half expected him to cup his ear and say, *I can't hear you!*

Amber was, presumably, in the kitchen, getting everything ready. It struck me again how big Callum was: around six two, broad with those hands that looked too big for the dexterity required for food prep. I'd seen him in action though, and although all I'd eaten so far were some crunchy vegetables, I'd heard the moans of ecstasy the meat eaters had made as they scoffed their appetizers.

'I know a lot of you are big fans of seafood,' Callum said, 'so for starters we have sea bass and crab fishcakes, with wakame salad. For the veggies, we have a pear, Stilton and walnut salad, which I would actually go for myself if I had to choose.' He winked at me and Sophie. 'We've got a gorgeous selection of bread too, all freshly baked, of course.'

'The butter comes directly from a farm in Somerset,' Georgina said.

'Like nectar,' said Callum. 'You'd think the cows had been grazing in the Elysian Fields.' He was a real showman, a P. T. Barnum of the kitchen. 'For mains, ladies and gents, we will be serving roast duck breasts with black figs, along with fried garlic and rosemary potatoes. The vegetarian option is a Wellington stuffed with kale, beetroot and red peppers, and don't worry, veggies – you won't miss out on the potatoes.' He paused. 'How does all that sound?'

There were exclamations of 'wonderful!' and 'delicious!', and Rohan said, 'I'm salivating.'

'Fantastic. Give us ten minutes, Rohan mate, and try not to dribble on the floor while you're waiting.'

He left to a ripple of laughter. Lily immediately got up from the table.

'Where are you going?' Georgina asked her.

She explained about the promise she'd made her children.

'I'll come with you,' I said. I wanted to see if I could hear that noise again.

'Wait for me,' Rohan said, taking his e-cigarette out of his jacket pocket.

'You want to call your kids?' Lily said to him.

'What? Oh. No, I was going to vape.' Seeing her reaction, he added, 'I'm sure they're all fine. My wife doesn't like it when I make a fuss.'

We left the dining room, Lily and Rohan hurrying ahead. I walked past the staircase – and sensed a movement above me.

I stopped. It had been a shadow, something glimpsed in my peripheral vision. A movement on the staircase.

'Hello?' I called.

Nothing.

I checked behind me. Finn was still in the dining room. It's the cat, I thought. It must have been the cat, although there was no sign of it.

What was wrong with me? All my instincts were telling me something was wrong, but I had no evidence to support the feeling. *You're just on edge because of the occasion*, I told myself. Then: *Rohan and Lily will be waiting for you.*

I hurried to catch up.

They weren't waiting. They were already at the front door, Lily twisting and tugging at the handle.

'This is embarrassing. I can't work out how it opens,' she said.

'I'll do it,' said Rohan. 'You have to press this in, then turn this, and . . . oh. Let me try again.'

'They have some fancy security system,' I explained to Lily. 'The front door and windows are controlled using an app.'

'It's not working,' Rohan said, squinting at the control panel beside the door. 'I don't get it. I'll find Theo.'

'I'm a geek, and even I know that sometimes old technology is best,' Lily said as Rohan ran up the stairs. 'What's wrong with a good old-fashioned key?' Then Theo appeared.

Despite how many glasses of wine I'd seen him consume, he seemed sober again. He approached the door confidently, did what Rohan had done and stepped back, saying, 'Oh.'

'Can you use the app?' Rohan asked.

'Not when the internet is down.' He peered at the control panel, pressing several buttons. 'Hmm. This is meant to override it and disengage the locks, but it's as if the whole system is glitching.' He tried the sequence again. Frowned, puzzled.

'Is there someone you can call?' I asked. 'Do you have a landline?'

'There is, and we do, although we only ever get junk calls on it so we unplugged the phone. Let's see if we can figure this out. Come on, Lily, you're good with this sort of stuff.'

'You sound like my dad. *Lily knows everything about computers.*'

'Well, you do, don't you?'

'Not *everything.*'

Theo headed towards the rear of the house. 'There's a central hub in the cupboard.'

'Which cupboard?'

He opened a door. 'The "cupboard" is what we call this room.'

Lily, Rohan and I went over and looked inside. The little room contained the security system's hub, the boiler and the gas and electricity meters. The wi-fi router sat on a shelf, its lights a solid red. There were several packing crates, some old coats and bags hanging on hooks, a mop and bucket and the rest of the cleaning equipment. Beside the router was another box, with the logo of a security company on the front.

Lily approached this box, tapped the greyed-out screen and began to scroll through the menus.

'I need some space,' she said, and the rest of us went out into the hallway.

'Has this happened before?' I asked Theo.

'The internet frequently goes down, but not the security system.'

'You seem very relaxed about it.'

He shrugged. 'It's annoying, that's all. Believe me, I deal with worse problems than this at work every day. We got cyber-hacked a couple of months ago. Absolute nightmare, but we fixed it eventually. I just don't want Lily to be upset and worried about her kids. Maybe I should call the security company now.' He paused. 'Hmm, where did we put the old phone?'

As he scratched his head, movement came from further down the hall. Amber, carrying plates out of the kitchen. The starters. Then Georgina appeared, looking for Theo.

'There you are,' she said. 'What on earth is going on?'

Theo explained.

'That bloody system,' she said. 'I told you—'

'Let's not argue about that now. Please. It's cool. I'm going to call them, get it sorted.'

Georgina had the air of a woman whose plans for the perfect dinner party were about to go terribly awry. She hissed through clenched teeth: 'They're serving the starters now.'

Lily appeared from the cupboard, frowning. There was a sprinkling of dust across the shoulders of her jacket.

'Any joy?' I asked.

She shook her head. 'I haven't seen a system like that before. I could probably get the internet working, though, if you give me a laptop I can use to connect to the router.'

Georgina was not happy. 'The food is going to be cold.'

'I need to speak to my children.'

'Wait here,' Theo said, ducking back into the cupboard. He emerged seconds later with the old landline phone in his hand.

'Here,' he said. 'Lily can make a quick call now, before we eat.'

'Fine. Whatever. But then, please, come straight up. We don't need the internet. We're not at Thornwood now, trying to launch a bloody website.'

She turned and marched up the stairs.

Theo pulled a comical, exaggerated expression. 'The nearest phone point's in here. You phone your kids and then I'll call the security company. And maybe if the internet doesn't come back on its own you can try to fix it after dinner.'

Dinner.

Right now, I didn't feel particularly hungry. The front and back doors were locked, along with the windows. We had no phone signal and no internet. Both Lily and I had heard strange, pained noises when we were outside. And then there had been the creak upstairs and the movement I'd just seen on the stairs.

Was there someone else in the house?

Someone making sure we were unable to get out?

The hairs stood up on my arms and a cold sensation spread beneath my skin, before I managed to get a grip of myself. There was a simple explanation for everything. Technology is always going wrong. Keys get lost. The cries we'd heard probably *had* been a nearby baby, the creak just the house breathing, and the movement was almost certainly my imagination or the cat. I was being stupid, and I needed to relax and enjoy myself.

'Are you coming?' Georgina called from above.

Repeating to myself that everything was okay, I left Lily and Theo in the hallway and went back up to the dining room.

Chapter 12

I took my place at the table, my starter waiting for me. I had expected it to consist of a single slice of pear, a lone walnut and a sliver of Stilton, maybe a couple of green leaves, but it was a generous portion. The fishcakes which had been placed before the meat eaters were substantial too.

I had Sophie to my right and an empty chair where Lily would be sitting when she finished her call to my left. Across from us were Finn and Rohan. Georgina was at the head of the table, next to Sophie, and Theo, who had just come in, was at the other end. Amber finished serving the food and went around with two bottles of wine, one white, one red.

As the chatter across the table recommenced – Rohan was telling Finn about his business idea – Sophie jabbed me with her elbow and whispered out of the side of her mouth: 'You need to chill out.'

'What are you talking about?'

'You keep staring at Finn. Talk to me. Tell me about, I don't know, your students.'

I was delighted she was showing an interest, of course I was, but I couldn't help but be distracted. Finn was acting like he was listening to Rohan, but his eyes darted towards me and Sophie, and he leaned forward as if he was trying to hear what we were saying to each other.

Having talked myself down only minutes before, watching Finn immediately brought back my fears. He had been missing when I'd heard the first creak upstairs and I was sure it hadn't been an innocent trip to the loo, but he was in here when I saw the movement on the stairs.

Was there someone else here?

Someone Finn was working with? A person he'd sneaked into the house?

What could he be up to?

The obvious thing seemed to be a burglary. There was a lot of valuable stuff here. Jewellery. Technology. Paintings. There might be cash too. My best theory, which had been half formed when I spoke to Sophie a little earlier, was that he had told the Howards a string of lies about being Sebastian's assistant in order to get an invitation into their house. Was he planning to rob us all? Demand we hand over our wallets and watches and any jewellery we were wearing? Could Amber be his accomplice? No, she'd been downstairs when I saw the movement, and I thought she'd been in the kitchen when I'd heard something earlier too.

'You're not eating,' Theo said to me as Sophie took a break from our chat to work on her starter.

'I thought I should wait for Lily,' I said.

'Don't be daft. Go ahead.'

I did need to eat. But the fear was growing and accelerating now, my imagination feeding itself, and my appetite had gone.

Everyone was eating and chatting happily now, including Finn, but they stopped and looked at me.

'I really feel like I should wait for Lily,' I said, groping for an excuse.

As if summoned, Lily came into the room.

'There you go,' said Georgina.

'Everything okay with the kids?' I asked Lily as she sat down. I half expected her to say the landline wasn't working, but she nodded.

'Yes, thankfully. The children actually sounded disappointed to hear from me because it meant it was bedtime.'

Sophie and Georgina were laughing together, some story about Theo making a fool of himself in the dads' race at sports day. Under the cover of their raucous laughter and Theo's cries of protest I said in a hushed voice, 'Did you get anywhere with the security system? Any idea what's wrong with it?'

'It's not really my area of expertise. It appears to have gone into lockdown mode. As far as I know, it's for use in an emergency, like if civil unrest breaks out.'

'Jesus.'

'Yeah, I know. The rich, sheltering in their west London townhouses while the rest of us batter each other to death. There must be a way to override this lockdown mode, but I couldn't figure it out.'

'Do you think it could have gone into that mode on its own? Like, random gremlins?'

'Anything's possible,' she said. 'But the system seems robust. I don't understand it. But Theo—'

She was interrupted by the appearance of Callum and Amber.

'How is everything?' Callum asked, and everyone said how amazing it all was.

'Will you come and live with me?' Sophie said, to much laughter.

Lily held up her empty glass towards Amber, who went off to fetch more wine, Callum accompanying her. Lily had been going to say something about Theo when she was interrupted. But I was prevented from asking her what by Finn, who had snagged her attention.

'Rohan was telling me you're a coding genius.'

Lily had a mouthful of food, and he had to wait a moment for her answer. 'I don't know about "genius".'

93

'Didn't Sebastian tell you about her?' I asked.

There was that discomfort that came into his eyes whenever he was asked anything about the professor. 'A little. You created the algorithm for his dating site, I know that.' A smug smile. 'What are you working on at the moment?'

'A project.'

A beat of silence. Finn laughed. 'Is that all you're going to tell us?'

'Uh huh.'

'It's top secret?'

'Something like that.'

Amber arrived and filled Lily's glass before stepping back from the table and waiting to see if anyone else needed more to drink.

'It's exciting, actually,' Lily said after taking a sip. 'And it's something I'm doing myself, for me.'

'Sounds intriguing,' Theo said. 'Something you might need funding for? Perhaps we should talk.'

Across the table, the look on Rohan's face was priceless.

Georgina asked Amber to fetch more water, then Finn said to Lily, 'Can you not tell us anything more about your secret project?' He was leaning forward, as far as he could, and it struck me: perhaps Lily was his target. Was he trying to get information about this project she was working on? He had certainly seemed very concerned when he thought she wouldn't show up, hadn't he?

'It's the project my whole life has been leading me to,' Lily said.

'Is it somehow related to your work with Sebastian?'

'Why do you ask that?'

'It's just,' he said, his voice heavy with portentousness, 'everything echoes, doesn't it?'

Finn looked at each of us, quickly, smoothly, in turn.

Clearly waiting for some kind of response. I followed his eyes. Everyone was impassive and, although he was trying hard not to show it, it seemed to me he was disappointed by our lack of response.

To my surprise, though, Finn didn't pursue it. Instead, he turned to me.

It was my turn to be put on the spot.

Chapter 13

'Will, I've been told you're a writer,' Finn said. 'Are you working on anything at the moment?'

'I bet he's writing about us,' said Rohan. Then, seeing my reaction: 'Oh! You are.'

'Is that true?' Sophie asked. They were all staring at me. Finn had sat up straighter.

'I'm playing with an idea,' I said.

'What, set at Sebastian's house? That summer?'

'Yes . . . well, a fictionalized version of it. With made-up characters.'

'But based on us?'

'Loosely.'

This was disingenuous. In the notes I'd already made, the characters were very much based on the people around this table. In fact, in the first draft – which I'd recently made a start on – I had used their real names, intending to change them later.

'What exactly is going to happen in this story?' Rohan asked.

'I haven't figured that out yet.'

'Is Sebastian in it?' Finn asked.

'There's a professor of psychology,' I replied, annoyed that he'd joined in. Had started it, in fact.

I was waiting for someone to say they found the idea of it exciting: to be immortalized in print. But none of them did. They all looked horrified.

'Listen,' I said. 'It's embryonic at the moment. I've barely started. But this is what novelists do. We take people and events from real life and use them as inspiration.'

'Is that why you came tonight?' Georgina asked. 'Why you accepted our invitation? Is this research?'

Rumbled. I thought again about the blinking cursor on the screen of my laptop. The story waiting to be written.

I hoped she couldn't see me squirm. 'No. I wanted to see everyone. To celebrate Sebastian.'

It was only half a lie. I *did* want to see my old colleagues, especially Lily, *especially* Sophie. But would I have come if I hadn't had the idea for the book?

'Is Dominic in it?' Rohan asked.

A hush fell over the table.

I'd been waiting for this. For someone to mention what had happened to him. I glanced at Sophie, wondering how she felt about it.

About Dominic's death.

I'd received a message just a week after we left Thornwood, the only contact I had from the Howards until Sebastian's death. *Sad news. Dominic passed away a few days ago. Thought you'd like to know. He drowned in the lake.* I'd been momentarily stunned, unsure how to feel. I hadn't liked him and had no intention of attending his funeral, but I was still stunned to hear that someone I knew, someone so young, had died.

I had replied, expressing my shock, but Theo hadn't answered. I sent a message of condolence to Sebastian but never heard back from him. Maybe if I'd liked Dominic more, if I hadn't still been confused and disappointed by the way the summer had ended, I might have enquired about his funeral. But it would have been hypocritical of me to go. And I didn't have the contact details of any of the others. I had no mobile phone and the company email addresses we'd used while at Thornwood no longer existed.

Now, I said, 'Does anyone know how it happened?'

'It was an accident,' Theo said. 'I got the impression he had been drunk. Probably stoned.'

'I always thought he was destined for tragedy,' Sophie said.

I couldn't stop myself: 'Is that what the Tarot cards told you?'

The look she gave me made me instantly regret my words.

'Did any of you go to his funeral?' I asked.

'We fell out, remember,' said Rohan.

'Theo and I were in Ibiza,' said Georgina. 'We went there the day after we left Thornwood.'

'Plotting our next move,' added Theo.

'I was never friends with him,' Lily said, matter-of-factly. 'Sophie?'

She stared at her plate. 'I would have gone, but I didn't see Theo's email until it was too late. After Thornwood I went back to my gran's, and she didn't have the internet in 1999.'

'So none of you went,' said Finn. 'Maybe you can make something of that, Will. In your book.'

I was about to ask if anyone had spoken to Eve since we left Thornwood, but Amber distracted me. As she leaned over the table to collect some of the dirty plates, she said something, very quietly, into Finn's ear.

He had been in conversation with Lily, but he instantly stopped listening and his head snapped towards Amber, who was already walking from the room.

'Excuse me,' he said after a few moments, getting up. 'Popping to the little boys' room.'

This was the second time he'd claimed to have needed the loo in an hour.

This was my chance to find out what he was up to.

'I'll be back in a moment,' I said to Sophie.

'Where are you going?'

I wanted to tell her, but last time I had tried to talk to her about Finn she had accused me of being paranoid. I needed facts. Proof.

'I need the bathroom too,' I said, then left quickly, without looking back. Out in the hallway, there was no sign of Finn or Amber. I paused outside the bathroom, listening, wondering if they'd gone in there. If Finn had an accomplice, someone else hiding in the house, was Amber in on it too? Was she involved? Earlier, I'd suspected that she knew him . . . I was becoming increasingly worried and unsure about what was going on.

I pushed the door open, unsurprised to find it empty.

I was about to go downstairs when I heard a light thump from above. More than a creak. This time, I was absolutely certain someone was up there.

I didn't hesitate. I felt like the tension in my body could have powered all the lights on the street as I went up the stairs, convinced we were locked in this house with people who were up to no good. Thank God Theo had called the security company. I wondered if they'd given him any indication how long it would take for them to turn up.

I went along the landing. The bathroom was empty, as was the former nanny's room. That left the daughters' rooms. Olivia and the younger daughter. Mia, that was her name. Theo had opened this door earlier to let the cat in, and the door was still shut, which told me it couldn't have been Claude I'd seen on the stairs.

I put my ear to Mia's door. There were no sounds coming from within and it felt wrong going into a teenager's room, like I would be violating her space somehow.

But I needed to see. Gently, I pushed open Mia's bedroom door and peered inside. There was no sign of the cat, which surprised me. *Had* someone been up here to let him out?

Something else was different in here too. What was it?

It came to me quickly: when Theo had opened the door to let the cat in, the computer screen had been black. Now the screensaver was on, a series of bright patterns drifting across the screen. Someone had turned the computer on, or at least the screen. Had it been Finn, or Amber, or the unnamed third person, snooping around?

I backed out of the room and looked around. I could check Olivia's room, but it felt wrong going into a missing teenager's room. What if someone came up and caught me? Nerves jangling, I decided to check the ground floor first, to see if Finn and Amber were there.

I went down. The dining-room door was wide open and Finn's chair was still empty. I went past before anyone saw me. If I didn't find him on the ground floor, I would come back.

Downstairs, I headed straight towards the rear of the house, thinking it was most likely Finn and Amber, and possibly the third person, would be in the family room or the 'cupboard'. Whispering. Discussing their plan, whatever it was. Burglary, stealing ideas, some con I couldn't even imagine. I had my phone in my hand, ready to record them if I got the chance.

But they weren't in either room. Could they have gone down to the basement? Checking over my shoulder to see if anyone was coming, I opened the door closest to the family room, revealing another staircase that led down to the cellar. I poked my head inside. Again, silence.

Unless the security company had opened the front door remotely, or they'd found the back-door key – or had it all along – and gone outside, the kitchen was the only place Finn and Amber could be. Except Callum would be in there, putting the finishing touches to the main courses. Was there another room I didn't know about?

'What are you doing?'

I whirled around.

It was Sophie, halfway down the staircase, furrowing her eyebrows at me. I gestured for her to come down. There was no point lying to her now.

'I'm looking for Finn,' I whispered.

'Oh, for God's sake.'

'No, listen.' I rapidly explained how I was now sure he and Amber knew each other. 'She whispered something to him, and now the two of them have disappeared.'

'Maybe she asked him to help out in the kitchen,' Sophie said, but, finally, she looked doubtful. Like she might actually believe me. 'He did say something else that was odd. At the table. We were talking about the professor and he got the name of his house wrong. He said Thornside instead of Thornwood.'

'I told you! He keeps slipping up. But I can't find him. I think there might be someone else here too. I've heard or seen movement upstairs three times now.'

I could see I was losing her faith in me again.

'Let's ask the chef,' I said. 'Find out if he's seen Finn.'

We edged towards the kitchen. I was worried Georgina was going to appear at any moment, asking why half her guests had disappeared. Then I'd have to explain everything to her.

We reached the kitchen door – and at that exact moment, a crash came from inside. A shout. A strangled yell of distress.

Sophie and I stared at each other.

'He's attacking Callum,' I said. I could see it in my mind's eye. Both of them: Finn and Amber, maybe the mysterious accomplice too, trying to overpower the chef. Because Callum had found out whatever it was they were planning? Or was this part of their scheme all along? In a second, I went from being uneasy to feeling very scared. The doors were locked. None of our phones were working. We were trapped.

'What shall we do?' Sophie whispered.

I looked along the hall. The landline. 'I'm going to call the police.'

There was another yell from the kitchen. A woman's voice: 'Shut *up*.' A grunt of pain. And before I could move towards the phone, the kitchen door was pulled inwards and, in a second, I realized two things.

I was right to be scared.

But I'd been wrong about Finn.

Because he wasn't the one pointing a shotgun at me.

Chapter 14

Finn had blood on his face, a cut lip, and one eye was swollen shut. A couple of buttons were missing from the top of his shirt so it gaped open, revealing a hairless chest. His head hung forward and I was sure that if Callum hadn't been holding on to him, he would collapse.

In his free hand, the one that wasn't gripping Finn by the elbow, Callum carried a shotgun, the kind farmers or hunters use. Amber, who was slightly behind the two men, was holding one too. I had temporarily gone into freeze mode, hardly able to take in what I was seeing. Beside me, Sophie was similarly frozen.

The moment he saw us, Callum raised his gun and pointed it straight at me.

'Don't make a sound,' he said. 'Amber – watch them. Don't let them move.'

He shoved Finn to his left, fully revealing Amber, who gripped her shotgun with both hands. She was panting slightly, her face flushed pink, beads of sweat on her upper lip. Her green eyes blazed with elation.

'Do not try anything,' she said in a hiss.

'We're not going to,' I said, finally able to speak. I was registering what I was seeing but not feeling it yet. Not believing it.

Out of the corner of my eye I could see Callum dragging Finn along the hallway. Finn, who had his hands secured behind his back with a cable tie, tried to struggle, and Callum, who was about the same height but stockier and more powerful, jabbed the end of the shotgun into his side. Then he opened the door of the cupboard, the room with the router and the hub and the cleaning equipment, and ordered Finn inside.

Finn hesitated and Callum shoved him, making him stagger forward, then followed him in.

There were several awful thumping sounds. A whimper of pain. Sophie and I flinched with every noise while, beside us, Amber grinned, displaying her perfect white teeth. She licked her lips. Another exhalation of pain, then silence.

Callum emerged. There was blood on his knuckles.

'Did you kill him?' Sophie's voice was an octave higher than normal.

Callum came towards us, nodding towards the stairs. 'Move.'

But Sophie stayed still. 'Is he dead?'

'Nobody's dead yet.'

I reached out and took Sophie's hand. It was trembling. I squeezed it, then nodded for her to go first. It might not make any difference, but I could provide a shield between her and the guns.

Slowly, she went up, and I followed, Callum and Amber behind us. Stories from true-crime documentaries and newspapers came back to me; awful tales in which the victims of home invasions were forced to do terrible things. I tried not to let my imagination run out of control. Prayed it was nothing more terrible than a robbery.

As we got nearer to the dining room, music drifted towards us, a Radiohead album we used to listen to at Sebastian's house. Thom Yorke singing about karma. That was why the rest of the party hadn't heard the commotion downstairs. There was chatter too. Theo, Georgina, Lily, Rohan.

They all looked up as Sophie and I walked into the room. 'Where have you—'

Callum and Amber entered the room behind us and Georgina fell silent.

'Sit down,' Callum said to me and Sophie. The music was coming from a smart speaker, which – with the internet down – must have been connected to someone's phone. I saw Callum tune in to it. 'Radiohead? At a dinner party? What is wrong with you people?'

Everyone stared at him as he strode across to the smart speaker and jabbed at the volume button with one of his huge index fingers, until Thom Yorke's voice fell silent.

'That's better.'

He saw that Sophie and I were both still standing, immobile.

'Oh,' he said. 'Are you confused? Do you think we're playing musical statues and that when the music stops you have to freeze?' His voice was so calm, like a sarcastic teacher, which made it more chilling. I wanted to move, to do as he'd ordered, but I couldn't make my legs work, not until Sophie grabbed my elbow and pulled me towards my seat.

'That's better,' Callum said. He took a few steps away from the table, giving me a moment to breathe. Lily had gone utterly pale. Rohan was staring in shock, his mouth open slightly. Georgina had her wine glass in her hand, and she seemed not to know whether to put it down or drink from it, so she stayed immobile, only her eyes moving, flitting between Callum and Amber.

Opposite her, at the other end of the table, Theo looked not scared but outraged.

'What is this?' he demanded. 'A robbery?'

Callum went over to him, and I braced myself, expecting him to mete out more violence.

Instead, in an even voice, he said, 'All you have to do is obey me. Easy. Couldn't be simpler. And here's your first order: I want everyone to hand over their phones.'

So it was a robbery. Relief washed through me. I could handle that, and not just because I had little to lose. My phone was insured, I had some bank cards in my wallet, around £20 in cash. Nothing I would miss. We all produced our phones, and Amber went around the table collecting them in a bag while Callum watched coolly, tapping his foot.

Rohan must have been thinking the same as me; that they were going to take all our valuables. 'Please. This watch was my dad's. It's the only thing he left me.'

'How interesting,' said Callum.

'You want money?' Theo went to get up from his chair. 'I can wire you money.'

Callum put a hand on Theo's shoulder, preventing him from standing, and said, 'Hush.'

He took a few steps away from the table, keeping the gun trained on us. The bag, which now contained all our phones, hung from Amber's shoulder.

'Okay,' Callum said. 'Are you capable of listening carefully?'

Nobody spoke or moved, except Georgina, who was still holding her glass. She kept putting it down then picking it up without drinking from it, like a robot that had malfunctioned.

'For Christ's sake,' Amber snapped, going over and snatching it from her. She was still panting a little but lifted the glass to her lips and drained it. Then she placed it carefully on the table and went back to her position beside Callum.

'You okay?' he said to her.

'I am now.' She blew out a breath.

'Good.' He cleared his throat and looked around the table at all of us before his gaze settled on Theo. 'We're not here to take your stuff. You'll get your phones back at the end of the night. We're here . . .' There was a long pause, like he was about to announce the winner of a competition: '. . . we're here to find out a secret.'

A secret?

He went on: 'This could all be over very quickly and easily, with minimum fuss and pain.'

'Where's Finn?' Lily said suddenly, like she'd just realized he wasn't there.

'He's not important,' Amber said. I'm sure she was going to say more, but Callum shot her a warning look and she pressed her lips together.

'They beat the crap out of him,' I said.

Amber swung her shotgun towards me. Instinctively, I raised my hands.

'Put your hands down.' Callum sighed. 'Just . . . hush. Stop *chattering* for a minute.'

Nobody spoke.

'That's good. I knew you could do it. Now, listen.'

Another of his pauses. He was enjoying this.

'There is a secret in this room,' he said, walking around us. 'A secret that dates back to the summer of '99. To something that happened at Sebastian Marlowe's house.'

He went over to the other side of the table, all our heads turning to follow him.

'One of you knows it. Maybe some of you. Maybe *all* of you. And before the end of the night *we* are going to know it too.'

Rohan stood up. 'This is crazy. A secret? Do any of you know what he's talking about?'

Callum jerked the gun in his direction. 'Sit the fuck down!'

Rohan dropped back into his seat like a puppet whose strings had been cut.

'Amber,' Callum said.

Amber crossed the room, her gun tucked under her arm, and closed the curtains. She then went around the table, collecting the cutlery. She blew out the candles and took the candlesticks. She put everything into the bag that contained the phones and passed it to Callum.

'Well?' he said. 'Anyone want to answer Rohan? Anyone know what I'm talking about and want to tell us now? Stop this game before it even gets going?'

Nobody spoke. He waited. We all just stared at him, silent.

'Yeah, that's what I thought would happen. Okay. Amber and I are going to leave you to talk. Amber will be outside the door, so don't even think about trying to get out. If you try to break a window, if we so much as hear a swish of a curtain . . .' He didn't feel the need to complete the sentence.

'What if none of us has a secret?' Sophie asked.

'Oh, you do. For a start, Sophie, *everyone* has secrets. We're looking for your biggest. Something that happened in 1999.'

'Wait,' I said. 'Do you know what this secret is?'

'We wouldn't be here if we already knew it, Will. But I promise you this: we'll know it when we hear it. We all will.'

'But if you don't know what the secret is, how do you know it exists?' That was Lily.

'You don't need to know that, Lily.' He checked his watch. 'It's nine o'clock now. I'm going to leave you to talk among yourselves and figure out what the secret is. I'm going to come back in one hour. At the end of that hour, well, I'm hoping the person or persons with the secret will be sensible enough to spill it.'

'And if they don't?' Theo asked.

Callum grinned. 'That's when the fun will begin.'

'Hold on,' Theo said. Callum turned back. 'What if we refuse to go along with this?'

'That,' he said with a sigh, 'would not be a wise thing to do.'

Part Two

Chapter 15

Silence.

Seconds stretched in time with our breathing. Ticked by on the faces of our watches. I glanced down at mine. It was two minutes past nine. A hundred and twenty seconds had passed since Callum and Amber had left the room. A hundred and twenty seconds of quiet. A shocked hush.

Until everybody spoke at once, all the voices merging and overlapping so it was hard to know who had said what.

'I don't have a secret.'

'An hour? Did he say an hour?'

'What are we going to do?'

'Who *are* they?'

'A secret? I really don't have any secrets.'

And then:

'*Quiet!*'

That was Georgina. We all looked at her, there at the end of the table. She was breathing steadily, nostrils flaring, and I guessed she was doing something she had learned at yoga, some meditative practice. Calming herself.

'Thank you,' she said as we all fell quiet again.

I glanced at Sophie next to me. She seemed okay, but when she lifted a hand to push her hair away from her face I saw how it shook. On my other side, Lily was motionless. Rohan, now sitting beside an empty seat, had the air of a man on Death Row who had just been told he'd lost his final stay of execution. Finally, to my left, at the other end of the table, Theo kept opening his mouth to speak, but nothing came out. While everyone else in the room appeared to have been drained of blood, his face was flushed pink, sweat popping on his forehead.

He reached for his glass but knocked it over, and red wine raced across the table, heading directly for Lily's lap. It stirred her into motion: she jumped up, her chair clattering to the ground behind her.

The door opened immediately, Amber coming in, shotgun in both hands, pointing it directly at Lily.

'What's going on?' she demanded.

I wanted to get up. To stand between the gun and Lily. But I was paralysed by the sight of the gun. The violence I'd seen downstairs reverberated through my veins, shaking my bones, while the wine dripped at my feet.

Amber assessed what had happened and marched across, barking an order at Lily.

'Pick up your chair and sit down.'

Unsteadily, Lily obeyed, while Amber snatched up a handful of napkins from the table and tossed them at me. 'Clean it up.' Then a smile crept on to her lips and I saw she was grinning at Sophie.

I followed Amber's gaze. Tears pooled in Sophie's eyes, threatening to spill.

Amber tossed a napkin at her too. 'Oh, diddums. What's the matter? Run out of jokes? Here's one: there's no point crying over spilt wine.' To Theo, she said: 'What time is it?'

He gawped at her.

'Are you that drunk? I asked you the time.'

'It's five past nine.' That was Rohan, glaring at Amber with fire in his stare. If he'd been in denial a minute ago, as the situation we were all facing sunk in, he had very quickly moved on to anger. How long before we got to bargaining? I wondered.

'You've got fifty-five minutes left,' she said. 'You'd better get on with it, hadn't you?' She paused on her way out and turned back, taking us all in, one by one. She made me think of one of the other lecturers at my college, walking into a classroom to find she'd been given the very worst students.

'Look at you all,' Amber said, her voice drenched in contempt. 'Revolutionaries? Professor Marlowe would be ashamed.'

She had, I noticed for the first time, a middle-class accent. She sounded like one of my friends who'd grown up in the rural villages around Rye. Not as posh as Georgina, but not far off. I could see now that she was actually a little older than I'd first thought: mid-forties, about my age. When I'd first seen her I'd thought she was Eve, hadn't I? She could easily have come from the same part of the world. Could have been one of the locals we'd seen on the rare occasions we'd gone into the village. Possibly an artist or a musician with that tattoo. An ordinary woman.

What on earth had brought her to this point, wielding a shotgun at a dinner party?

The moment she left, Sophie snapped out of her trance.

'No use crying over spilt wine?' she said. 'Did she really think that was a funny joke?'

I swivelled towards Lily. The floor by our feet was dark and sticky. The napkins I'd used to mop up the wine from the table looked like they'd been employed to clean up a crime scene.

'Are you okay?' I said to her.

'*They* cut the internet off,' she said, with the voice of some-one waking from a dream. 'Sabotaged the security system.'

I reminded myself that no one else had been suspicious that Finn had been up to something.

I spoke up. 'I knew something was wrong, but I was sure it was *Finn*. That he was pretending to have been Sebastian's assistant. That's why I went downstairs. I was looking for him and Amber.' I didn't mention that I'd thought there might have been a third person in the house, though it still didn't make sense why I'd heard and seen movement upstairs when I was sure Finn, Amber and – indeed – Callum had been downstairs. It was too much to think about right now.

I told the group what Sophie and I had witnessed. How Callum had shoved Finn into the cupboard and the sounds of violence that had come from within.

'Why didn't you say something?' Rohan asked. 'About your suspicions?'

I flicked a look at Sophie, who, gratifyingly, said, 'He tried. He spoke to me about it, and I told him he was being paranoid.'

'Oh, nice one, Sophie.'

I leapt to her defence. 'I *was* wrong about Finn.'

Rohan didn't let it drop. 'You still could have warned us you thought something was wrong.'

'I didn't know for sure though.'

'Yeah, but—'

Sophie cut him off. 'Rohan. It's not Will's fault.'

'No, it seems more like it's yours. And what a surprise – he listened to you because he's still desperate to get into your—'

'*Stop it!*'

Georgina had come down from her yoga cloud with a furious bump. Rohan, who had always been intimidated by Georgina, gave me and Sophie a final dirty look then sat back, arms folded, scowling.

Our hostess had all our attention now. All except her husband's. She snapped her fingers. Once, then twice more. 'Theo. Theo!'

Groggily, he lifted his head.

'Did you call the security company?' she asked. 'Are they on their way?'

He put his face in his hands and groaned.

'What is it?' she said.

'I didn't phone them. Lily was so desperate to speak to her kids I let her go first and then never got round to making the call. I thought I'd do it after dinner.'

'Oh, Theo! You idiot.'

We all stared at him. I couldn't believe it. The imminent arrival of the security people was the thing that had been stopping me from going into panic mode.

'Wait,' Lily said. 'That's not exactly what happened. When we were on the way to use the phone, Callum came out of the kitchen, don't you remember? He wanted to ask you some questions about the servings. You told me to go ahead, call my kids.'

'Oh. Yes. Of course.' He rubbed at his brow with his knuckles. 'And then the food was ready so I came up here.'

'You need to sober up, mate,' Rohan said.

'He does.' Georgina walked around the table to her husband. He looked so stricken I thought she was going to hug him, comfort him.

Instead, she picked up a glass of water and threw it in his face.

'What the hell?' he said, spluttering, water dripping from his chin.

'Has that helped?' she asked.

'For God's sake, George.' He grabbed a napkin and wiped his face then patted his lap, where some of the water had spilled. He did seem a little more sober though. I was tempted to empty a glass over my own head. Not that I felt tipsy any more. The shock of what I'd seen had worked as well as any cold liquid to the face.

Georgina went back to her seat and Sophie turned to her. 'Callum and Amber. Where did you find them?'

I remembered something she had told us earlier. 'You said you hired the caterers from an agency, didn't you? Is it one you've used before?'

'Yes. Lots of times.'

'And have they sent Callum and Amber before?' I wanted to know if they were real caterers who had gone rogue. After all, they had produced an impressive meal – or half of one, at least.

'No. We were expecting a different chef. One who catered our last dinner party.' She addressed Theo. 'You let them in. What did they say when they got here?'

'That Marissa and Seamus had been double-booked so the agency had sent them instead.'

'You didn't ask for ID? Proof of who they were?' Rohan asked.

'No. Why would I? One doesn't expect one's caterers to be replaced by imposters.'

'*One* wouldn't know,' Rohan said. 'When I have friends to dinner, I cook, or my wife does. Oh . . . Anika.' Out of all of us, he was the only one with someone waiting for him at home. I wondered if he was thinking about how he hadn't wanted to call them. If he was regretting it.

'If she doesn't hear from you, will she call the police?'

He looked at me like I was mad. 'No. Not unless she can't get hold of me for twenty-four hours.' His voice dropped. 'Things have been difficult recently. I quite often stay over in a hotel.'

'Where are the real caterers?' Sophie asked, breaking the awkward silence that followed. 'You don't think . . .' *You don't think they're dead?* That's what she was going to say.

Lily put her hand to her lips. 'The cries we heard, Will. I bet that's who it was.'

Could she be right? I pictured the scenario: the two of them heading to this house that they'd been to before. Callum and Amber appearing, intercepting them. Had it happened right outside here, on the street? And they'd been dragged into one of the empty properties? Tied up and left there? Or maybe they were in a vehicle. I tried to remember if there had been any vans parked outside.

While this had all been going through my head, Lily had told the others what she and I had heard.

Rohan was still sceptical. 'I didn't hear anything. You two must have super hearing.'

'Or you're a bit deaf,' Lily replied. 'Two of us heard them, and that means someone else might, if they're still able to make noise. Someone walking by the house. If they find them and rescue them, they'll send the police here.'

'Oh, come on,' Rohan said. 'You think these two would take a risk like that? Leave the people whose place they've taken somewhere nearby, where they can make enough noise to alert the cops?'

'He's right,' Sophie said.

Lily refused to give up. 'But we did hear something. Maybe they left them gagged and they managed to get the gags off.'

Rohan shook his head. 'Except if you two were talking about it downstairs, you probably alerted Callum to his mistake and that's what he's doing right now. Dealing with it.'

No one had anything to say to that.

'We have to face it. We can't rely on anyone to come to our rescue.' Rohan looked around the table. 'We're on our own.' He turned to Theo. 'Do you have any weapons in the house? A gun?'

'What? No. Don't be ridiculous.'

'Samurai swords?'

'What?'

Rohan wasn't kidding. 'I've got one on my wall at home. A proper samurai sword. This guy I used to do business with refused to pay me so I took it off his wall. You don't have anything like that?'

Georgina spoke up. 'The only weapons we have are kitchen knives.'

Rohan wasn't impressed. 'You don't have anything else? I thought you were into all that shooting and fishing stuff?'

'That was Georgina, when she was a teenager.'

'I haven't been shooting for years,' she said.

Theo remembered something. 'I've got some golf clubs in the cellar.'

'Golf clubs!' Rohan was scathing. 'That's going to be really helpful. We can all grab one each – mine's the nine iron – and whack them over the head . . . oh, but we have to sneak past the woman with the shotgun first.'

This tirade of sarcasm appeared to help Theo shake off the last of his drunkenness. The glaze vanished from his eyes. 'Screw you, Rohan. Even if I had a gun in my bedside cupboard, we'd still have to get past our armed guard.'

The silence returned. This time, Sophie broke it. She whispered so the others had to lean closer to hear.

'What do you think they'll do if we don't tell them whatever it is they came here for? Do you think . . . they'll kill us?'

'Please don't say that,' Lily said.

'But we have to think about it, don't we? He said if we don't tell them the secret, that's when the fun will begin.'

'And the only way they can possibly get away with this is if they kill all of us,' Rohan said. 'I mean, we've all seen their faces. That's why we need to fight.'

'Except they haven't done anything really terrible yet,' Lily said.

'What? They've threatened us. Kept us prisoner.'

'That's very different to actually murdering us.'

Georgina said, 'Please, do we have to keep talking about killing and murder? Rohan, can you stop?'

'How can I? If that's what they've got planned for us . . .'

'They didn't kill Finn,' I said.

Now all eyes were on me.

'They could easily have shot or stabbed him. But they didn't. They beat him up, locked him in the cupboard.'

'That's right,' said Lily. 'They won't murder us. It's not logical. Not if they're trying to get information out of us. They can't kill the person with the secret before they find out what it is.'

'They could hurt us though,' I said. 'In fact, I'm certain they will if we don't play along.' I addressed Rohan. 'We're not going to get past Amber. Nobody's coming. I think, right now, we only have one choice.'

Sophie finished what I was going to say. 'We have to try to figure out what this secret is. They said it was related to something that happened in '99. I can't think of any big secrets they'd be interested in.'

'Neither can I,' said Lily.

'Nor me.' Georgina said it, then Rohan, then Theo. All of us. I looked at Sophie.

'I'm trying to think of one,' she said.

Maybe there was no Big Secret. Maybe this was all some kind of twisted game, cats tormenting mice, or a smokescreen for something else. Surely everyone in this room had a secret of some kind.

I certainly did. Something that affected several other people in this room.

It couldn't be my secret that Callum and Amber were after?

Chapter 16

July 1999

After the Belbin test and the Big Five personality test, Sebastian was keen to tell us all about Tuckman's model of group development. Forming, storming, norming and performing.

We were somewhere between the forming and storming stages, a week into our stay at Thornwood, when I realized I was falling for Sophie.

I was in the office, seated behind my blueberry iMac. Sophie's grape model was opposite mine, though she wasn't in her chair at the moment, having gone to the kitchen to get a drink. The only person who didn't have a colourful iMac was Lily, who said she needed a 'proper' computer to do her work. According to Theo, whose desk was in the corner so he could keep an eye on us while we worked, Lily's PC was one of the most powerful and expensive on the market, a Dell Dimension XPS T600 running Windows NT 4.0. If anyone went near it with a cup of tea or the dogs strayed too close, Theo would leap up and yell. I was never sure if Sebastian had tasked him with this job or if it was something he'd taken upon himself.

Lily had her headphones on, listening to her MP3 player, and I was staring at an almost blank Word document. At the top of the page I had written 'SITE NAMES'. This was the first job I'd been given. Over the past week I had sent Sebastian a hundred suggestions – Someone 4 U, PsychDate, PerfectMatch, etc., etc. – all of which he'd rejected.

'I want something striking, Will,' he said. 'Something that will speak to people. This is love we're talking about here. Be *poetic*.'

Poetic. I couldn't stop thinking about it. In bed, on the loo, cleaning my teeth, trying to have conversations: words and puns would float in and out of my head, becoming meaningless, like a giant vat of Alphabetti Spaghetti.

'This is impossible,' I said aloud, prompting Lily to remove her headphones and raise her eyebrows questioningly. I explained my predicament, expecting sympathy.

Instead, she tutted. 'Well, of course he wants it to be perfect and poetic. You can't change the world with a bad name.'

'You really think this site will change the world?' I asked.

'Why not? If the professor believes it, I believe it.'

'Will hasn't experienced love yet. He hasn't felt its power.'

I swivelled my chair, cheeks turning red, to see Sebastian had entered the room. He strode over and clapped me on the shoulder. 'I used to be a cynic too, Will. Until I met my Barbara.'

I gawped at him.

'And it's nothing to do with being a hippy. It's science, Will. Brain chemistry. Have you ever felt it? That intoxication? The way all your senses sharpen and the world looks and smells and sounds so much better?'

'Not . . . yet.'

'You will. One day. Maybe our unnamed website will help you. In the meantime . . .' Was that a hint of warning in his voice? Impatience? 'Use your imagination.'

He tapped my shoulder again, quite hard, then strode out of the office.

I opened Netscape Navigator, went to Yahoo! and searched for 'love poems'.

'What are you doing?'

I turned in my chair again at the sound of Sophie's voice. She was in the doorway, leaning against the frame. The light washed her out, like an over-exposed photograph, so her face was obscured and all I could see was the shape of her body. Then she took a step forward so I could see her face and her skin and her hair.

I don't think I'm going to need your site, professor, I thought.

She approached my desk. 'Love poetry?'

'It's . . I'm still trying to come up with a name. Sebastian told me to make it poetic.'

'Why don't we just give in and call it Sophie dotcom? It means "wisdom", you know.'

'Wisdom of God,' said Lily.

'Perfect. *Our God-like computer algorithm will use all its magical techie wisdom to match you with your one true love.* There you go. I've even written the mission statement for you. I think I should be getting your salary too, Will.'

'I'm going to kill myself,' I said.

'As long as you don't make a mess,' Theo called across.

'No blood on Lily's PC, please.' Sophie shook her head at the blank document on my screen. 'Want to go for a wander?'

I stared at her, and that was when it hit me. Elation. Pure pleasure at the prospect of being alone with her. This was more than a mild crush.

I was in trouble.

'Will?'

'Yes. I do. I really do.'

I saw Theo check his watch as Sophie and I left the room. Ignoring him, I followed Sophie along the hallway. She was wearing a short dress and, not for the first time, I marvelled at her impressive calves, a result of the horse-riding lessons she'd had as a teenager, something she and Georgina had bonded over. Rohan and Georgina had arrived several hours after Sophie and me, ferried by Dominic from the station. Rohan seemed to model himself on the working-class City traders you often saw on TV, turning up to work on his first day in a suit and describing himself as a 'go-getter'. He told us his two passions were football and money, and that his ambition was to be rich enough to buy the team he supported: not some tiny local club, but Manchester United. One had to admire his ambition.

He and Dominic had already become friends, in the manner of small boys in the playground, kicking a football around on the lawn after work and talking about sport incessantly.

I hadn't spoken to Georgina much yet. I'd never been on a horse, and that was just the start of our differences.

'Let's go down to the lake,' Sophie said as we stepped into the sunlight, so bright after the dim of the library it almost blinded me.

We walked down across the lawn, which was turning yellow. It hadn't rained for weeks. Across the way, I spotted Dominic, lounging on the grass with his shirt off. I raised my hand in greeting. He nodded a reply then waved, which confused me for a second until I realized he was waving to someone coming down the drive behind us, gravel crunching beneath her feet as she pushed a bicycle. A young woman. She was tiny with vivid, copper hair and very pale skin.

The redhead waved back at Dominic but leaned her bike against the wall and headed to the house, disappearing through the front door. As she vanished inside, Dominic strolled over to us. He was wearing nothing but a pair of denim shorts and he ran a palm from his bare chest to his navel, stroking his own smooth skin. I noticed Sophie watching him. Did she like him? Dominic was happy to walk about almost naked, knowing he looked good, his skin lightly toasted, smelling of sunscreen. He had that naughty posh-boy thing going on too. Sophie was bound to fancy him.

'Who's the ginger?' Sophie asked.

'That's Eve.'

'An original sinner, eh?'

Dominic's grin was wolfish. 'Let's hope so. Uncle Seb's hired her to help out around the house. Prepare meals for you lot, clean up, get the shopping in . . .'

'Keep the nephew happy.'

His laugh was so loud they must have heard him in the library. 'I won't tell her you said that. Anyway, who said I'd be interested? She's fit, but she's not the fittest girl around here.'

The look he gave Sophie dripped with meaning.

I butted in. 'Come on, Sophie, I can feel myself burning.'

'Me too,' said Dominic.

I ignored that. 'I need to get into the shade.'

'Gotta stay pale and interesting, eh?' Dominic said, not looking at me, his attention still on Sophie. 'I'll probably join you for dinner later. See what Eve cooks up for us.'

'Apples all round, I expect.'

He wandered away and Sophie turned to me, a smile on her face. 'What is it? You don't like him, do you?'

'He's just so . . .'

'Arrogant?'

'Yeah. *Brideshead* bad-boy chic.'

To my immense gratification, she laughed almost as loudly as Dominic had and, even better, took my arm.

We entered the merciful shade of the woods. There was a faint smell of smoke from somewhere in the distance; the rumble of a tractor from a neighbouring farm. The path beneath our feet was dry, baked hard by the heat. Walking, even at this leisurely pace, was making me sweat, the heat playing havoc with my libido, which, being twenty-two, was on a constant simmer anyway. I wondered how Sophie would react if I made a move to kiss her, right here beneath the trees in the middle of the working day. Would she kiss me back? My great fear was that it would make everything horribly awkward. I wasn't confident enough to try it. I was also concerned that it might be frowned upon by Sebastian and jeopardize my job here. At the same time, I could see that if I didn't do something soon we would find ourselves in the friend zone, a terrible place from which there was no way back.

Sophie said, 'I found out why he lives here, by the way.'

I woke from my daydream. 'Dominic? I guess his parents aren't, um, around . . .'

'They died together in a car crash when he was sixteen, driving home after dropping him off at boarding school.'

'How awful.'

'I know. Get this though: the car they died in, it's the one he drives now. The one he picked us up in.'

I stopped walking. 'The Jag?'

'Yep. He told me he had it repaired. Can you imagine, wanting to drive around in the car that killed your parents?'

'Maybe it reminds him of them in some way?'

We walked on, and Sophie said, 'Perhaps. Though the way he told me, well, he didn't exactly seem sad that they were dead. He seemed distinctly happy that he got to leave his school and come to live here with his uncle.'

'I guess he wasn't close to them. If they sent him away to school . . .'

'Hmm.'

I glanced at her. Did she feel sorry for him? This was an extra ingredient that would make him even more appealing.

Good-looking, arrogant, rich – and he had a sad backstory. The abandoned orphan boy. How could I compete with all that?

We came out of the woods by the lake, shining gold in the afternoon sunshine. Something hovered near my face then darted away. A dragonfly. I went over to the little rowing boat which was tied up beside a wooden dock. It was magical here. Beside me, Sophie crouched to unlace and remove her Converse, then walked into the water until it reached her knees.

'Ah, that's good. Join me.'

I was wearing jeans, socks and trainers. Ridiculously over-dressed for this weather. I had an urge to strip to my boxers and plunge into the water. Would that make Sophie think I was wild and free? Would it impress her? I knew staying fully clad beside the lake wouldn't, so I took off my trainers and socks then rolled my jeans up as far as they would go. I waded into the water and sucked in a breath through my teeth. It was icy. But Sophie was right. It did the trick. Lowered my body temperature, even though I was standing right next to her.

'Do you believe in that stuff?' I asked.

'Huh?'

I gestured at the necklace that hung an inch below her clavicle.

'Oh, my evil eye? My gran gave it to me when I was a little girl, and I've always worn it. I'd feel naked without it.'

I swallowed.

'I do believe it protects me, although maybe it's the belief that's the important part. Like with the Tarot.'

'You mean the cards?'

'Don't look so sceptical, Will.'

'I'm not.' Of course, I thought stuff like that was nonsense. The necklace was a pretty object and the cards could be beau-tiful and fun, but protection from evil? Reading the future? It wasn't rational. I didn't tell her this though. I didn't want her to think I was being dismissive.

'Did you bring a pack with you?'

'I did. I'll give you a reading sometime.'

'Cool.' I liked the sound of anything that would involve us spending time together. 'We're meant to be brainstorming site names.'

We spent twenty minutes saying names until all words sounded meaningless. I was stressed. If I didn't come up with a name soon, Sebastian might fire me. Find a better wordsmith. I had only been here a week, but I couldn't bear the thought of it. Leaving. Before anything had happened with Sophie.

'I have a question,' she said.

Was she going to ask me if I liked her? If I would kiss her? I dared not speak.

'What happened to Sebastian's wife, Barbara?'

I exhaled, disappointed. 'Why do you ask?'

'Well, I'm assuming at your interview that he told you how he'd met her through some computer-dating thing. And there are pictures of her all around the house, from when they lived in Boston. Wedding photos too. The way he talks about her . . . I'm guessing they're not divorced.'

'You think she's dead too? Like Dominic's mum and dad?'

'She must be, right? I just can't help wondering what happened to her. I actually tried to ask Dominic and he changed the subject. There's something else too.'

I waited.

'I was talking to Dominic last night and asked why Sebastian had come back to the UK. And guess what he said? He told me his uncle had had no choice. I tried to get more out of him, but he clammed up. Intriguing, right?'

It was.

We waded back to the shore and sat on a log, legs stretched out so the sun could dry our feet. A pair of butterflies, cabbage whites, danced together above the long grass.

'I'm going to find out what happened,' she said. 'You know, there's nothing I like more than a mystery. A secret.'

'Nancy Drew.'

She smiled, pinching the evil-eye necklace between forefinger and thumb. 'That's me.'

Chapter 17

When Sophie had arrived tonight, I had known straight away there was something different about her. I don't mean that she was twenty-five years older. It had nothing to do with the altered timbre of her voice, the lines of experience on her face. It was something else. Something that, to most people, would seem trivial.

I leaned over to her. 'You don't wear the evil-eye necklace any more.'

She put her palm on her upper chest. 'I usually do. But . . . when I was getting ready to come here tonight, I thought . . .'

'What?'

'I thought you'd take the piss if I was still wearing it after all these years.'

'Why would I do that? Also, why would you care what I think?'

'I don't know, Will. Maybe I didn't want any of you to think I haven't grown up. Anyway, it was obviously a bad decision, wasn't it? The one day I don't wear it.'

I didn't know what to say to that. Did she really believe her necklace would have warded off Callum and Amber?

There was no time to pursue the thought, because a voice to my left boomed in my ear.

'Everybody, stop talking.'

Theo had got up from the table. His fringe was damp where Georgina had thrown the water at him, but the soaking had performed a magic trick, bringing back the old Theo, the one I'd known twenty-five years ago.

Actually, that's not quite right. He'd always had two sides. During the day, he had been a hard taskmaster, watching us carefully, ensuring we didn't slack off, but also helping us, giving us guidance, problem-solving. On the Belbin, he was the coordinator and the shaper, the person who organized us and drove us forward, making sure we stayed focused and knew what our objectives were. In tandem with Lily, it was his role to turn Sebastian's concepts into something tangible.

In the evenings, however, he had relaxed. Become a lot more passive, friendly. Happy for us to take the piss out of him and keen to be liked, especially by Georgina – who, it turned out, he had fancied from day one. From her interview, in fact, though he swore he hadn't pressured Sebastian to employ her because he had the hots for her. He'd kept quiet, thrilled when it turned out the professor agreed she would fit well into the team.

I remembered Rohan making a joke, saying, 'Meet Theo. Sheepdog by day, herding and directing the rest of us, and golden retriever by night.'

It was the border collie we needed now. The leader.

He walked around the table in the same way Callum had, pausing behind Georgina for a moment to squeeze her shoulder. He glanced towards the closed door, Amber presumably still on the other side.

'You all claim not to know what this secret is, yes?'

A collective nod.

'Let's take a step back. Try to be logical and figure this out.' He looked straight at Lily, knowing the mention of logic would appeal to her. 'Callum claims there's a secret in this room, something from when we were at Thornwood. But if it's a secret, how does he know it even exists?'

'Maybe he knows what it is,' Sophie said, 'but is trying to get us – whoever it is – to admit to it. To confess.'

'Maybe. What did Callum say? *We'll know it when we hear it.* Let me ask you this. Have any of you ever encountered Callum or Amber before?'

We all said no or shook our heads.

'Have any of you ever shared some big secret from that summer? Pillow talk with a lover? Pouring your heart out in an AA meeting? Posting on a forum?'

Again, we all shook our heads. I studied the rest of the group. It was impossible to know if they were telling the truth, but no one looked particularly shifty. No one was staring at the surface of the table, avoiding eye contact, showing any obvious signs they were lying. The predominant emotion was confusion – but also, a sense of relief that our former leader was taking charge.

'If that's the case, I really can't see how these thugs could possibly be telling the truth when they say they know one of us has a secret. Not without knowing what it is.'

'What are you thinking?' Lily asked.

'I'm thinking this is probably bullshit,' Theo replied. 'A tactic to keep us busy and distracted.'

'While they do what?'

'Well, the obvious thing would be that Callum is going through the house helping himself to all our valuables.'

'But why make up something so elaborate?' Sophie asked. 'They're already keeping us in here at gunpoint.'

'Like I said, it's a distraction technique. No different from giving little kids pens and paper to keep them busy in a restaurant.'

'You think they're just helping themselves to our stuff?' Georgina looked up at her husband.

'I think there's a good chance of it, darling. Filling a bag with loot while we're cowering in here, trying to figure out what this big secret is.'

'If that's the case, it's good, isn't it?' Georgina's voice ached with hope. 'Once they've got everything, they'll go. Everything's insured, isn't it?'

'Of course.' A pause. 'Except . . .'

'Except what?'

'It doesn't matter.'

'Come off it.' Rohan spat the words across the table. 'You can't not tell us.'

Theo went back round the table and sank into his seat with a sigh. 'The safe. There are papers in there.'

Georgina sat back. 'Ah.'

'What papers?' I asked.

'Stuff from work. Documents that I shouldn't really have at home, to be honest.'

'You think that might be what this is about? Some stupid documents?' That was Sophie.

'You don't understand. It's . . . I can't divulge exactly what these documents are about, but they contain information that could make some people extremely rich. And others could be, well, wiped out. If it leaked, I mean.'

'Hold on,' I said. 'If this is about industry secrets, and they're after what's in your safe, why aren't they marching you there at gunpoint and demanding to know what the combination is?'

'He's right,' Lily said. 'It can't be that.'

Theo suddenly seemed doubtful. A little relieved, in fact.

I looked around at the others. I could see that everyone wanted to believe this was a burglary. *I* wanted to believe him.

But there was so much about that scenario that didn't make sense. For a start, Callum had seemed extremely convincing when he'd been in here with his shotgun. Why go to all the trouble of making us believe there was a secret? Why not simply lock us in this room? On top of that, if *I* was a burglar, and in possession of a gun too, I would march Theo and/or Georgina up to the safe and demand to know the combination, whether or not I knew of the existence of these important documents. The safe is always where the most valuable stuff is kept.

I tried to argue with myself. Maybe they didn't know there was a safe – but wouldn't they assume there would be one in a house like this? If they didn't come across it, surely they would demand to know where it was.

What else? Well, Theo was right that Callum's claim to know there was a secret without knowing the details of that secret was far-fetched. But it *was* possible. There had to be information we didn't know yet. Things Callum wasn't telling us.

It felt very much to me like this was a game. The beginning stages of a game where the rules had not yet been fully revealed. It was, in my opinion, foolish and dangerous to think it was a smokescreen.

But everyone in this room was looking for a leader. That's what happens in groups. You don't need a behavioural test to tell you that. And although I had been pleased a few minutes before that someone, our old project manager, had stepped forward to do just that, now I was fearful of where he might lead us.

'What do you think we should do?' I asked, although I already knew what he was going to say.

'I think we should sit tight and wait. My strong feeling is that once they've got everything, they'll leave, laughing at these fools who spent the last hour trembling and trying to figure out what their big secret was.'

Once again, I looked at the others. They all wanted him to be right. I wished for it too.

But I had an awful feeling that this course of action – of *in*action – was riskier than any other. More dangerous, even, than running at the intruders and trying to grab their guns – not that I had any plan to do that.

'I don't agree,' I said. 'I think we need to keep talking, figure out what this secret is and who has it. I think it might be something to do with how it all ended. That last night – the night of the party. I mean, does anyone know why Sebastian closed the website down so suddenly?'

'There was no more money,' Theo said. 'We would have needed substantial extra investment to fix the flaws in the algorithm.'

I glanced at Lily, who didn't react, though I imagined Theo's words must have stung.

'But what about James?' He had been Sebastian's angel investor. 'Couldn't he—'

I was cut off by the door opening.

Callum entered the room, the shotgun held down by his side.

'I need a volunteer,' he said.

Nobody spoke.

'Don't all rush.' He eyed me and Rohan, then pointed at me. 'You. No need to look so worried. You're not going to miss any of the excitement.'

He gestured for me to follow him into the hallway.

'This is the point where you're *supposed* to be chattering,' he said to the others. 'The clock's still ticking, you know. Tick tock. Tick fucking tock.'

Amber stood outside the door, eyes shining. I noticed her pupils were large. Was she on drugs?

'Why are you doing this?' I asked her directly.

She seemed surprised by the question, but it made Callum laugh.

'She can't help herself,' he said. He reached out and stroked her cheek with his knuckles and she closed her eyes for a second, drew in a sharp breath. For a second, I was sure they were going to kiss. Was this something else? Bonnie and Clyde? One of those *folie à deux* set-ups? Somehow, that seemed even more dangerous than the other scenarios. More volatile.

Callum withdrew his hand from Amber's skin and she opened her eyes again. Her pupils shrank then expanded and I realized she wasn't high. Not on drugs, anyway. It was excitement.

Chapter 18

Callum made me go first, directing me into the sitting room. My legs felt weak. Why had they singled me out?

'You look like you're going to crap yourself,' Callum said with a sneer. 'Relax. Just don't think about trying to get out.'

I took several breaths before replying. 'What would be the point? You've sabotaged the security system. Locked all the doors.'

'True. Although, funnily enough, we didn't lock the back door. It was already locked and I couldn't find the key.'

'I don't believe you.'

He shrugged like he couldn't give a damn if I believed him or not.

I looked around me. There was a pile of stuff on the floor beneath the painting of Thornwood. A jewellery stand that had various chains and earrings hanging from it, diamonds and emeralds catching the light. A couple of laptops and several bottles of wine and Scotch, presumably the most expensive stuff they'd been able to find. There were more clothes, a couple of Chanel bags, a box with the Rolex logo across it, and a vintage lamp. There was also, on the floor next to this stuff, the landline phone Theo had found in the cupboard. It had been stamped on and smashed to pieces. He had been busy in the thirty minutes we'd been locked in the dining room.

Did this mean this was a burglary, after all?

'That's a Tiffany,' Callum said. 'Know how much it's worth?'

'I have no idea.'

'Me neither, but my mum will love it. What's that reaction, Will? Surprised I have a mother?'

'What? No, I—'

He cut me off. 'My mum used to clean houses like this. You want to hear a story? I know you like stories.'

His gaze became softer, almost dreamy.

'She took me with her sometimes, you know, when it was the school holidays. Give me a comic and tell me to sit still, not touch anything. But of course I was a kid. A restless kid, always in motion, and I couldn't help but touch things. Can you guess what happened?'

'You broke something.'

'Very good, Will. I broke something. A lamp, in fact. One very similar to this. Knocked it over. The lady of the house came running when she heard the crash – first time I'd ever seen her get off her arse – there was a big hoo-hah, and my mum got fired.'

I waited.

'Do you know what I remember? This woman – she came from money. Everything she had in her life had been handed to her on a silver fucking platter. And there she was, screaming at my mum, who came from nothing, who had nothing, not about me breaking this beautiful object that meant a lot to her but about how much it cost. That was all she cared about.'

I was expecting him to tell me about some lesson he'd learned. Some moral. Instead, he said, 'Anyway, the story has a happy ending. Years later, when I was grown up, I went back. I knew they kept the spare key under this stone lion in the garden. She was asleep in bed, drunk in the middle of the afternoon. I put a pillow over her face. Said my mum's name, so it was the last thing she heard.'

I stared at him.

'So yeah, this lamp will be a nice, belated souvenir.'

I was shaken and unable to speak for a second.

'Is this personal too? What you're doing tonight? Has somebody here wronged you or Amber?'

'I'd never heard of any of you until last week.'

I looked at the pile of swag. 'So this is just a burglary?'

'No, Will.' He grinned. I could see that one of his front teeth was chipped. Then he took something out of his inside pocket. A knife.

I took a small step back.

'It's not a burglary. This is just a little bonus, some stuff we can sell for petty cash. It's the magpie in me. I can't resist pretty things. Like this knife. Japanese steel. Know how much these cost?'

He thrust the knife towards me, making me jump back further, and suddenly he was right there, his breath in my face. This man who had just casually told me about smothering a woman in her bed.

'I was just thinking, it might make you more interesting. I can see Sophie going for a bloke with a cool face scar.'

He moved the knife so it brushed my cheek. I was frozen rigid, my other cheek pressed against the wall. His breath was warm on my face. I was convinced he was going to slice my cheek open. Maybe worse. Take out an eye. Decide he was sick of me and slash my throat.

'Sure you don't want one?'

I was terrified that if I spoke the knife would pierce my flesh, so I stayed silent. Rigid.

'Spoilsport,' he said, withdrawing the blade and tucking it back inside his pocket, stepping away from me and going over to the drinks cabinet. I expected him to pour himself something but instead he picked up a slim sheaf of papers, standard letter size. He leafed through them, then turned one round to show me.

It had my face on it. My Facebook profile picture. Beneath the photo, half a page of text. He turned it back and perused it. As he did I saw that the sheet below bore Lily's photo.

'Will Harper,' he read. 'You're a lecturer. Creative writing. Wannabe novelist too. Not good enough to be published though.' He looked up from the paper, directly into my eyes. 'Are you the one with the secret? Because if you are, all you have to do is tell me, right now, and Amber and me, we can go, leave you to your dinner party. I didn't prepare a main course, but you could always make an omelette or something. Break a few eggs.'

'Why should we play along? We've all seen your faces. How do I know you won't kill us all the moment you learn the secret?' I had to force these words past a knot in my throat.

'I promise you. Whoever's still alive when we hear the secret will walk out of here in one piece.'

Whoever's still alive.

'We're not planning on sticking around after this. All this stuff – I can sell this shit in five minutes, and then—' He made a speeding motion, a fighter jet taking off. 'You can describe us to the police all you like, but they'll never find us.'

'But how do you even know there is a secret?' I asked. 'You need to tell us that.'

'Oh, it's complicated, Will.' He went over to the painting of Thornwood. The gun was propped up against the wall below it. 'Do you know the phrase "everything echoes"?'

I was startled. Finn had said that earlier.

'Remind me,' I said, trying to act cool.

He didn't reply. Instead, he tapped the painting of Sebastian's house. 'You all need to think about what went on here, Will.'

'I *have* been thinking.'

144

'Have you all, though? You're going to have to persuade your friends to try harder. Persuade them to be honest.'

'At the moment they think you're bluffing. That this is a burglary.'

The anger returned in a flash. 'I am not fucking bluffing.'

He yelled it and, at the same time, stabbed the painting, right in its centre, piercing Thornwood's front door. He sliced downwards, so the canvas flapped open – revealing the wall behind.

Except it wasn't the wall.

'Well,' he said, peering through the hole he'd created. He reached up and lifted the painting down, tossing it to one side.

There, on the wall, was the safe.

He rapped it lightly with his knuckles. 'I wonder what's in here?'

The safe was almost as big as the painting that had concealed it, with a keypad at its centre. Callum picked up the papers. 'Dates of birth,' he said to himself, then went to the keypad, prodding it. 'Nope. Know their kids' birthdays?'

I shook my head.

'Of course you don't. Not seen each other for a long time, right?' He tilted his head, like a dog hearing its name, and regarded the safe one more time before seeming to lose interest.

'I expect you're wondering why I brought you out here.'

'For a chat?'

That brought a cold-eyed smile. 'As much as I've enjoyed it, no. I've got a mission for you, Will. Something to add a little extra spice to the game.'

A mission?

He reached into his pocket, and I thought he was going to pull out another knife. But it was something small. Something that sparkled.

'I found this upstairs,' he said, holding the diamond ring between his thumb and forefinger, turning it slowly so it caught and reflected the light, which danced across the walls. 'Gotta be worth a packet, right? Someone could sell this, raise a bit of capital for themselves.'

'What are you talking about?'

'This is your mission, Will. I want you to offer this to Rohan. Tell him you found it out here among all the other stuff and picked it up when I wasn't looking. I heard you talking to him earlier about how desperate he is to get his new business up and running. The money he'd get from flogging this would come in *very* handy.'

He held out his hand to give me the ring. I didn't take it.

'You want me to offer this to Rohan?'

'Yeah. I want to see if he accepts it.'

'But why?' I didn't get it.

'Let's just say I'm interested in human nature.' He pushed the ring towards me again, but I still didn't take it. And now darkness fell across his features. 'I'm not giving you a choice, Will. You're going to do this.'

'What if I refuse?'

'I've seen the way you look at Sophie. I'm guessing she's the main reason you came here tonight. You could walk out of here hand in hand, maybe, depending on how things play out. But if you don't encourage your friends to do as they're told, she's not going to be *walking* out of here – hand in hand or otherwise.'

He touched his pocket where he'd put the knife. It was enough to make me snatch the ring from his hand.

He grinned. 'Thought that would motivate you.'

'I still don't get why though.' I was also trying to figure out if this weird mission meant he was more or less likely to let us survive the night.

146

'You don't need to know. You just need to do it. I'll ask you later if he accepted it or not.'

'But . . .'

'I'm bored now. You can go back. And by the way, you've got fifteen minutes before the hour is up. Lots to think about, eh, Will? Now, move it. And the mission – don't breathe a word, all right?'

Chapter 19

July 1999

'I've got the results of the tests,' Lily said, emerging from the woods and waving a handful of papers.

That day, the temperature inside the office had hit the mid-thirties, or ninety-five on the ancient thermometer on the wall that only showed Fahrenheit. Of course, there was no air-conditioning, just a bunch of fans that rotated slowly back and forth. Sebastian had come into the office in the afternoon, his shirt unbuttoned to reveal his greying chest hair, and had distributed orange ice lollies he'd dug out of the freezer, though they had partially melted in the minute it had taken him to get to the office from the kitchen.

He went around the desks, checking how we were getting on. This was something he did every day, and I had come to both anticipate and dread these visits because his mood was so unpredictable. Some days he would radiate stress, usually after a meeting with his angel investor, a guy called James who would turn up occasionally in his Porsche, complaining about how the bumpy roads played havoc with his suspension. Neither Sebastian nor Theo would tell us much about James except we knew he was putting up the money for this first stage of development and when he visited it was like the Queen was in town. On those days, Sebastian was like a bear that had been awoken from hibernation too early, 'prowling and scowling', as Sophie put it.

'Come on,' he would snap. 'We're going to run out of money before we're ready to launch at this rate. What are you gawping at, Rohan? Look at the mess in here. You're worse than the psychopaths I worked with at Fredericks. I thought they were a filthy bunch. Eve!'

He would storm off, dragging Theo with him and shouting for Eve to come and tidy up. Theo would come back, shaken, and pass on our boss's displeasure with our progress. I'm annoyed to admit that it did actually make us work harder. Also, it didn't make us like our boss any less – because when he was nice, he was delightful. He was one of those people who, when he gave you positive attention, it felt as if the sun was shining on your face. We all wanted to please him.

Today Sebastian had been in good spirits, praising our work, coming out of a meeting about the user journey with Sophie with a grin on his face, discussing the PR strategy with Georgina and slapping Rohan on the back when he informed our boss he had negotiated a discount from our hosting company.

'Come up with a name yet?' he had asked, stopping by my desk. I had been working on the text for the registration page. 'I'm going to have to give you a deadline. Five o'clock tomorrow.'

He had walked away without giving me a chance to respond.

Around six, unable to stay in that sweat chamber of an office any longer, we had gone down to the lake, all except Lily – who arrived a bit later, her sheets of paper in hand.

Sophie and I were in the rowing boat. Sophie had found a bottle of cherry wine at the back of a cupboard, and Dominic, who was there too, had told her his uncle wouldn't mind if she took it.

'Disgusting stuff,' he said. 'Like drinking sugary blood.'

'Hmm, delicious,' Sophie said, the two of us passing the bottle back and forth. I felt woozy, and Sophie was very close to drunk. Seeing Lily emerge from the trees, she cried out, 'Lils!' and tried to stand, the boat rocking violently.

Suddenly, Sophie was on top of me, the bottle knocked from my grasp, wine spilling.

'Oops,' she said. She had landed so she was sitting in my lap, and her face was mere inches from mine.

It would have been so easy to kiss her.

I was tipsy, and if we'd been on our own I probably would have done it. Risked the rejection I feared. But we weren't alone. Everyone was looking at us.

'Sorry, Will.' Sophie extricated herself, picking up the bottle and moving back to her end of the boat.

'There's really no need to apologize,' I muttered, rowing the short distance to the shore, where all the others – except Dominic, who sat a little way apart, on the edge of the grass – gathered around Lily. I couldn't hear what she was saying at first, not until we reached the shallows and jumped out of the boat.

'What's happening?' I asked as we joined the group.

Rohan replied. 'Lily's got the dating matches.'

I immediately knew what he meant. This was what we were here for, after all. The whole point of the still-unnamed site. For the past two weeks we had been testing the system that Lily had programmed, using the questionnaires Sebastian had devised, which were partly based on the original 1960s computer-dating questionnaires but updated to heavily make use of the five-factor model of personality, along with Sebastian's own research. It was modernized, too, so the questions were less prim and more reflective of late-nineties dating mores. This had been one of my initial tasks, ensuring these questions were phrased in an informal and accessible way.

I spent a lot of time rephrasing questions from the five-factors test because Sebastian insisted he wanted the language to be 'twenty-first century'. *Do you feel more alive when you're hanging with a crowd or just chilling? How much do you enjoy being able to banter with your other half?* There were situational questions: *It's your partner's birthday but your boss asks you to stay behind to talk about a potential pay rise . . .* There was a section of sexual questions too, asking people to rank how much they enjoyed certain activities, from 'Oh my God yes!' to 'I would rather die a virgin.'

'Compatibility around sexual preferences is so important,' Sebastian said in one of our meetings. 'For example, if Will here likes to watch himself and his partner in the mirror when he's having sex—'

'He shouldn't date a vampire,' said Sophie.

Sebastian made us come up with a list of every sexual practice and potential kink we could think of, an activity Dominic eagerly volunteered to take part in.

'There's nothing I won't do,' he said. 'As long as it's not, you know . . .'

'Pleasurable for your partner?' That was Sophie again.

'Hilarious. They always come back for more.'

'Yeah, like Oliver Twist asking for a second helping of gruel.'

I hated it when they flirted. I also found it highly embarrassing sitting in a room with Sophie and the others discussing spanking and dirty talk and dressing up in furry animal costumes, which Lily insisted was a thing with numerous communities active online. 'There's a message board for everything.'

Once all these questions had been answered, Lily's algorithm took care of the rest, creating an 'affinity' score. The maths involved in this was far too complicated for me to understand, no matter how many times Lily tried to explain false positives and logistical regression models. All that mattered to me was whether it worked. Lily told us the algorithm was able to predict how compatible a couple were likely to be in different situations. For example, it told us whether a couple would be suited for marriage or a holiday romance. It could detect inconsistencies too. Tell when people were not being honest or trying to make themselves look better.

'Our aim is to help people find love,' Sebastian said. 'Of course, the site can also be used for casual relationships, but love is the important thing.'

In order to prove the accuracy of Lily's model, the site needed to go through a beta phase, a soft launch that would involve giving free memberships to several thousand singles in one location. However, before we even got that far, we needed to test it on a smaller cohort. That meant we had been feeding the system as many profiles as we could get hold of. Lily and Theo had started this months ago, distributing questionnaires at the University of Kent to students and paying them a nominal fee to complete them. Sebastian had also roped in as many people as he could from the local village, stressing it wasn't real – yet – but that it was important to complete it accurately.

And of course, everyone at Thornwood had taken the test too: all 387 questions.

These were the pieces of paper Lily was holding now. The results that told us who we had matched with, complete with a photo of the match and some basic biographical details. I wasn't particularly excited about it. A match with some random student in Canterbury, a person I would never meet in real life? I had, however, been diligent when completing the form, thinking carefully about my answers and attempting to represent the real me.

When the site launched, users would be given a list of matches, which would continually update. But for now, Lily had only printed out our very top match, the person the algorithm thought we had the strongest affinity with.

Her eyes shone with a sense of achievement. Here it was: something tangible. Real-life results.

'Rohan, here's your match.' Lily handed him a sheet of paper. 'She's a geography student. Twenty.'

'She's cute,' he said, holding up the printout to show us. 'Introvert. Workaholic. Likes football, and her ideal man is an entrepreneur. That's me!'

'They both like football and money.' Dominic's voice drifted over. 'Is that it? Is that all the algorithm does?'

'It's far more complex than that,' Lily said, not looking at him.

'Yeah, maybe. But none of it would mean anything if Rohan didn't think her picture was "cute".' He made air quotes with his fingers. 'Sorry, mate. Just being honest.'

'It's fine,' Rohan said. 'I'm not looking for love, anyway. All that stuff is a distraction from the important things in life. Like football and money.'

Dominic and Rohan high-fived, and Lily rolled her eyes at them.

'Theo, your top match is also a student at Kent.' She handed him his printout. 'Georgina, yours is a local guy. A farmer from the other side of the village.'

'How many acres?' Georgina asked.

'Size isn't everything,' Sophie said.

Theo was looking at his sheet of paper with dismay.

'What's the matter?' I asked. 'Don't fancy her?' Over his shoulder, I could see he'd been matched with a young woman with a pixie cut and big eyes, rather like a manga character.

'Not really.' He glanced at Georgina. 'I can think of other women who are far more my type.'

At that moment, Sophie said, 'Hey, Dominic, don't move. There's a butterfly in your hair.'

Of course, he shook his head, and the butterfly flitted away, but not far, landing on a long blade of grass. It was a beauty, pale blue and black, much larger than the red admirals and cabbage whites we usually saw.

'It would look good pinned and framed,' Dominic said.

'You're awful,' said Sophie.

'Shame I don't have a butterfly net.'

'Butterfly net.' This was my eureka moment. 'That's it. That's what we should call the site. Get it? Butterfly dot net.'

'Oh, I like it,' said Sophie. 'It's about catching something beautiful and fragile. It's poetic. Exactly what the professor's after.'

We smiled at each other. In my excitement, I had to fight the urge to kiss her, or to make some wild proclamation. At the very least, this felt like a good time to give her a hug.

'Butterfly net? I'm going to vomit,' said Dominic, puncturing the mood.

'You're such a dick,' said Sophie to him. To me, she said, 'Ignore him. It's great, especially the dot net part, if that domain is still available. I reckon Sebastian will love it.'

Butterfly.net. Had we finally cracked it? It was certainly better than LoveMatcher, which was the current front-runner.

'Anyway,' Lily said, drawing our attention back to her. 'Amazingly, we have a match right here, in this house.'

She handed a sheet to me.

There, in my hands, was Sophie's profile, complete with the photo she'd taken using our office digital camera. *Sensitive. Careless. Curious. Interests: Tarot cards, seventies music, vintage magazines.*

'What are the odds?' said Rohan, winking at me. I looked at Sophie, who was standing a few feet away, avoiding my eye. Hope flared. Had she matched with me too?

Finally, Sophie looked up, then over at me. What was that

expression? Was she mortified that she'd been matched with me? She didn't seem drunk any more, and I was getting a headache: an instant hangover from the sweet wine.

'Who did you get?' Georgina asked Sophie.

She held up the sheet, and it was like a punch in the solar plexus. 'Some guy called Guy.'

A random stranger. I didn't care who he was – although I did notice he looked a bit like Dominic. The important point was that she hadn't been matched with me.

'Unrequited love,' said Dominic. 'Tragic.'

'Get stuffed,' I said, which made him snigger.

'How about you, Lily?' Theo asked, seemingly oblivious to the tension. 'Who did you match with?'

'Oh, some skater girl from Brighton.' She sounded disinterested but said, 'She certainly seems like my type on paper.'

'What about me?' Dominic asked. The butterfly had gone, and he had pushed himself to his feet and come towards us. 'Didn't you put my questionnaire through?' he asked, frowning at Lily's now-empty hands.

'Um, yes, I did.'

'And?'

'It couldn't find you any matches.'

'What do you mean?'

'It couldn't find anyone you're compatible with. I think it must be a bug in the system. I'll look into it.'

'Don't bother. It's all bullshit, anyway. I'm too . . . unique for your stupid site.'

'That's one word for it,' I said.

'Fuck you, Will.' He glared at me, then returned his attention to Lily. 'Your algorithm probably realized every girl in the world would want to get with me and it couldn't cope.'

Lily stared at him like she couldn't believe what she was hearing.

'Screw this.' He stormed away, heading into the woods, calling back, 'I'm going to find Eve. She's the only person here who isn't a wanker.'

We watched him go.

'Wow,' Sophie said.

'I feel sorry for him,' Lily said, sitting down on a rock. 'This family . . . it's had to face so much tragedy.'

'Like his parents dying in a car crash?'

'Exactly. And that's not the only thing. I'm guessing you don't know what happened to Sebastian's wife?'

Theo spoke up. 'I'm not sure the professor would want us gossiping about that.'

'It's not gossip,' Lily argued. 'It's public knowledge, and I'm sure people have been wondering.'

Sophie and I exchanged a look. We were going to find out and hadn't even had to do any sleuthing.

'She was murdered,' Lily said. 'When they were still living in Boston.'

'Murdered?' That was Georgina.

Lily nodded. 'By a serial killer.'

Chapter 20

Callum put his hand on my back and shoved me into the dining room, slamming the door shut behind me. Everyone at the table stared at me, Rohan turning in his seat, Theo swivelling.

Sophie jumped up and came over to me. 'What happened? What did he want?'

I couldn't tell them about the mission, but what was I supposed to say? I deflected.

'He's got a pile of stuff down there. Jewellery, some bags and clothes, some old vintage lamp . . .'

'A lamp?' That was Georgina. 'What did it look like?'

'He said it was Tiffany.'

Georgina's hand went to her chest. 'The Dragonfly?'

Theo had gone over to her. 'All of this stuff can be replaced.'

'That can't. You bought me that for our tenth anniversary. It's a one-off. What else was there, Will?'

A huge fuck-off diamond ring that I've got in my pocket. But Theo was smiling. 'Can't you see, this is good. It shows I was right. It's a burglary, nothing more. All this stuff about the secret is a ruse to keep us distracted. It's—'

'No!'

I shouted it, so loud that Sophie took a step back as if blasted off balance. Theo's eyebrows went up.

'It's *not* a burglary. Your possessions – that's just a bonus to them. Callum was very clear. He's convinced one of us has a secret.'

I met each of their gazes in turn. It was vital they took this in. My time with Callum had convinced me this was real. It was not a burglary. 'If we don't do what he says . . .'

'What?' Theo asked. 'He didn't say he was going to kill anyone, did he?'

I hesitated, not wanting to cause panic. But I had to tell them what Callum had said. They needed to be scared. I recounted my conversation with him.

'He said, "Whoever's still alive when the secret is revealed will walk out of here."'

They all stared at me with horror, but Theo still wouldn't accept it. 'He didn't actually say he was going to start killing us?'

'No, he didn't use those actual words, but it was pretty bloody clear what he meant.' I turned to the others. 'We've only got about ten minutes left till the first hour is up.'

'Oh, come on. You really think they would fire a shotgun, here, on a residential street?' Theo scoffed. 'Do you know how much noise it would make? Someone would hear and call the police.'

'Theo, he's carrying one of your Japanese kitchen knives too. He held it to my throat. Threatened to cut me.'

Also, I was sceptical about them not wanting to use guns. I'd heard distressed noises this very evening and hadn't done anything about it. This was leafy west London. No one walking by would think they'd heard a shotgun being fired. They'd probably think someone had their TV up too loud.

But I could see the others were desperate to believe Theo. Behind him, Rohan was nodding. Georgina seemed to agree with her husband too. I wondered when I was supposed to offer Rohan the ring. Not right now.

'Please,' I said. 'We don't have long.' I thought I might explode with frustration, but I was still reluctant to tell them what he'd told me about murdering his mother's former employer. I wanted them to be scared, but not to panic. 'I am certain this isn't a burglary.'

'What if it's what Theo said before?' Rohan asked. 'Industrial espionage?'

'It's not.' Hearing how dry my mouth was, I went to the table, grabbed a glass of water and downed it. 'Callum took down the picture of Thornwood—'

'He found the safe?' Theo was aghast.

'Yes, but he wasn't even that interested in it. I get the impression this secret is a lot more valuable than anything in this house.'

'But what could that possibly be?' Sophie asked.

'I don't know. And no, he didn't give me any hints.'

Sophie sat down and faced Lily. 'Something from 1999. They couldn't have taken part in the dating-site trial, could they?'

Lily shook her head. 'I don't remember the names of everyone who took part. But it was only us, a load of students from Kent and some locals.'

'So maybe they were from the village.'

Could they be aggrieved locals from near Thornwood? Amber, at least, had the right accent for that part of the world. We hadn't been into the village much – at least, I hadn't – but there had been someone at Thornwood who came from there.

'Could it be related to Eve?' I asked. 'Does anyone know what happened to her?'

Most of the group looked blank, but Lily said, 'She moved to London. She tracked me down to ask for a reference two or three years after that summer. Working for a charity.'

I was able, even under so much stress, to be happy to hear that. I'd liked Eve a lot. Knowing she'd got what she always wanted – unlike most of us – was a small bright spot on this dark evening. And it killed my theory that Eve might somehow have put Amber and Callum up to this, before it even formed. Why would she? She was the house cleaner. It made no sense.

Theo spoke up before I could come up with any new theories.

'I really don't think these people know anything. It's a robbery. Trust me.'

'No, Theo—'

It was too late. The door swung open and Callum entered, followed by Amber. They both carried their shotguns under their arms.

'Time's up,' Callum said.

Chapter 21

It was there in the pit of my stomach: cold, immobilizing dread. I was still on my feet, at the corner of the table between Theo and Lily. As Amber closed the door and stood with her back to it, I knew, without any doubt, that whatever was about to happen was partially Theo's fault, partially mine. I had failed to make him sufficiently afraid.

I sat down beside Sophie and found her hand beneath the table, holding it. Her eyes met mine. She had no idea about Callum's threat. Or the extra responsibility I carried. I also knew, in that instant, that any negative feelings I might have been carrying since 1999 had dissolved. There was a connection between us. Always had been – even if the algorithm had only matched us one way.

'So, you've had an hour.' Callum was walking around the table, as he had the last time he was in this room. Amber remained by the door, the silent sentry, but I could feel waves of excitement coming off her. 'Which one of you is going to speak up?'

A moment followed in which everyone did the opposite of speaking up – and then Theo said, 'Come off it, mate, we know this is bullshit. Can't you see how much you're frightening the ladies?'

'The *ladies*?' Callum stopped by Theo's chair. 'I'm not frightening *you*?'

'No. Actually, you're not. I've been through a lot worse than this.'

'Did you hear that, Amber? He's been through a lot worse.'

Theo didn't give Amber the chance to respond. 'I have. My daughter going missing, for one.'

Callum shifted the shotgun from one hand to the other. 'Ah, yes. Olivia.'

Immediately, Georgina said, 'How do you know her name?' She got to her feet. 'Do you know something about where she is?'

'Sit down. Sit. *Down!*'

Slowly, she did as he demanded.

'For all I know,' said Callum, 'Olivia is living on the International Space Station. Though I'd say it's more likely her body is at the bottom of the Thames, don't you think? Or maybe she's been abducted and trafficked, and right now she's tied up in some brothel somewhere.'

'You bastard,' Theo said.

'Just being realistic. I suppose it's possible she ran away and is now living her best life, barefoot and pregnant on a farm in Cornwall. Let's try to imagine that happy outcome, shall we? Now, Theo, please tell me: do you have the secret?'

Theo made a mocking noise. 'Are you still insisting that there is one?'

Callum took a step back. 'You honestly believe we're only here to rob you? Or what? We're just having fun? A pair of sadists terrorizing the wealthy for shits and giggles?'

'I'm not wealthy,' Sophie said quietly.

'Me neither,' echoed Rohan, reminding me about the diamond ring in my pocket.

'Listen, if you want money, I can get you money.' Theo seemed weirdly smug, like this turn in the conversation showed he was right all along. 'Switch the internet back on or turn off the mobile blockers – you're using blockers, right? – and I'll transfer you money from my bank right now. Tell me how much you want. We can organize it so it's not traceable, it's easy—'

Callum banged the table with his fist. The remaining cutlery rattled. Glasses shook. Water splashed. Callum roared: 'Quiet!'

A thick vein throbbed in his temple. He shouted in Theo's face, spraying him with spittle, 'Are you going to shut up? Are you. Going to. Fucking. *Shut up?*'

Finally – *finally* – Theo looked scared. His Adam's apple bobbed. And he nodded.

'Good.' Callum stood straight. He sucked in air and his cheeks puffed out as he exhaled. Calming himself down, like Georgina with her yoga breaths. After a few deep inhalations he said, 'Let's start again. Which one of you relatively or not so relatively wealthy twats has the secret?'

Nobody spoke. He walked back around the table.

'Rohan? Not you? Georgina? Will, we've already done you . . . What about the lovely Sophie here? Or you, Lily? Theo . . . no point asking you because you think this is all bull-shit, don't you, *mate?*'

He swung his shotgun over his shoulder and walked over to Amber. A sickening tension hung in the air. I felt pain in my hand and realized it was Sophie, squeezing hard.

Callum spoke to Amber in a soft, resigned tone. 'Looks like we're going to have to play the game.'

If Amber had seemed excited before, she now looked like she might burst with it. Like this was everything she'd hoped for. The Christmas of her dreams.

He turned back to us. 'It's time to find out which one of you is lying.'

'And how do you intend to do that?' Theo asked, a new wobble in his voice. I inwardly cursed him. His denials had cost us precious time, when we could have been figuring out what Callum wanted to know.

'I'm not,' Callum replied. 'You are.'

'What are you talking about?' I asked.

He grinned and I could almost see the ripple of anticipation that went through Amber.

'You're going to vote,' he said.

Chapter 22

'Did you say *vote?*'

'Yes, Georgina. Your ears are working perfectly.' Callum had gone to the windows. Those of us with our backs to him twisted in our seats. I could still feel the echo of that cold steel knife against my cheek, and while Amber licked her lips in anticipation, I shivered with dread.

Callum patted the pockets of his chef's jacket, then pulled out a crumpled pack of Marlboros and a Zippo. Out of the corner of my eye I saw that Georgina was still able to be horrified by this.

Callum nodded at Amber. 'Want one?'

'I quit, remember.'

'You quit a lot of things.'

I registered her lack of amusement before Rohan said, 'Do you mind if I vape?'

Callum laughed. 'Be my guest. Not sure your hosts will approve though.'

Rohan had already got his vape out. 'Sorry, Georgina. I need it.'

She didn't even glance at him but aimed a withering look at Callum. 'What do I care?'

'That's right. There are far more important things to worry about.' He lit his cigarette. 'Like, who do you think has the secret?'

'None of us does,' said Theo.

'Wrong wrong wrong. I have it on excellent authority that one of you does, but – unfortunately for the rest of you – they're too gutless to speak up. So, unless that person comes forward right now, this is what's going to happen. We are going to go around the table and you are each going to tell me who you think is most likely to have the secret. Fun, huh?'

'And what happens to the person who gets the most votes?' I asked.

'They win a cuddly toy,' said Sophie.

That made Callum laugh again. 'Ah, Sophie,' he said. 'You never take anything seriously, do you?'

'You don't know anything about me.'

'Oh, I do, Sophie. Born in Trinidad and Tobago. Dad died when you were still a kid. Brain tumour, right? You've never been married and you make a pittance selling tat online while living off your tiny inheritance.'

'He's been researching us,' I said, remembering what I'd seen in the sitting room. 'He's got printouts. A kind of file on all of us.'

'What?' There was horror in Sophie's voice. Beside her, Lily looked shocked too, and I saw Theo's jaw drop a little. 'Why didn't you tell us that?'

'There's been a lot going on.'

Callum dropped his cigarette and ground it out on the polished floorboards. I thought Georgina was going to rush over to inspect the damage, but she managed to keep control of herself.

'Some of you are easier to research than others,' Callum said. 'Lily is a mystery woman. Barely seems to exist online at all, despite being a techie. Rohan, your LinkedIn profile makes you sound like London's most successful businessman, so I know you're a liar. Will, I found a lot of comments about you by former students. There's a whole thread about you in a writing subreddit.'

'What?'

'Relax: most of them like you. No female students complaining about you being a sex pest or anything. I mean, you sound a bit woke for my tastes, but whatever. Theo and Georgina are all over the interiors magazines with their *beautiful* house, though it's funny how Olivia's disappearance hasn't had much media coverage. A missing pretty white teenager? I thought the papers would be all over that.'

'It's a private matter.' Theo looked sick now, his confidence drained away. 'We didn't want to be splashed all over the media.'

'So you didn't do press conferences. Appeals for her to come home. I know I teased you about her being abducted, but it seems to me you know she's a runaway. That she left this house because she couldn't stand living here any more. What happened? Get between her and her boyfriend?'

That was close to what Theo and Georgina had told us, wasn't it? How did he know all this?

'Or was it something else?' The twist on his lips was cruel. 'Daddy try sneaking into her room at night?'

Theo launched himself at Callum. For a microsecond, I saw the flash of surprise on Callum's face, but he was fast, side-stepping the attack as Theo tried to grab him. Theo stumbled forward, losing his balance and landing on all fours. Georgina jumped out of her seat and hurried to him, crouching beside him as he stayed in that position, head down, face red, panting.

Callum's hand went to his pocket, and I was certain he was going for the Japanese knife, but he appeared to change his mind.

'Get up,' he said.

Georgina looked up at him. 'You're a bastard. Maybe Olivia did run away, but it has nothing to do with anything that happened here.'

'Oh, really? You—'

'Callum.' That was Amber. A gentle, warning tone. Like he'd been about to say something he shouldn't. 'The game. I want them to play the game.'

'Of course.' He exhaled. 'Theo, Georgina, get back to your seats.'

Georgina helped Theo up and the two Howards went back to their chairs at opposite ends of the table.

'Let's start,' Callum said. 'Amber? You want to lead?'

'I want to watch.'

He grinned. 'Kinky. You've made your prediction?'

She patted her back pocket, which made him laugh. Prediction? What were they talking about?

'Who's going to go first?' Callum said. 'Rohan, how about you?'

Rohan looked stricken. 'Me?'

'You've got it?'

'No, no – I mean, why make me go first?'

'Jesus Christ, Theo, were they always like this? How did you manage them, get them to do anything?'

Rohan took an anxious suck on his vape, but still didn't do as he was asked.

Not until Callum pointed the gun at him.

'Give me a second!' He looked around the table, eyes wide, flicking between me and Lily.

'One. Your second is up.'

Rohan exhaled. 'I think it's Theo.'

Theo, who was pink and shining with sweat, still recovering from his exertions and his outrage, snapped his attention to Rohan.

'Why Theo?' Callum asked, his tone neutral.

'I'm sorry, mate, it's just . . . If it's something from Thornwood, you were in charge, weren't you? If there was some big secret, you'd be most likely to know about it. Plus, the way you were trying to persuade us this was just a burglary, it was like, well, you didn't want us even talking about what the secret might be.'

It made sense. Echoed what I'd been thinking.

'This is stupid,' Theo said. 'I genuinely thought it was a distraction. I don't have any secrets.'

As he said that, he appeared to go a shade pinker and he glanced down at the table. If this was a game of poker I would absolutely think that was a tell. I'm sure Lily and Sophie noticed too.

'One vote for Theo,' Callum said.

'Wait.' Theo pointed a finger at Rohan. 'This is because I wasn't interested in hearing about your shitty business idea, isn't it?'

Rohan put down his vape. 'What are you talking about?'

'I'm not an idiot. I know that's why you came here. You wanted to pitch me some crap proposal. You need to face up to it, Ro. You're not a businessman. The same way Will's never going to be a successful writer.'

Ouch.

'You need to move on. Get a proper job. Christ, I'll give you a job. I'm sure we can find you something on the ground floor. I mean, you're a bit old to start out, but . . .'

He realized he wasn't doing himself any favours. Shut his mouth.

Callum looked delighted. 'One vote and there's already drama. This is better than TV. What about you, Theo? Who do you think our secret-keeper is?'

I was convinced he was going to go tit-for-tat and say *Rohan*. He didn't. He said, 'I think it's Will.'

I stared at him. 'You're not serious.'

'I think you could be in cahoots with these two.' He gestured at Callum and Amber. 'Why else did Callum get you to leave the room? You just spent fifteen minutes with him, probably plotting against the rest of us.'

'That makes no sense,' I said. 'This is about finding the secret. If I'm working with these two, then obviously I can't be the one who's keeping it, can I? Not that I *am* working with them.'

'I agree with Theo,' Georgina said, unprompted. 'I think it's Will.'

'Come off it. You're just saying that so someone has more votes than your husband.'

'It does sound like that,' Callum said, moving towards Georgina. 'Come on, why do you think it's him?'

She looked directly at me. 'I'm just not sure he's trustworthy.'

All the energy drained from my body. I knew exactly what she was talking about, and it wasn't my secret 'mission'.

'Two votes for Will, one for Theo.' Callum stood behind Rohan and nodded at Sophie. 'Your turn. Hopefully you'll take *this* seriously.'

'Fuck you.'

'Oh, not such a wit now. Come on, let's have your vote.'

She didn't hesitate. 'I think it must be Theo too, for exactly the same reasons Rohan said. Although, personally, I don't believe anyone here has this secret, not really. I think you *are* a pair of sadists who are enjoying this. And if you're going to kill us all, I want you to know I think you're scum.'

'Wow. Nice speech. Did you hear that, Amber? The female Peter Pan here doesn't like us.'

Amber traced a pretend tear beneath her eye. 'I'm so sad. I thought we were going to be bestest friends.'

'Right, that's two all, Will and Theo. This is fun, isn't it? Will, now you can take your turn.'

'I don't want to.'

Callum sighed. 'Come on . . .'

'If I have to choose someone, it's Theo. For the same reasons. And because I know it isn't me.'

Theo folded his arms. 'This is ludicrous. It's all ludicrous.'

'Three for Theo, two for Will. One vote left,' Callum said. 'Lily. What are you going to do? Going to make it a draw? Make Theo our winner? Or are you going to surprise us?'

'I don't know,' she said.

That *was* a surprise.

'It could be any of us. Can I abstain?'

Callum went around the corner of the table towards her. 'No, Lily. That would be unfair, wouldn't it, and I know you wouldn't want that.'

She cast her eyes down. 'I need longer to figure it out.'

I held my breath. The only way she could stop Theo from receiving the most votes would be to choose me. I wasn't sure what would happen if it was a draw. Would Lily go that way so it wasn't her who condemned Theo to . . . well, we still didn't know what would happen next. Though my squirming guts told me it wasn't going to be anything good.

'It's not me,' Theo said to her. 'I promise, Lily. I'm boring. I don't have any big secrets.'

But we had all seen his tell, the way he had gone extra pink and looked down, including Lily. He sounded insincere now too.

'I'm sorry,' she said.

'Oh, you bitch.'

'I choose Theo.'

Callum didn't bother totting up the scores. He raised his gun and pointed it at Theo's forehead.

Everybody else, including me, recoiled, drawing back from the table. Georgina tried to stand, but Amber strode over and, with one hand on her shoulder, shoved her back into her seat.

'Spill,' Callum said to Theo.

'But I don't have a secret.' There was no bravado left in Theo's voice now, not with the barrel of a shotgun inches from his face.

'I'm going to count to ten,' Callum said. 'And I'm not interested in any recent secrets you might have. I don't care if you're embezzling your company or screwing your secretary, and I also don't give a shit if you were messing with your daughter.'

'You're disgusting.'

'All I care about is what happened in '99. Got it?'

'But I don't—'

'Ten. Nine. Eight . . .'

'I don't have any secrets! I told you, I'm boring. I was just the project manager.' He looked at Georgina, imploring her to do something, pleading with his eyes, but what could she do?

'Seven, six . . .'

'Okay!' Theo yelled it. 'There's something.'

I could hardly breathe. Was this it? Had Rohan, who was staring at Theo with his mouth hanging open, been right?

'I blackmailed James.'

I hadn't been expecting that.

'Who the hell is James?' Callum asked.

Theo sucked in a breath. 'He was the guy who bankrolled Butterfly Net. Sebastian's main investor.'

I could picture him. James, rolling up outside Thornwood in his little red Porsche, complaining about how the countryside stank of manure and moaning about the bumpy driveway. He'd always worn a blazer, even on the hottest days, and his hair was permanently damp with sweat. I saw distaste cross both Sophie's and Georgina's face at the mention of his name, an unconscious reaction, because he had always sought them out, coming into the office and leaning over their desks,

174

breathing heavily as he asked them what they were working on, laying a hand on their arm. I wondered what had happened to him. He'd been around thirty-five then, so would be around sixty now.

'And?' Callum demanded.

'He asked if he could use one of our laptops one day, when he was waiting for Sebastian. Afterwards, I checked his browser history.'

'He'd been looking at porn?'

Theo spoke quickly. 'No. An escort site. He was staying in Tunbridge Wells and he'd been on there to find . . . company for the night. It probably wouldn't have been that bad, except he was married. Recently married, and I knew for a fact that it was his father-in-law who ran the investment house he worked for.'

'Ah.'

Theo went on. 'I knew I wanted to get into investment banking, but I also knew I'd messed up my exams, that I was only going to get a 2:2. It wouldn't be good enough for the kind of position I wanted.' Again, I was shocked. 'I needed help, a reference, an introduction. The next time James came to Thornwood I made it clear that I knew what he'd been up to and told him what I needed. He had no choice.'

Callum and Amber exchanged a glance, and Callum nodded deeply. I could see that Georgina was shocked. She hadn't known this.

'So,' Callum said. 'All this – your house, all the stuff you've acquired, your whole, fabulous life – it springs from some sleazebag cheating on his wife.'

'You could put it like that.'

Theo seemed lighter, in the way people do after they've been unburdened of a secret. But there was still a gun in his face. And then Callum said, 'It's interesting. Kind of impressive.

But it's not the secret we're after. What else have you got? Five, four . . .'

Theo was stunned. 'But that's my secret.'

'Yeah, and it's not the one I'm looking for. And if you're not the one with the secret, I don't need you any more.'

He put his finger on the trigger.

I will never forget Theo's expression. The shock. He shook his head, went pink again. Tripped over his tongue as he tried to speak.

'Three, two . . .'

Theo made a dash for the door. Amber ran towards him, trying to intercept him, yelling at him to stop, and Theo shoved her with both hands, sending her crashing to the floor.

He grabbed the handle and yanked the door open, and Callum – momentarily distracted by Amber's fall – refocused, the gun squarely aimed at Theo's back. I jumped up, intending to launch myself at Callum, my only thought being that if I could shove him, Theo would be able to get out of the room. But I was too slow. Lily was in my way.

Callum pulled the trigger.

Theo was framed by the doorway, his back to us. In a way, I'm glad I couldn't see his face as it happened, but the rest of it, I will never forget.

The roar of the gun. The dark bloom on the back of Theo's white shirt, between his shoulder blades.

Georgina's cry as Theo crashed down on to his front, a metre away from where Amber sat, her face alight with shock and wonder.

I found myself fixating on the soles of his shoes. There was a stain on one of them, a circle of white like he'd trodden on paint. His feet twitched, once, twice.

And then: he was still.

Chapter 23

July 1999

Every day, Sebastian would come into the office and tell us a thunderstorm was forecast. But the storm refused to break. Relief never came.

The heat crawled through my veins, a million tiny fires dancing in my bloodstream. Nothing would douse those fires – because it wasn't the weather setting me aflame. It was Sophie. When she left the room I was keenly aware of her absence. If she smiled at me or touched me casually during a conversation I would experience a rush of elation and longing. I closed my eyes and saw her face. *So this is love*, I remember thinking. Despite all the songs and the books and the movies, I'd never believed it would feel so close to sickness.

The problem was, thanks to her reaction to the dating matches, I didn't think she felt the same way about me. Surely, if she did, she would show me, because I was certain she knew I liked her. She must have known she could make a move on me with no fear of rejection – but she didn't. She continued to be friendly, and we hung out together a lot of the time we were off duty. I convinced myself she saw me only as a friend and colleague, and even though I didn't want to be in the friend zone, I valued even that too highly to risk ruining everything by blurting out how I felt.

So I stayed quiet, while still spending as much time in her company as I could.

Like tonight. Or rather, this morning. We had taken to staying up till the early hours, sitting out beneath the stars. Sebastian had set up some tables and chairs on the lawn near the house, and I sat there now with Sophie and Eve. Dominic and Rohan were inside, rewatching a tape of the Champions League final for the umpteenth time, and Georgina and Lily had gone for a walk. Georgina was in a bad mood because she'd been trying without success to get hold of her parents; something to do with them selling the pony she'd had since she was little. 'Every time I call it goes to their stupid answerphone, which they never even listen to. It drives me insane.'

Theo was here too, lounging in a deckchair, half asleep. Sebastian had given us an old boombox to use and I had put Moby's *Play* album on, one of the albums that soundtracked that summer, along with Radiohead and Travis, all taken from the wallet of CDs I had brought with me.

'Do you not have any Britney?' Eve asked.

Eve had been with us for three weeks now, having arrived a week after the rest of us. She didn't live at Thornwood – she cycled home to her house on the edge of the village in the evenings after completing her duties, cooking dinner and clearing up, coming when Sebastian yelled about the mess in the office – but tonight she was still here, sharing a bottle of wine with Sophie while I drank beer.

'I'm going to feel like death in the morning,' Eve said, the corner of her mouth curling up as she leaned forward to tap ash from her cigarette. She was pretty, her auburn hair making her look a little like Gillian Anderson. 'And the professor wants to talk to me about preparing some Boston-themed dinner party.'

The mention of Boston reminded me of what we'd learned about Sebastian's wife, but I had to park the thought as Sophie said, 'How come you didn't go home this evening? Couldn't tear yourself away from us?'

'Something like that.' She took another cigarette from the pack. Chain-smoking. 'Sometimes I just can't bear it.'

I knew that she lived on a new-build estate on the far side of the village, a development that wasn't finished yet. Every morning she would arrive on the rusty old bike she told us she'd had since she was twelve. She was so petite the bike was still the right size for her, though the brakes made a terrible squeaking sound as she pulled up.

'I have this fantasy,' she said, 'that I discover I was adopted and that the professor is my real dad and then I come and live here and have someone to cook and clean for *me*.' A bitter laugh. 'Not that my mum and dad would ever have adopted a child. They can't stand the kids they've got.'

'How many siblings do you have?' Sophie was an only child so found this topic fascinating.

'Four. Three brothers and a sister. I'm the youngest. One too many, my mum says. Do you know, sometimes when she cooks dinner she puts out six plates, and when I turn up she says, "Shit, I forgot about you."'

'That's awful,' I said.

She shrugged. 'I'm used to it. I'm saving up money from this job and then I'm out of here. I've got a friend in London and I'm going to go there to live with her.'

Sophie tipped the last few inches of wine into her glass and said, in a mildly teasing tone, 'I thought maybe you were hanging out here tonight so you could spend more time with Dominic.'

'Huh.' She looked around, palms raised. 'Where is he? Watching that stupid football match again? He's like one of my brothers. Expects me to fetch him snacks while he stares at the telly.'

179

'You don't fancy him then?' I had been hoping there was something between her and Dominic because, well, it might stop him making a move on Sophie. Every time Dominic and Sophie were in the same vicinity I would see him making eyes at her.

'Hmm. I mean, he does have something about him.'

'He has a nice car,' said Sophie, and the two of them cracked up.

'His dead parents' car,' I said.

They both stopped laughing, and Sophie rolled her eyes. 'Thanks for killing the mood, Will.' To Eve, she said, 'I think he likes you.'

'Almost as much as he likes football.' Eve shook her head. 'Let's be honest, he'd shag anything.'

'The boy's a total slut,' said Sophie, and that set them off again, laughing drunkenly, Eve holding her ribs and saying, 'Oh, it hurts.'

Eve lit another cigarette. 'If I was looking for a boyfriend, and thought he wanted an actual relationship rather than a shag, I might be interested. But I don't want anyone tying me down to this place, not when I'm planning to move away. And I might snog him, but I'm not into one-night stands. Never had one.'

'Really? I—'

I never got to hear Sophie's response because a scream rang out across the lawn and we all turned to look in that direction. 'What was that?'

Somewhere in the distance, down towards the woods, a woman yelled, 'Help!'

'Georgina and Lily,' I said, and Theo leapt out of his deckchair. I'd almost forgotten he was there he was so quiet. Without a word, he pelted towards the noise. I followed, running at top speed after him.

The sky was cloudless and bright with stars, the moon a sliver shy of being full, casting a silver sheen across the land. Georgina was standing on the rough ground between the lawn and the entrance to the woods, flapping her arms and making distressed, breathy noises. A few metres away, Lily was jumping up and down on the spot, saying, 'I don't know what to do.'

I arrived a few seconds after Theo, pulling to a halt just in front of where Georgina stood. It took a few moments for my eyes to adjust to the light, but then I saw that around Georgina – who was little more than a silhouette in the moonlight – small dark shapes were darting and circling. I wasn't sure if my eyes were playing tricks, but then I heard it: buzzing. They were wasps. Georgina was standing on a nest.

I discovered later, after talking to Sebastian, that while most wasps build nests in trees or buildings, one common species, the German wasp, builds its nests in holes in the ground. There was one right here, close to the path, and Georgina had strayed on to it. The whole colony hadn't come out – not yet, anyway – but there were dozens of them flying around her, defending their territory.

Georgina was frozen to the spot, still making those breathy, gasping noises. Then she cried out in pain, and suddenly the air around her became thicker as more wasps came swarming out of the ground.

'Run!' I shouted, but she wouldn't – couldn't – move.

She yelped with pain again, then again. I could see them crawling on her bare arms and legs and landing in her hair. 'They're all over me,' she said, her voice strangled by a sob. Then, while I continued to shout at her to move, Theo ran forward and scooped her up, lifting her from the ground, carrying her like she was a child – and he ran, down towards the lake, the wasps chasing them.

We all followed. By now, Sophie and Eve had reached us,

and Dominic and Rohan had come out too, drawn by the screams. Georgina was still yelling, wasps all over her. I realized exactly what Theo was doing. I was also impressed by how strong he was. Georgina wasn't tiny like Eve, but he was moving like she barely weighed anything at all.

He ran straight into the lake. Georgina cried out again, presumably because the water was cold, but Theo kept going until they were almost fully submerged. I heard him say something to her, and then they both plunged beneath the water.

The wasps, losing their quarry, buzzed around for a few more seconds, confused, then flew back over our heads towards their nest. In the next instant, Theo re-emerged, water pouring off him, and he carried Georgina back out of the lake, setting her down gently on the bank.

'Give her space,' he said as we all crowded around.

'How many times have you been stung?' Sophie asked Georgina.

'I don't know. Loads.' She was still breathing heavily.

'We should get you back to the house,' Lily said. 'Find some antihistamines.'

'Put vinegar on the stings,' Sophie said.

Theo, standing close to Georgina, who was still sitting on the ground, the two of them dripping wet, looked down at his arms.

'Did they get you too?' I asked.

'A few times. But it's fine.'

Eve clasped her hands to her chest. 'I can't imagine anyone doing that for me.'

Theo shrugged, but Georgina looked up at him and said, 'Thank you,' and I could see that, to him, the pain was worth it.

He crouched beside her. 'Do you want me to carry you to the house?'

'No, I'm fine. I can manage.'

But he helped her, encouraging her to hold on to his arm, even where he'd been stung, and she leaned her head against him as they walked back up towards the lawn, giving the nest a wide berth.

'I'll deal with them in the morning,' Dominic said. 'Kill all the little bastards.'

'I hate them,' said Eve. 'They're evil. Nature's psychopaths.'

And that reminded me of what I'd wanted to say earlier, when Eve had mentioned Boston.

As Dominic went up towards the house, I tapped Sophie's arm and said, 'Hold up a sec.'

We hung back. Lily and Eve stopped too.

'What is it?' Sophie asked.

'Did you see Sebastian earlier?'

He had been sitting out at one of the tables while we were having dinner, reading a book. After finishing my meal I had come outside for a smoke, just as he had thrown the book down in apparent disgust, shaking his head and storming past me.

'I picked the book up,' I said. 'It's about psychopaths. This other professor has written a book about how to identify them. I had a flick through, and it looks really interesting.'

'Right,' said Sophie, as if it sounded the exact opposite of interesting. Her eyes followed the others as they neared the house. She was distracted, I realized.

'I just thought . . . His wife was murdered, right? By a serial killer? I thought it was interesting that he was reading a book about psychopaths.'

'I'm surprised. He told me he wasn't researching them any more,' Lily said.

We both looked at her.

'We talked about it at college, when he first came up with the idea for Butterfly Net.' This name had been settled on

183

now. Sebastian loved it, thought it was perfect, and although the domain name was already taken, though not being used, he had persuaded James to buy it from the company who owned it. 'He told me he'd spent so long obsessed with the dark side of humanity that he wanted to go in the opposite direction. Focus purely on love. Bringing people together. I guess he can't completely let go.'

'I can't blame him,' I said. 'If someone I loved was murdered . . .'

'Yes, me too. He told me he had spent a long time thinking about it. Identifying people with psychopathy or sociopathy – which are pretty much the same thing, actually – and figuring out if it was possible to cure them.'

'Cure them? How?'

'I'm not sure. I asked him, and he just made some comment about how difficult it was to get funding for the research he wanted to do. Made some cryptic comment about ethics committees.'

'That sounds . . . dodgy.'

'Yeah. It was weird. I actually wondered if I'd misheard him.'

Sophie yawned, apologizing by saying she was exhausted, not bored, then Eve – who had been watching Dominic as he walked up the lawn towards the house – said, 'Everyone in the village was surprised when he came back.'

'Who, Sebastian?' I asked.

'Yeah. I mean, I was a kid, so I don't remember that clearly, but my parents talked about it when I told them I was coming to work here. My dad said Thornwood was up for sale, then suddenly it was off the market and he was back.'

'Surely he came back because his wife died?'

'No. It was a couple of years after her death, at least. Maybe more. My dad is a bullshit merchant and a massive inverted snob, so I'm not sure I trust him as a source, but he said he'd heard – in the pub, I assume – that the professor had been forced to quit Fredericks. That he'd come back under a cloud.'

'Did you know that?' I asked Lily.

'No. To be honest, I find it hard to believe. It sounds like typical small-town gossip to me, and not the kind of thing you should go around spreading.'

Eve looked shocked. 'I was just repeating what my dad said.'

'Yes, and as you told us, he's not reliable.'

'You shouldn't say anything negative about the professor in front of Lily,' Sophie said, nudging Lily with an elbow. 'It's like slagging off Santa Claus.'

'He's a far better man than Santa,' Lily said, with such seriousness that Sophie and I burst out laughing.

'Why do you like him so much?' Eve asked.

Lily didn't answer straight away. She found talking about anything emotional awkward and exposing. 'When I was in the first year at Kent, the family business started to do poorly and my parents kept telling me I needed to leave college and go home to help them. The professor found me crying in the library one evening. I'd decided I needed to do what they said, even though I really didn't want to. Sebastian got it all out of me, and then he phoned my mum, told her how important it was that I stay at uni, how talented and "special" I was.'

I could tell how embarrassed she was, repeating these words of praise.

'He told my mum that if they let me stay, the whole family would benefit in the end because I would almost certainly end up doing great things and making lots of money. He spoke to my dad too. Charmed them both. By the end of the call, they were completely won over, although it has left them with the conviction that I'm going to be a millionaire by the time I'm twenty-five.'

'Hopefully you will be.' Sophie rubbed her palms together. 'Maybe we all will be.'

'I hope so too. Anyway, after that, Sebastian took me under his wing, even though I wasn't majoring in psychology. He's always looked out for me.'

We walked back up towards the house. Halfway there, Lily said, 'I'm interested to hear the professor is still reading about psychopaths. You know, in his study, he has a whole cabinet full of papers, and I'd like to read this book too – the one you mentioned.'

'You're interested in them too?'

'Only because he is. I'd like to help him, Will.'

She didn't say any more. But I could see that the whole conversation had set her brain in motion.

By the time we got to the house, Theo and Georgina were sitting at one of the tables, close together in the half-light. I couldn't hear what they were saying, catching little more than murmurs – and the smell of vinegar, so strong it made my eyes water. They hadn't noticed Lily or me, and as we passed them Georgina appeared to make a decision, leaning forward to kiss Theo on the mouth, and his hand came up to her cheek, and the kiss took on the heat of the night, so much so that I had to look away.

I had two conflicting emotions. I was envious because I wished it was me and Sophie. But I also felt that little kick you get from seeing two lovers falling for each other. We had all known Theo was crazy about Georgina. Tonight, he had proved himself, and here she was, responding. Forget what the algorithm said: they were good together. Of course they were. Casting a final glance at them, arms around each other, kissing deeply, I was sure this wasn't a summer fling. This was real.

This was for ever.

Chapter 24

Chaos. Shock. Georgina had thrown herself down on her knees beside Theo, and Amber stood over her, seemingly stunned herself, unsure what to do. *She's an amateur*, I remember thinking, among all the other strands of thoughts that attempted to form themselves in my head, my ears still ringing from where the shotgun had gone off so close to me. Sophie and Lily hadn't moved, but Sophie was crying, and across the table, Rohan stared straight ahead, unable to look at the body, immobilized by terror – or was it guilt? He had been the first to name Theo, after all, although I had voted for him too, hadn't I? Voted to save my own skin. Unlike Rohan, though, I couldn't help but stare at Theo, barely able to believe what I was seeing. Our host, our leader: dead. My insides vibrated with the horror of it. But even then, there was a dark part of me that wanted to yell at him, *See, I told you. I warned you. This is real.* It was no comfort to think I had succeeded in my mission: to get them to play along.

'Theo. Theo, Theo . . .'

It was Georgina, saying her husband's name over and over. I clamped my hands over my ears, which only made the ringing worse, but I wasn't the only one being driven mad hearing Theo's name repeated. I kept seeing them in the past, Theo rescuing her from the wasps. Their first kiss. The wedding photo, in which they looked so happy. The family portrait. A family that barely existed any more.

'Make her stop,' Callum hissed at Amber, who snapped out of her stupor. She grabbed Georgina by the arm, attempting to haul her to her feet.

Georgina resisted. 'You killed him. *You killed him.*'

Callum stepped forward and pointed the gun in her face. 'I'll kill you too.'

'Go ahead. Do it. I don't care.'

He bent forward. 'You want your younger daughter to be an orphan, huh? Both of them, if Olivia's still alive?'

'She *is* still alive,' Georgina said in a trembling voice.

'Then get up and get back in your chair.'

Refusing to break eye contact with him, she obeyed. Her trousers were creased and her eyes were ringed with smudged mascara. She swayed, and I was sure she was going to fall. Instead, she took a long, deep breath and, moving like a ninety-year-old, went back to her seat.

Callum immediately went over to the window and pulled the curtains aside, peering out, clearly worried someone might have heard the shot.

Seemingly satisfied, he came away from the window and went over to where Theo's body lay, shaking his head.

He pointed at me, then at Rohan. 'You, and you. Give me a hand.'

We both got up. I noticed Rohan still couldn't look at the body, whereas I was glad Theo was lying on his front so I didn't have to see his face.

Callum went past us into the hallway, opening the next door along: the study. He came back and gestured. 'Let's get him in here. Take a wrist each.' His voice was hard and cold. 'Come on.'

I could hardly believe how much effort it took to move Theo. Beside me, Rohan made a grunting noise. The body moved a couple of inches.

Callum huffed, exasperated. 'Are you about to start crying, Will? For fuck's sake. Put your bloody backs into it.'

We did it. Dragged him down the hallway into the study. We left him there, still face down, lying adjacent to the desk. I shuddered as I took in the trail of blood smeared on the floorboards, marking Theo's undignified journey.

Callum saw me looking. 'Don't worry. I'm sure they pay their cleaners more than minimum wage.' He lit a cigarette.

'Can I have one?' Rohan asked.

'You've got your vape.'

'Please.'

With a shake of the head, Callum stuck a second cigarette between his lips, lit it, then passed it to Rohan, clearly thinking it was too risky to give him the lighter.

'What if he was the one with the secret?' Rohan said.

'We heard his biggest secret.' Callum was calm, like nothing had just happened. 'Blackmailing James.'

'But how do you know for sure?'

'Trust me, Rohan. He was trying to save himself. Situations like that, people tell you what they think you want to hear. That was the biggest thing he had.'

His confidence made me realize something: Callum had done this before.

Amber came out of the dining room. 'What's going on?'

'Smoke break,' Callum said.

'That arsehole hurt me.'

'Not as much as I hurt him.'

'Don't you care?' she demanded.

He ignored her, giving me his attention instead, flicking a glance towards Rohan. In the aftermath of what had just happened, it took me a second to realize he was trying to remind me about my mission.

Amber's reaction told me she was in on it too.

'Give me one of those,' she said, gesturing to the cigarettes. They moved along the hallway a little, their heads bent together as they shared a flame, leaving Rohan and me alone for a moment. I remembered Callum's threat towards Sophie. I had no choice.

I sidled up to Rohan, who had almost finished his cigarette. His hand trembled as he took a final drag.

'Here,' I whispered. 'Take this.'

'What is it?' he whispered back.

I didn't speak, just tried to push the diamond ring into his hand. Seeing what I was trying to give him, his eyes went wide.

'What the fuck?' he hissed.

'I spotted it among the stuff Callum had piled up. Took it when he wasn't looking. Take it. You can use it—'

I held it out to him again. Callum and Amber, at the other end of the hallway, were facing in the other direction. I still didn't understand the point of this mission. All I knew was that I was scared of what they'd do to Sophie if I didn't play along.

'I don't want it.'

'Go on. You can sell it. Use it to start your business.'

He stared at the ring. I could see him thinking, trying to figure out how much it was worth. Picturing himself with the cash. Using it. Getting started. A story of temptation flickering in his eyes.

'No. I don't want it.'

Callum hadn't told me I needed to persuade Rohan to take it, had he? He'd just said I needed to offer it. And the look Rohan was giving me now – appalled, shocked – made me wonder if this was why Callum had done it: to sow distrust between us, although I had no idea how that helped his cause. I wanted to tell Rohan I'd been put up to it, but it would be easy for Callum to quiz Rohan, to find out if I'd broken the secrecy rule. So instead, I returned the ring to my pocket and turned away, silent, cheeks burning.

'Right, come on then,' said Callum, striding back towards us and not giving any indication that he knew what had just happened. 'The break's over.'

We went back into the dining room. Callum motioned for us to sit down. Sophie tried to catch my eye, clearly wondering why we'd taken so long, but I could hardly look at her.

'Do you finally get it now?' Callum asked the group. 'Perhaps I need to reiterate. One of you has a secret. One of you just got Theo killed.' He paused. Let it sink in. 'We're going to give you another hour. That takes us up to eleven thirty. This time, I hope whoever it is will speak up.'

Beside him, Amber still seemed annoyed with her partner – but also exhilarated.

'If you want to speak up before the hour is over, give Amber here a shout. Otherwise, I'll be back at eleven thirty. If no one confesses, we'll take another vote. And if I don't hear what I'm after . . .' Callum pointed towards the study. 'One of you will be joining old Theo.'

I always told my students to avoid clichés. 'Find another way to say "my blood ran cold".' But right then, that was precisely what it felt like. The liquid in my veins cooling. Ice in my arteries.

One of us was dead, we were locked in this house with two people who had just shown they were willing to kill, and nobody was coming to save us.

Chapter 25

Mia

The gunshot made Claude fly off Mia's lap, his claws digging into her thighs. She only just managed to stop herself from crying out, slapping her palm over her mouth.

She pressed herself against the wall of Olivia's walk-in wardrobe, beneath the clothes that still hung there like she would return any day, and watched as the cat shot out into the bedroom, praying he wouldn't create a commotion and cause whoever had fired the gun to investigate.

Because what would they do if they found a sixteen-year-old girl hiding upstairs?

At one thirty that afternoon, Mia had said goodbye to her parents and, carrying her backpack, had gone to a cheap little café down the road. She had sat there with a big mug of tea, scrolling through her phone. There was some drama going on at school – some girl had written a spicy story about one of the teachers and got caught sharing it – but that was trivial compared to the dramas in Mia's life.

No one else at school had a big sister who'd gone missing.

Mia thought back to earlier. Dad had been at work, and she knew Mum always went on her Peloton in the early afternoon, if she wasn't teaching a yoga class. With the trainer yelling at her through her headphones, urging her to pedal faster or whatever, Mia had been confident her mum wouldn't hear her sneaking back into the house.

Sneaking back and installing the listening device in the dining room.

She had already downloaded the app and connected it to her phone. After that, all she'd had to do was stick the little device – the bug – to the picture rail in the dining room and test it, shutting Claude in the room and listening to his mews of protest through her AirPods. Loud and clear.

At first, when the adults had gone into the dining room, it had all worked exactly as she hoped. The quality of sound transmitted by the bug was average, but she could still make out what the adults were saying.

And then the internet had gone down and the bug, which relied on her phone being online, stopped working.

The broadband failing was something that happened a lot in this house. Despite Dad's love of high-tech shit like the security system, for some reason he wouldn't replace the router with one that didn't go down every other week.

Mia had left the room, thinking she might be able to sneak downstairs to restart the router while the adults were busy eating.

Which was when she'd seen the redhead on the landing.

Holding a gun.

It was a proper WTF moment. The dining-room door was closed, her parents and their guests presumably inside. Mia had immediately crept back towards her room – then changed her mind. She'd already had one scary moment, thinking she was going to be discovered, when Mum had come into Mia's room earlier, looking for the back-door key, which Mia had in fact used earlier that day, when she'd let herself back in. It was still in the pocket of her jeans. But she couldn't tell Mum that, could she? Not if she wanted to stay hidden.

And now she *definitely* needed to stay hidden. Olivia's room, she decided, was safer. So she'd come here, to the wardrobe, Claude following her in, and she'd sat here, not knowing what to do. She couldn't call for help because not only had the internet failed but she couldn't get a signal on her phone.

She was trapped. Clueless as to what was going on downstairs.

Until she heard the gunshot.

Watching Claude flee the wardrobe, his thick tail snaking out of sight, she had a strong urge to follow him. To find out what was happening.

Slowly, she stood and crossed the carpet to the bedroom door. Even more slowly, she opened it a crack and peered out.

No one had come up here. Then, from below, she heard a door open. Voices. Movement.

She had to see what was happening.

Taking inspiration from Claude, she dropped to her hands and knees and crawled, slowly, silently, towards the railing.

She peeked down through the banisters and saw a man emerge, broad and powerful-looking, holding a shotgun. He went along the hallway, opening the door of Mum's study, before going back towards the dining room.

'Let's get him in here,' she heard him say. 'Take a wrist each.'

And then he turned towards her and she scuttled backwards, out of view, flattening herself on the floor. From below, she heard grunts of effort, the sound of something being dragged.

An injured person?

A . . . body?

She tried not to breathe, tried not to make the slightest sound, as she crawled back into Olivia's room.

Chapter 26

The second Callum and Amber left the room, Sophie, Lily and I got up and went over to Georgina. Sophie tried to hug her, bending forward awkwardly, but Georgina didn't respond.

'We're going to get out of this,' I said. 'They're going to pay.'

They sounded like lines from a movie, with no power behind them. No conviction, just wishes.

I wasn't expecting Georgina to speak – thought she was too deep in her state of shock – but she surprised me by lifting her chin and saying, 'How? How are we going to get out?'

Was that an accusing glare? Was she angry because the group had voted for Theo instead of me? If so, I understood. But I also knew I wasn't to blame. None of us were. The only villains here were Callum and Amber.

'We have to tell them the secret,' Georgina said, answering her own question. 'Which one of you has it?'

'It's not me,' Rohan said, still refusing to meet my eye. I dearly wished I could tell him why I'd offered him the ring.

'I swear it's not me.' That was Sophie.

Lily shook her head, pale and mute.

'It's not me either,' I said. 'Unless I've got a hole in my memory. I just can't think what it would be.'

My voice trailed off. I knew exactly what my own secret from that summer was and I was certain it couldn't be what Callum was after. It was something personal. And the only

197

person it really affected . . . well, unless the afterlife was real and they were listening in, they would never know or care.

We had all gone back to our seats again, except Sophie, who paced the room in silence. I didn't know what to do. All I could see was Theo falling.

Sophie's voice shook me out of it. 'We have to give them what they want. Let's think. What do we know?'

I replied. 'All we know is that the secret wasn't that Theo blackmailed James.'

'Could it be something to do with James though?' Sophie asked. 'I mean, if he's still out there, which I assume he is. Maybe he's harboured bad feelings all these years and when he heard about Sebastian's death it triggered him, made him decide to get revenge.'

'He is still out there,' Rohan said, everyone's attention snapping to him. 'I follow this stuff. He's even richer than you, Georgina. Runs one of the biggest firms in the City.' Less than an hour ago, Theo had told us about the classified papers in the safe. That already felt like ancient history.

'I know how rich James is,' Georgina said. 'The papers Theo was talking about . . . it was a hostile takeover. James's company was behind it.'

'Wow,' said Rohan.

'That's one of the reasons Theo has been drinking so much. The stress. That, and Olivia . . . He didn't even want to have this dinner party, not really, but I told him it would take his mind off things.'

I frowned at her. 'Didn't Theo still have the blackmail material?'

'I didn't know anything about that. But it was twenty-five years ago, and James has had at least two wives since then. The takeover was his revenge, and it was all going ahead. He has no reason to send thugs here to intimidate us. If anything, killing Theo would spoil things for him. Take away his fun seeing Theo lose the company he's built up.'

'Okay, so it's not anything to do with James,' Sophie said. 'Why won't they give us a hint? It doesn't make sense.' She marched over to the door and, before anyone could stop her, shouted, 'We need more information. Come on, you arseholes. Give us some clues!'

'Sophie . . .' I began.

She rounded on me. 'Don't tell me to be quiet.'

'I wasn't going to. Please, sit down. I think I *have* a clue.'

Now everyone was looking at me.

Sophie took her seat beside me. 'What is it?'

It had come back to me, perhaps shaken from my brain by the shock. The fear of what might happen next.

'It's something Callum said, when I was helping him carry stuff downstairs. He said, "Are you familiar with the phrase 'everything echoes'?"'

Rohan said, 'Finn said that. When we were eating our starters.'

'That's right. I thought maybe Amber had overheard, but I don't think she was in the room when Finn said it. She'd gone to get water. I'm still convinced Finn wasn't really Sebastian's assistant. He made too many mistakes. There was that whole thing with him writing in a notebook. Also, remember when Callum and Amber first appeared with their guns? Amber was about to say something about Finn, but Callum gave her a warning look. I think they knew him. I'd seen Amber looking at him too; whispering in his ear. I thought they knew each other, but maybe it was one way.'

'If they know him,' Lily said, 'he might know what they're after.'

'Or be able to point us in the right direction, at least,' I said. 'Shame he's locked up in the cupboard downstairs.'

We all fell quiet, thinking. As a group, we had reached an impasse. If someone in this room did have the secret, they weren't going to share it, even after what had happened to Theo. The minutes were ticking by. Soon, Callum would be back, forcing us to vote again. Finn had to know something, even if it wasn't the secret. Surely he would be able to tell us some information that would help point us in the right direction. Shake a memory loose. Something.

'There has to be a way,' I said, not realizing I was speaking aloud. 'A way to get to him.'

We all sat there, mute, thinking. If anyone was going to come up with a solution, I was sure it would be Lily. She was the genius. The problem-solver. But it was Rohan who broke the silence.

'I think I have an idea,' he said. 'We know they're not going to kill us unless they're sure we're not the ones with the secret, right?' Rohan looked around, seeking reassurance. 'Lily? That's logical, yeah?'

She hesitated for a moment. 'That seems to be the case.'

'Which means we have a certain amount of armour, for now, anyway. We need to use that to our advantage. It's like in *Mario*, when he grabs a super star.' His focus was still on Lily, and I remembered: 1999, the two of them passing a Game Boy back and forth, playing *Tetris* and *Super Mario Land*.

Lily knew what he meant. She got it. But Georgina, who had sneered at their love of video games, said, 'What are you talking about?'

'You know who Mario is, don't you?' Rohan asked.

'Of course I do. I have children. Even Theo . . .' She swallowed. Blinked. 'Even Theo liked those stupid games.'

Rohan flinched but went on: 'When Mario grabs a super star, he becomes temporarily invincible. Enemies can't hurt him. It only lasts for about ten seconds, and during those seconds you have to make as much progress as you can. I think that's what we have, between these votes. We can't be killed.'

Sophie covered her face with her hands. From behind her palms, she said, 'So what do you think we should do? Attack them?'

'No. A gun could go off. Plus, their self-preservation instincts are still going to be stronger than their desire to know the secret. But we could cause a distraction, so someone can get down the stairs to Finn.'

The five of us came together in a huddle, and Rohan, in a soft voice, told us his idea. It was simple. It could easily be foolhardy rather than brave. But – if he was right about our temporary invincibility – it could work.

'So who's going to do it?' I asked. 'Who's going to try to get to Finn?'

'I think it should be one of the women.'

'I'll do it,' said Georgina.

'I don't think—'

'What, you think I'm too fragile? Because I just saw my husband die? Or because you think I'm a spoilt rich waste of space who's never done anything useful in her life?'

Rohan's mouth opened and closed.

'We don't think that,' Lily said.

'Whatever. Right now, I don't really care, as long as you stop treating me like I'm made of glass. This is my house,' Georgina said. 'It's my territory. I can get to Finn faster than any of you.'

'That makes sense,' I said, fighting back guilt. Because I had thought those things about her. Not a waste of space, but privileged, used to others doing things for her. A person who hired caterers for her dinner party, who'd employed a nanny to help with her children. Georgina hadn't cried for Theo yet, but

I could see she was grieving and was currently in the second stage of grief: anger. That's what was driving her. And, as a group, we needed to use it.

'Do we all understand what we're doing?' Rohan asked.

We murmured yes, then broke from the huddle and went back to our seats, all except Georgina, who went over to the door and rapped on it lightly. 'Amber?'

The door was yanked open. Amber stood there, gun by her side. 'What is it?'

'I need to use the toilet,' Georgina said.

'I'll bring you a bucket.'

'Please.' She pointed across the hallway. 'The loo is right there. It's not like I'm going to be able to get out through the window.'

Amber's jaw flexed. It was as if they hadn't considered the possibility that we would need the toilet during the evening.

'Please,' Georgina said. 'If you want us to figure out who has this secret, we need to be able to concentrate.'

I could see Amber trying to decide what to do. I was also impressed by Georgina. She could have pleaded and tried to get sympathy, playing the 'you killed my husband' card. Instead, she sounded reasonable and calm. Not trying to appeal to Amber's better nature but just stating facts.

'Wait there,' Amber said, closing the door.

She shouted for Callum, and I heard his voice, deep and echoey on the stairwell, asking her what was going on. This was good. We wanted them both up here for Rohan's plan to work. Callum's footsteps stopped outside the door, and the two of them conversed.

The door opened again and Callum pointed a finger at Georgina. 'Be quick.'

'Thank you.' She hurried from the room, turning right towards the bathroom.

Callum remained in the doorway, watching us, while Amber followed Georgina. 'Close the door but don't lock it.'

We heard the bathroom door click shut, and that was our cue. Immediately, Rohan grabbed a glass from off the table and threw it, hard, against the wall.

'What the hell?' Callum strode into the room, to see all of us – me, Rohan, Sophie and Lily – grabbing the remaining crockery and glasses, snatching them up like chimps at a tea party. We threw plates to the floor. Smashed bowls. Flung glasses towards the windows.

'Stop!' Callum yelled. He had the shotgun in both hands but didn't know who to point it at.

I threw a dinner plate at the wall and watched it explode into shards. It felt good. Beside me, Sophie snatched up a vase, tipped out the flowers and flung it with all her strength into the corner, screaming with the release of it. We weren't only causing a distraction: we were letting out some of our rage. Lily roared as a glass she had thrown shattered against the wall.

'Stop it or I'll fucking kill you!'

I wanted to throw something at Callum but knew that could be a fatal error, that Rohan was right: while we deliberated, they would only kill us if they had to, in self-defence or anger. We were protected by their need to know the secret. But where was Amber? For the plan to work, we needed her to come into the dining room so Georgina could get past her and downstairs. Amber must have still been guarding the bathroom door, despite the mayhem. Maybe we *did* need to attack Callum to make him call her.

I grabbed a glass which was half full of water. It was one of the few items left on the table. I turned towards Callum, my arm raised. He turned towards me, and I found myself staring straight into the barrel of the shotgun. My heart flipped in my chest. I held the glass above my shoulder, primed, aimed at Callum's face. Water splashed out, dribbled down the back of my shirt.

'Go on then,' Callum said.

I hesitated.

'I know you think you're protected by the secret. We won't kill you till we know you're not the one hiding it, right? Well, you've forgotten something. I don't have to *kill* you. I could hurt you. Maim you.' In a sing-song voice, he said, 'Cut off a finger. Slice up an eyeball.'

I lowered the glass.

'Good boy.'

He smiled with one corner of his mouth, and the arrogance on his face almost made me change my mind about throwing the glass. The room had fallen silent. Everyone had stopped throwing stuff, the mad energy that had filled the room draining away.

'Amber!' he shouted over his shoulder. 'Get that bitch back in here.'

We heard the bathroom door, female voices, and seconds later Amber pushed Georgina into the room. They both looked furious, especially Georgina, as if we had fucked up and let her down. Then I saw something else come into her eyes. Determination. She flicked a glance at me – her back was to Callum and Amber, so they didn't see – then strode over to the far wall. There was a shelf there, with some knick-knacks, another vase, an ornamental plate. She grabbed the plate and threw it in Callum's direction.

'That's for Theo,' she yelled as the plate sailed over Callum's shoulder, missing Amber's head by inches and smashing against the doorframe. Then she grabbed the vase.

'You crazy—' Callum strode towards her, Amber following him. The vase flew past them, landing on the table and exploding.

Georgina let out a scream, and the others – Rohan, Sophie, Lily – were infected by her energy, her rage, or maybe they understood her plan, and suddenly the room was full of flying objects again. The remaining crockery. A chair that Rohan picked up and bashed against another. Callum barked orders – *Put that down!* – and Amber tried to grab hold of Sophie, who was picking up shards and flinging them towards the windows.

I was frozen for a second. Paralysed. But then I met Georgina's eye and saw it. The doorway was clear. Callum and Amber weren't looking in my direction.

As quietly and quickly as I could, I slipped through the door and ran towards the stairs, taking them two at a time, almost losing my balance and having to grab the banister to stop myself from toppling. I jumped down the bottom few steps. There in front of me was the pile of loot, waiting to go home with Callum and Amber. I was barely thinking by this point. Not worrying about whether there was any hope that I'd be able to get back into the dining room without Callum and Amber noticing I'd gone. All I knew was that I needed to find out who Finn was. What he knew. I prayed he would be conscious. Lucid.

I executed a U-turn and sprinted towards the cupboard. A voice in my head screamed at me to go into the kitchen, grab another of those expensive knives, but I stuck to my priority: get to Finn. A knife would achieve nothing against two shotguns.

I reached the cupboard. There was still no sign of Callum or Amber. The smashing and thumping sounds had stopped, but Callum was still shouting, sounding increasingly angry and frustrated.

I yanked open the door.

Finn was on the floor, lying on his side, hands secured behind his back. His eyes were closed, and my first impression was that he was unconscious. But as I entered the little space, which was now filled with light from the hallway, he moved his head, flinching as if expecting a blow. There was a gag in his mouth. A dishcloth. Had they not known Finn was going to be here?

'Finn,' I said, crouching beside him and whispering. 'It's Will. I need to talk to you. I don't have much time.' I wanted to apologize to him for being suspicious, thinking he had been in league with Amber, that he might even have had another accomplice hiding in the house. But what was the point, now?

He turned his face towards me. One of his eyes was swollen shut, fat and purple, with a cut on his cheekbone. He managed to open the other eye. It was bloodshot, watery. I reached out and untied the dishcloth, pulling it away gently and wishing I'd brought some water with me. He tried to speak and blood dribbled from his mouth, then he spat out a tooth. Jesus. Callum had really hurt him. It sickened me almost as much as what he'd done to Theo. The brutality. I could easily be next.

'You weren't really Sebastian's assistant, were you?'

He shook his head, made a low grunting noise.

'Who are you?'

He licked his lips. I wasn't sure if he'd be able to speak, but he managed to get a couple of words out.

'Private. Detective.'

I stared at him, taking in what he'd said. 'Why are you here?'

Even now, he didn't want to tell me.

'Finn,' I said. 'Do you know anything about this secret Callum and Amber are after?'

He blinked, uncomprehending.

'When you said, "everything echoes", what did that mean?'

He opened his mouth, and the faintest sound emerged. Maddeningly, I couldn't make it out. I put my ear to his lips, and he said it again. 'Pocket.'

His jacket hung open, exposing the inside pocket, and I reached inside. Of course: it was the little notebook he'd been writing in earlier. I quickly shoved it into my own back pocket.

'Is the answer in here?' I asked.

His eyes widened, like I'd said something revelatory. 'Yes?' I urged. 'What is it?'

And then I realized. He wasn't staring at me. He was looking behind me. I had been so engrossed, so desperate to get him to speak, that I hadn't heard the footsteps coming down the hall. Hadn't noticed the shadow fall over me. Hadn't heard Callum breathing.

He grabbed the back of my collar and yanked me towards him, tipping me off balance so I fell from my crouching position on to my back, clearing the path between him and Finn, who flipped on to his front, trying to wriggle away on his belly.

I tried to get up, attempted to speak, to ask Finn again why he was here. Why a private detective had come to dinner, pretending to be Sebastian's assistant.

But I didn't get the chance.

Callum stepped over me.

He shot Finn between the shoulder blades, then turned the gun on me.

Chapter 27

July 1999

Sebastian's study was directly above the library/office. I would often hear him moving around up there during the day while we were working on the website.

'What are we going to do if he catches us?' I asked Lily as we went up the stairs towards the study. Sophie was with us too, wearing a pair of cut-off denim shorts and a vest top, so much skin on display that I found it hard being near her. *I'm on fire*, I kept thinking.

I had noticed Lily look at Sophie too, with a little raise of the eyebrows. Did she fancy her too?

'Will, are you listening to me?'

'Huh?'

Lily sighed. 'I was answering your question.'

'He's nervous.' Sophie winked at me. 'Not a fan of subterfuge, Will?'

'It's not that.' *I'm acting like a moron because proximity to you melts my brain.* I could hardly say that, could I? Or maybe I should. Sophie still hadn't given me any sign that my feelings were reciprocated. In fact, with every passing day we headed deeper into the friend zone.

'Don't worry,' Lily said. 'Sebastian's gone into Tunbridge Wells for a meeting with the bank.'

It was the last day of July. Twenty-four hours had passed since Lily had come up with her idea. As if she wasn't busy enough trying to finish Butterfly Net, she wanted to create this new program.

A test to tell if someone was a psychopath.

Sophie trailed her long fingers over the surface of the banister as we climbed the stairs. 'Dominic gave him a lift. I've asked him to text me before they head back so the professor doesn't catch us.'

'Wait.' I stopped. 'You told Dominic what we're doing?'

'No. I told him I was planning a spot of topless sunbathing. He doesn't know anything about this. He wouldn't approve.'

'Did he ask for a photo as payment?' Lily asked.

'Of course he did.'

'And you're going to give him one?' I was appalled.

Sophie slapped my arm with the back of her hand. 'You're such an idiot. Of course I'm not. I just told him I didn't want his uncle catching me slacking off. I promised him a Tarot reading in return.'

'I'm still amazed you managed to dissuade him from killing all those wasps,' Lily said. After the incident with Georgina the previous week, Dominic had threatened to 'nuke' the nest. Sophie had persuaded them that wasps deserved their place on this planet too, and that they in fact provided a valuable service by eating aphids. Georgina hadn't been happy, nor had her new boyfriend, Theo, who was so lovestruck it made me feel slightly sick – although, on the plus side, he'd been a much more pleasant supervisor since he and Georgina had got together. Every morning he would appear at breakfast with his hair sticking up and a dopey grin on his face, then he'd spend the day yawning. Georgina would arrive ten minutes after him, looking immaculate, and she would ignore Theo all day, except at lunchtime, when they would sit out on the grass sharing sandwiches.

Love was in the air, adding to my torment.

We reached the study door, and Lily beckoned us to follow her inside.

'Remember,' Lily said. 'We're looking for anything on the subject of diagnosing psychopathy. Papers, journals, notes . . .'

Sophie gestured at the crammed space. Bookshelves, crammed with leather-bound volumes and dusty paperbacks. More books stacked in wobbling, precarious towers on the floor. A dark wood desk, piled high with journals. Cabinets. Drawers. Everywhere: paper.

'This could take hours.'

'We don't have hours.'

There were framed certificates on the wall, along with several photos. I found myself transfixed by one that featured a younger Sebastian with big seventies hair, wearing a corduroy jacket and pointed collar, his arm around the shoulders of a woman with the same hairstyle as Joni Mitchell about the time she released *Blue*. They stood on a lawn beside a tree with bare branches, a red-brick building with multiple windows in the background. I had rarely seen such a happy-looking couple. The way they looked at each other – it was how I longed for Sophie to look at me.

'Fredericks University,' said Lily, joining me. 'And that's Sebastian's wife.'

'Barbara,' I remembered.

Lily reached out to touch the frame of the picture. 'They were living together on campus, but one night Barbara went back to her parents' home to sort through her belongings.'

'And she never made it?' Sophie had come to join us.

'They found her body the next morning, in a parking lot. Strangled. They caught the guy two weeks later. He attacked another woman in the same area, but she managed to get away and a police car happened to be cruising by. They stopped, chased the attacker, shot him.'

'They killed him?'

'Yeah. And they found souvenirs in his apartment. Underwear taken from four women he'd killed, including Barbara. They found notebooks in which he'd written out his plans, drawn maps and routes. Turned out he'd been seeing a psychiatrist and had confessed to deep misogynistic feelings. A belief that he had been judged and rejected by the world's women. The psychiatrist blamed his mother, of course.'

There on the desk, on top of a stack of papers, was the book I'd seen Sebastian reading. *Without Conscience* by Robert D. Hare. I picked it up, flicked through it. One of the early chapters contained a list of criminals. Conmen. Murderers. Serial killers.

'Not all serial killers are psychopaths,' Lily said. 'And not all psychopaths are predators. A lot of them are just getting by, living their lives without doing anyone any harm. But Sebastian believes, and I agree with him, that if we can identify psychopaths and study them, the world will be a less dangerous place. He was frustrated that he wasn't able to work with Barbara's killer.'

'Wait.' Sophie put down the journal she'd been leafing through. 'He wanted to study the guy who killed his wife?'

'How else are we supposed to negate the threat posed by violent psychopaths? The first step, of course, is identifying them. And that's where my test comes in. I want to know how they react to other people and to emotional situations. Sebastian always says that they are masters of camouflage. That they learn to act normal. To blend in. How do the experts see through the disguise and know a person is pretending to have normal feelings and reactions? I want case studies. Details of successful studies and experiments.'

I passed the book to her and began flicking through the journals, setting aside any that looked interesting. *Diagnosing Child Psychopathology: Three Case Studies*; *Nature vs Nurture in Sociopathy*; *The DSM and Antisocial Personality Disorder*. I found myself putting nearly everything on to the pile, confused by the terminology and the denseness of the academic language in these essays.

Then I came across a magazine called *Psychology Matters*, which appeared to be aimed more at the layperson. It contained an article about Robert Hare, summarizing his work, particularly his psychopathy checklist, which was designed as a tool for professionals.

Hare's checklist describes the symptoms that are shared by people with psychopathy. For example, Hare states that psychopaths seek excitement but are irresponsible; they practise deceit and enjoy manipulating others; they are not troubled by remorse or guilt or empathy. These people have superficial charm, and their emotions are shallow. They often behaved badly as children and are antisocial as adults. Finally, their egos are large and they are prone to grandiosity.

I showed this to Lily, who tapped the book and said, 'That list is in here.'

'Do you think you're really going to be able to devise a test to find out if a person has those traits?'

'I'm certainly going to try.'

'This is locked,' Sophie said, rattling the drawer of a metal cabinet.

Lily glanced over. 'It's probably got his own papers in it. His own notes.'

'Or his collection of *Playboy*.'

'Sebastian wouldn't have those kind of mags.'

'Of course. A man who's even greater than Santa wouldn't look at—'

Sophie's phone beeped, and she produced it from her pocket. It was dark blue and silver, a Nokia with a small grey screen.

'They're on their way back,' she said.

'Do you really like having that thing?' I asked as she put it away.

'My mobile? Of course.'

'I'm never going to get one.'

She laughed. 'Of course you will. You like video games, don't you? Just think, you could be playing Snake.'

'What's that?'

She stared at me. 'Are you from another planet?' She got her phone out again and came round the desk. She perched beside me on the edge of the desk, her hip touching mine. 'Let me show you.'

Of course, I had played Snake before. Lots of my friends at uni had owned phones. I suppose I should be ashamed to admit it, but I just wanted Sophie's attention. Wanted her beside me, leaning in to me and showing me how to play this primitive game. I caught my breath when she passed me the phone and her fingers brushed mine. I wondered if she could feel me trembling, hear my heartbeat. I could smell her, the heat coming off her body, the faint odour of fresh sweat mixed with a perfume I couldn't identify. It made my head swim.

I'm sure she must have known the effect she was having on me, because she was silent. We both were, just breathing. I stared at the game on the tiny screen, but I hardly took in what she was showing me. It was as if the universe had paused, and all I wanted to do was touch her, kiss her, undress her right here on the floor of this dusty office, finally throw off my inhibitions and show her how I felt.

'It needs a name,' Lily said.

'Huh?' Both Sophie and I snapped our attention to her. I

214

was light-headed, like I'd stood up too fast and there was no blood in my head.

'My test. I want to call it something.'

I handed the phone back to Sophie – we didn't look at each other – and reached for the Hare book, desperately trying to drag my attention back to what Lily was talking about, but before I could open it Lily said, 'Wasps.'

'What's that, Lils?' Sophie said.

'Did you hear what Eve said when Georgina was stung?'

I remembered. 'She said wasps are nature's psychopaths.'

'It's not true though,' Sophie said.

'We know. They eat aphids. You love the little stripy bastards.'

She batted me with the back of her hand, and a thrill went through me, before I noticed Lily giving us one of her looks. *Children. Stop it.*

'We've got Butterfly Net,' she said. 'Maybe we can do something with "wasp". The wasp test?'

'The wasp trap.' It came to me in a flash of inspiration. 'A test to catch a psychopath.'

Lily beamed. 'I love it.'

She scooped up journals and papers and nodded at the pile on the floor. 'Grab those, Will. We'd better go. I think I have everything I need here.'

I glanced at Sophie. Everything *I* needed, and wanted, was right here too. Would something have happened if Lily hadn't been here? I tried to catch Sophie's eye, but she avoided it and, again, I was left not knowing how she felt, and too nervous to ask.

Later that afternoon, we were back in the office, talking about what we were going to spend our riches on. As the site got closer to completion and we could see that Lily's algorithm actually appeared to work, it was hard not to get caught up in the excitement that came with being right there in the dotcom bubble. Every day, we heard tales about some start-up going public, making anyone with stock options instantly rich. Companies were selling for millions. Rohan had been talking about how he was going to use his to set up his own company when Georgina raised her head. 'Can anyone else smell smoke?'

I sniffed the air, one of the dogs emerging from beneath the desk and imitating me. 'Now that you mention it.'

When we got outside, we saw that the smoke was coming from further down the lawn, towards the woods. It rushed up towards the perfect blue sky, black and acrid. Beneath the stink of smoke was a sweeter smell: petrol.

Someone stood nearby: Dominic. There was a second figure there, too, a little further off. Eve.

'What are you doing?' I asked as we approached. But I could see the answer. Dancing in the smoke were dozens of tiny black dots.

He was burning the wasps' nest.

'What the hell?' said Sophie.

Dominic grinned at us. 'Yeah, I know I said I wouldn't, but one of the little bastards stung Eve. They needed to be dealt with.'

Dominic looked past me at Georgina, who hadn't ventured on to the lawn. From where I stood, I couldn't see her expression, but her arms were folded.

'You're an idiot,' I said to Dominic. 'You're not supposed to burn their nests. It's . . .'

'What?'

'It's caveman behaviour. It's also fucking dangerous.' As I said this, a furious wasp buzzed by my ear.

'I hope they sting you,' said Sophie, glaring at Dominic.

'For fuck's sake,' he said. 'Vegetarians. Wasps are evil. They deserve it.'

'He'll have killed the queen,' Lily said.

Dominic took a step towards us. 'So what?'

Sophie looked like she was going to cry. 'I can't believe you broke your promise to me.'

'Yeah, well, like I said, one of them stung Eve.'

I looked over at Eve, who was standing well away from the smoke, clearly ashamed of her role in this. The surviving wasps were still buzzing around, but there weren't many of them left now.

We watched the nest burn for a minute, then most of the others went back into the house. Sophie shook her head again, and a thrill ran through me. She was pissed off with Dominic. This was good.

There was a moment when I could have put my arm around her, to comfort her and show we were united. But just as I was about to do it she turned too, and followed the others, leaving me there with Dominic.

'Still haven't made a move, eh?'

'I don't know what you're talking about.'

'Oh, come off it, mate. You know when you show one of the spaniels a piece of meat and they start drooling, but they're too well trained to grab it? Afraid they'll get a smack on the nose. That's you, that is.' He chortled.

'I haven't seen you making a move,' I said.

'That's where we're different, Will. I let them come to me. Like, well, wasps to sugar.' He lowered his voice. 'Eve here is desperate to crawl all over me. Sophie's not far behind. You'd better make a move soon, mate. Unless you want my sloppy seconds.'

'You're disgusting.'

He laughed again, then strode away, past the burning nest,

to Eve, and flung his arm around her shoulders. As they walked up towards the house he turned his head and winked at me.

I had never hated anyone as much. And part of it was, I knew he was right.

Chapter 28

Mia

Another gunshot.

Mia hugged herself. Since the last one, she'd been hiding back here in Olivia's wardrobe again, completely unsure of what to do. Nothing in her sixteen years on the planet had prepared her for this. She kept flashing to scenes in movies she'd watched. Horror films in which the final girl went creeping into the basement to confront the killer. Since hearing the first shot and seeing the big guy with the gun, she'd told herself she wasn't going to be that girl.

But the second shot changed her mind.

She couldn't stay here. She had to do something to get out.

And that started with finding out what was going on.

With a glance back at Claude, who was now lounging on Olivia's bed, she went out into the hallway and tiptoed to the staircase, peering through the banisters again. The shot had come from further away this time. Were they all downstairs on the ground floor? There were dark marks on the wood below. Was that . . . blood?

She wanted to creep down a few steps to get a better look, but then the redhead came out of the dining room and she heard movement from further below. Footsteps coming up the stairwell.

Mia shuffled backwards so she was out of sight. But instead of going all the way back to Olivia's room, she lay on her belly, listening.

'What happened?' a woman, presumably the redhead, asked.

A man with a gruff voice replied. 'Will here got our private-dick friend shot.'

A pause. 'You killed Finn?'

Mia put her hands over her mouth again. Finn was *dead*? She reeled from this news and missed the next part of what was said.

When she recovered and tuned back in she heard the man with the gruff voice say, 'In there.'

After a pause, the woman swore. 'Did he tell Will anything?'

'I don't know. I don't think he had time.' The man sounded furious. 'This lot. They are giving me. A fucking. *Headache*. I was this close to shooting Will in the face.'

Another pause. 'You need to try to stay calm.'

'I *am* staying calm. Look. Totally, perfectly calm.'

Mia was surprised to hear the woman laugh, then say, 'I think this might be the best night of my life.'

'Better than our first night together?'

'Well . . .'

There was another pause. Oh Jesus, were they *kissing*?

When she next spoke, the woman sounded breathy. 'Maybe we should call—'

'No! Not yet.'

Then Mia heard them both go into the dining room, slamming the door behind them so she couldn't hear any more.

She lay there on the carpet, waiting for it all to sink in.

Finn was dead.

And it was her fault – because she had brought him here.

*

Of all the people who had promised to find her sister, Finn was the only one she'd had any faith in.

Olivia had gone missing in March 2023. A Tuesday. Mia had been away at school, and Mum and Dad hadn't even told her about it until she'd got home that weekend and asked where her sister was. She'd expected them to say she was out with friends, or that maybe she'd got back together with Felix, even though Mia was pretty certain Olivia was finally over him. He'd turned out to be a gaslighting narcissist with major ego problems. There had been a point when Olivia had spent a lot of time in her room crying, or staring at her phone, waiting for it to light up with a message from that loser. But after Christmas, through January and February, Olivia had seemed to finally get the message. He wasn't interested, and he certainly wasn't worth it. She had seemed happier and lighter. She had started making plans to go away for the summer before taking her place at Durham in the autumn.

But then, that last weekend before she disappeared, Olivia appeared to relapse. Started acting weird again.

And when Mia came home the following Friday, Olivia wasn't there.

The police, as far as Mia could tell, were useless. Olivia was an adult. There was no evidence that anything sinister had happened to her. They had interviewed Felix, who had an alibi. They had, apparently, checked all the CCTV cameras in the area and hadn't been able to find her. There had been several sightings that led nowhere. The cop who was assigned to the case had told them she believed Olivia had gone of her own volition. A runaway. It happened a lot, apparently. The main evidence supporting this theory was that Olivia had withdrawn £10,000 from her uni fund before she vanished. This, according to the cops, was proof she must have planned to disappear, and her parents appeared to accept this too. It was why they hadn't done a TV appeal. Why they hadn't made a bigger scene in public, although Mia thought it was also because they were embarrassed. The Howards were supposed to be a perfect family. They didn't want everyone scrutinizing them, all those internet sleuths trawling through their history, every social media post they'd ever made, pointing fingers, speculating.

'She'll come back when she's ready,' Mum said.

'We think she's had some kind of . . . breakdown,' said Dad. 'She's out there somewhere, healing. Finding herself. I know she's going to come home. I know it.'

It all made sense. Olivia had been hurt by Felix. Even though she'd seemed to be getting over it, it could easily have been a pretence. The withdrawal of all that money seemed to point to one thing.

But Mia simply couldn't believe that Olivia would vanish without saying goodbye to her. Without giving her some hint that she was okay.

She wouldn't be that cruel. Dad said Mia had to understand that Olivia wasn't herself. That if she wanted a complete break, she wouldn't have been able to risk Mia giving her away. Mum agreed.

Mia couldn't accept it. She spent months trying to persuade her parents to put more pressure on the police. Then, finally, one of her friends, Fatima, had said, 'The feds are shit, fam.' Fatima's parents were multimillionaires from Surrey, but Fatima spoke like she had grown up in the 'ends'. 'Why don't you hire a private detective?'

'Where would I find one?'

Fatima had shrugged. 'Google, innit.'

So, that evening, in her room at school, Mia had searched 'private detective London' and had been amazed by the number of results. It seemed like most of them were set up to catch cheating spouses or find out all the deets about your daughter's new fiancé. There was a lot of boring talk about fraud and financial investigations. Trawling through their sites, Mia learned a lot about trackers and bugs and 'the ten signs your partner is playing away'.

She found Finn on page four of the results. There was a picture of him on his home page. He looked . . . nice. Like the big brother she'd always dreamed of having. But how much did he cost? Her allowance was quite generous, but surely it wouldn't be enough to cover a private investigator?

'Only one way to find out, sis,' said Fatima. 'Call the dude.'

So Mia had. And yeah, he wasn't cheap. Hiring him would cost thousands, which she didn't have.

She had agonized over it for days, making her mind up on the Friday, before she went home. That Saturday, Mum and Dad had gone out, and Mia had searched the house, looking for something valuable they wouldn't miss. Her mum's jewellery was out. So was her collection of antiques, like the Tiffany lamp she loved so much. She couldn't sell any of their art. Finally, she realized she had something valuable of her own. Granny's bracelet. She'd left it to Mia when she died, back when Mia was little. Mia actually thought it was kind of ugly and had stuck it in a drawer. But it was covered with diamonds and emeralds, and she thought it was probably worth loads.

She'd taken it to a dealer in Hatton Garden. Made herself look as old as she could, dressed smartly and grabbed Olivia's ID before she went, knowing she could pass as her sister. She'd told the dealer she wanted to sell it to pay her way through uni, and he hadn't appeared to give a shit. She knew he'd ripped her off, but it was still enough to hire Finn.

She remembered their first encounter. She'd bunked off school and gone to his office, close to Upper Street. He'd raised his eyebrows at the sight of her school uniform but had invited her to sit. He appeared to be a one-man operation, working out of a single room.

She'd told him about Olivia. Persuaded him to take the work – she got the impression he needed the money – then given him all the information she had.

And now he was dead.

Mia made her way back along the hallway and into Olivia's room. She could think in here. Assess the situation.

All the adults, including the two with shotguns, were in the dining room. There had been two shots. At least one person was dead, and another was either dead or injured.

How long before they killed someone else?

What if they came exploring the house?

She took her phone out of her pocket and looked at it. The dead broadband. The lack of mobile signal. The intruders had clearly done that.

But she had one advantage over them: they didn't know she was here.

If she could get downstairs, she should be able to get out and call for help.

The front door was fiddly. It beeped when you pressed the keypad to open it. But, and she patted her jeans to make sure, she still had the back-door key.

The question was, how the hell was she going to get down the stairs?

Chapter 29

Callum escorted me up the stairs with the gun at my back. Amber was there on the landing, waiting.

'What happened?' she asked.

I was in a daze, not listening to them, until Callum punched me on the arm. 'Wake up. I said, what happened with Rohan? Did he accept the ring or not?'

'Huh? No. He was disgusted with me.'

'Yes!' exclaimed Amber. 'Told you.'

'Bollocks.' Callum swore, but he was smiling. 'I was sure he'd take it. I guess I owe you a quid.'

I couldn't believe my ears. 'Wait. The mission. It was . . . a bet? For a pound?'

'Yeah. I thought Rohan would bite your arm off, and Amber said he'd refuse. I guess she has more faith in human nature than I do. Now, the ring, give it back to me.'

I fished it out of my pocket and handed it over. Then he opened the dining-room door and told me to go back in. As I went through I heard Amber say, 'You can pay me another way if you prefer.'

I turned back and saw Callum step towards Amber and kiss her. A proper, full kiss.

Well, that explained some things. Then Callum, with his lips still on Amber's, reached out and pushed the door shut.

'What happened?' Sophie said from behind me. 'We heard another shot. I thought you were dead.'

I took in the devastation. Broken crockery. Glittering shards of glass. Splashes of water and red wine on the walls. Upended chairs.

'It's Finn,' I said. 'Callum shot him.'

Sophie stared at me. 'He's dead?'

All I could do was nod. I was about to tell everyone what I'd just seen in the hallway when the door opened and both Callum and Amber came in. Amber strode straight towards Georgina, grabbing her arm.

'Give me the knife,' Amber said to Callum.

'Get off me,' Georgina demanded, struggling to escape Amber's grip. But Amber's fury gave her strength.

'What are you going to do?' Callum asked.

'She needs to be punished.' She pushed Georgina against the wall between the windows. 'Need the bathroom, do you? Going to piss yourself? Callum, give me the knife. Look at that perfect face. No amount of Botox or surgery will fix what I'm going to do to you.'

Callum laughed.

Amber wasn't smiling. 'I bet there's acid in this house somewhere. Drain unblocker. Where do you keep it?'

Georgina, who had been doing a very job of looking like she wasn't afraid of this woman, suddenly seemed terrified.

'I'm sorry,' she said.

'What?'

'I apologize. I shouldn't have lied to you.'

Amber fell silent but continued to hold on to Georgina's arm. Sophie said, 'Let her go,' and Callum snapped, 'Shut up.'

He took a step towards Amber and Georgina. He still hadn't taken the knife out of his pocket.

'Are you going to cooperate, Georgina?' he said. 'Play the game?'

She nodded.

'What about the rest of you? No more screwing around. No more *distractions*.'

We were silent.

'Jesus Christ, did you hear me?'

'Yes, yes.' We all said it.

Callum had the knife in his fist now. 'There are worse things than getting shot in the back. Far, far worse ways to go. No one will care if you yell and cry out either. We've fired a gun twice and no one came.' He chuckled. 'In Notting Hill, no one can hear you scream.'

He tucked the knife into his pocket, sure we'd got the message.

'Let her go,' he said to Amber and, like a cat reluctantly giving up a mouse, she loosened her grip. Georgina crossed the room back to the group.

'You've got twenty-eight minutes till the next vote,' Callum said.

They left the room, slamming the door behind them.

The moment they left, everyone gathered around me, except Georgina, who sank into a chair and turned a piece of broken vase over in her hands.

'Tell us what happened.'

I raised my hands. They trembled, and I realized I was still in shock. In the last hour I had seen two men die right in front of me. My brain was still struggling to process it, but my body – the chemicals and primal hormones that drive us, no matter how far we think we get from our origins – was reacting as bodies always react to horror. My stomach was cold inside, my heart racing. It took effort to get the words out.

'I got to him. Then Callum arrived. Shot him in the back.' I put my hand over my shoulder, touched the spot between my shoulder blades.

Rohan goggled at me. 'Did he say anything before . . . I mean, did you speak to him?'

'Yeah. Briefly. He was really badly beaten and it was hard for him to talk, but he told me why he was here. He's a private detective. *Was* a private detective.'

There was disbelief on Sophie and Rohan's faces. Lily's too. 'A detective?'

We all rotated at the same time, like a dance troupe executing a move, to face Georgina.

'Did you know?'

She didn't reply immediately. I could see her thinking, trying to decide what to tell us.

'Georgina? You knew, didn't you?' I couldn't believe it.

As if defeated, she sighed and said, 'Okay. Yes. I knew.'

'Jesus wept.' Rohan stared at her in disbelief.

'What was he investigating?'

She put down the piece of vase. 'What do you think? Olivia's disappearance.'

Her eyes flicked towards the door, telling us that she didn't want Callum and Amber to overhear, and the four of us moved closer to her, so she could speak more quietly.

'It was Mia. She was frustrated with the police and their lack of progress, so she went on Google and found an investigator. This was a couple of months ago. When she eventually told me what she'd done I was . . . well, I was cross with her, of course, going behind our backs, but I was also impressed. We always encouraged the girls to use their initiative. To solve problems. I wasn't so impressed to hear she'd sold a bracelet my mum left her to pay for it, but that's another story.'

'But why was he here?' Sophie asked. 'Tonight?'

'And did Theo know?' That was Rohan.

'No, Theo wasn't in on it. He genuinely thought Finn was Sebastian's assistant, which was the cover Finn suggested he

228

use, though he slipped up a few times, didn't he? It's my fault. I was meant to brief him properly earlier but was too busy preparing for the party.'

'You were right,' Sophie said to me. 'About Finn not being who he said he was.'

I took no pleasure from this. Not now.

'Do you think Callum and Amber knew he was a private detective?' Lily asked.

'I don't know.'

I interrupted. 'I think they must have.'

'But how?'

None of us knew the answer to that.

'You still haven't told us,' I said to Georgina. 'Why exactly was he here at the dinner party? And why didn't you tell us you knew he was a private detective the moment you had the chance?'

'I didn't want them to know.' Meaning Callum and Amber. 'I didn't know if they were always listening. I only went along with your plan just now because I thought it might give me a chance to talk to him. See if he'd found anything out.'

'What do you mean?' I asked.

She hesitated. 'He was here because he thought one of you might know something.'

'About what?' Rohan asked.

'She means about Olivia.' Sophie sounded amazed. Horrified.

'What? You thought one of us might have done something to your daughter?'

Georgina flapped her hands at us. 'You're all getting too close.'

Again, like a synchronized line of dancers, we backed away.

'Thank you.' She took a deep breath. 'It was Mia's idea. You don't know what it's like. When one of your children vanishes, you'll do anything to keep the other one happy. I was terrified that if I didn't go along with her plans she would leave too, and I know that's irrational, but this whole thing with Olivia has made me crazy. You have to remember, too, that I didn't know what Mia was up to for ages. This whole thing was presented to me as a fait accompli. Finn told her, and then both of us, that he suspected Olivia's disappearance was somehow related to the summer we all worked together, which made us think maybe one of you knew something.'

'And that's why you threw this dinner party?' Rohan said.

'Why did Finn think one of us might know something about Olivia?' I asked, trying to sound calm. 'None of us have seen you for years.'

With what appeared to be great effort, Georgina lifted her head and met my eye. 'If Mia was here, she could explain it all better than I can. But it's because Finn went to visit Sebastian before he died. It's all because of something the professor said to him.'

I heard the words in my head and knew exactly what she was going to say.

'Everything echoes.'

'Yes.' She blinked at me. 'That.'

Chapter 30

Mia

How to get to the back door? It was impossible. Mia was too scared to go downstairs, to pass the dining room. Because what if the man with the gruff voice or the redhead came out and saw her? She thought about the bloodstains in the hallway.

There had to be another way out of here.

She went over to Olivia's bedroom window. It looked on to the garden, while her own bedroom was on the side of the house, overlooking the empty place next door. No good for trying to attract the attention of passers-by, and too high up to climb out of.

She sat on the bed, stroking the cat, wondering what was going on downstairs. Why had they killed Finn? She recalled the conversation she'd overheard between the man and woman with the guns. He'd called Finn a private dick, which meant they knew who he was.

Did that mean them being here was related in some way to Olivia's disappearance?

Did they know where she was?

She looked around Olivia's bedroom. A couple of years ago, Olivia had taken down all her posters of the bands she liked and replaced them with tasteful framed pictures of 'inspirational figures'. Greta Thunberg, Nelson Mandela, Rosa Parks,

Malala Yousafzai. Then her eyes fell upon a photo of Olivia on the dressing table. In it, she was wearing her My Chemical Romance T-shirt, and that triggered a memory. Olivia had been wearing that T-shirt that final weekend, music blaring from her Bluetooth speaker, so loud that it had brought Mia in here to ask her to turn it down.

She had known straight away that something was wrong.

'Do you want to talk?' Mia had asked, and yes, Olivia had. Though it was less talking, more rambling. A stream of consciousness that didn't make an enormous amount of sense. She was bug-eyed, pacing the floor. She kept saying, 'I don't know what to do. Maybe I shouldn't do anything. But if I don't do *anything* – that's wrong.' And then she said, 'I'm going to talk to him.'

Mia asked her, 'Who?'

But Olivia wouldn't answer. 'No, I don't want to burden you with it.'

And then she had said, 'I wish I hadn't . . . I wish I hadn't gone in there.' Claude had come into the room at that point and Olivia had yelled at him, 'It's your fault.'

Olivia was making less and less sense. She was yelling at their cat as if he had done something wrong. She kept talking about wasps, which made Mia think she must have been referring to when their parents met, that famous time when Dad had rescued Mum from a swarm of wasps. Their origin story.

Then, finally, she had ushered Mia out of her room. Except she had said one more thing, almost to herself.

'I need to talk to him. About what he did.'

Mia had said, 'Who?' and Olivia had stared at her like she was stupid and hadn't been listening.

'The professor,' she had said.

Months later, she had repeated this whole conversation to Finn.

'I hardly saw her for the rest of the weekend,' she had told him, that first day, after he'd agreed to take the job. 'I went back to school on the Monday wondering if the whole thing had been some weird dream – then, when I came home the following Friday, she'd gone.'

'Who's the professor?' he had asked.

'I don't know for certain, but I guess she was talking about Sebastian Marlowe.'

She told him what she knew. About how Mum and Dad had met.

'And do you know if Olivia did speak to him? Have you tried to contact him?'

She told him she hadn't, then Finn told her he would do some research and give her regular progress reports. He said he intended to visit Professor Marlowe, but arranging a meeting proved difficult. Finn's emails and calls to the professor went unanswered for weeks, then Christmas got in the way, and it wasn't until the early weeks of January, when she went back to his office, that Finn was able to give Mia a detailed update.

'I decided to turn up at Thornwood unannounced,' he said. 'It's a creepy place. Overgrown vegetation. In a state of disrepair. There was no answer when I knocked on the door so I started to wonder if it was abandoned. I was about to go but decided to try the front door – and it opened.'

Mia had been enrapt, transported in her imagination to a Gothic castle from a fairytale.

'It was so strange. I went in, calling his name, thinking there was no one there, but I could hear this faint beeping.'

'Beeping?'

He made the noise. 'It led me to what I think had once been a dining room, with a hospital bed in it – you know, the kind that can be lowered and raised with the touch of a button.

There was a drip and a monitor, which was where the beeping was coming from, and in the bed . . .'

'Professor Marlowe.'

'Exactly. I couldn't believe how ancient he looked. Much older than his years. Frighteningly thin, and his lungs made a dreadful squeaking noise, like a door that needs oil.'

Mia had shuddered.

'He was clearly at death's door. On heavy painkillers: morphine, probably. I didn't understand why there was no one there, looking after him.' It was his turn to shudder. 'I couldn't tell if he was awake or could hear me, but I told him who I was and why I was there, and when I said your parents' names he definitely reacted.'

'And you asked him about Olivia? If she'd been there?'

'Of course. That's when it got really weird. He opened his eyes and grabbed my wrist.'

'Oh my God.'

'I nearly had a heart attack.' Finn had laughed. 'But then he started talking. "The girl," he said. He sounded distressed. I asked him if she'd been there and he looked me right in the eye and said, "Everything echoes."'

Mia repeated the phrase beneath her breath.

'I asked him to tell me more, but he couldn't, and I could see I was losing him and didn't have much time. I remembered what you told me, about how Olivia had been talking about when your parents met, and I said, "Is this about 1999? About something that happened then?" and he said, "That summer." And then, before I could say anything else, a man strode into the room. Sebastian's nurse, demanding to know who I was.'

'Where had he been?'

Finn had shrugged. 'In the loo, I think. I explained that I was a private detective and that I was looking for someone who I thought might have come here. A nineteen-year-old woman. He said no one had been there, and when I told him that Professor Marlowe had reacted quite strongly, the nurse said, "He's dying. Off his head on opioids." Then he escorted me out, telling me not to come back.'

'Did you believe him?'

Again, Finn had shrugged. 'I don't know. But it had been so easy for me to get in to see Sebastian, I can easily believe Olivia could have done the same. Marlowe certainly reacted strongly when I mentioned her. *Everything echoes.* That felt like it meant something.'

Now, she sat on Olivia's bed, gently stroking Claude's soft fur, and her thoughts returned to the pressing problem of how she was going to get out of here.

There was something in what she'd remembered that was niggling at her. Something Olivia had said that last weekend. Something she had wondered about at the time and then forgotten.

What was it? It was as if there was an itchy spot deep inside her brain; an itch she couldn't reach. It made her want to punch something out of frustration. And as she tried to relax, her thoughts returned again to that meeting with Finn.

'I need to talk to your mum and dad,' he had said. 'I need to ask them about that summer.'

Reluctantly, she had agreed.

Or rather, she had agreed to let him talk to Mum.

Chapter 31

Georgina continued in her quiet voice, not wanting Callum and Amber to hear. I was so absorbed by her second- and third-hand tale – Mia said this, Finn did that – that I had temporarily forgotten that the deadline was approaching fast.

'So what happened?' Sophie asked. 'Did you talk to Finn?'

'Yes, Mia agreed he needed to speak to me or Theo.' It clearly hurt her, saying his name. 'She decided in the end she wanted him to talk only to me because she thought Theo would be furious with her for hiring an investigator behind our backs.'

'And what was *your* reaction?'

'I was shocked, but as I said, I also admired her determination. I wish I'd done it myself.' She cleared her throat. 'I spoke to Finn, and he described the meeting with Sebastian and asked me if I had any idea what it all might mean. Why might Olivia have gone to see the professor?'

'And?' Rohan asked.

'I told him I had no idea. Finn asked me if he could go through Olivia's laptop and phone. The police had already done this and found nothing useful, and they'd given them back to us, and I told him it was fine. The police had unlocked them for us, and I handed them over. He came back to me a few days later, saying he'd taken the laptop to an expert, who'd recovered her search history.'

We all waited.

'The week before she disappeared, she had looked all of you up on Google. Social media too. LinkedIn, Facebook, all of what Mia would call the "old people" sites.'

She looked around the room. Me, Sophie, Lily, Rohan.

'She never contacted me,' Sophie said.

'Nor me,' the rest of us echoed.

Georgina didn't respond to that. Did she believe us? Was someone here lying?

'Finn, Mia and I talked about what to do – and then we heard: the professor had died. That's when we came up with the plan. Theo and I had received an invitation to the funeral. Finn suggested he should go too, because we thought you guys, or at least some of you, might be there. It also gave us a chance to introduce Finn to Theo, telling him Finn had been Sebastian's assistant. I feel terrible about that now, but we still thought Theo would react badly and start loudly pointing fingers if we told him Mia had hired a detective. I knew we needed to be subtle. And then, of course, none of you were at the funeral.'

'I didn't know he'd died,' Rohan said.

Sophie and I nodded in agreement.

Lily said, 'I heard about it. But I couldn't . . . I just couldn't bring myself to go.'

'You were still angry with him for closing down the site,' Georgina said, and Lily didn't argue. Georgina continued. 'That's when Finn and Mia came up with the idea for this dinner party. We would invite you all, and Finn would come too so he could get a look at you all and subtly try to find out if any of you had talked to Olivia. Find out if any of you had told her something that had shocked her and caused the behaviour Mia had witnessed, a few days before Olivia disappeared.'

The rest of it was unspoken. *Or she met up with one of you and you did something to her.*

Sophie didn't let it stay unspoken. 'You think one of us might be directly responsible for Olivia's disappearance.'

Georgina's gaze was unflinching. 'I no longer know what to think, Sophie. All I know is that Finn thought – because of his encounter with Sebastian and what the professor said – that Olivia must have found out something that happened that summer. Something that echoed.'

'A secret,' I said.

'Exactly. And then Callum and Amber turn up looking for a secret from '99, and I thought it had to be connected. I still think that.'

'You still haven't told us why you didn't tell us about Finn being a detective,' I said.

'At first it was because I didn't want Theo to know. I thought maybe I could still keep it secret from him. Then I saw what they did to the person who received the most votes, and I was scared.'

'You thought if we knew you'd been lying to us about Finn that we'd vote for you.'

'And they'd kill me. Yes.'

There was a long silence while we absorbed everything Georgina had told us. How did it all fit together? All I knew was that Olivia hadn't contacted me, and I wasn't that difficult to find. My name and email address were listed on the college website, and I was easy to contact. Had she reached out to me and I'd missed it? Could it have gone into junk? Were Sophie, Rohan or Lily lying when they said Olivia hadn't been in touch with them? Could they really have told her something that had led to her disappearance? Done something to her?

'Hold on,' I said. 'How do we know Callum and Amber didn't encounter Olivia?' I was trying to make sense of it all. The novelist in me knew there must be a thread; a connection. 'I have no idea what she might have uncovered or how she did it, but maybe something she did or said to them, some information she shared, brought them here.'

'How would she have encountered them?' Georgina asked.

'I have no idea. But like I keep saying, I'm sure Amber knew Finn. There must be a connection. Maybe—'

I stopped.

Callum was standing in the doorway. His grin was back. Amber stood behind him.

Callum came into the room. 'Oh, it's all a big puzzle, isn't it?' His tone was mocking. 'How does it all connect? Who's lying? Who what where why when?' The smile fell away. 'I'm getting bored. Really fucking bored. Let's get this over with. It's time to vote again.'

Chapter 32

August 1999

Lily ushered me into the sitting room and said, 'Take a seat.'

The curtains were drawn to keep the sun and heat out of Sebastian's sitting room, an immaculately tidy space that smelled of furniture polish. In the corner was a twenty-seven-inch Sony television set with a video attached. I surmised Sebastian must use this room sometimes, though it was hard to imagine him doing anything as lowbrow as watching TV, and I guessed he'd bought the set for Dominic to watch football on.

On the coffee table between the sofa and the TV was Lily's laptop, with numerous cables snaking out of it.

'Put this on,' Lily said, holding up a plastic clip with a wire attached. I squeezed one end to open it and clamped it over the tip of my left index finger.

'This is to measure my heart rate?'

'Your pulse. Yes.'

The wire led to a small plastic box, clearly home-made, with a sound-level meter set into it. The needle was currently resting to the far left.

'It's a volume unit meter,' Lily said, seeing me peering at it. It was the kind of thing one might see on an old-fashioned tape recorder. If the needle tipped to the right, into the red, it meant you were being too loud. Presumably this meter would register my heart rate and swing into the red if my pulse increased suddenly.

'I'm going to put the box out of your sight,' Lily said. 'I don't want you looking at it when you're taking the test.'

'Where did you get all this stuff?'

'I got Dominic to drive me to Canterbury last week. I borrowed the finger clip from the university. Everything else is easy to buy at Tandy. The guys in the shop were really helpful, actually, when I told them what I was making. One of them had a friend who'd done something similar, and he emailed me the diagrams. They even showed me how to record the readings automatically using this clever program on the computer.'

Lily explained that I was the first one to sit the test, but that everyone at the house, including Dominic and Eve, had agreed to take it. 'Everyone except Sebastian, that is. I'm only going to tell him about it if it works. My gift to him, to do with as he wishes.'

I had been there when Lily had first raised the idea of the test. Most of the group had agreed to it immediately, all except our golden couple.

'I really don't think we can afford any distractions right now,' said Theo.

'I have capacity.'

'I don't think you do. I don't want you to burn out when the beta site is almost ready.'

He looked around at us, seeking an ally. I expected Dominic, our chief cynic, to pipe up, but it was, of course, Theo's girlfriend who took his side.

'It sounds like a waste of time anyway,' Georgina said. 'I know you're meant to be a genius, Lily, but I can't see how even you could create a test that a psycho couldn't fool.'

'I think I can.'

'Also, isn't this just going to remind the professor of what happened to his wife? Do we really want to put him in a darker mood, especially at such a crucial time?'

'Well said.' Theo squeezed her knee.

'He thinks about it all the time anyway,' said Dominic with a sneer aimed at Georgina. 'I think it's a good idea. When he gets bored of the dating site, which he will—' Dominic never missed an opportunity to express his disdain for Butterfly Net. 'He's going to need another project to keep him busy. I say go for it. Plus, I'd quite like to know if I'm a psycho. All the nice girls love a bad boy.' He grinned and winked at Sophie.

Theo still looked uncomfortable. 'I think there's something unethical about it. You know how difficult it can be to shake labels, Lily. We studied that. If you attach a psychopath label to someone it could have serious consequences.'

'I really don't think any of us is one,' Lily said.

'But you don't know that for sure.'

'Let's vote,' I suggested. 'That's fair, right, Theo? If Lily believes she's got time to do it, what harm can it do? It's fun, that's all.'

He sighed. 'Fine. Whatever. But if it screws up the site launch, it will affect all of you.' He looked at Rohan. 'Could delay us getting our stock options, going public.'

Theo, Georgina and, yes, Rohan voted against. But Sophie, Dominic, Eve and I voted in favour.

Lily spent little time setting everything up. She switched on the TV and popped a video cassette into the video recorder. 'The test is in three parts. First, I'm going to show you some images and short video scenes, and you'll be shown multiple-choice questions that ask you how you feel. Just click the most accurate word. At the end of the test all the results will be fed into the algorithm and it will assign you a score out of a hundred. Under sixty, not a psychopath. Sixty-one to seventy-four: borderline; some signs of a disorder. Over seventy-five—'

'Everybody run.'

A faint smile.

'I know. They're not all bad. This isn't the movies.'

'Quite. Psychopathy is a spectrum, and there are other factors that play into whether someone with this kind of brain wiring actually poses a threat, like the man who killed Barbara. Also, even with a test like this a clinician would still need to interrogate the results, assess the subject, ask follow-up questions. It's a starting point, really. But I do believe that if anyone scores very high – say, eighty or higher – there can be very little doubt.'

Maybe it was the mention of Barbara's murder but, as she spoke, doubts crept into my mind.

'What if we *do* uncover someone like the guy who murdered Sebastian's wife? Isn't it dangerous to expose someone like that? I worry it would be, well . . . it would be like poking a wasps' nest.'

But Lily was too far gone. It was all about the challenge of creating the test and seeing if it worked. And I was too fascinated to really press the point. Even though there was suddenly part of me that worried we might be about to open Pandora's box, that we were playing with explosives, I wanted to see what happened. So I stopped arguing and went along with it.

She pressed play on the remote and, over the next ten minutes, I watched a series of still images and short clips taken from movies, TV shows and adverts. The images ranged from pictures of plane crashes and roadkill, paintings depicting scenes from hell and crying children, to scenes of kids blowing out birthday candles, athletes lifting trophies, and tumbling puppies. Some of the video clips were familiar: the home invasion from *A Clockwork Orange* and the neo-Nazi violence in *American History X*. News reports of disasters and murders. There were clips from pornography and 'Lovers' Guide' videos, sex that was brutal or loving. Scenes of babies being born and ducklings following their mother. My gaze flicked between the TV and the laptop, where I chose words from the multiple-choice options: disgusted, sad, aroused.

Lily instructed me to remove the clip from my finger so I could take the second part of the test.

'You'll see a series of statements on the computer, again with multiple-choice options. Rather like the dating question-naire, but designed to find out if you meet any of the criteria on Robert Hare's PCL-R checklist. Glibness. Grandiose self-worth. Lack of empathy. Et cetera, et cetera. Some are easier to formulate questions for than others. Again, it's important that you're honest. There's no point trying to fool or manipulate it. Okay?'

'Yes, of course. I genuinely want to know how high I score.'

It took about thirty minutes to complete. The initial statements were straightforward:

I have no qualms about telling a white lie to get what I want.
I sometimes lie awake at night regretting or feeling embarrassed about things I've said or done.
I deserve to be more successful than the average person.
I get nervous about speaking in front of people I don't know well.

Agree or disagree. There was no 'Don't know' or 'Somewhat' option.

After these questions Lily had written out a number of 'What would you do?' scenarios.

You live alone in a flat. You frequently hear fighting between the couple who live downstairs and are convinced the man is violent towards his partner. You are the only witness and you believe the woman is too scared to leave. What do you do?

Your widowed mother has met a man with whom she wants to spend her twilight years and plans to remarry. The man is a decade younger than her and you believe when she dies her considerable estate will go to him instead of you. Which of these emotions do you feel?

Your ambition is to be a successful screenwriter, and you have written several screenplays without success. Your best friend writes one script 'for fun' which he sells immediately for big money. How do you feel?

There were occasions, answering, when I had to force myself to be honest. I didn't want to admit I might do nothing, or feel aggrieved or jealous. I also knew that it was quite natural to do or feel the 'wrong' thing without being a psychopath. I guessed Lily would be looking for patterns, a consistent lack of feeling or elevated sense of self-worth.

After thirty minutes, I handed the laptop back.

Then came part three, the polygraph part of the test.

'I'm going to do this in the same way the police do it,' Lily said. 'I'll start by asking you some questions I know the answers to, then carry on from there. Yes or no answers, please. Is your name William Harper?'

'It is. I mean, yes.'

'Do you come from Rye, East Sussex?'

'Yes.'

Glancing down at the needle on the meter, which had presumably not moved, she asked her next question:

'Do you fancy Sophie?'

I laughed. 'I wasn't expecting these questions to escalate so quickly.'

'Yes or no only, please.'

My pulse was accelerating. I could feel it: the quickening

246

of blood rushing through my veins. I wasn't sure how the polygraph read answers that were truthful but that made your heartbeat race. 'Yes.'

'Are you in love with Sophie?'

I opened my mouth to protest the question, but Lily shot me a warning look.

'Yes.'

'Do you dislike Dominic?'

I hesitated before saying, 'Yes.'

'Are you worried that Sophie likes Dominic more than she likes you?'

Lily had obviously been watching me more closely than I'd realized. Answering in the affirmative again, I guessed the needle must be going crazy.

Still speaking in her calm, scientist's voice, she asked, 'Are you going to do something about it?'

My mouth was dry. 'I don't know.'

'Yes or no?'

I took a deep breath. 'Yes. Yes, I am.'

'When?'

I jerked my head towards her. 'What?'

She had put her pen down and was no longer avoiding my eye. 'When are you going to tell her how you feel?'

'Is this part of the test?'

She ignored the question. 'She likes you too, I'm sure of it.'

'Really?'

'Ninety per cent sure. What's stopping you?'

'Isn't it obvious? Fear of being rejected.'

She tutted. 'So what? If she says she just wants to be friends or whatever, just accept it and move on. That's got to be better than never knowing.' She waited for my response. 'What is it?'

'I'm scared that she'll laugh at me. It happened at uni. I asked out this girl that I really liked and she laughed then told all her mates, who took the piss out of me. Why would a nerd like me ever think he stood a chance with someone so hot? It was humiliating.'

I expected sympathy. Instead, Lily rolled her eyes and said, 'Jesus, Will, that is so typically male of you.'

'What do you mean?'

'Scared a woman will laugh at you. There are much worse things, you know.'

I felt a deep, instant shame.

'Besides, Sophie's not going to laugh at you, even if she doesn't like you in that way.'

'But what about the algorithm? It only matched us one way.'

'I only showed you your top match. But when I looked at the data, you got a high score both ways. You're compatible, Will.'

I stared at her. 'Why didn't you tell me?'

'I was hoping you'd see it yourself. And have the guts to do something about it. You need to be brave, Will. Take a risk.'

What was the needle on the meter doing? My stress levels were surely high enough to make Lily's home-made polygraph explode.

'I know. I know.'

'So?'

'I'll do it the night of the party.'

We had been planning the party for a while now. A week from today, we were going to launch the site in beta and invite a select number of people in Kent and Sussex to start using it, with free memberships. Live testing, with real people going on real dates, feeding back to us how it had gone. To celebrate the beta launch, we were going to throw a small party. Just us, the people at the house. Booze, music, dancing and takeaway pizza. Sebastian had given us a budget and we were all excited.

'We're all going to be working so hard until then,' I said, pre-empting Lily's next question. 'Sophie's going to be distracted and busy. The night of the party, she'll be relaxed. It will be better.'

'You're not going to chicken out?'

'No. Absolutely not.' I swallowed. 'I'm going to do it.'

'Good.' She leaned over and clamped a hand on my shoulder. 'I think it's all going to be fine, Will. All I ask is that the two of you name your first daughter after me.'

I had this image, then, of Sophie and me, not at a wedding, not on a maternity ward, but at a dinner party. Lily would be there. Hopefully Rohan and Georgina and Theo too. Maybe Eve. It seemed clear to me that we would always be friends. That if this summer gave me nothing else – if it didn't make me rich; if it didn't work out, for whatever reason, with Sophie – it would give me that. Lasting friendships. A bond that would stretch through my life.

'I assume that wasn't part of the test. When are we going to start the third part properly?'

'Now, Will.'

We did the polygraph test proper, with the computer recording whether I lied or told the truth. It took around ten minutes and I made sure to tell the truth each time, even when the questions made me uncomfortable. Have you ever told someone you love them to get them to sleep with you? Have you ever shoplifted? (No and yes, though the shoplifted item was a lollipop that I'd accidentally pocketed in a sweet shop when I was nine.)

'Right, you're done,' Lily said at the end. 'Can you find Rohan and send him up? He's next.'

Chapter 33

Callum picked his way through the shattered plates, deliberately crunching a pile of glass beneath his boot.

'Anyone ready to confess now?'

Silence. And in that silence, it hit me: I didn't need a test or clinical study to tell me. Here was a psychopath. The *dangerous* kind. The type I had been afraid we might antagonize when we sat Lily's test.

And I wondered, too: had our actions back then led us, somehow, to this now? Was what was going on here tonight part of a chain reaction that started when Lily devised her test that summer? We hadn't trapped a psychopath; we'd drawn one to us, like kids who play with a Ouija board and unleash an evil spirit. Wasn't it more than likely that it was related to the test and that Callum was the evil we had set loose? I didn't know, at that point, the steps that had led him, and us, to this point. But the more I thought about it, the more I felt there had to be a connection.

'No confession?' Callum pretended to be shocked. 'Better get voting then. Who's going to go first?'

He rocked the nose of his shotgun back and forth, as if silently going 'tic tac toe' in his head. Before he settled on anyone, I said, 'What's the point?'

The gun went still, the barrel pointing directly at my belly. 'What's that, Will?'

'None of us has this secret. We would have told you by now

if we did. Nothing happened in 1999. Nothing worth all this carnage. Olivia couldn't have found anything. It's—'

He cut me off. 'Olivia? This has nothing to do with Olivia.' He tilted his head. 'Well, I suppose, in a way . . .'

Georgina was suddenly in his face, standing between me and the gun. 'What do you know about Olivia? Did you do something to her?'

'Of course not. I'd never even heard of her until—'

'Callum.' Amber said his name quickly. Warning him. For a second, he looked mollified.

'Sit down, Georgina,' he said. 'All of you. Around the table.'

One by one, those of us who were standing did as he asked, glass crunching beneath our feet.

'You can go first,' he said to me.

'I'm not going to do it. I watched you kill Theo. I saw you kill Finn. I'm not going to sit here and take part in a point-less game that leads to someone else being murdered. You're going to have to find another way to get this secret, if there even is one.'

Was I doing the right thing? The truth is, I had no idea. Despite Callum's threats to hurt us, all I knew was what had happened last time – and isn't the definition of insanity doing the same thing repeatedly and expecting a different result?

Beside me, I felt Sophie tense. I put my hand on hers.

Amber saw, and smiled. I realized immediately I'd made a stupid mistake. Because it reminded Amber that Sophie was my weakness.

She pointed her shotgun at Sophie and said, 'On your feet.'

'No,' I said.

'I wasn't talking to you. Get up, Sophie. Stand and walk over there.'

Callum furrowed his brows, then realized what Amber was

doing. He grinned and grabbed Sophie's upper arm, hauling her to her feet.

'That hurts! Get off me.'

He shoved her into the middle of the space between the table and the windows. Amber walked around the table towards Sophie, gun trained on her.

'Tell Will, if he doesn't vote, I'm going to shoot you.'

I stood, dodging Callum, who tried to push me back down. 'Leave her alone.'

Amber arched an eyebrow.

I jabbed a finger at Callum. 'You told me if I completed my mission you wouldn't hurt Sophie. And that's what I did.'

Everyone, including Sophie, stared at me. 'Mission?' she said.

Callum snorted. 'I didn't say that exactly, Will. And your efforts barely made a difference.'

'What are you talking about?' Georgina asked.

'When Callum made me leave the room, it was so he could give me a mission.' I had decided there was no point keeping quiet now. He was already threatening Sophie. 'He gave me a diamond ring and told me to offer it to Rohan, who refused to take it.'

'A diamond ring? What ring? Show me.'

'Callum's got it.'

'That sounds like bullshit,' Rohan said. 'Why would Callum make you do that?'

'It was a bet, between him and Amber. Some stupid game they were playing. I only went along with it because Callum said he'd hurt Sophie.'

That made Sophie gasp.

'And what are you going to do now, Will?' Callum seemed to be enjoying himself again.

'You won't kill her,' I said. 'Not if you think she's the one with the secret.'

'Did we say we'd kill her?' Amber asked. 'I told you, there are worse things than death. Ever seen someone shot in the kneecap? Of course you haven't. But I think you can imagine the pain, right? Now, stop fucking around. Vote.'

What choice did I have?

'Give me a second. I haven't even thought about it.'

I obviously wasn't going to vote for Sophie. I couldn't ever see myself voting for Lily either. That left two, and Georgina had just watched her husband die. I couldn't vote for her.

I could sense Rohan reading my mind.

'Just get it over with,' he muttered.

'If I have to vote, even though I don't believe anyone has the secret you're after, it has to be Rohan.'

Callum nodded. 'Why?'

'I don't know. Because I think the others are even less likely to be hiding something.'

'Not good enough. I need a reason.'

'I don't know.' I groped for something to say. 'He was friends with Dominic. Sebastian's nephew. If anyone did anything dodgy back then, it would be Dominic, and he and Rohan used to hang out together and watch football. They were mates.'

Rohan was disgusted. 'That's your reason? Dominic and I both liked football?'

'They're forcing me to choose. I'm sorry.'

Rohan snorted. 'Let me vote next. I vote for Will.'

'Here we go,' said Callum. 'Why?'

'Well, first of all, this mission stuff – it sounds made up to me.'

'I didn't make it up,' I protested. 'Callum, tell him.'

Callum laughed, and Rohan went on:

'More than that, he's writing a book about us all. A novel about what happened that summer. I've been thinking about this. How can he write the story if he doesn't know everything that happened? If he doesn't know all the secrets?'

'That's a very good point,' said Callum.

I was appalled. 'It's fiction! It's made up.'

Rohan wasn't impressed. 'You told us it was based on us. Our story.'

'Based on. Inspired by. That's just the setting. Any secrets, any twists, will be made up. That's what writers of fiction do.'

'Yeah. Well, they say you should write what you know. And my feeling is that after twenty-five years of failing at fiction you've decided to write a true story.'

'*Interesting*,' Callum said, approaching me. 'Is he right? Do you know more than you're making out?'

I squirmed beneath everyone's attention.

'No! I don't know anything. It was going to be . . . well . . .' My squirming intensified. 'A love story.'

Callum hoisted himself up, planting his bottom on the table between me and Sophie. 'Oh, a *romance*. Between the two of you? This is beautiful, Will. Almost brings a tear to my eye.' He cupped his hand around his mouth and leaned towards my ear. 'Tell me. Does it get raunchy? Do you and Sophie here get up to all sorts of deliciously unspeakable acts?'

'Pervert,' Sophie said.

Callum mock gasped. 'Did you hear that, Will? She called you a pervert. I think I'd like to read this book if it's kinky.'

'Perhaps he could give us a reading?' said Amber. She was excited again. Her irritation with Georgina and the rest of us appeared to have abated, replaced by the thrill of the game.

'Have you memorized any of it, Will?' Callum asked.

'I haven't started it yet.'

'What's that? Your voice is very quiet.'

'I said, I haven't started it.'

Callum jumped down from the table. 'Of course you

haven't. All mouth and no trousers. Just like Sophie in your book.' He slapped me on the shoulder.

I tried to whisper an apology to Sophie, but she wouldn't meet my eye.

Callum was still talking. 'Where were we? One for Rohan, one for Will. Who's next? Let's go with Lily.'

She stared at the tabletop, unable to look at any of us. 'I don't know.'

Rohan spoke up. 'Come on, Lily, you know what I said makes sense. Will's reason was pathetic.'

I wished I hadn't voted. That I'd stuck to my guns. The moment I'd given in, the game had started, and now it was unstoppable. We were all going to vote. Someone was going to get shot at the end of it.

'I'm sorry, Will,' Lily said.

It looked like the person getting shot was going to be me.

'Lily,' I said. It stung like betrayal. But I couldn't blame her, could I? Like Rohan, she wanted to survive and get home to her children.

'Georgina?' Callum said.

The silence that followed was like none I'd ever known. She looked from me to Rohan and back.

'I have children,' Rohan said.

Both Sophie and I, the two of us who didn't have kids, stared at him. It was a low blow. But I could see it gave Georgina pause. If she condemned Rohan, she'd be robbing two children of their father. Who did I have? A cat. I really didn't believe that being child-free made me a less important member of the human race, but we were in an impossible situation where we were all being asked to make impossible choices.

But I wasn't that worried. There was a good reason why I didn't think Georgina would vote for me.

'Come on,' Callum snapped at her.

She turned her face towards Rohan. He groaned.

'Will,' she said. 'For the reason Rohan gave.'

I couldn't believe it. Across the room, Sophie gasped. Her vote wouldn't be needed. With three votes, I had lost. Lily and Rohan wouldn't meet my eye. In fact, Lily had her hands over her face, as if that would render her invisible.

Callum walked around the table so he was beside Rohan and opposite me. 'You know how this works, Will.' He sighed. 'Such a great loss to naughty literature, but those are the rules.'

All evening, since Callum and Amber had told us why they were here and outlined the rules of their game, I had been trying not to think about this happening. Put my head in the sand and prayed it wouldn't come to this.

My secret.

I knew it wasn't big or consequential enough to be what they were after. But I had one.

I had a choice. I could refuse to tell it. I could take it to my grave. Or I could share it and, unless the rules changed or a miracle happened, probably die at the end anyway. It didn't seem like much of a choice.

Except . . . the survival instinct is stronger than everything. Telling my story would buy me ten or fifteen minutes. Maybe a miracle *would* happen. An alien invasion. Nuclear war. An earthquake. We could but hope. And who knew? Perhaps unburdening myself of it before I left this mortal coil might make my spirit lighter as it flew up – or plummeted down.

'Go on,' said Georgina. 'Just get it over with.'

'Are you sure?' I asked her.

She shrugged. 'Why should I care now? Tell them, Will.'

Chapter 34

I drank for courage. I drank because it was a party. And I drank because we'd all been working so hard over the last week, readying the site for the beta launch, putting in sixteen-hour days, living on adrenaline and team spirit. There's something intoxicating about a deadline when you're with a group, all of you focused on the same goal. Sebastian spent most of the week with us, there in the office, with Theo going from desk to desk too, both mucking in. Sebastian had his shirtsleeves rolled up to his elbows, perched on a chair with a laptop balanced on his knees, inputting data with two fingers. I can still see him all these years later, stabbing at the keyboard, face screwed up with concentration, dark stains spreading beneath his armpits. I knew Lily hadn't told him about her test and I wondered how he would react when she revealed her project, which she was going to do next week, after the launch, though she had promised to tell us our personal psychopath scores over the weekend.

We worked our arses off and then – on Friday afternoon at 4.48 p.m., twelve minutes before our target time – Lily said, 'I think we're ready.'

Everyone gathered around her computer. There it was, the home page, with the Butterfly Net logo – a butterfly, of course, with symmetrical hearts on its wings – that Sophie had designed because Sebastian didn't like the logo the agency came up with. There was a photo of a happy couple, embracing and smiling, loved up and unable to keep their hands off each other, all because of the power of the algorithm.

'It looks amazing,' Sophie said.

'Lily, you did it,' said Rohan.

'You all did it. Together.' Sebastian clapped us all on our backs. 'My revolutionaries.'

The plan was that on Monday morning, invitation emails with codes would go out to a list of single people across the south-east, a mailing list that Georgina had sourced. On top of that, articles were due to be published in local papers across the area – *New dating website harnesses scientific matchmaking to help singles find love* – and Sebastian was booked to appear on several radio stations over the following week. There was talk of Meridian, the local ITV network, running a piece. Georgina had been busy and, listening to her on the phone, I'd been amazed by how persuasive she was. It also helped that her parents knew a lot of people who ran newspapers and other media outlets, having gone to the same schools as them.

'Wonderful,' Sebastian said as Lily gave us a tour of the finished site. 'You can all take the weekend off. I think you'll need to, to cope with your hangovers.'

As he spoke, I heard an engine outside, tyres on gravel, and went outside to investigate. It was Dominic, behind the wheel of a van, with Eve beside him in the passenger seat.

He got out and opened the van's rear doors, gesturing for me and Rohan to help.

'Wow.' I had never seen so much alcohol outside of a supermarket's shelves. Crates of beer and boxes of wine. Champagne and cider. Vodka and gin and Pimm's. There were boxes full of snacks too, and cans of Pepsi for Rohan.

'Right?' Dominic grinned. 'Uncle Seb pushed the boat out. I need you to help me get all this in the fridge.'

Rohan and I helped him carry the booze to the kitchen. Theo came out to help too and, I noticed, Dominic quickly disappeared. Sebastian came into the kitchen and told us he'd given Dominic cash to order pizza from a place in the village.

'I'm not going to cramp your style.' There were half-hearted murmurs of protest. 'I hope you all have a great night. You deserve it.'

Sophie had already gone off to start getting ready. Lily, who had promised to join us, was missing too. Apparently, there were a few bugs that needed to be fixed, though she promised it wouldn't take long.

Dominic appeared and took a couple of bottles of Grolsch out of the fridge, popping the cap on one and handing me the other. Rohan cracked open a Pepsi, and then Eve appeared, mixing Pimm's and lemonade in a jug which she filled with strawberries.

We sat out at the tables on the lawn, drinking and smoking. Then Sophie and Lily appeared, along with Theo and Georgina. All eight of us, a small but lively party, euphoric to have hit our deadline. It was another hot night. We talked about what we were going to spend our money on when the site became massive and the value of our shares ballooned. At one point Dominic ordered the pizzas and time skipped forward and the pizzas were there, half a dozen of them, and we stuffed ourselves and kept drinking.

'Have you got the results of the psychopath test?' Sophie asked Lily.

'They've been generated. I just need to check them over. But maybe later. Tomorrow morning at the latest.'

I watched Sophie talking to Lily, and nerves fizzed in my stomach. Lily caught my eye a couple of times, reminding me of my vow. Tonight, I was going to tell Sophie how I felt about her. But in order to do that I needed to get her on her own, and there was no sign of that happening. All I could do was stare at her, in her vest top and her shorts and her Doc Martens, skin shining in the golden hour of that evening, the most beautiful woman I would ever see.

'Can I just say something?'

We all looked at Eve, who had tapped the Pimm's jug to get our attention.

'I want to thank you all for being so nice to me this summer. I know I'm an outsider, that I'm not a brainy graduate like you lot—'

'That's rubbish,' Sophie said.

'Yeah. This lot aren't brainy.' Dominic grinned. 'Except Lily, who's a freak.'

'Well, I think you are all super clever.' Eve was a little drunk. 'The website's amazing. I'm proud that I could be involved, even if it was just cleaning up around you.'

There were murmurs of protest.

'Anyway,' she went on, losing her courage a little. 'When you're all rich, think of me. I'm going to be out of here in a couple of weeks. Going to find myself somewhere in London and start my life properly.' She raised her glass. 'To life, and being young, and the future.'

We all joined in the toast.

'Let's go down to the lake,' Dominic suggested, clamping a hand on Rohan's shoulder, and we followed him down there, except Lily, who said she still had a couple of things to do. We protested en masse, but she wouldn't be dissuaded.

I grabbed the boombox, checking it had batteries in it, and carried it with me. We passed the burned-out remains of the wasps' nest. At the edge of the lake, I set down the boombox and riffled through the wallet of CDs I'd brought along too, selecting the Radiohead album we'd been listening to all summer. But as soon as the opening guitar chords of 'Airbag' rang out, Eve said, 'Do we have to listen to this depressing stuff?'

Dominic, who was sitting very close to her on the grass, said, 'Yeah, come on. It's a party. Haven't you got anything the girls can dance to?'

That made both Eve and Sophie groan, but Sophie asked me to throw her the CD wallet. 'Haven't you got any Britney? Will, your tastes are so "approved by the *NME*". This'll do.' She plucked out the Fatboy Slim album and soon 'Right Here, Right Now' was blasting out across the lake.

'That's better, eh, babe?' Dominic said, nodding along and laying a hand on Eve's bare leg. She immediately jumped up to dance, as did Sophie, and Georgina dragged Theo up by the hand. Rohan joined in, and then there was just me and Dominic sitting on the grass. I had a moment where I felt rooted to the ground, unable to make my body move because I was worried about what Sophie would think. What if she believed that old maxim about being able to tell how good someone will be in bed by how well they move on the dance-floor? I danced like an uncle at a wedding.

But I couldn't be on Team Dominic, no matter how awkward I felt. I drained the rest of my beer – my fifth or sixth bottle, on top of several glasses of Pimm's that I'd downed – and jumped up, locating the beat and doing my best to follow it. Sophie's proximity, the beer, the warm summer air . . . It all went to my head and into my feet, and soon I was lost in the music, and someone passed me another beer, and I danced and I danced, my friends surrounding me, feeling young and not just alive but immortal. Looking back, I know the other reason I did it. This was dancing as an avoidance strategy. All the while I moved to the music, I couldn't tell Sophie about my feelings.

The CD ended and somebody put another one on, then

another, and another: The Prodigy, The Chemical Brothers, Orbital. It got dark, the moon so big it seemed uncanny; stars blazing in a cloudless sky. I was drenched with sweat. I'd been dancing with my eyes closed, letting out all the stress of the past few weeks, and hadn't realized that half the people there had drifted away. Only Rohan, Eve and I remained.

'Where is everyone?' I said, stunned that I hadn't noticed Sophie leave.

Rohan sipped from his can of Pepsi. 'You mean everyone else? Theo and Georgina went off to shag, presumably. I think Sophie and Dominic went to fetch more alcohol.'

I checked my watch. I couldn't believe it: it was already eleven. I also realized, as I almost tripped over a tree trunk, that I was a lot drunker than I'd thought.

I waited, chatting distractedly with Eve and Rohan. I remember talking about the psychopath test we'd all taken a week ago. Rohan, with his naked desire to be a business tycoon, took offence when I said that a lot of CEOs were psychos. Eve talked more about her plan to move to London to get away from her toxic family. I half listened. I needed to find Sophie. To finally tell her how I felt.

'I can't put it off any longer,' I said, their reactions telling me I'd spoken aloud.

Eve gave me a hug. 'Good luck.'

'Yeah, good luck, mate.' Rohan got up too. 'I'm going for a slash.'

He went into the trees, and I staggered up the lawn, thrumming with energy and determination. This was it. I was going to do it. No holding back. You only live once, and life is short. I reached the house and went inside, realizing I needed a pee too, so I went to the bathroom on the ground floor, then headed to the kitchen, expecting to find Sophie there. No sign of her. In fact, there was no one around.

Had she gone to bed? Had I missed my chance? I was disgusted with myself. If I'd had a mobile phone I could have called or texted her to find out where she was, if she was asleep.

I went into the hallway and paused at the bottom of the staircase. If I'd been sober I probably would have grabbed more beer and gone back to find Rohan and Eve. But the alcohol that was already in my system propelled me upstairs. Along the corridor.

I stood outside Sophie's room. Hesitated for a second, then knocked lightly.

There was no response.

'Sophie?' I whispered, pressing my lips to the doorframe. Again, no reply.

I made a decision. I would go in and leave her a note. Put it on her pillow. Tell her I loved her, that she was the most amazing, gorgeous, funny, brilliant, sexy person I'd ever met and that if she liked me too I would be waiting in my room, that I would wait up all night for her.

I opened the door before I could change my mind and took a step inside.

It wasn't fully dark. A pair of candles burned on her dresser, casting yellow, flickering light against the walls, and revealing that the room wasn't empty.

Dominic sat on the bed.

We stared at each other in silence. He had that patented Dominic grin on his face, the one that – even in different circumstances – made me want to punch him. I couldn't move. All I could do was gawp in disbelief.

Then Sophie's voice came from the en suite. 'I won't be a moment.' A laugh. 'Hope you're still up for this.'

'Oh, I am,' he said, not breaking eye contact with me. At the same time, he reached into his pocket and pulled something out, holding it up for me to see.

A condom in its wrapper.

That was when I noticed the clothes Sophie had been wearing – her vest top and shorts – lying on the carpet. Dominic saw me notice. He winked at me.

I almost fell out of the room backwards. He must have stood up because, a second later, the door closed, and I heard Sophie's voice again, a low murmur, the way you talk to a lover.

I lurched down the hallway, convinced I was going to be sick. Dominic! How could she? Why *wouldn't* she? It was my own fault. I'd waited too long, been too much of a stupid chickenshit idiot. I'd blown it, and I was furious: with myself, but with her too. Dominic was *awful*. What was she thinking?

I was almost at the end of the hallway, unsure where I was going or what I was going to do, when a door opened.

Georgina appeared.

'Are you okay?' she asked. 'You look like someone just died.'

I couldn't speak.

'Do you want to come in for a minute? Tell me about it?'

Yes. That would help. Someone to talk to. I felt like someone had plugged me into the power grid. I followed her into her room.

'Where's Theo?' I asked.

She tutted. 'We went back to his room and he immediately passed out, drunk. Where's Sophie?'

'In her room. With Dominic.'

'Oh. That's not good.' Her eyes widened. 'You're crying.'

I hadn't realized until she said it.

'Come here.'

She pulled me into a hug, squeezed me tight. Her body was hot, like someone suffering with a fever. Her hands stroked my back and she whispered soothing words in my ear. 'It's okay. You'll be fine. She's not worth crying over.'

And that's when it happened. I don't know how it started; who started it. There were no more words exchanged. I'm pretty sure her eyes were closed. But we were kissing, and I felt her hands go to my fly, into my jeans, her fingers curling around me, and then we were on the bed, her skirt hitched up, underwear pulled to one side, and she pulled me against her and I was inside her. There was a book on the bed, a diary or journal, and I banged my head on it, grabbing it and throwing it aside.

It was over in two minutes. And I knew immediately I'd made a terrible mistake.

Chapter 35

'Wow.' Callum applauded, crossing the room and nudging Amber with his elbow. 'I wasn't expecting that. Were you? Looks like the main character in your book was going to be quite the lothario, Will.' He turned to Georgina. 'And you. Cheating on Theo. It's always the posh girls. You're a proper Lady Chatterley.'

The glare Georgina sent his way could have killed. 'Not that it's any of your business, but we hadn't even discussed being exclusive at that point.' She took in a deep breath. 'It actually made me realize how much I liked Theo. How I wanted it to be serious. It was a moment of madness which I regretted instantly. I'm pretty sure, from the way he almost ran out of my room, looking utterly horrified, that Will felt exactly the same.'

'That right, lover boy?' Callum said with a grin.

I ignored him and, instead, forced myself to look at Sophie. 'I'm sorry.'

I found it hard to read her expression. Shock? Disappointment? No, it was more . . . bemusement.

'Oh, Will. How could you?'

'I'm sorry, I shouldn't have—'

'I don't mean "how could you sleep with Georgina?" I mean, how could you think I screwed Dominic? He came to my room for a Tarot reading. That's all.'

I tried to speak, but nothing came out.

'I wouldn't have let him anywhere near me.'

That made Callum clap his hands together with glee.

Sophie went on. 'We got chatting about it when we were by the lake and you were dancing. He told me he was worried about the future and didn't know if he should stay living with Uncle Sebastian or move out. I told him the Tarot might be able to give him the answer. He whispered something about Eve too. Wanted to know if the cards would tell him if she liked him.' She rubbed at her forehead. 'I was pretty drunk, and you weren't showing any signs of making a move, so I told him I'd give him a reading.'

'It must have been a ruse. A way to get into your room.'

'I don't think so. I know he was a cynic about a lot of things, but he seemed to believe in the Tarot. He told me he was sure he'd seen his mum's ghost once, shortly after she was killed in that car crash, so he was open to that kind of thing.'

I could hear her unspoken words: *unlike you*.

'Also, he didn't really like me, not in that way. He pretended to in front of you because he liked winding you up, but when we were alone he showed no interest. He knew there was no chemistry. He was only interested in Eve.'

'So when you were in the bathroom . . .'

'I was probably getting changed. It was boiling, wasn't it? I would have been all sweaty from dancing.' She thought about it. 'Actually, I'd already been into the bathroom to get changed, had thrown my dirty clothes out, and went back in to do my ritual. I haven't read the Tarot for years, but I always used to have to psych myself up, get into the zone. It's something I could only do when I was on my own. Oh, Will, I cannot believe you thought I'd slept with him.'

But I had thought that. All these years, I'd believed it without question. I'd seen what that dark, insecure part of me had wanted to see – helped along, of course, by Dominic. Then I'd had sex with Georgina – for comfort, for revenge; I'd never really questioned why I'd done it – and the next morning . . . well, we had all gone our separate ways. I'd never had the chance to ask Sophie or Dominic about it.

'The next morning, when I told you you should get a phone, it was because I had been trying to find you. To tell you I wanted to talk to you.'

'What about?'

'What do you think, you idiot? I was sick of waiting for you to ask me out. But I couldn't find you so I went to bed.'

I couldn't believe what I was hearing. I couldn't do much about not having a phone in the summer of 1999. But the rest of it: if I hadn't jumped to conclusions. If I'd stayed to talk to this young woman I was besotted with. I knew now what she would have said.

I had well and truly blown it.

'Mate,' said Rohan.

'Where were you?' Sophie asked. 'I knocked on your door after Dominic left. Were you still with Georgina?'

'He was only with me for two minutes.' Georgina delivered her line drily, and Callum sniggered.

This was getting worse. 'After . . . what happened with Georgina . . . I went back to the kitchen to get more beer. Then I went to my room.'

'I must have just missed you.'

'I'm so sorry.'

'You don't need to apologize to *me* for sleeping with Georgina, Will.' Sophie looked over at our surviving host. 'Theo's the one you betrayed.'

Silence settled over us for a minute, until Callum said, 'I suppose it's a good thing old Theo wasn't around to hear your secret, Will.'

'Fuck you.' I clenched my fists.

Georgina lifted her chin, voice wobbling as she spoke. 'He would have forgiven me. And now you know my secret too.'

'We got a two-for-one,' Callum said. 'Plus some juicy entertainment. Shame, really.'

I braced myself. I knew what was coming. Beside Callum, Amber perked up, her eyes shining with the thrill of it all.

'I mean, as funny as it was to hear about old Will here getting the wrong end of the stick and realizing he blew it with the woman he loves, it's not the secret we're after.'

'Of course it isn't.' I got up from my chair and faced him. 'But it's the only secret I've got.'

'Me too,' whispered Georgina, also getting to her feet. 'What are you going to do to us? Because you don't need us any more, do you? We're eliminated from your stupid game.'

'You said it, sweetheart. Get over there.' Callum gestured to the far end of the room. A painting hung there: an abstract piece of art, black and white with a red streak across it. I pictured my own blood spattered there, crimson on top of crimson.

I didn't want to move. But I didn't want to die as Theo had, shot in the back, or Finn, lying on the floor, in pain. I was going to make Callum look me in the eye. Also: I had already disappointed Sophie tonight. If she was going to be there during my final moment, I didn't want to beg or embarrass myself. I needed her to see that, during the past twenty-five years, I had shed my chicken feathers and discovered courage.

I'd wasted twenty-five years when I could have been with her. Of course I knew the chances were our relationship wouldn't have worked out. But I hadn't even allowed us to have a chance.

If I was going to die in front of her, I was going to do so with dignity.

I crossed the room to the painting and stood with my back

to it, holding myself tall. Georgina hesitated for a second, then followed.

'Which one first?' Callum asked Amber.

'One each? Same time? I'll do our hostess.'

Georgina sneered at her. 'Just get it over with.'

I put my hands behind my back and swallowed hard. I was being brave, but my insides were liquid. At the table, Rohan was visibly shaking. Sophie, I was gratified to see, had tears spilling down her cheeks. Lily, again, was covering her face with her palms, unable to watch.

'Last chance,' Callum said as Amber stood beside him, and they both raised their guns. 'If either of you has another secret, now's the time to tell it. I'm going to count down again. Five. Four.'

I reached out to find Georgina's hand. I wanted to say something to her about how she'd soon be with Theo again, that I'd see her on the other side, but I didn't think she believed in any of that. I wondered if she was thinking about Olivia, knowing she was about to go to her grave without knowing what had happened to her. Perhaps she was worrying about her other daughter, Mia, oblivious at her sleepover. I glanced at her and saw that her chin was held high.

'Three.'

I met Sophie's eye and tried to smile, to reassure her, and realized that this was the moment to say it, to tell her, even though I thought she already knew.

'I still love you.'

Callum smiled. 'Two.'

I took in Sophie's face, more beautiful with age, with its lines and shadows. If this was the last thing I ever saw, that was fine. 'I should have told you I loved you back then.'

'Too late,' said Callum, flexing his finger on the trigger. 'Amber . . .'

She did the same, her gun aimed at Georgina's heart.

'One.'

I drew in a breath and closed my eyes and—

'Wait!'

A pause. I opened my eyes.

It was Lily. She was on her feet. Her face was wet with tears and her hands shook.

'It's me,' she said.

We all stared at her.

'Don't kill them. Please.' She said it again: 'It's me. I'm the one with the secret.'

Chapter 36

August 1999

Lily

When she left the others by the lake, Lily had only been intending to fix a bug that was bothering her, a minor glitch in the grand scheme of things but one that stopped her from being able to relax and enjoy herself. She would love to be able to let herself go – to drink and dance and laugh – but she had accepted a long time ago that this was part of who she was. Imperfections niggled. All she could see was that stray piece of code, the gremlin in the system.

So she'd come back to the office and booted up her PC, thinking it would only take fifteen minutes, thirty tops. After that, she'd rejoin the party and actually take the time to celebrate what she'd achieved. Because most of it, the creation of Butterfly Net, the beautiful algorithm that made it all work, was down to her, wasn't it? Yes, it had been the professor's idea. Theo had managed the project efficiently. The others had played their part, doing the stuff Lily found difficult – words and design and marketing. But she had always known she was the most important person here. Furthermore, she was doing this for other women in tech. The industry was so male, and although there were a few prominent women in the dotcom boom, they weren't coders. It was important for Lily, because she knew her work would undergo more scrutiny, that her work was flawless.

Of course, that meant that in the process of squashing one bug she found another, losing herself in the work, in the sweet satisfaction of fixing a problem, and when she looked up from her screen it was half midnight.

Great. She had missed the party.

But she wasn't tired now. Her brain was fully awake. And part of that was because there was something else she was dwelling on.

Earlier that afternoon, while she was waiting for a software update on the Butterfly Net beta site to complete, Lily had gone up to her room to do something she'd been intending to do all week, that the others had been hassling her about.

Check the results of the tests. See if she'd trapped any wasps.

She was frustrated with herself because, after testing everyone, she'd realized there was an error in the code that meant it wasn't interpreting the results correctly. It had taken several nights of thinking about it, exchanging messages with a couple of friends from the webdev message board she frequented, one in Texas, the other in South Korea. At one frustrating point she thought she might have to get everyone to resit the tests so she could try again with clean data, but, at three o'clock this morning, she'd had a revelation. She'd jumped out of bed, opened her laptop and worked until the sun was high in the sky. She'd fixed it. She went down to breakfast and a full day's work on Butterfly Net, leaving her laptop in her room processing the data and spitting it out. She had taken a printer to her room and instructed her computer to output the results as soon as they were complete.

At just after 4 p.m., she had sneaked upstairs to inspect the printouts, stomach fluttering with anticipation as she approached the printer. Eight sets of results sat in the tray: hers, her five colleagues', plus Dominic's and Eve's. As she'd explained to Will and everyone else who had taken the test, they had all been given a score. Above seventy-five meant that, according to the criteria in Robert Hare's book, and all the other research Lily had read and devised the program around, the subject was psychopathic. Of course, as with all tests of this kind, it would need to be backed up with observation, interviews and assessment over a longer period, but Lily truly believed her test was accurate. If someone scored over seventy-five, they were probably a psychopath. Over eighty, she didn't believe there was any doubt.

She didn't know what the results would be because, after conducting Will's test, treating him as a guinea pig because she was certain he was more ladybird than wasp, she had left the others to watch the video and answer the questions on their own. The only part she'd needed to be present for had been the verbal lie-detector section and, realizing she might influence the results via her reaction to where the needle landed on the meter, she hadn't looked at it; she'd let the computer record the readings using the program the nerds in town had told her about.

With a tingle of excitement, she had leafed through the printouts, each of which had the name of the subject at the top, a breakdown of each stage of the test, with a score from each, and then the overall result at the bottom of the page.

She looked at her own first. Sixty. Not low, but then she had always known she struggled a little with empathy and, yes, maybe she was a little egotistical. She was certainly sure of her own abilities. But not a psychopath.

She checked the other scores. Will's, at 31, was the lowest, as she had suspected. Eve's was low too, at just 33. Theo (58), Rohan (39), Georgina (49) and Sophie (38) were all in the middle. Theo's was quite high, but she had expected that. He had that slightly ruthless streak that attracted him to positions of power.

Finally, she came to Dominic's.

Eighty-three.

She drew in a sharp breath. She had suspected it. Of course she had. His borderline-gleeful reaction to his parents' deaths, driving around in the car they'd died in. The sadistic way he had burned the wasps' nest. His whole manner. He displayed very little warmth, had clear predatory inclinations, a huge ego and a cruel streak. She was not a professional psychologist but the more she read, the more she had become convinced that Dominic was going to score high.

Still, to see it there, in black and white. It made her go cold.

It also meant she had a quandary.

Despite her suspicions, she had clung to the belief that Dominic would come out the right side of the line. She certainly didn't think he would score *so* high. Now what was she supposed to do? She had created the test as a gift for Sebastian, and she couldn't present it to him without the sample tests, but how would he react if she showed him evidence that showed who his nephew really was?

Second, how would the rest of the group react? They had been clamouring for the results all week, and she couldn't lie and say it hadn't worked because she'd told them the results were on their way. How would they feel, knowing they were living with a psychopath? She thought Will would be particularly freaked out, especially as he disliked Dominic so much already. Also, how would Dominic react? He must already know he was different, and he might be furious that his cover was blown, his camouflage ripped away. Because that was one of the things that, according to the studies, many of his kind did. They went through life pretending to be normal.

Finally, there was a more fundamental ethical question. If she had uncovered a bona fide psychopath, did she have a responsibility to do something about it? To warn the world about him? Again, from her reading she knew not everyone with this disorder was dangerous; not criminally, anyway. There was plenty in the literature about how people who shared these traits became successful politicians or CEOs. Their lack of conscience made it easier for them to climb ladders. There were theories that many of the most powerful people in the world were psychopaths, and some of them were able to do more damage than their criminal counterparts.

But even if someone didn't become a CEO or a world leader or a serial killer, they could do plenty of damage to the people around them. The co-workers from hell. The nightmare neighbour. The toxic spouse. All the seemingly ordinary citizens who cause havoc and harm wherever they go. Many of them became parents, creating a world of misery for their children.

Dominic could easily be one of these people. But although Lily didn't believe someone with psychopathy should be put on a register, forced to live their life as if they were already guilty, she also knew she would want to know if a predator was coming her way.

It was all so confusing, and she needed to talk to someone about it. There was only one candidate in this house. Sophie. But then, that afternoon, Lily had been drawn straight back into working on Butterfly Net, and the party had kicked off immediately after that, and Lily hadn't been able to get Sophie on her own. The task was made even harder by Will, who had spent the early part of the party giving Sophie meaningful, moony glances. Realizing he was trying to get Sophie on her own too, Lily had given up. She needed to work. She'd shown her face at the party; it was more important to squash that bug.

Now that was done. It was half midnight. And as she got up from her PC, wired and wide awake, Lily's thoughts returned to the results of her test.

What was she going to do? Now, finally, she might be able to find Sophie – assuming she wasn't in bed with Will. Knowing how he'd been earlier, she thought that was unlikely. He'd still be trying to gather the courage.

She tried Sophie's room first, rapping on the door. No reply. She thought about trying Will's room, in case she was there, but she really didn't want to disturb them if a miracle had happened and they were having sex. She would check downstairs first.

There was no one in the kitchen. Faintly, she heard the noise of a TV and went to the sitting room, where she found Rohan, watching that football match he was obsessed with, a can of Pepsi in his hand. He startled when he saw her.

'I can't sleep,' he said, raising the can. 'Too many of these.'

'Have you seen Sophie anywhere?'

'Not for hours. Will went to look for her but didn't come back.' A pause. 'He was pretty wasted.'

She turned to go, then paused in the doorway. Rohan was acting strangely. Shifty.

'What is it?' he asked. Yeah, he was definitely acting like he was up to something.

'You seem nervous.'

She could tell he was making a great effort to appear normal. 'Do I? I told you – too much caffeine. It makes me jittery. Also, this part of the match . . . No matter how many times I watch it, it gets my blood pumping.'

Lily squinted at the screen. There were five minutes to go and the team in red appeared to be losing. Rohan had turned back to the TV, leaning towards the screen as if he'd never seen the match before.

She went outside. The air was warm, the gentlest of breezes stroking her skin. Could Sophie be down by the lake? It was worth checking. And maybe a walk in the night air would do her good. The sky was clear, alive with a million stars, and the moon hung like a lamp, illuminating the estate, so it was easy to find her way down towards the woods.

She heard the noise as soon as she entered the woods. Low voices, one male, one female. Sophie and Will? They were too faint for her to tell. She followed the path, the moonlight penetrating the trees just enough for her to see where she was going. The trees were dense either side of her, in full foliage, the ground baked hard beneath her feet. It was pleasingly cool here, the air a little fresher. Ahead of her, somewhere to the left, she could hear murmuring. The male voice speaking for a while, then a short response from the woman, then back to the male.

She was wary again. What if she came across two naked bodies writhing in the moonlight? It would be *so* embarrassing. Perhaps she should turn—

She didn't get the chance to decide. Because suddenly the female voice went from a murmur to a cry of protest – a clear 'No!' – and then a male cry of pain, followed immediately by the sound of thrashing in the trees ahead of where Lily stood.

A woman emerged, about fifteen metres ahead of Lily. Lily was about to call out – get the woman's attention – but everything happened too fast. In the next second, the man appeared out of the trees, reaching out to grab the woman, who shouted again and ran.

Now Lily could see who it was. Eve and Dominic.

He chased after Eve, sprinting towards the lake.

Later, Lily would ask herself why she didn't yell and let them know she was there. The truth was, she was afraid. Only hours had passed since she had discovered Dominic's true nature. She was so used to using logic, thinking through everything step by step, relying on her intellect to guide her through life. But here, suddenly, her body had taken over, and fear and shock froze her brain, stilled her tongue.

By the time she was able to move again they were out of sight. She heard them before she saw them. Eve was shouting.

'I'm going to tell everyone. Tell your uncle. No, get away from me!'

'Eve, come on. I was messing around, that's all.' He was panting.

They came into view. They were both standing on the very edge of the lake, silhouetted against the water, moonlight rippling across its surface.

'No you weren't. Everyone's going to hear about this. I'm going to show them. Look, you ripped my dress.'

'You scratched me.'

'Yeah. This blood is yours. Everyone is—'

It happened in a moment. A blur. Eve's voice went up several octaves on her final word as, in one swift motion, Dominic stooped to grab something from the path. A thick, broken piece of branch.

He swung it. Struck Eve on the side of the head.

Lily didn't think. She sprang into motion, rushing at Dominic, launching herself at him. This was instinct. The need to do something, to save Eve, to stop this man, this psychopath, all thoughts for her own safety vanishing.

She crashed into his back and, having not seen or heard her coming, he went down on his front, into the water, which was just deep enough to cover his head and shoulders. He was still for a second. Lily could just make out a dark shape beneath the water, beside his head. A rock. Later, she realized he must have struck it and been knocked unconscious for a second. But now he was awake again, and struggling, trying to push himself up,

282

but she was kneeling on his back, her hands on the rear of his shoulders, pinning him down, and his arms were trapped behind him, so all he could do was attempt to rock from side to side. There was water in her eyes so she could hardly see, and there was a terrible noise which – she realized – was her, roaring. Dominic was silent, unable to make any sound, trying to turn his head. Behind her, Lily could sense Eve, present but absent, and then Dominic went still too.

You can save him, said a voice in her head. *Pull him out of the water.*

And in return, another voice said, *But he's a psychopath.*

He had just attacked – killed? – a woman. He was extremely dangerous. A predator by nature. The test had proven it: he wasn't wired like other people. He didn't have a conscience. If he thought he could get away with it, he would hurt people. Hurt more women.

Save him, said the first voice, the one that had urged her to pull his face from the water. *He's going to rot in jail, anyway.*

But would he? Look at where he lived, the car he drove. He'd be able to afford a great lawyer. She'd seen it so many times in the news and on TV: rich men walking free after murdering women. Even if he went to prison, think of the havoc he could cause. He could manipulate guards and other prisoners. He would be sure to behave well, get an early release. He'd be free again. Free to destroy lives. Maybe – probably – he would even come after Lily.

All this flashed through her head in a second.

He had scored eighty-three. He couldn't be rehabilitated. He would always be a threat.

So she left him lying there while she pushed herself up and crawled over to Eve, wiping the lake water from her own eyes and checking Eve's pulse. Nothing. Eve lay there, eyes still open, unblinking, blood matted in her hair. She was clearly, undoubtedly, dead.

Lily got to her feet. Afterwards, she didn't remember the walk back to the house. She didn't recall skirting the woods, passing the burned-out remains of the wasps' nest, crossing the lawn. She didn't remember going back into the house. The next thing she remembered was knocking on Sebastian's door, almost falling into the room. He was still up, still dressed, a book lying face down on the couch.

'Slowly, come on, breathe. Tell me.'

It all came rushing out. Sebastian loved her, she knew that. She was his favourite. He'd told her so many times she was the best student he'd ever taught. His genius. The daughter he'd never had. She didn't tell him how she'd had the chance to pull Dominic from the water, that she'd wrestled with her conscience. She made it sound like she'd pushed him once, he'd gone down and struck his head and she'd rushed back here immediately.

But she did tell him about the test, all of it coming out in a jumble, so he had to keep getting her to stop and repeat herself.

When she told him about Dominic's score she saw a look come into the professor's eyes. He wasn't surprised. Perhaps he even looked a little angry with himself for not spotting it. Or perhaps it confirmed something he already suspected.

It didn't matter. What mattered was what he did next.

'It's going to be all right, Lily,' he said. See, she was his favourite. He did love her. 'I want you to go back to your room, change out of these wet clothes and put them in the washing machine. Then stay in your room.'

He had touched her on the shoulder, told her to stay calm. 'It's going to be all right, Lily,' he said. 'I'll deal with it.'

Chapter 37

'I didn't sleep. I spent the whole night reading through my papers about psychopaths, trying to justify it to myself. Telling myself I'd made the right decision. I kept thinking that the professor would come to my room and tell me what he'd done and what was going to happen. I was frantic with worry, half convinced he was going to call the police. And then the next morning . . .'

I finished Lily's sentence. While Lily had been talking, Callum had gestured for Georgina and me to retake our seats. 'He sent us all home.'

'Yes. When I came downstairs Sebastian was arguing with Theo in the hallway. Theo was saying he didn't understand, that if there was a problem surely it only needed some more tweaking and testing, and Sebastian just kept repeating that he'd made his mind up. He told Theo – who was so hung-over his skin had a green tinge – to go and wake everyone up. Sebastian had already ordered taxis to take us all home. Separately.'

I remembered. The cars hadn't taken us to the station. They'd driven us all the way home.

'So it *was* your fault.' Rohan spat the words at Lily. 'I thought it was because you'd fucked up the algorithm. But this . . .'

Lily spat back. 'Dominic murdered Eve. I think that was a little more important than you not getting your share options.'

He shut his mouth, chastened.

It was all so clear in my memory. The confusion. The

285

disbelief. When Theo had come to my room and – looking like he might puke, cry or both – told me to pack my bag I thought he must have found out about Georgina and me, that she'd woken up and, racked with guilt, confessed. Thank God, I'd thought when I realized that wasn't the case, I hadn't blurted out an apology.

I had been relieved, in my callow way, not to have to see Georgina. Sophie too . . . well, actually, I'd been torn. But then, when I was in the taxi, she came up and gestured for me to wind the window down.

'What happened?' she had asked. 'Last night? Where were you?'

I had stared at her, fifty per cent ashamed and fifty per cent angry. 'What do you care?'

She furrowed her brow.

'You didn't seem to care where I was or what I was doing last night.'

She started to say something, then stopped. I guess my expression – that mix of fury and shame – made her lose the will to explain. 'You need to get yourself a phone.'

'Whatever,' I said, and the taxi pulled away. Tears pricked my eyes and I was instantly filled with regret. I should have stopped the cab, got out, run back to her. But I did nothing.

My God, I had been an idiot on so many levels.

'What happened with Dominic's Tarot reading?' Rohan asked now. 'I'm trying to get my head around the timeline here. He was in your room between eleven and twelve, right? When Will was shagging Georgina.'

I hardly reacted. After what Lily had just told us my and Georgina's secret seemed unimportant.

'Yeah, I don't remember the exact timing, but he must have been with me for about forty minutes. He asked if the cards would tell him what would happen with Eve.'

286

'And?'

'Oh God. I remember laying down the Two of Cups. That indicates a new union. The Lovers card was in the spread too. Mutual attraction. I think I'm going to be sick.'

I recalled now that Sophie had read Eve's cards a week or so before this. Eve had been excited, saying the Tarot had fore-seen an exciting future for her. Escape, and travel. I imagined Sophie was remembering the same thing.

Her voice cracked as she spoke. 'He left around midnight. He was bouncing like fucking Tigger.' To Lily, she said, 'So Sebastian didn't say anything to you? About Dominic and Eve, I mean? He didn't tell you what he'd done with the, you know, the bodies?'

'No. He came to my room later that night and we talked, well, business.' I could tell that this part of it, almost as much as everything else, still caused her pain. 'We all know what happened the next morning, and I went along with it, when I should have gone to the police, handed myself in. And then . . .' Lily's eyes were wet. 'I got Theo's email about Dominic. Sebastian had already told me he was going to wait a few days before telling you all Dominic was dead. He wanted to ensure you were all settled back at your homes and were unlikely to come rushing back, though I told him none of us had been good friends with Dominic, that even Rohan had fallen out with him.'

I was barely aware that Callum and Amber were there. All I cared about was the group. My old friends. The survivors of that summer. We had all listened to Lily with open mouths, with gasps of shock, but we'd all had so many questions we hadn't quite taken it in – until now.

'Sebastian covered up a murder,' I said. In the plan I'd written for my book about that summer, I'd been planning on hinting that my fictional professor had a dark past – I'd been mulling over making him somehow complicit in the murder of his wife; that seemed like the kind of twist that would surprise readers – but I could never have invented something like this.

'I'm not shocked,' said Georgina.

'Really?'

She shrugged. 'Sebastian always had a darkness about him. His obsession with psychopaths. I mean, talk about a red flag.'

'His wife was killed by one.'

'Remember how Eve told us he'd come back from Boston suddenly, under a cloud,' Sophie said, her voice quiet. 'And he could be horrible, couldn't he? Stomping around, shouting at us about mess and deadlines.'

'I know, but . . . covering up a murder?'

'It was his nephew,' Rohan said. 'Wouldn't you do the same for one of your relatives? I would. If it was my son. I'd do anything . . .'

Now was not the time to think about this turnaround in Rohan's priorities – earlier, he hadn't even wanted to call his kids to say goodnight – because I was busy trying to figure out how I would answer his question. The truth was, I didn't know. I wasn't close to my nephews or nieces and I didn't have kids. But it was believable that Sebastian would do it. Awful, but understandable. Except . . . Dominic was dead. It was Lily he had been protecting.

We all turned back to look at her.

'I loved him,' she said. 'You knew that, though. The way I used to defend him. And I think he loved me too, like the daughter he might have had if Barbara had lived.'

A tear rolled down her cheek. 'You know, I locked myself away for months. Barely ate. Barely slept. I kept expecting the police to turn up, but they never did. I'd killed someone. Whether or not Dominic deserved it didn't matter. I'll never forget that noise, when he hit her. And the blood. The end of the stick he used was coated with it. I couldn't—'

Georgina interrupted her. 'You lied. About Eve moving to London.'

Lily couldn't meet her eye. 'I killed someone. I've had to live with that my whole life. Worse – I failed to save her. If I'd called out. If I hadn't frozen.' She sucked in a breath. 'I couldn't talk to anyone about it. Couldn't go to a therapist or even, later, confide in my wife. The only way I could cope with it was to deny to myself that it had ever happened. To invent this alternative future – not for Dominic, but for Eve. I was reading a lot of quantum physics at the time. Multiverse theories. I started to believe that we were living in a different timeline, that I'd saved her and she got the future she wanted. Getting away from her family. Coming to London.'

But Georgina was not sympathetic: 'You've sat here all evening, knowing you were the one with the big secret. How could you do that? If it wasn't for you, Theo would be alive.'

Lily hung her head, tears dripping into her lap. I didn't know what to think, how to feel. Georgina was right, in a way. If Lily had spilled her secret straight away, the whole evening would have gone differently.

'Or maybe we'd all be dead already,' I said, looking at Callum, seeing how the corner of his lip curled up, a twitch of amusement. He'd told me that whoever was alive when the secret was revealed would walk out of here. But that was before I'd seen him murder two men. How could I still believe that?

'So what happens?' I asked him. 'Now you've got what you came for?'

He smiled fully, putting the shotgun over his shoulder and walking a semicircle in front of the table where we all sat. Amber was over by the window. She seemed frustrated. Was she itching to put an end to this? To get on with the massacre?

'I'm very glad Lily felt able to speak up,' Callum said. 'But . . . well, do you want to tell them, Amber?'

She stepped forward and regarded all of us in turn.

'It's not what we're after,' she said.

'What?' Several of us said it at the same time.

'It's not the secret.'

Callum left the room without saying another word. We waited in silence, too shocked to speak. Downstairs, I heard a clicking noise, the sudden sound of traffic from the street. A change in air pressure. Then footsteps.

Was that more than one person, coming up the stairs?

Callum entered the dining room first, followed seconds later by another man. He was bald and stocky, with greyish skin. Another stranger.

Until I looked at his vivid blue eyes and the cruel shape of his mouth as he smiled and said, 'What happened to my invite?'

It was Dominic.

Part Three

Chapter 38

Mia

Someone else had come into the house. She felt the change in air pressure, the rumbling of male voices below, heavy footsteps on the stairs beneath her. Claude felt it too: he jumped to his feet, tail puffing out like a dog had just walked in.

It brought Mia to her senses. She had been paralysed, trying to remember what was niggling at her and attempting to figure out how she could escape. Sitting here in Olivia's room wasn't doing anyone any good. What if they were about to ransack the house? To search for valuables? Staying in one spot was making her itchy. She needed to move. And if she couldn't go down, she would have to go up.

Mum and Dad's room.

Slowly, silently, she pushed open Olivia's bedroom door and checked there was no one around, then turned left towards the staircase that led up to what had once been the attic. It had been converted into a suite – a bedroom and bathroom – a long time ago. Mia tiptoed up the stairs and into the bedroom, with its sloping ceilings and exposed brickwork, gently pushing the door closed behind her.

When she was really little, Mia had come up here a lot, bouncing on the king-size bed, playing hide and seek in Mum's gigantic wardrobe. But then, when she was around four, Mum and Dad had installed a fancy new bathroom, and suddenly Mia and Olivia, who was eight by then, weren't allowed up here any more. 'It's our private space,' Mum had said, and, to be honest, Mia hadn't really cared, though she knew in later years the teenage Olivia had sneaked up sometimes to borrow a squirt of expensive perfume or to steal one of the many fancy candles Mum kept in the bathroom.

As soon as she entered the room Mia checked the windows, wondering if it would be possible to get on to the roof. But as she peered through into the darkness of the night she quickly realized she would likely plummet to her death if she tried. And even if she could get on to the flat part of the roof, what good would it do her?

She wandered into the bathroom, wondering if she might be able to find a weapon, something she could use as protection if the intruders found her. But there were just the plastic razors the whole family used.

She went into the wardrobe where Mum kept all her designer clothes and shoes and bags. There were no weapons in here either, although she briefly had the absurd image of herself trying to fight off the shotgun-toting redhead with a Burberry handbag.

She heard a chirrup behind her. Claude had followed her. He slunk past her legs to the far side of the wardrobe, stretching out his paws to claw at the shoe rack.

Mum would be—

And that's when it came to her. What she'd been trying to remember.

Olivia, yelling at Claude:

It's your fault.

Olivia had said something else too, just before that. What was it? It came to her quickly: *I wish I hadn't gone in there.*

'Gone in where?' she whispered to the cat. Could she have

meant in here? Mum and Dad's bedroom? Olivia had always been paranoid about Claude going missing. He'd stayed out for three nights once, and Olivia had been frantic. If she didn't see him for a couple of hours she would search the house for him.

All this would have been meaningless if it hadn't triggered another memory. One from further back, when Olivia was still with Felix.

One afternoon, a month or two before Felix had dumped Olivia, Mia had overheard the two of them in the house when Mum and Dad were out. Mia remembered it clearly because it was obvious the two of them had just *done it*. Olivia's hair was all messy and Felix was swaggering around, looking at the portraits, inspecting the artworks with this sneer on his face. 'It's so bourgeois,' he said at least twice. 'Even your cat has a posh name.'

'I know,' Olivia had said, in a voice Mia didn't recognize, like she was trying to sound like she hadn't gone to private school. 'It's so cringe.'

Then Felix had said, 'Do you really think it exists?' Mia had heard him tapping the walls. 'It does sound kind of hollow.'

'I think that writer made it up to sound more interesting.'

'That's a shame. If it exists, there might be treasure in there.'

'Or thousands of spiders, more like.'

Hold on. Was that what she meant when she said, *I wish I hadn't gone in there?*

Olivia and Mia had only been six and two when their parents had bought this house. Mia remembered that when she was about five, and Olivia nine, Dad had told them about the mythical secret passage, and said he would give a prize to whoever found it first. But after weeks of searching, of looking in cupboards and behind bookcases, they had concluded it was just a story.

But what if the 'there' Olivia had been talking about *was* the secret passage?

For the time being, she parked the question of why going 'in there' had caused Olivia so much distress. Because right now, the important thing was this: if the passage existed, it might be her way out of here. A way to get downstairs and, hopefully, out of the house.

She crouched and whispered to the cat: 'Did you find the secret passage? Is that why it's your fault?'

He blinked at her.

Okay, she wasn't going to get any help from Claude. But she was sure she was on to something. The passage could be real.

All she had to do was find the entrance.

Chapter 39

Dominic was alive.

Lily was staring at him like her brain had short-circuited, as if, after a lifetime of scepticism, an actual ghost had just entered the room – although if this had been a spirit, I didn't think it would look like this: middle-aged, sallow, bald. His ghost would still be good-looking, youthful, with that floppy hair that made him look like a nineties Brideshead resident.

Out of all of us, Dominic's appearance had changed the most, and it wasn't just his physical features, the extra weight, the hair loss. It was his entire demeanour.

Gone was the perma-smirk, the God's-gift strut. There was little trace of that arrogant young man, the one I was convinced Sophie had fancied.

Despite his initial wisecrack about not being invited to the dinner party, this Dominic looked extremely pissed off to be here. Angry not just with us but with Callum too.

The first thing he did after entering the room and making the dinner-party comment was turn to Callum and say, 'You told me this would be easy.'

Callum immediately went into self-defence mode. 'Yeah, well. You didn't tell me what your friends are like. I'm starting to think this secret doesn't exist.'

'It does! He wouldn't have made it up.'

Who was 'he'? It had to be Sebastian, surely.

I looked around. Everyone was shocked, but none of us

looked as stunned as Lily. The rest of us had only heard about Dominic's death in an email. Lily thought she'd killed him. It must have been like seeing someone rise from the dead.

Dominic crossed the room to the window, where Amber stood. How had he got through the front door? Presumably Callum had been able to bring the security system out of the lockdown mode he'd put it into. I had to assume he'd locked everything down again after letting Dominic in.

I was growing numb to shocks, but when Dominic pulled Amber into an embrace and hugged her, planting a kiss on her lips, my jaw dropped. I thought of Callum kissing Amber in the hallway. But she was with Dominic? Now, that was interesting.

Dominic let go of Amber and came back towards the table. He seemed to take in his surroundings for the first time.

'You've done well for yourself,' he said to Georgina. 'Of course you have. Though it looks like your cleaner's going to have her work cut out clearing this mess up.' He wiped his slick forehead with his fingers. 'I'm sorry we had to kill Theo.'

'*Had* to,' said Georgina, glaring at him with fury.

He took another step towards her. 'All you needed to do was reveal the secret. Whichever one of you has it. Nobody had to die.'

Behind him, Callum raised his eyebrows.

'So come on, then,' Dominic said. 'Who's going to confess?'

We were all quiet.

'I told you,' said Callum. 'It's like trying to get blood—'

Dominic interrupted him with a roar. '*Fuck!*' He marched back over to Amber and said, 'Give me the gun.' She handed it over and he turned back to the table, pointing the barrel at each of us in turn. I had started the evening wondering if Finn was a psychopath, was almost certain Callum must be one – but here was someone who we knew to be psychopathic, and he had a shotgun in his hands.

'Come on!' he shouted. 'Who is it? Are we going to have to start torturing you all?'

Nobody spoke.

Dominic addressed Callum. 'Who hasn't spilled any secrets yet?'

'Rohan and Sophie.'

The barrel of the shotgun swung towards Rohan. Instinctively, he put both hands up, level with his shoulders. 'It's not me. I swear.'

Dominic narrowed his eyes, and Rohan said, 'Mate. What happened to you? Where have you been? We thought you were dead.'

Of course, they had been friends back at Thornwood. The two lads: the ones who liked football and cars and who thought the indie music I listened to was for wimps. I felt a flare of hope. Perhaps Rohan could get through to Dominic, even if he had scored eighty-three on Lily's test. Maybe we all could. Callum and Amber were strangers to us, but we all had history with Dominic. Even if I had hated him at the time, we had a connection, and the way he was looking at Rohan, the gun trembling in his hands, made me wonder. Perhaps he did feel some affection for his fellow Man United fan, in the same way psychopaths can like cats and dogs.

Then Georgina interrupted the moment:

'Do you know where my daughter is?'

Dominic, and the gun, turned several degrees towards her. She was still at the end of the table. Still glaring.

'No, Georgina,' he said. 'I don't have a clue. But she kind of started all of this.'

'What?'

'The detective you sent to look for her. It's because of him . . .' He trailed off.

Georgina shot out of her chair. 'What are you talking about?'

'The detective. Finn.'

'Someone else you *had* to kill,' said Sophie.

He glanced at Callum. 'That wasn't part of the plan.'

I don't think Dominic saw Callum's reaction to this. The little shake of the head. The curl of the lip.

'Aren't you going to answer Georgina's question?' Sophie asked. 'If you know anything about where Olivia is . . .'

'Yes.' Georgina looked like she might throw up. 'Please.'

'I told you, I don't know anything about that.'

'Come on—'

'Shut up!' He yelled again, rubbing his face as his shout echoed around the dining room. 'Jesus Christ, none of you are any less irritating, are you? I have absolutely no idea where your brat is, Georgina, and frankly, I don't care.'

'Maybe you should care,' I said. 'Because she might be the person who knows the secret you're after.'

'What?' He seemed utterly confused by this. 'No, it's one of you. Uncle Sebastian told me.'

'He told you one of us has a secret?'

'Yes.'

'But not who? Or what the secret is?'

A shake of the head.

I went on: 'Did he not even tell you what it's related to?'

He didn't reply, and for the first time since Dominic had entered the room Lily spoke up.

'How?' she said. 'How are you even alive?'

Dominic smirked. 'Wouldn't you like to know?'

'For fuck's sake.' For a second I thought Callum was going to punch Dominic in the face. 'Just tell them. We need to shake this secret loose.'

'He's right,' said Amber, stroking Dominic's upper arm. 'It might help. Go on, baby.'

Callum's expression almost made me laugh.

'Go on,' Amber said again, and Dominic – making his mind up – smiled. It was another glimpse of the old him.

'All right,' he said. He pointed at Lily. 'A lesson for you: if you think you've killed someone, always double-check before you run off and leave the body.'

Chapter 40

August 1999

Dominic

He came to – and tried to breathe. Instead of air, his mouth and nostrils were flooded with water. In that split second, his body sent signals to his brain from every direction. His shoulders told him his arms were positioned behind his back. His chest and belly told him he was lying flat on his front. There was a pain emanating from his skull that was unlike anything he'd ever known. And his face, his eyes and lips and nose, were performing the corporeal equivalent of a wailing red alert. Move. Now. Move. *Now.*

He managed to roll on to his side and lift his head free of the water, gasping and sucking at the air, then coughing and retching as he got up on to all fours. His knees were on dry land, his hands and wrists in the lake, the tip of his nose inches from the surface as he spluttered and spat.

When he'd finally stopped coughing he hauled himself fully on to the bank and sat there, shivering even though the night was still warm. Most of the pain appeared to be coming from a spot on his hairline and, tentatively, he touched it, wincing at the sting and staring at the blood that clung to his fingertips.

What had happened?

It didn't come back to him until he saw the shape lying there in the moonlight.

He got up on his knees to get a better look. Eve had her back to him, but he knew who it was. Of course he did. And it all came rushing back. What he'd done.

He just didn't understand what had happened next. Who had crashed into him, sent him plummeting into the water.

Nor did he have any idea what he was going to do next.

He had killed a woman. And somebody, whoever it was who had pushed him into the lake, must have witnessed it.

His instinct was to run. Get to his car. Go far away. But he didn't even have his car key with him, let alone his wallet. Could he get to his room, get changed and pack a bag, grab everything? He could head for Dover, which wasn't far, get out of England through the Channel Tunnel or on a ferry before morning. Then what? Phrases like 'extradition treaty' and 'border checks' made the throbbing in his head worsen like someone had whacked it with a hammer.

He was well and truly fucked.

Maybe it wouldn't be too bad in prison. It might not be any worse than boarding school, anyway. He might get a pleasant cellmate and the screws might respect him and treat him well because of his accent and . . .

Ah, who was he kidding? They'd call him Posh Boy and kick the crap out of him every day. They would—

His imagination stopped spinning. There was a noise in the trees. Footsteps on the path. Someone was coming.

Dominic didn't get the chance to scramble up from where he was sitting and hide before the person appeared.

Uncle Sebastian. Dominic blinked, wondering if the blow to his head was making him hallucinate, but no, Uncle Seb really was pushing a bicycle. Eve's bike.

His uncle saw him sitting there and froze.

'Well. It appears news of your death was exaggerated.' He came closer, inspected the wound on Dominic's head. He seemed thoughtful, like he'd just had an idea. Some academic shit, no doubt. 'Lily thought she'd killed you.'

Lily. So that's who had pushed him into the water. That *nerd* had almost killed him? He opened his mouth but found he couldn't speak. All he could do was watch as Uncle Seb lay the bicycle down carefully, then crouched beside Eve, checking her pulse, looking into her eyes. He shook his head and sighed, then got to his feet.

'She *is* dead. My God, Dominic. What a clusterfuck this is. She lives in the village, yes?'

Dominic gawped at him.

Sebastian marched over, bent down and slapped his cheek, hard. Dominic couldn't believe it. No one had hit him since his father had died. Since he'd left boarding school and the bullies and the masters behind. He stared up at his uncle, the pain reverberating through his head.

'Wake up! Do you want me to hit you again? No? Good. Now, tell me about this girl. Does she have a boyfriend?'

'No.'

'Oh, you *can* speak. Good. What about her family? Does she still live with them?'

All Eve ever did was talk about how much she hated her folks. Her neglectful parents, her slacker siblings. How she was planning to move to London after this summer and didn't plan to ever speak to them again. 'They won't miss me,' she had told everyone.

Still in a daze, and finding it hard to get the words out in the correct order, he conveyed all this to his uncle.

'Well, that's good,' Sebastian said, looking down at the body. 'She disappears, and everyone will assume she moved away. It sounds like her family won't even bother looking for her.'

'They definitely won't report her missing.'

'Good. Good.' Sebastian tilted his head to one side and stroked his chin. 'Were you thinking all that when you did it? That she would be easy to murder because no one cared about her? Yes, that sounds right. Clever. Calculating.'

What was he talking about?

'Tell me, do you feel any remorse? Did you feel your heart rate increase as you swung the weapon?' He waved a hand. 'Don't answer. There'll be plenty of time to go over this. Come on. I need you to fetch the rowing boat. Get up.'

Sebastian helped Dominic to his feet. The boat was about twenty metres along the shore, at the spot where the group usually gathered. They'd been playing music and dancing there only a couple of hours ago. With his head still throbbing, and with pains in his back and shoulders, he made his way to the boat and dragged it along the waterline. Only panic and adrenaline were keeping him going.

While he did this, Sebastian crouched close to Eve. Dominic couldn't work out what he was doing until he got closer and saw that he had removed the thin leather belt she had been wearing around her jeans.

'Help me get her into the boat.'

It wasn't easy. Even though she was small and skinny, death seemed to have doubled her weight. It wasn't just that. Touching her, feeling how cold she was, made him want to vomit. He had done this. Eve would never get to achieve her dream of moving to London. At least, he supposed, she was free of her family now. She would never grow old. She had died quickly, without pain.

They dropped the body into the rowing boat, less gently than either of them had intended. She lay in the damp base of the boat on her back, hidden mercifully by shadows. Dominic stood by the water's edge as his uncle went over and lifted the bike, bringing it over and putting it into the rowing boat, on top of Eve. Then he knelt beside her and used the belt to attach the bike to Eve's body.

'That should hold,' he said. 'A lot easier than using rocks to weigh her down. We don't want her floating to the top.' He stepped out of the boat. 'Right, go on then. Take her to the centre of the lake, the deepest point, and push her into the water.'

And so he did. He climbed into the boat, the body and the bike taking up most of the space and making it difficult to move the oars. But it actually felt good to concentrate on something physical for a few minutes. Pulling the handles of the oars towards him, gliding across the dark water in the moonlight. The lake wasn't huge and it didn't take long to reach the centre. He stopped rowing and pulled the oars into the boat, then looked down at the tangle of flesh and metal before him. Was he going to be strong enough to get her into the water without capsizing the boat?

Somehow, he managed it. Eve and her bicycle plunged into the water, sinking and disappearing from sight immediately.

He sat there for a few seconds, waiting for his pulse to slow down, then rowed back to shore and his uncle and whatever fate awaited him.

Chapter 41

'You dumped her in the lake.' Sophie's voice was strained. 'Is she still there? Twenty-five years later?'

Dominic nodded. 'You don't need to look at me like that. I feel shit about it.'

'No you don't.' That was Lily. 'People like you, they're not capable.'

Dominic took a menacing step towards her. 'That's what you think, isn't it? Because of that stupid test.'

'It wasn't stupid.'

'Oh, it was, Lily. That fucking test ruined my life.'

'What are you talking about?'

He handed the shotgun back to Amber. They were such a mismatched couple. She was striking, with that red hair and her sharp cheekbones, her English-rose complexion, while he looked like any average middle-aged bloke: puffy and gone to seed.

He patted her on the bum, his hand lingering for a moment. She didn't react at all, but I watched Callum's face. Disgust. Jealousy, perhaps? What exactly was the dynamic here?

'Tell them,' Amber said. 'Tell them what it's been like for you all these years.'

Dominic removed his hand from her backside and grabbed the chair Theo had been sitting in at the start of the meal, sitting in it like he was joining us for dinner.

'Wait,' I said. 'What happened that night? After you . . . after what you did with Eve?'

'Uncle Seb sent me back to the house. He told me to ensure no one saw me. He said not to worry about you, Lily. That he'd already told you to go to your room and wait for him to deal with everything. He said he wanted to check around, make sure there was no evidence left. That Eve hadn't dropped anything. I just remember sitting on my bed, shivering, thinking, *What have I done?*'

'Self-pity,' said Sophie. 'Worried you were going to jail.'

'Of course I was scared about that. But I felt awful about Eve too. Like, I couldn't understand what had got into me. What made me do it.'

'Come off it,' Sophie said. 'Lily told us. Eve rejected you. You got angry, like so many men before and since. Then she frightened you by saying she was going to expose you. It doesn't take a genius to know why you did it.'

Dominic's response surprised me. 'I can't even explain what happened. It was like – like something took possession of my body. I was wasted. Drunk and high. I don't think any of you knew how badly messed up I was by everything that had happened in my life. My parents. The school they sent me to. I was lost, and none of you even realized it. I was filled with remorse. I liked Eve.'

'This is bullshit,' Lily said, addressing the rest of us. She could hardly bring herself to look at the man she thought she'd killed. 'He's incapable of remorse. Maybe regret, but that's purely self-preservation. His crime is exactly the kind of thing someone who fits his profile would do. He would have felt enraged because Eve wouldn't give him what he wanted. What he believed he was owed. Then, when she threatened to tell everyone, he would have been alarmed. Sebastian told me that the most dangerous psychopaths spend their lives trying to blend in. They have this need for people to think they're normal because it makes everything easier for them.' She paused. It was almost like she was talking to herself. 'Although I'm wondering if that applies with Dominic. I don't think he knew he was a psychopath at that point.'

Dominic sneered. 'You really were Sebastian's mini-me, weren't you, Lily? I've heard all this shit from him. Over twenty years of it, starting that night. Do you know what happened after we hid Eve's body? Uncle Seb came to my room and told me, first of all, that he was going to shut down Butterfly Net. You all know that. He couldn't have anyone wondering where Eve had gone, asking questions, trying to find her. But also, I think he suddenly became sick of it, lost interest. He had something new, something that was far more interesting to him.'

'The wasp trap,' Lily whispered.

'Exactly. And, more importantly, a wasp of his own to study. A real, live psychopath to be his subject. One he could do what he liked with. No restrictions. No ethical codes to worry about.'

We all stared at him.

'That was the agreement. He would protect me, ensure no one ever found out what I had done, but I had to stay at Thornwood and allow him to carry out psychological tests on me. Let him finish what he'd started at Fredericks University, before they stopped him and he came back to England.

'You all knew he was interested in psychopaths,' Dominic went on. 'What none of you realized was how obsessed he was. Before Auntie Barbara was murdered, his specialist area was social psychology in general. Then he switched completely. He had a thesis—'

'Wait – did he tell you all this?' Lily asked.

'Yes, Lily. Your precious professor told me everything, usually late at night when he'd had a few whiskies. His thesis was – get this – that love could suppress madness.'

Lily shook her head, like she couldn't believe what she was hearing.

'He told me he had suspected himself of being a psychopath,' Dominic said. 'Or on the spectrum of psychopathy, anyway. Don't look so shocked. He had many of the traits: a love of power and status, extreme competitiveness, supreme intelligence. He told me that, growing up, he didn't care about anything except doing well at school, being top of the class, outperforming his classmates. Academia was the perfect place for him. He said he'd prepared himself for a life of serious study, where friends were not important and relationships were about networking, climbing. He was determined to make it to the very top and knew he was ruthless enough to achieve whatever he wanted. And then he met Barbara.'

'Through computer dating.' Rohan said it like he'd just remembered.

'Yeah. He only did it because he was looking for sex. But he met Auntie Barbara and . . . he changed. A part of him that he'd thought was dead came to life. Suddenly, he was less ruthless, more empathetic. He said it wasn't like a total transformation – he was just as ambitious – but he was sure that love had done this to his brain. To be honest, I didn't take all of it in. Something to do with oxytocin and reward circuits and the amygdala.'

Lily stared at him, then nodded like it made sense. She, of course, was the one surviving member of our group who had taken Sebastian's psychology class.

'So he started studying this?' Rohan asked.

'Not straight away. At first it was just an idea. Then Barbara was murdered – and that was when he became obsessed. He found all these people, these sociopaths and psychopaths, and brought them into his research centre. Tried to get them to fall in love. He gave them MDMA and other drugs, I'm not sure what, then encouraged them to screw each other. Sent them on romantic dates.'

'And did it work?' Sophie asked.

'Did it hell. There was some kind of side-effect to the oxytocin. They became possessive. Violently so, in a lot of cases.'

'Of course. Vasopressin,' said Lily. 'It's a peptide that makes people defensive, like a mother being prepared to fight to look after her newborn.'

'Sounds right. Uncle Seb was sent packing, back to England, where he vowed to change his ways. He stopped focusing on psychopathy, but he still retained that belief in love as—' He waggled his fingers. '"The Great Cure."'

Was that why he'd decided to create a dating site?

'And then . . .' Dominic went on. 'And then the incident with Eve happened and he flipped back. Now he had his own subject, someone he was convinced was psychopathic. A live lab rat. His own fucking nephew. The arsehole told you all I'd drowned, didn't he? And no one in the world cared or came looking for me, asking if they could go to my funeral. Not even you, mate.'

He said this to Rohan, who retorted, 'I emailed Sebastian asking about the funeral, but he never replied.'

'That's because there was no funeral. I didn't have any proper friends or other relatives. Like Eve, he knew no one would wonder where I was. He kept me hidden away. Like his own Mrs Rochester, locked up, hidden from the world, except I wasn't insane.'

He paused to let us absorb that point.

'I couldn't believe it when he told me I got eighty-three in the test, although I think I laughed because it sounded so ludicrous. He used that laugh as part of his evidence against me. That and what I'd done, of course. But I'm not – I never was a fucking psychopath.'

His voice cracked. He sounded so convincing – but then, I told myself, that was what people like him were skilled at, wasn't it? Pretending. Lying. I trusted Lily. Trusted her intelligence, her methods. Her test. And we knew for a fact that Dominic had murdered Eve. He wasn't denying that.

'Uncle Seb started running tests the very next day. He started with the exact test you'd devised, Lily, and then adapted it over the years.'

'Years?' I said.

'Yeah, Will. I told you. *Years*. It drove him insane, trying to replicate the results, which never came close. All the tests told him I was pretty much normal. Screwed up, yeah, but it was nurture. All the beatings and the bullying at school. My totally freaking dysfunctional relationship with my parents. Uncle Seb couldn't accept it. He had absolute faith in you, Lily. He became convinced I was such a clever, manipulative psycho that I could fake my own physiological responses as well as being an expert at lying.'

He paused again to allow us all a moment to take this in.

'He could never find proof I was a psychopath. I was a prisoner. Every time I talked about leaving, he threatened me. Even though he would have gone down for it too. He said he didn't care. He was old. All he cared about was completing his great study, with me as the subject. Like I said, his obsession, his refusal to believe I was normal and that he'd wasted all this time – it drove him mad. And me? I was too pathetic to leave.'

Callum spoke up. 'It wasn't only your fear of going to prison that kept you at your uncle's, was it?'

Dominic narrowed his eyes at the other man. This was interesting. They clearly weren't good friends. Again, I wondered how they knew each other.

'Callum's right,' Dominic said. 'Uncle Seb had another way to keep me under his control, to keep me there.' A pause for effect. 'His will. He promised me that if I cooperated, he would leave everything to me. Thornwood. His whole estate.'

Okay. That made a lot of sense. Thornwood alone, including its grounds, must have been worth millions.

'He told me everything would be mine when he died. But if I tried to go, or refused to take part in his stupid tests, he would change the will and leave everything to Eve's family. A mysterious gift for some local folk who would spend their lives wondering why Lady Luck had smiled on them.' He muttered several swear words.

'So yeah, I had a good reason to stay. And then Sebastian got sick. Cancer. Aggressive cancer that rampaged through his body. Finally, the old bastard was getting what he deserved.'

I looked around the table. The others were as stunned as I was. Yes, Sebastian had closed down the site suddenly. He had always been temperamental, prone to outbursts. But we had all believed that, essentially, he was a good man. A scientist, dedicated to helping people.

And Dominic's story . . . I was still convinced he was a psychopath, that he was in denial or lying about that. But the rest of it: I believed him. I didn't want to, but I did.

'It was all looking good,' Dominic went on. 'Sebastian was getting worse and worse. I was looking after him. Like I keep trying to convince you, I'm not a monster. I didn't want him to suffer, despite everything. I was his nurse. But the end was getting close, and with it, finally, my freedom. And my inheritance.'

Everyone's attention was fixed on Dominic. Even Callum appeared fascinated, as if he was hearing details he didn't already know. I took a moment out from listening to him to reflect: no novel I could have written about that summer could ever have been so captivating. Perhaps that was why I had never written that great book. Something inside of me knew that my imagination could never match what had really happened.

Dominic was still talking. 'After all these years, it would be mine. My reward. I was almost there. All the pain of being psychologically poked and prodded and told I was a fraud and a liar, of being trapped in that house for all those years, would be made worthwhile. I'd be rich. I could sell the house, buy somewhere modern. Go out there and see the world. Do all the things I've ever dreamed of, with Amber by my side.'

I'm certain she grimaced, though Dominic didn't see.

'Then that private detective turned up, going on about missing girls.'

Chapter 42

January 2024

Dominic

Dominic escorted the private detective, who thought Dominic was Sebastian's nurse, out of the house. A missing teenager? Dominic was here all the time, and no young woman had been here. The only women who'd visited the house in the last six months were his uncle's cleaner – a woman from the village who was in her sixties – and Amber.

Oh, Amber.

He would never forget the first time he had seen her. Uncle Seb had still been in good health, and was working on a new study, looking at the links between psychopathy and addiction. This involved interviewing a number of 'case studies' who had been referred to him through his contacts in the psychology community.

Dominic had been hanging around in the corridor, waiting to speak to his uncle about a leak in the roof that needed to be fixed, when the door of the treatment room had opened and a woman had emerged, walking fast with her head down, heading straight past him without even looking.

Apart from the cleaner, Dominic didn't see many women. Most of Sebastian's patients were blokes. Seeing this curvy redhead with the elaborate tattoo – ecstasy, teardrops, wolves – did something to Dominic. Like a prisoner who had been locked away for too many years, he found himself unable to stop thinking about her. For the next week, he counted down the hours, praying she would return at the same time the following Tuesday, unable to believe anything that fortunate could ever happen to him.

But it did. She came. And when she exited her session with Uncle Seb, Dominic was waiting outside.

She paused by the front steps and produced a cigarette from her bag, struggling to light it in the wind. Dominic immediately approached with his Zippo.

'Do you live here?' she asked, after they had smoked in silence together for a minute.

'I do. I'm Professor Marlowe's nephew. His only relative.'

'So, one day, all this will be yours?'

And for the first time, she had properly looked at him.

He had been shy at first. He had been handsome once. Really fucking handsome, but years trapped in this place had robbed him of that beauty. Now, he could hardly bear to see himself in the mirror. When Amber looked at him and didn't flinch, he was distrustful. She was so hot; how could she like him? On top of that, the last woman he'd liked had rejected him, and Amber looked a lot like Eve, only older. Surely she couldn't be interested in him.

But when she told him why she was meeting with Sebastian he began to understand that she, like him, was damaged. She was a gambling addict who was in recovery. Her life had been glamorous once. Casinos, Monte Carlo, Las Vegas, underground card games and powerful men who had seen her not as a trophy but an equal. She explained that she hadn't gambled for money, primarily, even though she appreciated the good life. No, it was the thrill of the game that hooked her.

Competition, the roll of the dice, the turn of a card. She loved to win, but it was the game itself – be it poker or drag racing or dog fights or bare-knuckle boxing – that made her skin tingle, her pupils dilate, her breath catch. The gambling, which eventually led to bankruptcy and ruin, simply gave her a reason to take part.

Knowing she was damaged gave him the confidence to woo her. Now, every time she visited he would be there: solicitous, sympathetic, chivalrous, taking her wet coat, bringing her cups of coffee, lighting her cigarettes.

Then one day, after a long chat about his plans after he inherited Thornwood, she kissed him. The next time she came around, they went to his bedroom. And soon after that, she moved in.

This was around the same time Uncle Seb grew sick. They led a quiet life. Walks in the woods together. Old movies in bed. Dominic expressed a desire to learn to cook and she brought in an old friend of hers, a chef called Callum, to teach him. They stayed away from games and sport and anything that might trigger her.

Everything was good. Sebastian was dying. Dominic would very soon have it all: money and a beautiful woman to share it with.

And then the private detective turned up. And it all started to unravel.

After Finn left, Dominic had to spend some time calming himself down and waiting for his uncle to regain consciousness. He needed to talk to him. But Sebastian didn't wake up until the next day.

His skin sagged where he'd lost so much muscle. His breathing was shallow, eyes watery. Dominic pulled up a chair beside him and launched right into it: 'What were you talking about? With that guy yesterday? Why would he think Theo and Georgina's kid would come here? Did you tell them something?'

Sebastian didn't respond.

'Did you talk to Theo and Georgina? Tell them about Eve?'

He waited. He thought his uncle had fallen unconscious again. For a second he thought he might even be dead, and was leaning forward to check if breath still left his uncle's lungs when Sebastian said, 'I never told anyone the secret.'

Dominic was shocked. Not by the words, but because Uncle Seb sounded so lucid. Like his old self.

'I never even told *you*.'

Had he misheard? 'You didn't need to tell me. I did it.'

Still sounding normal, frighteningly lucid, Sebastian said, 'No, not just that you killed the girl from the village. The rest of it.'

'You mean Lily seeing what I did?' And trying to drown him.

'No. The rest of it.'

Dominic couldn't take this in. 'What are you talking about?'

There was a smile at the corners of his uncle's lips. The smile spread. Became a laugh. Dominic sat there, wanting to shake his uncle by the shoulders, to get it out of him. Was he delirious? Was it the drugs? No, he sounded like he knew exactly what he was talking about. Dominic had heard about this before: people who were at death's door having a spell of clarity, a good day, before they passed. Was Sebastian about to sit up, ask to go for a walk around the grounds? Suggest a game of croquet?

No. But his mind was obviously clear.

'You've been waiting for me to die, haven't you? I know that, Dominic. Your reward for all these years with me. And I want you to have it. You're my blood. The last of my blood.'

Without warning, his hand shot out and he gripped Dominic's wrist. Where was he getting the strength?

'But there's something I need to tell you . . . If it ever comes out, you'll lose everything. All of this. And my legacy, my work . . . my memory. You have to make sure they never tell.'

'Who?'

Sebastian's voice dropped to a whisper. His brow creased and he looked confused. 'One of . . . my revolutionaries.'

As quickly as he'd risen, he appeared to be fading again. To be struggling to remember their names, or at least the name of whoever had this new, unknown secret.

'Who is it?' Dominic pressed. 'Which one? Something else Lily knows? Will? Theo?' He said all their names, but Sebastian didn't respond differently to any of them.

His lips moved, and Dominic had to lean close, his ear to Sebastian's mouth, to hear. His voice was so faint that only a few words were clear. But those words drove splinters of ice into Dominic's heart.

Dominic listened. And, moments later, Sebastian was gone.

Dominic was in shock. This was it. The moment he'd been waiting for. Sebastian was dead. But in the last seconds he'd learned that it could all be taken away from him. Everything he'd waited for. Everything he *deserved*. It was like the opposition team getting a penalty kick in the last second, threatening to snatch glory away when it was so close.

Sebastian's final act of cruelty.

While the professor's body cooled and stiffened, Dominic went to the study and searched through Sebastian's papers, looking for some note, some evidence, some clue. At the bottom of the cabinet he found a file with 'DATING SITE' scrawled on the front. Inside were half a dozen CVs with photos attached. The six graduates who had come to work here that summer.

He looked at their pictures in turn. The so-called revolutionaries.

Could it be Lily? She had at least one secret – she had seen Dominic strike Eve and thought she'd killed Dominic. She'd made a deal with Sebastian to protect herself.

Could it be Theo or Georgina?

Or what about Will? He hated Dominic – thought that he'd shagged Sophie. Or could it be *her*? Sophie had known he was going to go to look for Eve after the Tarot reading. What if she'd tried to find Eve herself, after the professor sent them home the next day? Or could it be Rohan? He'd been around that night too and had been acting shiftily.

In the coming days, he tried to dismiss it – but it was impossible. It gnawed at him. The idea that one of the six graduates could destroy his life. How could he relax, knowing somebody had a time bomb?

He needed to know who it was. What it was.

Sebastian's solicitor told Dominic that the Howards would be attending the cremation, and Dominic's first idea had been to invite the rest of the group too. The problem was, they thought he was dead, didn't they? Lily thought she had killed him. He could imagine her shock, seeing his 'ghost' at the funeral, prompting her to reveal that she had seen him kill Eve.

He needed to find out who had the secret and deal with them before he let any of the group know he was still alive. That meant he couldn't reveal to the Howards that he was alive.

So he decided to stay at home. Sebastian didn't deserve Dominic's presence at his funeral, anyway. He would go for a walk instead. Around the grounds that, without this fucking complication, should be his.

He left the house and was stopped in his tracks.

There was a young woman – a girl really, fifteen or sixteen years old – coming up the drive towards the house.

The moment he saw her face, he knew who she was. She was like a clone of Georgina; an even younger version of the woman he'd known in 1999. He'd seen her picture online when he'd searched for Georgina and Theo. The family, on a newspaper website, posing in a room that looked exactly like the living room here. The younger daughter.

Mia Howard.

Chapter 43

Mia

Where was it? If the passage actually existed, if Olivia had been in there, where could it be? She thought back to when they'd searched the house. They'd looked behind the book-cases, in all the cupboards and nooks and crannies. Mia had been convinced at one point it must be behind the wall of her wardrobe because when she tapped the wall it sounded hollow. But she had explored every inch of that wall and found nothing.

If they hadn't been able to find it back then, when they were at leisure to explore the house, how could she expect to locate it now, when she was so restricted? It was insanely frustrating. But if she could figure out how Olivia had found it . . . Her only clue was that it was related to Claude, that he had led her there, but that was hardly any help at all. Cats are chaotic, random, impossible to influence.

Why had her life become about searching for things, and people, that were impossible to find?

She racked her brain, trying to remember if Olivia had said anything else. Or if Finn had uncovered something that might help now.

After Finn had told her about his visit to Sebastian Marlowe's house, and persuaded Mia to let him talk to Mum, she had felt more frustrated than ever. She had wished Finn had taken a proper look around. What if Olivia had actually been there? Mia had seen enough scary movies to know that Sebastian's big old house was exactly the kind of place where women might be held prisoner. Chained to beds. Locked in cellars. Or maybe there was some clue there, some proof that she'd visited.

Mia couldn't let the notion go, and when the day of the funeral came she'd had an idea. Mum and Dad were going, along with Finn, who Mum was going to introduce to Dad as the professor's former assistant – out of earshot of anyone who might know otherwise, of course. Surely, Mia had thought, Sebastian's house would be empty. This was the perfect opportunity for her to go and take a look. She was sure there would be somewhere she could sneak in. An unsecured window, a cellar door. So as soon as her parents left for the crematorium, driving down to Kent, Mia headed for the train station.

Except she screwed up. Timed it so she got there when Sebastian Marlowe's nurse, the one Finn had told her about, was coming out.

There was a weird moment when he seemed to recognize her. Then he demanded to know what she was doing.

She tried to make up a lie – something about searching for a lost dog – but he interrupted her.

'I know it's not a missing *dog* you're searching for. If you've come here to look for your sister, she was never here.'

She had blinked at him.

'I know who you are,' he said. 'Why don't you come in and tell me all about it? Maybe I can help.'

Sebastian's nurse had a whiff of weirdness about him. But he was really old – forties, at least – and unfit-looking, so she knew she could outrun him if necessary. Besides, she was desperate. He had presumably been with the professor for months. He might know something. She pictured herself out-witting him, finding Olivia and freeing her. Or getting some piece of information that would stun her parents and lead her to her sister.

'Don't you need to get to the funeral?' she asked, though he wasn't wearing a suit.

'There's plenty of time. Would you like a drink?' Without waiting for a reply, he had led her into a kitchen. There were dirty dishes piled in the sink and a calendar on the wall that was two years out of date. He filled a dirty glass from the tap and passed it to her. 'Tell me about your sister. What makes you think she came here?'

She had decided to be honest. He really seemed like he wanted to help. If he wanted to grab her and lock her in a room, wouldn't he have made a move already? She told him everything. Told him how her parents had lived here once, working on a dating site.

'We think Olivia found out something that had happened in 1999 and came here to look for answers.'

'You mean . . .' His Adam's apple bobbed. 'Like a secret?'

'I guess. My mum swears she doesn't know what it is.'

'What about your dad?'

'He doesn't even know I hired a private detective.'

'Ah. The guy who came here.'

'Yeah. Finn, his name is. He's going to talk to everyone who was there.'

'Oh, really?'

'Yeah. The plan is to throw a dinner party and invite every-one who used to work here with my parents. Finn is going to try to figure out if any of them had any contact with Olivia.'

He, the nurse, had seemed extremely interested in this.

'A dinner party?' He had interlaced his fingers and rested

327

his chin on them. 'They're all going to be there? So . . . when's it happening?'

She had told him, and then asked him if he was sure Olivia hadn't visited and if she could look around the house. He'd said, 'Sure,' and had given her a tour. It was crazy to think her parents had worked here once; even crazier to think it had been the base of a tech company. It smelled of dust and medicine. She had looked all around and, by the end of the tour, was satisfied Olivia wasn't here.

Leaving the house, she had realized that all her hopes lay in Finn finding something out at the dinner party, and had resolved to be there. To listen in.

And here she was, in her mum's walk-in wardrobe. Unable to listen to what was happening downstairs. Unable to call for help. And unable to think of anything Olivia or Finn had said that might help.

She crouched beside the cat again. 'How did Olivia find the entrance?' she whispered. 'We searched the whole . . .'

She stopped.

She had personally looked around the whole house. Every room. Every space.

Except she had never looked up here – in this room where she wasn't usually allowed to go.

Chapter 44

'As soon as Mia told me about the dinner party, about the six of you gathering together, I knew this was my chance.'

I had checked Georgina's reaction to Dominic's words. She seemed stunned. She clearly hadn't known her younger daughter had visited Thornwood and spoken to this person she thought was Sebastian's nurse.

Dominic went on. 'I knew one of you had this secret that might destroy my chances of claiming my inheritance. But how was I going to find out who it was? You all thought I was dead. That's when Amber suggested we enlist Callum. I was like, why would we need help from a chef?'

'Callum hasn't always been a chef,' Amber said.

'Let me guess,' I said. 'He was another of Sebastian's psychopathic test subjects. Of course a psycho would recruit another psycho.'

Dominic took a step towards me, jabbing my chest with a finger. 'How many times do I have to tell you?'

'Oh yeah, you're totally sane.'

Callum spoke up. 'I would never have let that old bastard experiment on *me*.'

'So what were you?' I asked him. 'Before you were a chef?'

'Callum was part of an organization,' Dominic said.

'You mean, like, a crime organization?'

Callum shrugged. 'Something like that. And you should all

think yourselves lucky. My first suggestion was that we should take the Herod approach.'

'Massacre the innocents,' Sophie said.

'Exactly. Kill everyone and you don't have to worry about figuring out who's guilty. Unfortunately, old Dominic here was worried that whoever had the secret might have left instructions. You know the kind of thing: *to be read in the event of my death.* He wouldn't take that risk, even though it would have been quite easy. Lock you all in, start a fire.'

A chill travelled through my veins because I could see it in his eyes: it was still an option. Perhaps becoming their only option.

'So you came up with this game instead?' I said.

As the words left my lips, I noticed how Amber shivered. I actually saw goosebumps ripple across her arms.

'Yeah. Well, I can't take the credit for inventing it. It's something we used to do . . .'

'We?'

'The elimination game was something we did if we knew someone in the organization had stolen from us but we didn't know who. We'd gather together every potential suspect, lock them in an empty warehouse and make them turn on each other, just like tonight. I learned how even people who are determined not to be caught will tell all their secrets when they think they're about to die. Human nature. I've been listening to all this bullshit about psychopaths and, let me tell you, it doesn't matter. Everyone is capable of selling out their friends. Everyone will kill or let their loved ones be killed.'

Was that true? I saw Lily's reaction, her downcast gaze, thinking about how she'd agreed to cover up Eve's murder, because of fear. Self-preservation.

'Dominic promised you a cut of his inheritance?' I asked Callum.

'I'm not doing this for shits and giggles.'

I guessed Dominic must have promised him a very large cut. No wonder he wasn't that bothered about what was in the safe. Thornwood was worth millions, and Sebastian probably had loads of money stashed away on top of that. Dominic must have promised Callum enough for him to get far away from here, to feel confident the police wouldn't find him, presumably borrowing against his impending inheritance in order to pay Callum quickly. To me, someone who had lived a quiet, law-abiding life, the whole thing seemed impossible. This was hardly the kind of crime the police would treat as low priority. Callum must have been extremely confident he could pull this off. *Delusions of grandeur*, I thought. *A belief that society's rules are for other, weaker people.* Sebastian would have loved to have got his hands on Callum.

Something worried me. Presumably, Dominic and Amber were planning to vanish too. But Dominic would need to stick around to claim his inheritance, to sell Thornwood. He couldn't disappear immediately. And now he'd shown his face . . . we were in greater danger than ever.

'Was Amber someone you knew in that old life?' I asked Callum. I saw the answer pass between them. She was more than just someone he knew. She had been a gambling addict. So . . . what? How would I write her if this was a story? A woman who had got into debt, owing thousands. And . . . Callum had fallen for her? Perhaps he had agreed to wipe her debt, or pay it for her. And she had somehow helped him escape the organization? Whatever the story, they had changed their lives – but were unable to stay away from their old vices. And from each other.

I studied Dominic. He must have known these two had a history. But I was also pretty sure he thought it was all in the past. He hadn't seen them, like I had. Wasn't aware how Amber felt about Callum.

'I thought I wouldn't have to show my face at all,' Dominic said. 'I thought these two would be able to get the information I was after. I agreed to wait outside in the van. I would only make an appearance if things weren't going well.' A pause. 'I thought the shock and the sight of the guns would mean the secret would be revealed straight away. I didn't think anyone would end up getting hurt.'

'I don't believe you.'

We all looked at Lily, surprised by her words. She was staring not at Callum but at Dominic.

'You're not sentimental. You don't care about any of us. You're not capable of caring. You're just a coward. Someone who didn't want to get his hands dirty.'

Dominic sneered. 'Aren't psychopaths supposed to be fearless?'

'Not all psychopaths are the same.'

'How many times? I am not—'

'He's just fucked in the head,' said Callum.

Dominic didn't see it because she was behind him, but Amber had to put a hand over her mouth to suppress a laugh.

'Anyone would be fucked up after all those years being a human lab rat.' We all turned to Rohan, who had spoken these words. He shrugged. 'Well, it's true. And he says Sebastian was never able to replicate the test. Maybe your method was flawed, Lily.'

She was adamant. 'It wasn't.'

'You don't want to kill us all, though,' Rohan said. 'Do you, mate? We were friends. Good friends. Remember how many times we watched that match together? I saw how excited you got when we scored that winner. I know you're not a psycho.'

Dominic clamped a hand on Rohan's shoulder and his eyes misted over. 'Thank you, mate.'

Rohan looked up at him. 'I really want to see my wife and kids again.'

'I know you do.'

'If you let me go home tonight, I'm going to change. No more pursuing all these crazy business ideas. I'm going to be a good dad, a good husband. Spend time with them. Money's not the most important thing, is it?' He looked at me. He had rejected the offer of the ring. I believed him. But at the same time, I could see he was being clever. Dominic's parents had been too busy for him. They'd sent him away to school. Rohan was simultaneously speaking the truth and aiming at Dominic's weak spot.

'I'd show you their pictures, Dom, if we had our phones.'

Dominic withdrew his hand from Rohan's shoulder like it was red hot.

Rohan realized what he'd done.

'Mate, I wasn't trying to get you to give me my phone. I really do want to show you pictures of my wife and kids.'

But Dominic wasn't listening. 'You really think I'm that stupid, do you? All this bullshit about us being friends. Did any of you ever like me?' He waved a hand. 'Not you, Will. I know you were jealous of me. Anyone? Georgina?'

She shrugged. 'I didn't have much of an opinion.'

He laughed bitterly. 'What about you, Sophie? You liked me, right?'

I could sense her mind racing, trying to decide what to say, making a political decision. But Dominic saw it too and looked crestfallen.

'I felt sorry for you,' she said. 'The orphan driving his dead parents' car. It was obvious your arrogance and bravado were an act.'

'Do you still feel sorry for me?'

'Dominic. You murdered a woman because she wouldn't

333

have sex with you. I don't feel sorry for you at all. I feel sick with guilt and, if I end up getting killed tonight, then, well, maybe I deserve it. But I'm fucking glad you've spent the last twenty-five years having a really shit time.'

Callum laughed, not even bothering to hide it.

Dominic had gone scarlet. Amber went over to him and whispered something in his ear. He nodded.

'Yes,' he said.

My insides went cold. This was what I had just seen coming.

'Let's go back to Plan A.'

'You mean it?' Callum said. He seemed impressed.

Dominic's lip curled. 'The Herod approach. Let's kill them all.'

Chapter 45

Dominic took the shotgun back from Amber and nodded at Callum. I am sure in the next second we would have scrambled, tried to get beneath the table. We were two seconds away from blind panic.

'Wait!'

For the second time tonight, Lily stopped the bloodshed.

'I can get you the secret,' she shouted, standing up, marching over to Dominic and standing in front of his gun.

'Don't listen to her,' Callum said. He stepped forward and made to push Lily out of the way, but she cried out.

'Please, Dominic. Listen.'

Dominic blocked Callum and said to Lily, 'Talk.'

She drew in a breath. 'I have a way to end this.' She turned around so she was looking at me, Rohan, Sophie and Georgina. 'Remember earlier, when I was talking about the new project I've been developing?'

'The top-secret one,' Rohan said.

'Yes. Well . . . it's a lie detector. It syncs up with a smart-watch. It actually uses some of the same principles as my wasp trap, but the technology is way more sophisticated now, and it's a lot simpler too. It literally just measures if you're telling the truth, and it's ninety-nine per cent accurate.'

Dominic did not look convinced. 'Why the hell should I trust something you designed?'

Lily stayed calm. 'I'm willing to concede . . .' She paused.

'Willing to accept that the test I created back then might have got it wrong. I can see now that you do feel emotions. I just saw how you reacted when you felt like Rohan was trying to trick you, like you were being betrayed. Your feelings were hurt.'

'Yeah, I was pissed off.'

Rohan spoke up: 'I wasn't trying to—'

Lily touched his arm. 'Rohan, it's okay. Maybe my test was flawed. I mean, it was developed incredibly fast. It wasn't tested. But this is a game-changer. There are already apps out there that claim to be able to tell if someone is lying, but most of them are just for fun. This one works. I promise. You can go around all of us and ask us if we have the secret you're looking for, which is going to be a lot easier now we – those of us who are innocent – know the nature of it. Something incriminating. Something that would stop you from claiming your inheritance.'

Dominic listened intently. To Callum, he said, 'Remind me who hasn't already revealed any secrets?'

'Hmm. Lily thought she'd killed you. Theo had blackmailed some rich perv. Will and Georgina shared bodily fluids. That leaves Sophie and Rohan.'

'It's not me,' Rohan said immediately. 'I don't know anything.'

'It isn't me either,' said Sophie. 'And I'm very happy to take a test to prove it.'

'It's possible one of them has more than one secret,' Amber chimed in. 'It could still be Will or Georgina or Lily.'

Her eyes were shining again. I knew there must have been part of Amber that wanted to kill us all, get this over with. But the game was too exciting. Too irresistible. And although I was still almost certain that, whatever happened now, Dominic planned to kill us, this would buy us some time.

336

Lily nodded. 'I think you know I've spilled my only secret, but I'm very happy for you to ask me whatever you like.'

Dominic went over to the window to confer with Amber. We all watched them. I still wasn't sure if Lily was up to something or if she genuinely was trying to find out who had the secret.

'All right,' Dominic said, coming back towards the table. 'Let's try it.'

Lily exhaled. 'Great. I'm going to need my phone and my smartwatch. You're going to need to turn the internet back on.'

'Let's *not* try it.'

'I need the internet to grab the latest version of the app from the server. You can hold the phone – I'll tell you exactly what to do.'

Callum came over. 'This is a bad idea. For all we know, the second we turn the internet back on her phone will fire off a load of messages telling everyone she knows that she's in trouble.'

'Why on earth would I have set my phone up to do that? I can promise you, no one is going to be wondering where I am. I spoke to my kids already. My ex knows I'm not going to call her. There isn't anyone else, and I'm not going to secretly try to call the police. Why would I? I kept quiet about a murder for twenty-five years. All I want is for this to be over. To go home. See my children again.'

Dominic looked over to Amber, who shrugged.

'You don't even need to keep the broadband on for long. It will download in five minutes. Like I said, I won't even need to touch my phone. I'll give you full instructions.'

Dominic went back over to the window. Light from the chandelier made his head shine. He was sweaty, clearly exhausted. But, even if he planned to murder us all, he still wanted to know who had the secret. 'Fine. Let's try it. Where's Lily's phone?'

Callum replied: 'In the kitchen, with all the others.' He had the air of a man whose teenage kids had just done something hugely disappointing.

'What's your problem?' Dominic asked.

'My problem? It's this. We've spent hours trying to get whatever this fucking secret is out of this lot. I'm sick of it.'

'It was your idea.'

'Yeah. Because the people we were dealing with when I did this before, they were straightforward. Honest criminals. These people? They're slippery as eels. I still think we should kill them all. Either that or torture it out of them. Pain is going to work a lot better than some stupid lie-detector test.'

A ripple of alarm ran through the group, until Lily said, 'Torture doesn't work. All the studies have shown it's a very unreliable method of extracting information. Sebastian used to cover that in one of his classes. All people do is tell you what they think you want to hear.'

Dominic nodded. He'd clearly heard that too.

'Callum, turn the internet back on,' he said.

Callum huffed, but Dominic caught his eye and a look passed between them. A look that told me they had an understanding. This was just a pause. The only way Dominic was going to get away with this was if they slaughtered all the witnesses.

Lily had bought us some time. Now we needed to use it.

Chapter 46

Mia

It would make sense if the entrance to the secret passage was up here, Mia thought. It was the only place they hadn't looked – because Dad had only told them about the secret passage after he and Mum had banned them from coming up here – and Mia knew that Claude often got himself trapped in this room. Mum was always complaining about him leaving fur on the bed or paw prints in her bathtub. She also remembered Olivia coming up here to look for him on several occasions, when their parents weren't around.

And if there was an entrance here, surely this wardrobe was the most likely place.

She got down on her haunches. The walk-in wardrobe was about two and a half metres square. One wall was taken up by a long rail on which Mum's clothes hung. Another was dominated by designer bags. The far wall was covered mostly by the metal shoe rack, which was about a metre high. But from down here on the floor, Mia could see there was darkness behind the bottom two shelves of the rack, on which Mum kept some of her vintage trainers. If, Mia figured, Mum had been wearing her rare Adidas or Nikes, there would be enough room for Claude to squeeze through into whatever space lay behind.

Mia tossed several trainers aside then took her phone out

of her pocket, switching on the light, which she shone through the gap.

There was what looked like a crawl space behind, stretching back beneath the wall. Easily big enough for a cat to stroll through, and just big enough for a slender person to commando-crawl into.

This could be it.

Excitedly, but carefully, afraid it might topple over and make a racket, Mia pulled the shoe rack away from the wall. Claude, disturbed by the movement, shot not into the space it revealed but into the main bedroom, causing her to doubt her theory for a moment. But she dropped down on to her belly and, holding her phone out before her, used her elbows to drag herself into the dark alcove.

It was dusty in here, and she had to fight against a sneeze. Clumsily, she dropped the phone, but snatched it up again, pointing it ahead of her. Her whole body, all five feet seven of her, was now in the space. She noticed too that the ceiling above her sloped upwards, so by the time she was fully inside the alcove she was able to push herself up on to all fours.

There in front of her, like something from *Alice in Wonderland*, was a little door, with a handle.

She reached out and opened the door, revealing a doorway that was exactly the right size for her to crawl through.

She didn't hesitate. She went through, immediately finding herself in a space that was big enough for her to stand up. It was dusty, and without her phone it would've been pitch black.

Olivia had been in here, she was sure of it.

For some reason, Olivia had regretted coming in here, but Mia wasn't thinking about that right now. All she cared about was finding out if she could use this passage to get downstairs. To the back door. Or maybe – better – it would lead straight out of the house.

Using her phone to light the way, she stepped forward, and discovered stairs that led down.

This was amazing. That crime-writer guy had actually done it. Installed a secret passage like, presumably, in his novels. Had he done it just for fun? Or had he wanted to be able to sneak around his house without being seen? Mia knew that once upon a time there had been servants living upstairs. Maybe the old bastard had been carrying on with a maid, or a manservant, and had used the passage to visit her, or him, without his wife finding out.

Whatever the reason, she said a silent prayer of thanks to Rupert Chadwick as she went down the narrow stairs. The passage was wide enough for her to stick both elbows out if she wanted to. She imagined it would have been a lot tighter for Chadwick. The stairs were solid and didn't creak, and she could hear own breathing. As she reached the bottom step a cobweb tickled her face and she had to quickly push away the image of a fat spider scuttling into her hair.

The passage branched out to the right and she realized this must be the middle floor, where her bedroom was. In fact, she was almost certain her own wardrobe was on the other side of this wall. That was why it had always sounded hollow. She had been right all along. She had a sudden, pointless urge to text Mum and Dad, to tell them she'd found the passage, and that made her thumb automatically move to open the app that connected to the listening device. It was still running, waiting for a web connection. It was intensely frustrating.

But maybe there would be an exit down here that would lead outside. She shone the torch to the right, into the stretch of passage that ran parallel to her bedroom, and saw a dark shape at the far end. A box, or a trunk. But there was no time to take a look: she needed to keep going downstairs.

She continued down the narrow stairwell, more confident

now, moving a little faster. She wondered if Claude had explored this whole space, if he came down here to hunt for—

She jolted forward, her foot not finding anything beneath it – one of the steps was missing! – and she found herself jerking forward, instinctively flinging her arms out to support herself against the wall, and dropping her phone. It disappeared somewhere below her. Plunging her into blackness.

She stood there, frozen on the step, too worried to try to move. She'd heard the phone land far below, probably into some hole, because she could no longer see anything. Not even her hands in front of her face.

Holding on to the wall, she tentatively reached down with one foot and was relieved to find another step. She descended, very slowly, in the pitch black, testing each step with one foot before continuing.

She went down one more step, and then there were no more. She was at the bottom of the staircase. Crouching, she felt around for her phone but instead discovered she had been right. There was a hole in the floorboards. Squinting into it, she could see the glow of the phone, which had clearly landed with the torch facing down, way beyond her reach.

She fought back tears of frustration but quickly got a grip. She stood, then stepped sideways into what felt like a wider space. She must be on the ground floor now. Where exactly? She tried to picture what was below her bedroom. The cupboard? If she was right, the router would be less than a metre away. Not that turning it on would do her any good now she'd lost her phone. She—

'Waste of fucking time.'

The man's voice sent a shock through her. It was as if he were right here in the passage with her. Her entire body tensed up, until she realized he couldn't be. He was on the other side of this wall.

It was the man with the gruff voice. It sounded like he was talking to himself. Grumbling, clearly pissed off about something.

Now she'd recovered from the shock of hearing him she pressed her ear to the wall.

'Yeah, Dominic, I'm gonna burn this house down. And when I've got my share I'm gonna burn yours down too, with you in it.' He muttered something inaudible then, 'Here we go.'

She heard a familiar beep. The sound of the internet coming back on. But she hardly took that in. All she could think about was what he'd said.

Gonna burn this house down.

There were no more steps. She was stuck. Stranded in the dark without her phone. But there *had* to be an exit. She had to get out.

Chapter 47

The moment Callum left the room, I turned to Dominic.

'You actually trust him? You're an idiot.'

He shot me a look of contempt.

'Callum and Amber,' I said. 'They're fucking.'

As soon as I said it, Amber took a step towards her boy-friend, opening her mouth to speak, but I talked over her. 'I saw them kissing, in the hallway. They're sleeping together. I'd put money on it.'

'Don't listen to him,' Amber said, trying to take hold of Dominic's arm, but he jerked away.

'You know it, don't you?' I said. 'You don't have to be a pro-fessor of psychology to see it. Maybe you did like Dominic, Amber. But this whole thing, this game, it's made you revert to how you used to be, hasn't it? You're the woman who fell for Callum again. I'm guessing the plan is to help Dominic get his inheritance then steal it from him. Or maybe just run off with Callum and his share.'

'This is bullshit,' she said, but it was so obvious I was right. And I could see it on Dominic's face. He knew it too. He must have already suspected.

'Baby, I'm not going to steal anything from you.'

'Shut up!' Dominic had gone red again. 'I'm gonna kill him.'

He flung the door open and we heard him stomping down the hallway towards the stairs, shotgun in hand. For a moment, Amber was alone and unarmed. We could have acted. The five of us could have overpowered her, and she must have realized this because she quickly followed Dominic, yelling for him to wait.

We were alone. This time there was no silence. I went to the door and peeked out. Maybe we could try to get out, but Callum and Dominic were out there with guns and we knew the doors were locked. We wouldn't get far. Instead, we all started talking rapidly, half of us standing, Georgina and Lily staying seated.

'Callum and Amber? Did you really see them?' That was Rohan.

Sophie said, 'Lily, do you really think your test was wrong?'

Georgina interrupted. 'Does it matter? I want to know what you've got up your sleeve, Lily. Is your phone actually going to alert the police as soon as it's turned on? Is it a trick?'

'No. I'm sorry.' Lily shook her head. 'I was telling the truth. I want to use the app to end this.'

Sophie spoke again, echoing exactly what I'd been thinking: 'They've murdered two people tonight, including Theo! You really think they'll let us go if they find out what this secret is? We're witnesses. This lie-detector test might delay them a bit, but they're going to kill us. We need to find a way out.'

'I'm starting to wonder if there even is a secret,' I said.

'Oh God, me too.'

I had a sudden urge to hug her. To feel her warmth against me. A craving I'd had twenty-five years ago and hadn't done anything about. But now I knew she had liked me too, and I wasn't that nervous twenty-two-year-old any more. This time, I didn't hesitate. I put my arms around her and pulled her in. She didn't resist. Instead she flung her arms around my back and hugged me hard, my face in her hair, the smell of her making me feel young again, and even standing here in the wreckage, with perhaps minutes of my life remaining, I had to fight the urge to kiss her.

'I still love you,' I whispered to her. 'I mean that. I'm so sorry about what happened with Georgina.'

She shushed me. 'I don't care about that.'

'You forgive me?'

'There's nothing to forgive you for.'

'Sophie, can we—'

She hugged me again. 'Let's talk about it afterwards. After we've survived.'

She kissed my lips, lightly. I kissed her back.

I saw the other three staring at us. Georgina looked horrified, Rohan impatient.

Then Sophie said, 'What's that in your pocket?'

Georgina groaned. 'This is not the time for stupid jokes and innuendo.'

But I was already reaching into my pocket.

'It's Finn's notepad. The one I saw him writing in.' With Lily's revelations and Dominic coming back from the grave, I'd completely forgotten about its existence. 'There might be something in here. Finn might have found something out or noticed something tonight when he was going around talking to us.'

I handed it to Sophie, who started to leaf through it. I thought it was highly unlikely there was anything useful in there. We knew all about Finn's investigation now. Knew why he was here. What could he have found out tonight? Even if he'd written, in block capitals, that one of us had a secret, would it do us any good? I was convinced that anything we did now was merely buying time. They were going to kill us, whatever happened. We had to focus on escape and there was no point just leaving this room without a plan. We needed to be clever.

'Is there any other way out of here?' I asked Georgina.

'What do you mean?' Georgina asked.

'Is it possible to get on to the roof, for example? Maybe if we could get up there we could make it along the row of terraces?'

At that moment, I heard a beep come from below us. Presumably that was the internet coming back on.

'I don't think so. If you could get out of one of the windows on the top floor you might be able to climb down a drainpipe, but the windows are all controlled by the security system and locked down. Also, how would you get into my bedroom?'

'Hey, guys,' said Lily, but we all ignored her.

Georgina was visibly trying to rack her brain. 'The only other way out I can think of is the cellar. There's a window down there that leads out to the garden. It's not connected to the security system . . . it's just a tiny window that might not even open because it was probably painted shut years ago.'

I tried to stay hopeful. 'It might not be though?'

'No, but come to think of it, it's high up on the wall. And it might not even be big enough for anyone to squeeze through.'

'But if we can get down there, it has to be worth trying?' Sophie said. 'I'm pretty good at getting through small spaces. Maybe we could create another distraction, like when Will got to Finn?'

'Because that ended really well,' said Georgina.

'None of this is going to end well if we don't do something,' I said. 'We have to—'

'Hello! Can you hear me?'

We all turned to look at Lily, who was waving a sheet of paper. We gathered round her.

'It fell out of that notebook,' she told us. 'When Sophie was looking through it.'

I took it from her. It was a printout of what looked like a text message, possibly WhatsApp. At the top of the sheet, someone – presumably Finn – had written DRAFTS FOLDER, 2 March 2023. I read the short message aloud:

I need to talk to you. I found something and I don't know what to do. I've left it where it was until I decide. It's all Claude's fault. He led me in there and now I'm really scared and confused. I don't even know whether to send this message. It's going to ruin everything. But maybe I need to be brave?

Georgina snatched the sheet of paper from me. 'This was in Finn's notebook?'

'Yes. Do you have any idea what it is? Who it's from and to?'

'None.'

'But it mentions your cat. Do you think it's from Mia, to Finn? Something she found out about Olivia?'

Georgina stared at the sheet of paper. Her jaw was rigid with tension. 'Maybe.'

'They're coming back,' Lily hissed. 'All three of them.'

While we were talking, I had been hoping to hear a gunshot. Dominic killing Callum. It appeared that he had been all mouth, or Amber had caught him and reassured him. I quickly folded the paper and put it back in my pocket, along with the notebook, which I took from Sophie.

The door opened and there they were again. Dominic, Callum and Amber. Dominic had a phone in his hand while the others carried the two shotguns.

'Make up, did you?' I asked.

'Fuck you.' Amber narrowed her eyes at me. 'You're a liar. There's nothing going on with me and Callum. Got that?'

I shook my head. 'Dominic . . .'

'Shut up!' He screamed it, a vein almost popping on his forehead. I recoiled. Of course he didn't want to believe his beloved was screwing Callum. He preferred to be deluded.

Dominic shoved the phone in Lily's direction. 'Let's get this over with. Let's find out which one of you is the liar.'

Chapter 48

Mia

Through the wall, she heard more people go into the cup-board. The one whose name, she now assumed, was Dominic, shouting at the other one, addressing him as Callum, accusing him of screwing Amber, who was presumably the redhead. It was confusing because Dominic was the name of Sebastian's nephew – she'd heard Mum and Dad mention him when talking about the old days – and his voice was familiar, but she didn't have time to think about that now. She hoped they would all shoot each other before Callum got the chance to burn the house down, but he mollified Dominic, denied the accusations, and then the three of them started talking about a lie-detector test.

She tuned out. Because something had struck her. If the internet was on, and her phone was nearby, she might be able to listen in to what was going on in the dining room. She already knew the app was still open, after all. She felt in her pockets and found her AirPods, thankful she still had them on her. She popped them into her ears and they connected immediately to her phone.

A woman was talking.

'. . . Sophie was looking through it.'

Then a man. She realized he was reading something out,

and when he said, 'It's all Claude's fault,' she couldn't believe her ears. She listened to the rest of what he said, and then Mum was talking, but it was what the man said next that really interested her: 'Do you think it's from Mia, to Finn? Something she found out about Olivia?'

And then the three who had been in the cupboard returned to the dining room and Mia plucked the AirPods out of her ears so she could think. She wanted to shout out, *No, it's not from me. It's obviously from Olivia!* She presumed the message was to Felix, but that wasn't important. What was important was this line:

I've left it where it was until I decide.

She didn't know what Olivia had left, but the fact she'd written 'he led me in there' made it pretty obvious where she had left whatever it was. It was in here. The passage.

Something important. Maybe – almost certainly – something connected to her disappearance.

Mia stood in the darkness, trying to see the path ahead. Her priority had to be to find her way out of here. To grope her way to an exit, in case that guy Callum really set the house on fire. But she also believed she had a little time. Callum and the others were in the dining room, doing something with lie detectors.

And Mia knew exactly where to look.

She went back up the stairs, feeling her way with her hands, being careful not to stumble over the missing step. She reached the middle floor and paused for a second, before continuing up. If she was going to find what she was looking for, including a way out of the house, she needed light, and she knew there were candles and matches in Mum and Dad's en suite. Loads of them, all around the edge of the bath. So she went all the way back up, through the crawl space, through the wardrobe, and grabbed as many of Mum's fat scented candles as she could carry. She crawled back into the passage and lit one, leaving it at the top of the stairwell so it cast just enough light for her to see where she was going.

She did the same on the middle floor, then lit another, carrying it with her towards the trunk or box she had seen earlier, praying she was right but deciding, if she wasn't, she was going to search for the exit. Get out of here. Call for help.

With the candle held out before her, she crawled along the passage and opened what she now saw was a trunk.

She reached inside.

Chapter 49

Dominic made us all sit around the table one last time. Downloading the app had, as Lily had said, taken only a few minutes. As soon as it had downloaded, Dominic had gone into Lily's settings and switched off the wi-fi connection, telling the phone to forget all networks and passwords. Finally, he took Rohan's Apple Watch and synced it with Lily's phone via Bluetooth, and told Lily to put it on her wrist.

'Let's start with you,' he said to her.

I think everyone in the room knew Lily had already spilled all her secrets. This was Dominic's way of getting accustomed to the program and seeing how it worked.

We were seated in the same places in which we'd sat for dinner. Georgina at the end of the table to my right then, clockwise, Sophie, me, Lily and, opposite me, Rohan. Dominic sat in Theo's place, with Georgina sending waves of hate in his direction. Amber stood behind Rohan with her shotgun balanced against her shoulder, while Callum wandered around, clutching his shotgun. I was unsure if he would still get a big cut of Dominic's fortune if no one confessed, but I couldn't see Dominic saying no to him. If the secret didn't come out now, I was certain Dominic would take the gamble, encouraged by Amber, and hope no one had left behind, as he had feared, something incriminating that would be revealed in the event of their death. Assuming that wasn't the case, the three of them were going to be rich, though I was also sure that at some point Callum – and probably Amber – would double-cross Dominic and take the rest. Live happily ever after.

Dominic opened the lie-detector app on Lily's phone and slid it across so it sat on the table before her. 'Tell me how it works.'

'It's simple. It's just like a classic polygraph, like the crude one I created back in the day. This uses current tech. It can be set so it asks you questions on the screen, but the answers always have to be given verbally because it analyses your voice along with registering your heartbeat. It also tracks your eye movements, which is why we need the camera on. It's a triple-action model. Eyes, voice, pulse. May I?'

She gestured to the phone, and he said, 'Go ahead.'

Lily picked it up and turned the front camera on. 'I need something to prop it up with. That smart speaker will do.'

Amber handed over the little device Theo had been using to play music at the start of the dinner party and Lily set it in front of her, then leaned the upright phone against it. Her face filled the screen.

'The app is running,' she said. 'All you need to do is ask questions and I'll answer them. Once you're done, you navigate back to the app and check the results. This app already knows my voice so you won't need to worry about asking me preliminary questions.'

'Do they need to be closed questions?'

'It works better that way.'

'This is such bullshit,' Callum said in a low voice.

Dominic glared at him. 'You completely failed to find out who has the secret. It's my turn.'

'Whatever. Go ahead. It's not going to work.'

But he watched, interested, as Dominic started the test, firing questions at Lily.

'Did you believe your secret was the one we were after?'

'Yes.'

'Do you have anything else to tell me?'

'No.'

She gave both answers calmly, and I would have been amazed if she'd been lying.

'Do you know who has the secret?'

'No, I don't.'

Dominic paused. He knew he was wasting his time with Lily. But he had one more question: 'Do you still think I'm a psychopath?'

'Hmm. I don't know.' She tilted her head; thought about it. 'No. I don't.'

'Thank you. Now, how do I check the results? Show me.'

Lily picked up the phone and opened the app. She held it out so Dominic could see the screen, though, annoyingly, this meant I couldn't see it.

Fortunately, he read the results aloud. 'Lies told: zero. Honesty rating: ninety-eight per cent.'

'There's always a little room for doubt,' Lily said.

Dominic moved the phone and speaker to the other side of the table so they faced Rohan. Lily removed the smart-watch and passed it over to Rohan, who strapped it on to his wrist. 'Your turn,' Dominic said. 'Do you have anything you want to tell me?'

Rohan shifted in his seat. 'No.'

Lily interjected. 'You need to ask more specific questions.'

'Yes, yes. I know.' He tried again. 'Do you have a secret from that summer?'

There was a long wait for the answer. Rohan shifted again. 'Shoot him in the kneecap, Amber,' Callum said.

That made Rohan speak. 'No, wait! I do. I do have a secret.'

Was this going to be it?

Dominic leaned across the table. 'Do you have a secret that could stop me claiming my inheritance?'

'For God's sake,' said Callum, coming closer. He had the Japanese knife in his hand, the shotgun tucked under his arm. 'Just get him to tell you what it is.'

'Callum,' Amber said in a warning tone.

Callum huffed and stalked away from the table again, still holding the knife.

Dominic leaned even closer to Rohan. 'What is it? What is your secret?'

Rohan rubbed his face. 'I'm not proud of it.' He turned to Lily. 'The afternoon of the party, when everyone was getting ready, you were still in the office working and I sneaked up to your room.'

'To look at the results of the test?'

'Not that. I wasn't worried about that at all. I wanted . . . to steal the code.'

'Of the wasp trap?'

'No. I didn't care about that. I was after the Butterfly Net algorithm. I knew you had the code saved on your laptop as well as your work PC. The PC was password protected and I had no idea what the password was, but when we were doing the psychopath test I watched you tap your password in on your laptop. It was "Sebastian".'

'Oh my God.'

'Why were you trying to steal the code?' I asked.

He wouldn't meet my eye. 'I was using this message board, a community for would-be entrepreneurs, and I guess I started showing off about how I was working for a site that was going to change the face of internet dating. How we had this amazing algorithm that was ready to launch. The next day I got a direct message from someone offering me a shitload of money in return for the code. It would have been enough to start my own business, to really invest in my own dreams.'

'And you did it?'

'I'm ashamed to say I would have. But as I was about to save everything on to a disk, I heard someone coming towards the room. I hid in the bathroom.'

Lily stared at him. 'Do you know what time this was?'

'Around three.'

'Then I'm sure it wasn't me.'

'I don't know who it was. They came in, and then about ten minutes later they exited. I was so freaked out I got out of there as quick as I could. I think in that five minutes I'd realized what I was doing.'

'Hold on. Were the results of the tests already printed out?'

'I don't know. There was something on the printer, but I didn't look. I was only interested in the code.'

'That's it?' Dominic said. 'That's your big secret?'

'It's the only one I've got,' Rohan said.

'You don't care that he was trying to steal from your uncle?' Sophie asked.

Dominic didn't answer. He snatched up the phone, took a cursory glance at the app – 'Telling the truth,' he muttered – then moved to Georgina, instructing Rohan to pass her the watch. As she put it on, she kept eye contact with Dominic, giving him a look of utter contempt.

'You already know my secret,' she said. 'My regrettable encounter with Will.'

'Shut up,' Dominic said. Rohan had irritated him. There were only three of us left now, and I knew the secret-keeper wasn't me. If Dominic didn't get what he wanted from Georgina or Sophie, he and his cronies were going to set fire to the house with all of us in it.

Dominic had already started quizzing Georgina, with a couple of questions about Theo's secret, blackmailing James. Then he moved on:

'Do you know who has the secret I'm looking for?'

'Obviously, I don't.'

He almost growled at her. 'Just say yes or no.'

'Yes, *sir*.'

He shook his head. 'Bitch.'

'Misogynist.'

His mouth opened and he looked to Amber, who was standing between Rohan and Georgina. 'I love women,' he said.

'Oh yes. You love murdering them and dumping them in lakes. Wait, except you were just following your uncle's instructions, weren't you? So pathetic, especially as you whined like a baby when he told you to get in the boat and—'

She stopped. We all stared at her. Dominic lurched to his feet, his chair scraping behind him.

'You saw me? It was *you*?'

'No. I . . .'

We didn't need a polygraph app, even though I assumed it would tell Lily that Georgina was lying. It was clear to anyone in the room. She'd made a mistake. She'd been there. How else could she have known Dominic whined about getting into the boat?

'It was you,' Dominic said, getting to his feet, pointing at Georgina. '*You* were the witness.'

'Hold on.' That was Callum, striding back over. 'Witness? You're talking like you know what the secret is.'

Dominic waved a hand at him. 'Shut up.'

But Callum didn't back off. We were all staring at them, trying to figure out what Dominic was talking about. What had he meant when he asked Georgina if she saw him?

'What's going on?' Callum demanded.

Dominic stood up straight. There was so much tension in his voice it had risen an octave. 'All right. Yes. Sebastian told me, on his deathbed. Whispered it to me. His final words.

360

Somebody saw me put Eve's body in the lake. Someone had evidence. That's what we came here tonight to find out. Who it was. What and where the evidence was.'

Callum was outraged. 'Why the fuck didn't you tell me that? You sent us in here with half the information. Amber, did you know?'

'No, I didn't.' She stared at Dominic, horrified.

Dominic explained his logic. 'I knew if you told them what the secret was, they might deliberately confuse things.'

'How?' Callum demanded.

'Well, they could all have claimed to be the witness. I thought Georgina and Theo would protect each other. Will and Sophie, too, maybe. They could all have given each other made-up alibis. Or turned on each other! Lied and wheedled and obfuscated. I needed to hear it direct from the person with the secret so I'd know they weren't lying. And now we do know: it was Georgina. *She* saw me put Eve in the lake.'

I tried to take all this in. To figure out why Georgina hadn't spoken up, but I didn't have time. Because Dominic and Callum were squaring up to each other, Callum yelling, 'I cannot believe this!' and Dominic shouting back at him.

In a rage, Callum snatched up Lily's phone from the table and threw it with all his considerable strength at Dominic. It missed but struck the wall so hard it made a shattering noise and fell, broken, to the floor.

And then Callum yelled, 'Will was right.'

'What?'

There was a look of pure glee on Callum's face. His voice suddenly became very calm and cold. 'Will was right, Dominic. About me and Amber. We've been screwing. And yeah, she's only interested in your money. You should hear the things she calls you when we're in bed. How grateful she is to be fucked by a real man.'

With a roar of anguish, Dominic launched himself at Callum, trying to take the shotgun from him, grabbing it with both hands and tugging. Callum didn't let go, but to get a proper hold of the shotgun he had to drop the knife.

Amber saw it and went for it.

Georgina was faster.

She threw herself on to the floor and grabbed it, this knife that belonged to her, to her family, this impossibly sharp and expensive item, and as Amber tried to rebalance herself, to point her gun at Georgina, Georgina kicked out at Amber's ankle. Amber stumbled and Georgina leapt up, swinging her clenched fist at the other woman. Amber screamed and fell to her knees, hands going to the knife – which was embedded in the side of her neck. She pulled it out and blood sprayed from the wound.

Amber made an awful gurgling noise then crumpled to the ground.

Callum and Dominic saw what had happened. Dominic pulled the gun from Callum's grip, which made Callum fall backwards on to his behind, and Dominic raced around the table towards his fallen girlfriend. But Georgina was closer to Amber. She grabbed Amber's shotgun.

Dominic didn't care. All he was interested in was getting to Amber. He threw himself on to his knees beside her. Across the other side of the room, Callum tried to get to his feet – and Georgina shot him in the chest. It blasted him backwards, and he crashed into the wall between the windows. But it didn't kill him. Somehow, like a movie monster, he started to get to his feet, and I realized the shell had struck the muscle just beneath his clavicle.

Georgina shot him again, right in the heart.

This time, he didn't get up.

'Come on!' I yelled, jumping up and opening the door. 'Let's go.'

'No!' Dominic shouted. He was on his knees in a puddle of Amber's blood, holding the gun he'd wrested from Callum. I had no idea where the knife was. Under Amber's body, presumably.

Georgina took aim at Dominic, but as he tried to get up he slipped in the blood, crashing to the ground, and Georgina held off from firing.

'Come on!' I shouted. Rohan, Lily and Sophie didn't hesitate. They shot out the door. But Georgina stood there, trying to aim at Dominic as he continued to attempt to get up, swinging Callum's gun towards Georgina, finger on the trigger.

I pulled her into the hallway before he could fire.

'I can take him,' she said.

I remembered how she had gone hunting when she was a teenager. Shooting pheasants. But Dominic had a shotgun. This was not like aiming at a defenceless bird.

'Your gun. Is it still loaded?'

'There will be one shell left.'

'One? For fuck's sake, it's too risky. The cellar,' I said. 'We can barricade ourselves in there and someone can get out the window to fetch help. Okay?'

'I agree with Will,' Sophie said. 'We're so close. Let's not take any risks now.'

Georgina shook her head. 'Fine.'

I wanted to ask her about witnessing what Dominic had done – about being the one with the secret all along – but there was no time. Above us, I heard the dining-room door open and footsteps run along the landing. The five of us ran past the cupboard, which was shut, and reached the cellar door. Georgina yanked it open and told us to go inside. Lily went first, then Rohan, then Georgina.

'Go on,' I said to Sophie, but we were too slow. Dominic didn't wait until he got to the bottom of the stairs. He leaned over the banister, yelling our names. I tried to shove Sophie through the cellar door, but Dominic had already aimed, and fired.

I felt the blast in my ears. I was dead, I was sure of it. The barrel had been pointed straight at me. But when I looked down at my body I couldn't see any sign of injury. Could feel no pain.

'Will.'

Something worse had happened.

Sophie was hit. Somehow, in the second following the shot, she had stayed upright.

Now, she collapsed to the floor.

Chapter 50

'Sophie!'

I threw myself on to my knees beside her. Dominic was almost at the bottom of the stairs now and Sophie was completely still – *dead*, I thought, *she's dead* – but I couldn't see where the shell had struck her at first. Then I saw it: it was her leg, high up on the outside of her left thigh. The shell had caught the edge of her leg, on the side that was furthest from me. Her tights were shredded above the wound and blood spread through the material.

I said her name again, trying to get her to come to. I guessed the pain and shock must have made her pass out. Her eyelids flickered. And then, just as Dominic came stalking down the hallway, his face a flickering whirlwind of anguish and fury, Rohan came back to the top of the cellar steps.

He grabbed Sophie's arms and yanked her through the door. I had a moment to make a decision. Dominic had raised his gun, aimed it at Sophie's back. I didn't have time to get through the door.

I slammed it behind Rohan and Sophie.

And stood face to face with Dominic.

'Get out of my way. It's Georgina I want. She killed Amber.' He sounded like he'd snapped. There were tears in his eyes. 'I loved her. You get it, right? You know what it's like.'

'You shot Sophie,' I said.

He stared at me like he didn't even realize what he'd just

done. I wondered how many shells were in his gun. Georgina had said the guns held three shells. Dominic had fired it once, but Callum had already used it twice, to kill Theo and Finn. Had Callum reloaded or was the gun empty?

It was strange. I wasn't scared. I felt very calm. All I could think about was buying the others time, to get out, to fetch the police.

'It's over, Dominic. You're not going to get that inheritance now. There are four dead bodies in this house . . .'

'I didn't kill any of them.'

'. . . and five witnesses who know what you did. Why don't you leave now? You'll have a chance to get away. Come on, we can figure out how to open the front door together.'

At the back of my mind, I was aware that Sophie would be losing blood. There was an artery in the thigh, wasn't there? The femoral artery. She'd need an ambulance. Surely the others would be able to tie something around the wound. Maybe one of them had already managed to open the little window Georgina had told us about and got out.

For a second, Dominic appeared to think about it, then he grinned. Laughed and made a sobbing noise at the same time.

'All those years,' he said. 'All those years being tested. All those years *trapped*. Can you imagine what that was like?'

'I can empathize . . .'

'And the rest of you, swanning about. Free! Having wonderful lives.'

We were still standing outside the cellar door. There was nothing here I could use as a weapon. No way I could get away without being shot. All I could do was try to keep him talking. To reason with him. It was all about buying precious seconds. Allowing the others to fetch help.

'I think only Georgina and Theo have had wonderful lives – and that was only until their daughter went missing.'

He ignored me. 'None of you deserves to live.' He saw me looking at the gun. 'You're wondering if it's empty, aren't you? Callum reloaded it.'

I put my hands up – but, to my surprise, he turned tail and marched towards the kitchen. I followed. What was he doing? In the kitchen, he picked up a bottle of vegetable oil and inspected it, then tossed it aside. He headed over to the sink and crouched, pulling open the cupboard. When he stood up, he was holding a large bottle of white spirit, and he took the top off straight away and began splashing it around the kitchen.

'It was Sophie's fault,' he said as he strode around the room, splashing the turpentine around. 'She told me Eve liked me, that it was going to happen between us. And Lily tried to kill me. Georgina saw us try to hide Eve's body. She could have stopped everything tonight before it had even started, if she'd confessed straight away. Why didn't she, Will?'

I didn't know.

The white-spirit container was empty now. He began to look around for some matches. At the same time, I edged towards the wine rack.

'You were always a dick to me,' Dominic said. 'Thought you were superior because you were into books and had gone to university.'

'That's not true.' There was a bottle of wine on the counter, a few inches of red left in the bottom. 'I thought you were better than me because you were confident with women and lived in a massive house.'

How wrong, and how shallow, I had been.

'Where the hell are the matches?' He grunted. 'Ah, here we are.'

He had found a box of chef's matches. Dominic had his back to me, holding the shotgun between his knees, opening the box and dropping the first match he fumbled out, then plucking a second.

'His fucking revolutionaries,' he said. He was rambling, muttering. 'I should have left that nest there. Let those wasps sting you all to death.'

He went to strike the match – and I smacked him over the back of the head with the wine bottle. It shattered as it struck his skull, the remaining red wine exploding all over me. Wine in my face, in my eyes, temporarily blinding me. I groped for a towel and wiped my eyes, and realized a shard of glass had cut my cheek, just above the bone. I hardly felt it.

Dominic lay still, motionless but breathing, on the kitchen tiles. I crouched to check him. He was out, but only temporarily.

I grabbed the shotgun and the matches, then paused. Callum and Amber had taken our phones. Where were they? I looked around but there was no sign of them and searching could take for ever. I needed to check how Sophie was so I ran back to the cellar door and knocked frantically.

'It's me,' I yelled 'Let me in.'

Rohan opened the door. 'Where's Dominic?'

'In the kitchen. Unconscious. How's Sophie? Have any of you got out yet?' I went down the stairs and found Sophie lying on the floor, with Lily and Georgina beside her. One of them had tied a cloth around her leg, but it was drenched with blood. She looked weak, her breathing shallow.

'The window won't open,' Lily said.

I lay the shotgun on the floor beside Georgina and inspected the window. 'Surely we can get the front door open now.'

'I don't think Callum reversed whatever he did to the security system. The door's still locked. But can't we use the landline? It's in the family room.'

'No, Callum smashed it to pieces. I saw it when he called me out of the room. I need to find our phones.'

I turned back towards the stairs.

There was an old double wardrobe propped against the wall at the bottom of the staircase. As I walked past it, its door opened and I yelped with surprise.

We all watched, frozen, as a teenage girl emerged.

'Mia!' Georgina got up from where she'd been crouching. 'What . . .'

She approached Mia, arms outstretched, ready to embrace her. Mia was filthy, covered in dust and with black streaks on her forehead. How long had she been here? Had she been hiding all along? She had a candle in her hand, which she dropped to the floor, the flame going out as it fell.

I saw her expression and stopped wondering. She was looking at her mother with horror.

'Get away from me,' she said.

Georgina stopped. 'Mia?' But I could tell, somehow, that she knew what was wrong. Georgina, the person who had been keeping Dominic's secret all along. She knew what we were all about to find out, but there was nothing she could do to stop it.

'It was you,' Mia said. I saw now that she had something in her hand. A book. A diary? She held it up. Her voice trembled with emotion as she spoke.

'You killed Olivia.'

Chapter 51

August 1999

Georgina

She watched Will leave her room. Scuttle, that was the word. Head down, mortified in a very ungentlemanly way. It was amusing, kind of fascinating, to see how he had been flooded with instant shame and regret the moment he finished.

It would be quite funny if he bumped into Sophie outside the room, smelling of sex. She liked the idea that Sophie would be upset by it. Sophie was one of those pretty girls who didn't have to make any effort to get boys to like her. Vivacious but immature, with ridiculous superstitions, protected by just enough family money to ensure she would never have to take big risks.

Family money. Everyone thought Georgina had plenty of the stuff.

Everyone was wrong.

She got out of bed and went into the bathroom. When she came out, she poked her head into the hallway. No commotion. Sophie clearly hadn't caught Will. He hadn't rushed to her room with a stupid urge to confess. Georgina was pleased, really. She wasn't sure if Theo would forgive her, even if they hadn't discussed exclusivity, and Theo was an important part of her plan. She deserved a good life – the best life. She'd been brought up to believe it was her birthright. Theo would help her achieve that. He would help her fit in.

Help her seem not just normal, but better.

A big house. A perfect family. A beautiful life.

That was all she wanted. And she certainly wouldn't achieve that with an arty loser like Will. No, she had already hitched her wagon to the alpha male of this house, the one with the most potential to make money. And if Will decided that his conscience was hurting him – something Georgina would never understand; a concept she only knew about through books and films – she would deny it. Say it was his sick fantasy. She had never had sex with Will, and he would never be able to prove they had.

She thought about going to bed, but she was too wired now. Perhaps she should go and see Theo, wake him up, have sex with him. But he'd been so drunk; he and his room would stink of alcohol and he would probably be greasy with sweat. It wouldn't be pleasant.

It was a nice night. She decided to go for a walk.

Halfway along the landing, she passed Lily's room, and thought back to earlier that afternoon.

Lily had told her that she'd left her laptop processing the results of the psychopath test. Georgina wanted to see them before anyone else. Lily and most of the others were in the library, working on getting the beta site finished. Rohan had gone off somewhere, acting weirdly shifty, though she didn't know what he was up to.

This was her chance.

She had seen straight away that there was something on the printer. Carefully, not wanting to make it obvious anyone had moved them, she picked up the sheaf of paper and leafed through the pages. Her results were halfway through. She flicked straight to the final score.

Eighty-three.

She knew what that meant. Lily had explained it to them.

It meant that she, Georgina, was a psychopath.

She wasn't shocked. She wasn't even surprised. It told her what she had suspected ever since they had all started talking about psychopathy here. She had looked through the books and papers Lily and the others had taken from Sebastian's study. Read the checklist in that book and the case studies.

Lack of remorse. A grandiose sense of her own importance. No empathy. An urge to do 'bad' things. Pleasure taken in others' suffering. An ability to blend in, chameleon-like. A craving for power. Bored easily. A strong libido but no emotional connection with the men she slept with.

Yes, she thought. Tick, tick, tick.

She had known, since she was a little girl, that she was different. She didn't understand why she got told off when she took other children's toys. She didn't get it when the other girls at her prep school cried when she told them they were stupid or ugly. She didn't see what was wrong with always wanting to beat everyone else in tests and getting angry when she didn't.

There were so many things. She remembered when their form teacher, Mrs Harket, a woman who was kind and sweet and who went out of her way to help everyone, stood before the class one day telling them she was going to 'take a break', tears shining on her cheeks. 'Girls,' she had said. 'There's something growing inside my head. It's called a tumour. But I'm going to beat it and then I'll be back.' All the other girls had cried and hugged Mrs Harket, but Georgina had been fascinated. How big was this tumour? What were their teacher's percentage chances of surviving? Would it make her act in strange, funny ways? Also, what was for dinner?

When they heard Mrs Harket had failed to beat the tumour and was dead, all the other girls cried again. By this point, the nine-year-old Georgina had learned she should make herself cry too. She practised for hours, thinking self-pitying thoughts, until she was able to squeeze out a few tears and fake the rest of it. She joined in with the wailing, but, inside, she felt nothing. Absolutely nothing.

Standing by Lily's printer, looking at her results, she had pictured what would happen if this label – psychopath – was attached to her. She would be ostracized. Feared. Maybe even studied, if Sebastian found out. Her future as half of a golden couple with Theo would be severely compromised.

She needed to do something.

She had gone over to the laptop. To her surprise, it was already open – not password protected – as if someone had just been using it. Maybe Lily had left it like this so it could process the results.

She opened the program. She was sure Lily hadn't already looked at these, so all she had to do was switch around two of the names. She noticed their gender and dates of birth were included too, so she would also need to change those.

It was obvious who she should pick. Dominic's score was forty-nine. Everyone thought he was the person most likely to be a psychopath so no one would question him getting eighty-three, and forty-nine would be a good score for Georgina. Well outside the range, but not too low to be unrealistic if Lily had any suspicions about her true nature.

It only took a few minutes to change the details for the two of them and reprint the results with the new names at the top of the page. She put them back in the pile of pages, in the correct place, and put everything back on the printer.

She had taken the original sheets with her, to be destroyed later. She'd found a floppy disk beside the laptop too, with

'Wasp Trap' written on it. She'd taken that too. It was the old shoplifting urge. It helped relieve the pressure in her head.

No one would ever know who she really was.

Now, in the aftermath of the party, after sleeping with Will, she walked past the spot where the wasps had attacked her. It had been the closest she'd ever come to proper terror, to feeling like a normal person. She stopped for a moment, remembering how Theo had saved her and how she had realized this was the perfect opportunity to begin their union.

She entered the trees, and heard someone coming. Was it Sophie, on the warpath, looking to have a pop at Georgina because she'd screwed her biggest admirer? Georgina didn't relish a fight – she might not feel anything on the inside, but she still experienced pain like anyone else – so she hid behind a tree.

She was surprised to see it was Sebastian, in a hurry. Soon, she heard him talking to someone else. Dominic. He sounded weird. Confused and contrite, whining like a child as his uncle admonished him.

She crept closer, peeked out from between the trees. There was someone lying on the path near the two men. They weren't moving. From the clothes the prone person was wearing, Georgina realized it was Eve.

Was she dead? She certainly looked dead.

Interesting.

Very interesting.

She could hear everything Sebastian and Dominic were saying. The moment it became clear Dominic had killed Eve and the professor was helping his nephew cover up this crime she knew she needed to record this in some way, and the solution came immediately. She took her mobile phone out of her pocket and quickly dialled her parents' house. As always, it went straight to the answering machine. In the darkness, she held her phone out at arm's length so it captured the conversation between the two men, and as they wrestled the body into the rowing boat, Georgina tiptoed out to get a better look, seeing something lying on the path. A piece of branch, with blood coating one end. Strands of ginger hair stuck to it. The murder weapon.

On impulse, a little idea forming, she took it and retreated back to her hiding place. Together, the branch and the answerphone tape would provide compelling evidence.

She watched as Dominic took the boat out. Heard the splash. Waited as Dominic rowed back to shore. By the time Dominic trudged up the path past her, heading back to the house, Georgina's idea had formed fully. She knew what to do.

She stepped out of the trees and said, 'Professor Marlowe.'

Chapter 52

'You did a deal with him,' said Mia, holding up the book. The journal. 'It's all in here.'

I was crouched beside Sophie. She was only just conscious, blood soaking through the makeshift bandage on her leg. We needed to get her help, urgently.

But Mia was monopolizing everyone else's attention. I noticed that, as well as the book, she had a tatty-looking backpack slung over her shoulder: a small one, like the type a kid would take to school.

She looked round at the rest of us. It was remarkable how much she looked like Georgina. 'It's Olivia's journal. I found it hidden in a trunk in the secret passage.'

She flung one arm towards the wardrobe she'd emerged from.

'Yeah, I found it. The passage. There's another entrance on the top floor, in Mum's wardrobe. It says here, in the journal, that Olivia heard Claude miaowing in the walls and followed the sound.'

Georgina didn't move. In that moment, she looked like an android that had glitched. Her eyes went blank and she froze. Then she regained her composure.

'That's absurd,' she said. 'It's fantasy. A . . . creative-writing exercise. I love Olivia, like I love you.'

If she was guilty, she was good. She remembered to stick to the present tense.

She put her arms out. 'Darling, come here. We can get all this confusion cleared up once we're out of here.'

Mia shrank away. She didn't seem to have noticed yet that her dad wasn't here. 'Get away from me. When Olivia went into the passage, she found where you kept *your* journals hidden.'

'I've never kept a journal.'

And I remembered.

'That's a lie. That night . . . when we slept together. There was one on the bed.'

She glared at me. 'It was probably my Filofax.'

'No. It was a journal. One hundred per cent. It had "1999" written on the cover.'

I watched Georgina's face. Everyone was staring at her, except Sophie, who lay on the floor, eyelids fluttering, clearly in great pain. That was my priority. Not what Georgina had or hadn't done.

'We need to get Sophie—'

But Mia spoke over me. 'How could you do it, Mum? How could you lie like that?'

And Georgina clearly decided there was no point lying any more.

'I should have sealed the entrance,' she said. 'Idiotic of me.'

There was a long silence. Lily and Rohan stared at Georgina. Mia waved the journal at her.

'You told the professor that if he gave you money, you would keep quiet about what you'd seen. He agreed, even though it was a lot, right, Mum?'

'Why did you need money?' Rohan asked. 'Your family were loaded.'

Georgina sneered. 'We were rich once, until my dad lost everything. Bad investments. We were completely broke, in tons of debt. Theo didn't have any money at that point either, even though he had a good job lined up. I knew we were going

378

to need cash to help us get started, to achieve what I wanted. This seemed like a good solution.'

'You didn't care about Eve dying? About what they'd done?'

'She couldn't care,' Mia said. 'She detailed that in her journal too. She switched the tests. Hers and Dominic's. It was you who got the high score, wasn't it, Mum?'

'Eighty-three.' She seemed proud.

Lily, who hadn't spoken since Mia had appeared, said, 'Oh.'

'Yeah.' Georgina shot her a look that dripped with sarcasm. 'You knew the tests were accurate. You were right. Well done, you. Dominic only got forty-nine.' She sighed. 'I should have destroyed my diary. I haven't even written in it for years. I just never thought anyone would find it. I thought I might need to keep it in case I ever had to go back to Sebastian for more money, so when we moved into this house and I found the secret passage, I put my special possessions there, and told Theo and the kids the passage couldn't really exist, made sure they never looked behind the shoe rack.'

On the ground beside me, Sophie was fading. I felt like I was the only person aware of the ticking clock. Sophie was bleeding out. Dominic was upstairs too, and who knew how long he would remain unconscious.

'We have to get Sophie to a hospital.'

'Shut up, Will.' Georgina swung the shotgun towards me. 'You think I give a fuck what happens to her? You want to know what I did, don't you?'

She jabbed the gun into my belly, making me take a step back.

'Olivia came to me, making all sorts of threats. *I had watched these men sink the body of this poor woman. How could I do it? I was a disgrace.* She was going to tell Felix. She was going to go to the police. It didn't matter if the whole family was ruined because of it. She didn't care. She was so virtuous. Such a social-justice warrior.'

379

'So you killed her,' Mia said. 'And you told us all she'd gone missing.'

'She didn't give me any choice. Believe me, darling. If there'd been any other way.'

'But . . . why did you go along with my plan? To throw this dinner party? Weren't you worried Finn would find out the truth?'

'No, of course not. I knew he wouldn't find out anything useful by talking to this lot. I thought if I let you do this, you'd finally give up. Let Olivia go. Which is what you need to do.'

That was the moment when Mia noticed Theo wasn't here. 'Where's Dad?'

Nobody spoke until Georgina said, 'I'm sorry, darling. Daddy's dead.'

Mia stared at her.

'It's just us now,' Georgina said to her. 'We're going to inherit all of Daddy's money. All we have to do is keep the secret. Me and you.'

'Um, except, we all know about it too,' said Rohan.

'Yeah. You do, don't you?'

She pointed the gun at him, and I could see it: the narrative she would construct. A dinner party with old friends. A home invasion. Some crazed guy from her past who'd always been obsessed with her. They killed Theo and Finn. Then they killed the rest of us before turning on each other. In the chaos, Georgina got hold of their guns – the other one, fully loaded, was lying right by her feet where I'd left it – and protected herself and her daughter.

'Dominic's still alive, right?'

I nodded.

'I'm going to have to kill him too. I don't need a bullet for Sophie. She's almost gone already.' She picked up the second shotgun, cracked it open and tipped out the shells into her palm, pocketing them before dropping the now-empty gun. She reached out with one hand to Mia. 'Come here. Come on, sweetie. Me and you. Like mother like daughter.'

I was certain Mia was going to tell her what to do with her offer. But, to my astonishment, after a few moments of hesitation, Mia crossed the cellar to stand by Georgina's side. She hung her head. Maybe she had figured Georgina was the only family she had left. Or perhaps it was simply years of conditioning. Of doing what her mum asked her to do.

But I had no time to think. To stand there and wait for Georgina to shoot us. Sophie was bleeding out. I had to act.

Georgina pointed the shotgun at Lily, obviously deciding to take her out first – and I threw myself at her.

We crashed into a pile of boxes and went down. She was much slighter than me, but she practised yoga. She was faster and fitter. I tried to grab the shotgun but she evaded my lunge and swung the gun towards me.

I grabbed it and pushed it upwards as she squeezed the trigger.

The shell blasted a hole in the ceiling, plaster raining on us, and I fell backwards, sprawling on the concrete. Georgina, on her knees, tried to take aim at me, but Rohan darted towards her and she pointed it at him.

'Get back!'

He froze. Beside him, Lily was paralysed too. Georgina swung the shotgun back in my direction. There were fragments of plaster in her hair, dust on her face, and her expression was one of pure fury and hatred. How different she looked to the immaculate, groomed woman she had always pretended to be. I was on my back, unable to do anything, and I braced myself.

That was when Mia struck.

None of us had noticed her opening the old backpack that was hanging from her shoulder and taking something out: a thick, knotty piece of wood, already dark at one end; a broken branch. It must be the one Dominic killed Eve with. Georgina must have kept it, sealed in plastic, all these years.

Was that the evidence? What Dominic had been looking for?

Georgina went down immediately, the gun clattering to the floor.

Rohan scooped it up and pointed it at Georgina, who lay on the stone floor. Like Dominic, she was still breathing.

'Will.'

A voice whispered my name. It was Sophie, lying still, her eyes closed.

'Will. I'm cold.'

I jumped up, yelling, all my words tumbling over each other. 'We have to get out of here. Find the phones? Figure out how to open the front door?'

I held Sophie's hand, and Rohan kept the gun trained on Georgina. Mia appeared to be in a trance.

'Hold on,' I said, telling Sophie I loved her. Lily's algorithm had been right. We were meant to be together. After all this time, I'd finally gathered the courage to tell her. She knew my secret too. Knew and didn't care.

'Please,' I said to the air around me. 'I don't think she's going to last much longer.'

I loved her.

I couldn't lose her now.

Chapter 53

It snowed the night before the funeral.

I woke up, opened the curtains of my flat and looked out to see that everything was white. The rooftops were smooth like the icing on Christmas cakes. The branches of the trees that lined the street shimmered in the morning sun. Children were already out there, playing, having a snowball fight in the field across the way. My cat, Bernard, jumped up on to the back of the sofa and looked out too, clearly displeased by the view and blaming me for it.

I showered. Put my black suit on, still groggy from another night of bad dreams. Two weeks had passed since the night of the dinner party and I kept seeing Callum shooting Theo and Finn. Seeing Sophie fall after Dominic shot her in the leg. I had developed an aversion to loud, sudden noises. Yesterday, I'd heard a bang from out in the street and it had taken ten minutes to calm down, to resist the urge to hide. I had an appointment with a counsellor booked for the following Tuesday. I knew there was a long road ahead. Trauma to deal with.

But I was going to face it with courage.

With no secrets.

Despite the snow, the trains were still running, though they were delayed, of course. This was London, after all. I took the train to King's Cross, then the tube to Notting Hill.

Walked to the crematorium.

The streets were wet, but much of the snow on the

pavement around the crematorium had already turned to slush, dirty where so many pairs of feet had trodden on it, including all the journalists and photographers who had come here hoping for a glimpse of Georgina, although we were all a little bit famous now. The survivors of the 'Nightmare in Notting Hill'. Faces all over the tabloids and social media.

Georgina, though, was the biggest celebrity by far. The yoga teacher who'd murdered her own daughter.

I pushed my way through the crowd, head down, and went through the gate into the grounds. The snow was still untouched here, covering the flowerbeds. The garden of remembrance. I wrapped my arms around myself and shivered, then heard a voice behind me.

'Chilly, isn't it?'

I turned.

It was Sophie, in a wheelchair, with Lily pushing her. I bent down and gave Sophie a kiss, which she returned.

'Please,' Lily said. 'Not here.'

'Sorry,' I said, standing straight.

'I guess you need to make up for lost time.' I thought Lily was going to wink at me. 'And you're both getting on a bit.'

'Hey, we all are.' I turned again, to see Rohan approaching. He hugged me and Lily, then bent to kiss Sophie's cheek. 'How are you?'

Sophie smiled. 'Lots of physio ahead, but it's healing well.'

It had been Mia who had saved Sophie's life. After snapping out of her trance, Mia had reached into her jeans pocket and produced the back-door key. I'd run out to the street and hammered on doors until someone answered, using their phone to call an ambulance, which arrived mercifully rapidly. Still, Sophie had lost a lot of blood, and one of the paramedics had told me that if it had taken another ten minutes we probably would have lost her.

That was another thing I kept dreaming about, and I would wake every time with a punch of relief in my guts.

We moved towards the building where the cremation was taking place. A joint one for Theo and Olivia, whose body they had found buried in the garden. Apparently, Georgina had done it one weekend when Theo had taken Mia to a concert, having kept the body hidden in the secret passage for a week or so. Finn's funeral was set to take place in a few days, and we would all be going to that too, even though we'd only known him for a few hours. I'd also heard that they'd found the real caterers, tied up in the empty house next door, the one that belonged to the oligarch. One of their gags had slipped, allowing them to cry out, and before Callum had let him into the Howards' house, Dominic had gone in and tied it more securely.

'Do you think they'll allow her to come?' Rohan asked, meaning Georgina.

'I can't see it,' I said. Georgina was in custody, though I wasn't sure in which prison. I wondered if she would even want to come here today. It wasn't like she cared, was it? If she came, it would only be for the attention.

We walked on. There, a little way ahead, was Mia, with an elderly couple who I assumed were her grandparents. My heart ached for her. She'd lost her sister and her dad. Her mother was not who she thought she was. But she'd been so brave. I could still hardly believe she'd been in the house that whole time, though I'd heard her upstairs, hadn't I? I'd thought it had been Claude, who, apparently, had been taken in by the grandparents too. She must have been there when I went into her room. I wondered if anything would have turned out differently if I'd spoken to her then.

She saw us and nodded in our direction. Everyone in the group turned to stare at us.

'Did you hear about Dominic?' I asked.

He was in custody too.

'He's telling everyone that he's a psychopath, that he shouldn't be in the general prison population but should be in a psychiatric hospital.'

'You know they found Eve's body too?' Lily said in a quiet voice. I knew she was still racked with guilt. There was still some fear that she might face prosecution, for keeping quiet about what she'd seen. Her lawyer was arguing it wasn't in the public interest and seemed confident she was going to be okay. She had attacked a man who had just murdered someone. She had been terrified, young, easy for Sebastian to coerce. And there was solid evidence that Dominic had murdered Eve and worked with Sebastian to cover it up. Hidden in the backpack along with the bloody branch that was covered with Eve's DNA was the answerphone tape from Georgina's parents' house, which she had retrieved the day we were all sent home. This tape contained the recording, captured on Georgina's Nokia phone, of Dominic and Sebastian discussing what Dominic had done and how they were going to hide Eve's body.

It seemed highly unlikely, in light of all this, that Lily would be charged. In the meantime, she was setting up her own company to market her lie-detector test. She was going to be wealthy, as long as she stayed out of prison. She was no longer going to be that person who helped other people – men – get rich.

Rohan, meanwhile, had decided he now had no desire to be a tycoon.

'I'm not a businessman,' he had told us when we'd seen each other a few days before. 'I've finally accepted that. I'm going to get a proper job. Spend time with my family. I feel kind of ashamed of my obsession with money. How I neglected them all because I thought I just hadn't had a break yet.'

'Nothing like a shotgun in your face to make you reassess your priorities, right?' Sophie had said.

'You can work for me,' Lily had said to him.

Now, I took the chair from Lily and pushed Sophie a few metres away, to a quiet spot.

'How are you doing?' I asked. 'Emotionally, I mean. Mentally.'

'I actually feel okay. I know it's a massive cliché, and the last thing I would ever want is to be one of those, but, like Rohan, I feel like this whole thing has woken me up.'

'The shotgun in the face.'

'Exactly. It's like I was sleepwalking through life for so long. Existing on that money my grandmother left me. Not growing up.'

'The female Peter Pan.'

'Exactly. You can be my Wendy, if you want.'

'I'll keep an eye out for crocodiles and pirates.'

I crouched beside her and took her hands. They were warm. 'I can't believe I was too scared to tell you how I felt back in '99.'

She laughed. 'You were pretty stupid. You can put it all in your book, anyway. How's it going?'

'I've actually started it.' In fact, I'd already had interest from an agent, though they wanted me to write the true story of what had happened rather than a novelization. I would need to figure that out. How was I going to do it without spilling everyone's secrets? This would be a proper test of my creative powers.

I kissed her lightly, and she said, 'Why don't you take me home after this?'

'I'd like that. I mean, I'd love that.'

'I need someone to help me change the dressing on my leg.'

'Romantic.'

She laughed. 'Come on, we'd better get back to the others.'

I pushed her up the path and we joined Rohan and Lily, who were still loitering on the edge of the bigger group. It seemed we were about to go in, to get proceedings started. A wave of melancholy washed over me, but there was gratitude too, the counting of blessings. Four of us were okay. We had survived. Like the others, I had been woken up too. I wasn't going to waste any more of my life.

As the doors opened and the people ahead of us began to file inside, Rohan said, 'You know, Sophie, it just struck me. You're the only one of us who never revealed any secrets.'

'Perhaps I don't have one.'

'Come on,' said Lily. 'Everyone does.'

Sophie had a twinkle in her eye. 'Well. You know what, why don't I throw a dinner party? Then you can all come and see if you can get it out of me.'

There was a silence.

'Yeah, I think I'm going to be busy.' Rohan grimaced.

Lily raised her palms. 'Me too.'

'Guess it's just me and you then, Will. What do you say? Want to learn my secrets?'

'Oh yes,' I said, bending to kiss her again. 'Every one of them.'

Epilogue

Mia

Mia still hadn't got used to being here at Nanny and Grandad's place. They were old and kept fussing over her, and Nanny was prone to bursting into tears. They were Dad's parents – Mum's had died several years ago; it was Mum's mother who'd left her that bracelet – and the house was full of photos of Theo when he was young. Olivia too. Nanny had already removed all the photos of Georgina and burned them in the fireplace.

At least Claude was here. He was curled up on the bed now, seemingly content. Mia didn't blame him for starting the chain of events that had led to her mother killing her sister. Why should she? He was just a cat, trying to catch a mouse.

It was nature.

And nature was something she had been thinking about a lot over the last couple of weeks.

Earlier this week, they had let her back into the house in Notting Hill, now that the crime-scene people were done. She had needed to fetch some clothes and a few other possessions. Grandad had waited downstairs by the front door, not wanting to venture any further inside.

Mia had rushed straight up and through the secret entrance in her parents' bedroom.

Because she had remembered seeing something else in the passage, near where she'd found the journal and the backpack containing the murder weapon. A little box with some odd items in, including an old floppy disk with 'Wasp Trap' written in pen on the label. It was only after she'd learned everything that had happened that she'd understood the significance of that disk, which Mum must have taken from Lily's room when she'd switched the results.

When she'd got home, she'd gone online and found an ancient laptop computer; one that worked with this crazy old technology.

Amazingly, the old disk still worked. It had contained Lily's original psychopath test program.

She sat in front of it now.

She didn't have everything. The videotape that contained the clips the group had responded to was missing. And she was having to measure her pulse separately, using her Apple Watch. But she was confident it was going to be good enough to at least give her a good idea of what she wanted to know.

Because she kept thinking back to that night.

Yes, she had been scared of getting caught. But had that just been self-preservation? Survival instincts?

Hearing that Dad was dead hadn't made her feel particularly sad. She'd thought about the things he wouldn't give her any more. Where would she get her allowance from now? But she hadn't cried, even at the funeral earlier today.

Everyone said grief affects people in different ways. Nanny said the tears would come later.

Mia wondered if that was true.

When she'd heard what Mum had done to Olivia, she had been genuinely upset. Outraged. Filled with anger because of all the lies, the betrayal, the wild goose chase Mum had allowed her to go on, pretending to go along with all the stuff with Finn even when she knew Olivia was already dead.

So maybe she *was* a normal girl.

But she knew herself. And she couldn't shake the niggling fear that what Mum had said in the cellar, when appealing to her, was true:

Like mother like daughter.

Mia guessed she would soon find out.

A Letter from the Author

Before you go further, a warning: this letter contains some spoilers, so please don't read it until you've finished the book.

Still here? Thank you for reading *The Wasp Trap*. Whether you're a long-time reader of my books, or this is your first, I'd love to hear what you thought of it. My email is mark@markedwardsauthor.com or you can follow and contact me on Facebook or Instagram, where my username is @markedwardsauthor.

On top of that, if you join my newsletter, you'll get a box set of short stories. Just go to www.markedwardsauthor.com/free and sign up.

The Wasp Trap is my sixteenth novel and one that has been, well, buzzing in the back of my mind for a long time. For years, I had wanted to write a book about a dinner party from hell. I had also, as a big fan of scary movies, wanted to write something involving a home invasion. I couldn't quite decide, though, how to make either of these ideas work – until I figured out how my guests, and the bad guys, knew each other. To do this, I took inspiration from my own past: a spell back at the dawn of the millennium when I worked for an internet start-up.

It wasn't internet dating, but an auctions site. And we didn't all live together either. But the business *was* based in my boss's big house in the English countryside. There were dogs running around our feet while we worked and, during breaks, we could go out into the fresh air and gaze across the vast lawn towards fields and woods, or walk up the long track that led to the nearby village. Like the characters in this book, we thought the dotcom boom was going to make us rich.

Unfortunately, it didn't work out like that, although I'm pleased to report that no one died. Nobody left that place with a dark secret (well, not as far as I'm aware, anyway.)

Once I'd figured out the backstory for my characters, the whole book began to take shape in my mind. An invitation. Locked doors. And a deadly game. Some books are sheer agony to write. But, partly because it allowed me to go back to that wonderful time at the end of the 90s, when the internet was new and before I owned a mobile phone, this one was a joy.

I hope you liked reading it as much as I enjoyed writing it.

Some thanks:

To my editors: Joel Richardson and Stella Newing at Michael Joseph, Sean deLone at Atria and Sarah St Pierre at Random House Canada. It's such a pleasure working with all of you and it almost goes without saying that this book is vastly better because of your notes, suggestions and red pens. Thanks, too, to my copy-editor, Sarah Day, who spotted numerous errors and helped ensure this novel makes sense; and to everyone else at the aforementioned publishers who has helped get *The Wasp Trap* into the hands of readers, including Maxine Hitchcock, Ellie Morley, Gaby Young and Maudee Genao.

A massive thank you to my amazing, tenacious agent Madeleine Milburn, and everyone else at the agency including Valentina, Rachel, Saskia and Hannah.

To my fellow writers, who are part of an incredible mutual support group, including Ed James, Susi Holliday, Caroline Green, Fiona Cummins, John Marrs, Cally Taylor, Elly

Griffiths, William Shaw, Claire Douglas, the QCs, the Colin Scott massive, the WMWC, and Lisa Jewell, for reading this book before anyone else and being so enthusiastic about it.

I am also lucky to have lots of loyal readers, many of whom have been there since my first book was published, so I'd like to thank everyone on my Facebook page and all the other book lovers who have helped spread the word and who keep me going when the writing gets tough, including the members of the Psychological Thriller Readers group and THE Book Club.

A special thanks to Jonas and Rania at Imagine Greece Retreats and everyone I met there.

Huge thanks to my family: Mum, Claire, Ali, Dad, Jean, all the Baughs, including Julie and Martin, and Auntie Jo, Louise and Martin.

And finally, the biggest thanks of all go to Poppy, Ellie, Archie and Harry, and right at the top, my wife, Sara, who has supported me every time I've felt the need to take a risk, and who is always there when my brain is in a dark forest or a locked-down house in Notting Hill.

And if you made it to the end of this letter – thank you again for reading this book.

Best wishes

Mark Edwards
Wolverhampton, February 2025